*At sunset, the Colors are
lowered with dignity and
the Evening Gun
is fired, signaling for all
an end to the day's
toils and struggles.*

THE EVENING GUN

a novel by

William H. White

Volume Three in the
War of 1812 Trilogy

PUBLISHING
St. Michaels, MD

Cover art: "Patrol" © 2001 Paul Garnett
Illustrations © 2001 Paul Garnett

Graphic design and production by:
Words & Pictures, Inc., 27 South River Road South, Edgewater, Maryland 21037

Printed in the USA by:
Victor Graphics, 1211 Bernard Drive, Baltimore, MD 21223 USA

Questions regarding the content of this book should be addressed to:

TILLER Publishing

605 Talbot Street, Suite Two
St. Michaels, Maryland 21663
410-745-3750 • Fax: 410-745-9743
www.tillerbooks.com

DEDICATION

My late mother, Claire Faitoute White,
a writer and poet in her own right, was
vitally interested in history and is most likely
responsible for my interest in both the written word
and the history of our country. This final volume in
the War of 1812 trilogy is for her, with thanks for
sending the muse to me.

ACKNOWLEDGMENTS

As with the other volumes in this trilogy, there are several people who must be acknowledged, for without their assistance, research would have been much more difficult, if not impossible, and I must thank them for the time and effort they expended on my behalf.

C. Douglass Alves, Jr., the Director of the Calvert Marine Museum in Solomons, MD, who opened the library and other resources of that marvelous facility to me and provided great assistance in checking out some local historical details for me.

Paul Berry, the Librarian at the same institution, along with **Robert Hurry**, the Registrar, were available to find materials, suggest sources that I had not even thought of, and make themselves most useful on a cold December day in Solomons.

Scott Sheads, Park Ranger and Historian at Fort McHenry National Monument, as well as author of several books on the Fort and Baltimore, gave up the better part of the day to give me a personal tour of the Monument, answering my never-ending questions with patience and clarity. He brought out maps and diagrams from the Fort's library to amplify his explanations and provided copies of any I wished, clarifying the British siege of McHenry and Baltimore in 1814. I hope I have done justice to his explanations.

Robert Paulus, a dear friend and graduate of the Merchant Marine Academy at King's Point, also an incurable collector of the esoteric. He provided me with factual material concerning uniforms, hats — even buttons — of the period, and always had me in mind when he discovered something he thought might be helpful.

Linda Wiseman, my sister, and an independent scholar of the decorative arts, interior design and way of life during the seventeeth, eighteenth, and nineteeth centuries, was always willing to research some minor detail for me — unless she already had the information at her fingertips.

These good folks gave of themselves, sharing their wisdom, talent, and specialized knowledge with me purely out of kindness.

To them I say thank you; any success this effort enjoys is partly yours, for without your assistance, availability, and expertise, it would have been most difficult to attain any significant level of accuracy and realism in the following pages. Of course, any omissions or errors are mine alone and not as a result of the efforts of these fine people.

Two others were indispensable in the creation of this book and its two predecessors and I would be inexcusably remiss if I did not publicly thank them.

Of course, without the wisdom, counsel, and expertise of **Jerri Anne Hopkins**, my editor at Tiller Publishing, we wouldn't be here at all! She provided her considerable skill to keep me on course and sailing full and by throughout all three volumes of this trilogy. And unquestionably led me through the maze of the seemingly arbitrary (to me) rules of punctuation.

Paul Garnett, artist, craftsman, and sailorman created some pretty spectacular covers and chapter head drawings for this volume and its predecessors. He was always available to discuss my ideas for each and put up with my silly suggestions with patience and understanding. He saw the needs of the books, frequently before I did, and was unstinting in bringing his considerable talents to bear with the impact of a broadside to make our vision a reality.

Finally, my wife, **Ann**, and sons, **Skip, John**, and **Joshua**, have been there for me whenever I needed encouragement, a little common sense, wisdom and, sometimes, a course correction. Their love and patience with me as I wove my way through the intricacies of meshing history with invention were like a sheet anchor in a storm — always there, ready to assist, and constant.

William H. White
Rumson, NJ

As 1813 waned, the tide of battle had turned dramatically. First, there was the shattering defeat of USS Chesapeake by HMS Shannon in June; then in October, Napoleon retreated to France and freed up English military assets, both ground troops and elements of the Royal Navy, for service in North America. The blockade on the East Coast of the United States was reinforced, trapping, among others, Stephen Decatur's squadron in New London and ending the year-long string of American naval victories. And with it, the American naval threat on the high seas.

At the same time, however, the Americans had enjoyed some success on the fresh water, most notably, on Lake Erie in September of 1813. These victories drove home the point to the British that they must relieve the pressure on their Canadian forces, both by strengthening them and by convincing the Americans to reduce their own commitment. The Chesapeake Bay, well scouted and mapped during 1813, and the Gulf Coast seemed ideal locations in which to mount diversionary efforts which would draw American forces from the New York/Canadian border campaigns. In the Spring of 1814, the British returned to the Bay to carry out this effort.

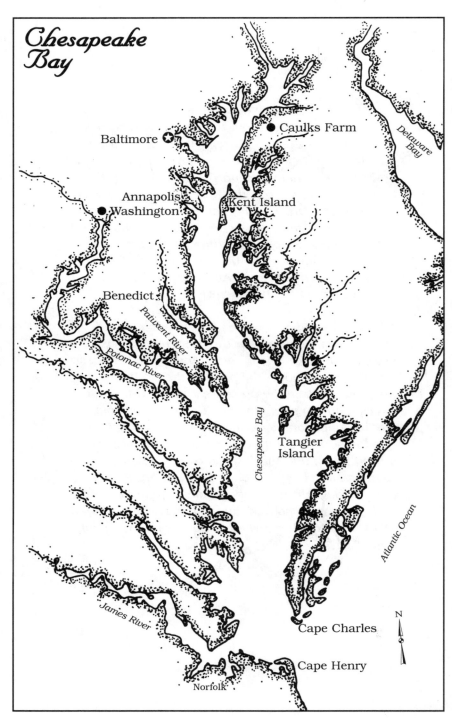

Chesapeake
Bay

Baltimore ✪

● Caulks Farm

Delaware Bay

Annapolis
● Washington

Kent Island

Benedict

Patuxent River

Potomac River

Chesapeake Bay

Tangier
Island

Atlantic Ocean

James River

N

Cape Charles

Cape Henry

Norfolk

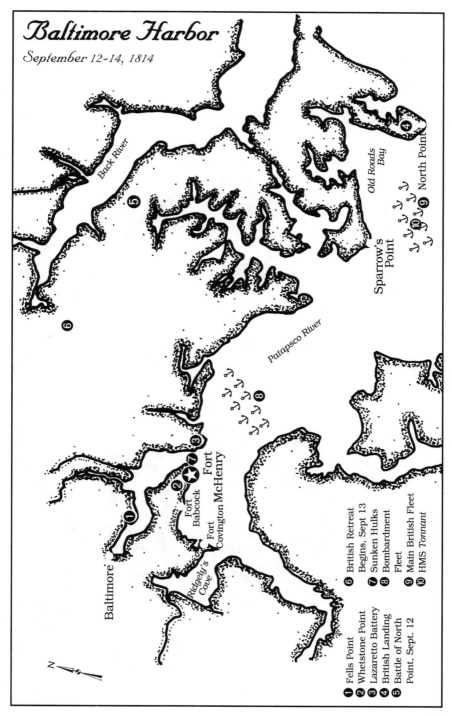

Baltimore Harbor

September 12-14, 1814

Back River

Old Roads Bay

North Point

Sparrow's Point

Patapsco River

Baltimore

Fort Babcock

Fort Covington McHenry

Fort McHenry

Ridgely's Cove

N

❶ Fells Point
❷ Whetstone Point
❸ Lazaretto Battery
❹ Battle of North Point, Sept. 12
❺ Battle of North Point, Sept. 12
❻ British Retreat Begins, Sept 13
❼ Sunken Hulks
❽ Bombardment Fleet
❾ Main British Fleet
❿ HMS *Tonnant*

11

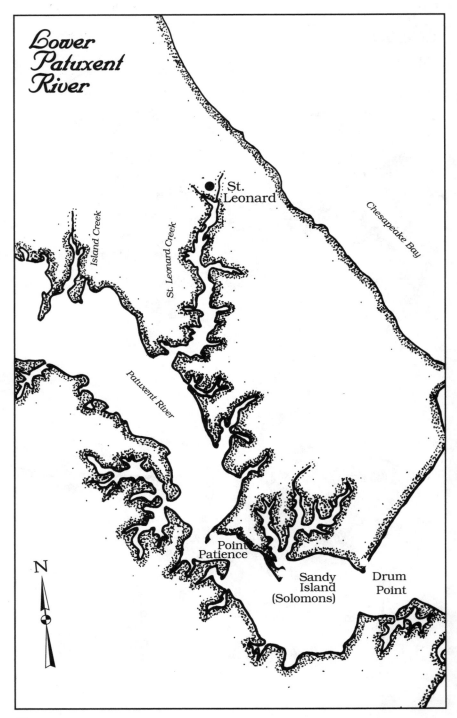

Lower Patuxent River

Island Creek

St. Leonard Creek

St. Leonard

Chesapeake Bay

Patuxent River

Point Patience

Sandy Island (Solomons)

Drum Point

N

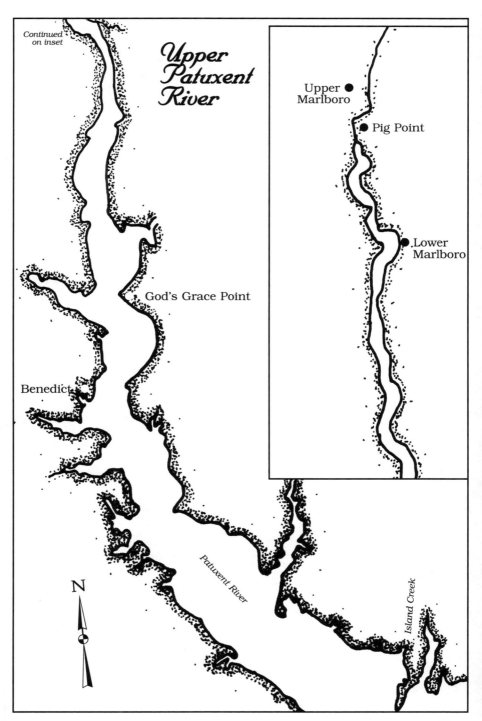

Upper
Patuxent
River

Continued on inset

Upper Marlboro

Pig Point

Lower Marlboro

God's Grace Point

Benedict

Patuxent River

Island Creek

N

CHAPTER ONE

The black-hulled sloop ghosted around the point and into the small bay; the men on deck were silent, unmoving. In fact, they were barely breathing. Standing next to the man at the tiller, Isaac Biggs strained his eyes through the Stygian darkness. Even though he had cut the point as close as he dared, few aboard had been able to make out any details of the land; it was merely a dim smudge darker than the surrounding night. Those aboard took comfort in knowing that they in turn would be as difficult to spot, should someone be looking. Now they had to find the object of their late-night foray without themselves being seen. A whispered voice, hoarse with excitement, floated aft.

"I think I got her, Isaac. Lookee there, just off'n the wind'ard bow. Looks like there might be a light showin' for'ard on her." Jake Tate hunkered down at the butt of the slender bowsprit, just inside the bulwark. Even with only the scant light from the few stars peeking through the overcast, his shaggy straw-colored hair seemed to glow, disembodied and suspended in the dark. He had the sharpest eyes aboard and, though he had but one arm, had made himself indispensable on this little vessel, contributing the knowledge gained through his many years sailing the waters of the middle and northern Chesapeake Bay.

Biggs strained his eyes to penetrate the darkness, wondering how Jake managed so effortlessly. Standing as tall as his five-foot-four-inch frame would allow, he peered resolutely into the night, striving to see what the young Bayman had spotted. He pushed a hand through his curly hair and with his sleeve mopped the beaded sweat off his narrow forehead. The Bay's oppressive heat had begun early this year and even nightfall did little to cool the air or ease the heaviness that almost made it hard to breathe.

As the sloop eased into Tavern Creek, the air became still; the breeze seemed to be caught and held by the freshly-foliated trees lining both banks. A faint glimmer caught his eye.

"I got her, Jake. Good eyes." In the next breath, Isaac whispered instructions to the helmsman to "bring her up a point" and felt, rather than saw, that the black-dyed sails were trimmed properly as the sloop made her way silently toward a cove about halfway into the creek. He knew that there was little chance of any but the most alert watchman on the British frigate noticing them; the arrogance of the Royal Navy and their certain knowledge that they had successfully cowed all the inhabitants of the region virtually assured him that the watch would be sloppy at best. More likely would be someone hearing them, and he had admonished his men to "be quiet as the dead, or we stand a fair chance of bein' dead". The only sound was the gentle rush of the water as it parted before the hollow bows of the rakish sloop.

Within a few minutes, the shoreline suddenly appeared, and Isaac, having taken over the tiller himself, stood on, easing the sloop into a spot Jake had described to him before they left Kent Island. He brought her head to the wind, now barely the memory of a breeze, and the crew handed the big mains'l silently at the first sign of a luff. The sloop, barely moving now, coasted less than a length and stopped, and the anchor was eased carefully into the still, black water. Any who might have heard the splash would have surmised a fish had jumped. The stays'l and jib dropped noiselessly and were lashed down on the deck. The square tops'l had been furled to its yard even before they entered the creek.

"Everyone below now, quick as you please, and not a sound." Isaac knew he didn't have to remind his crew how critical was complete silence now; mostly Maryland watermen, each was more than familiar with how easily sound carried across the water, especially on a still night. They'd been through this drill quite a few times now, and the American sloop was building an enviable success record harassing the British. With each little triumph, the British became more determined to catch this embarrassment to their might, but so far, Biggs and his small crew had managed to disappear in the confusion they caused.

The six men crowded into the small hold and waited silently for their captain to join them. A few shifted their feet, leaning on the bulkhead or the mast. One or two mopped their faces but, for most, the sweat ran down their necks unnoticed in the close quarters. The shirts of those who still wore them were soaked, dark with sweat. The hatch closed over their heads as Isaac appeared on the ladder. The heat built instantly; someone lit a small lantern which cast long shadows and a dim yellow light reflected on the glistening faces of the men. It gave them an even more sinister look than they already had.

"I ain't gonna tell you how important what we're doin' is; you all know that since we started doin' these little raids we been drivin' the Royal Navy crazy. Commodore Barney ain't got no plan to stop, an' gettin' caught up by them surely wouldn't be part of anyone's plan. Less'n a mile into the creek there's a British frigate. 'Cordin' to the commodore, it's the selfsame one what's been sending parties ashore to burn farms and steal livestock. I don't know that we can stop 'em, but we surely can let 'em know we're here. And mayhaps get us a little payback for the trouble they been causin'." He then outlined the plan again and, after putting out the light, climbed up and opened the hatch. The night air, hot though it was, flooded into the hold cool, smelling like the woods so nearby, and the men silently followed their captain onto the deck.

With practiced, economical moves, they quietly launched a boat and Isaac and five of his raiders nestled themselves in between the casks of powder and other supplies needed for their mission. Oars, their mid-sections wrapped where they rested between the thole pins, were wet, and a hissed command from Biggs moved the boat away from the sloop and toward the British frigate.

Jake Tate, now alone on the sloop, waved unseen as the boat quickly disappeared into the night. He listened intently, straining to catch the splash or creak of an oar; the silence of the middle watch hours was broken only by the rustle of the trees and the cheeps of the peepers which had emerged from the mud to fill the night with their rhythmic sounds.

Good luck, men. This one ain't gonna be easy as them others — not against a frigate, by God. Jake thought about the task his mates had before them, and wished he were with them instead of minding the sloop. *Well, reckon I couldn't be much help to 'em anyway. That surgeon on HMS Shannon took care o' that. Course, I could be dead or settin' with Charity an' her folks at the farm. Ugh!* The one-armed sailor shook his head at the thought of being stuck ashore, and worse, with those high-minded in-laws of his who thought this war was all a waste of time and money. And it interfered with their importing business. Bad business indeed to be on the "outs" with England. Tate spat over the side, and sat on the hatch top to wait, a pistol and cutlass in easy reach of his good left arm. He had managed to become adept at handling both weapons adroitly with what had been his 'off-side'. In fact, in the almost twelve months since he caught the ball that led to its amputation, his missing limb had become little more than an inconvenience to him.

The sloop had been swallowed by the darkness within moments of their shoving off, and Isaac now steered up the creek keeping close to shore; a dark, broken backdrop would make it more difficult for anyone watching to notice the small craft as it crept toward the British warship. Isaac concentrated with part of his mind on keeping the boat headed fair, watching for low branches and stumps as the shore slipped past; the other part of his consciousness reviewed their plan and, more importantly, their escape back to the sloop.

Satisfied with the plan he and Jake had worked out with Commodore Barney, whose local knowledge was as great as Jake's, that part of his mind turned to the recent past and how he and Jake wound up here in the Chesapeake sailing small boats against some of the best of the Royal Navy.

Shortly after Oliver Perry's September triumph in *USS Lawrence* on Lake Erie, the Navy recognized a greater need existed for sailors inland than on the coast. Hundreds were detached from blockaded frigates, brigs, and sloops and marched to New York state where their services were in desperate need. Isaac's two mates, Robert Coleman and Tim Conoughy, formerly Royal Navy and now seamen in the American Navy, had been included in the group sent inland. Biggs had remained with the Salem privateer *General Washington,* under Captain Asa Rogers, for another successful cruise after their harrowing rescue mission to Halifax.

Jack Clements, a former Navy warrant bosun who had been with Captain James Lawrence aboard the *Chesapeake* frigate in June of 1813, had been released from further obligation to the Navy in recognition of the injury he received when the *Shannon* had boarded and taken the American man-of-war. His ear had been cleanly, almost surgically, removed by a cutlass stroke during the brief but fierce hand-to-hand fighting on *Chesapeake*'s deck, and his wound had been treated by the British surgeon while they were en route to Halifax and the Melville Island prison there.

There was little chance that any shipping could escape the tight stranglehold the Royal Navy now maintained on the entire coast from the Carolinas to northern Massachusetts; if a vessel was in, it stayed in, and, if offshore, her master had to find another port from which to operate. Trade suffered, and with very few exceptions, the deep-water Navy and most of the privateer fleet remained harbor-bound.

This was the driving force that drew Clements and Isaac, accompanied by Jake Tate, back to the Chesapeake. Jake had also been in the Navy and, like Clements, had been released from further service due to the wound he received during his service on *Chesapeake*. He was headed, reluctantly, for married life ashore, feeling as he did that there was little chance of his finding a berth afloat.

The three left Boston a month after their friends marched inland, arriving in Baltimore just ahead of winter. It had taken them no time at all to find useful employment with Commodore Barney's small "navy." Jake, anticipating a life ashore with Charity, was understandably delighted to find that his services would also be needed — even with only one arm. He and Isaac had been sailing this sloop together for close to three months, and Jack Clements, with a wall-eyed waterman named Frank Clark, skippered a similar vessel. So far, both the former privateersman and the navy bosun, late of the *Chesapeake*, had enjoyed only success and the two seventy-foot sloops and Barney's gunboats, like biting flies around a horse, had become anathema to the ships of Captain Robert Barrie, who regularly sent out forces to find and destroy them. The gunboats, based further south in the Patuxent River, had almost been caught twice, but so far the sloops had operated unchallenged.

"Isaac! Lookee there. Ain't no one watchin' out." Sam Hay, crouched next to Isaac and elbowed him sharply in the ribs as he whispered his observation about the Royal Navy frigate. Isaac grunted in surprise, and peered through the black night.

"Aye, 'pears so, Sam." Indeed, they could make out no watchmen or any other on the frigate's deck. A dim lantern showed near the foremast, and Isaac could detect the faint aroma of tobacco in the still air. The watchmen must be hunkered down near the fore-mast having a smoke. "Easy now, lads." Isaac's whispered command took the boat alongside the towering sheer wall of the British frigate and the oars were silently boated. He steered to a position under her starboard main channel where it was unlikely they would be seen, and where they would set the first surprise for the Royal Navy.

A stout line was heaved 'round the shroud lanyard and secured in the boat. One of the Americans silently stepped with bare feet over his boated oar and shinnied up to the channel; a small cask filled with black powder was handed up him which he placed carefully between the hull and the lanyards, affixing a length of slow match to its top. After a brief pause, the powder-impregnated cord flared suddenly, then dimmed to a glow. The sailor slid down the line and back into the boat. The forward starboard channel received the same treatment. All remained still.

Silently, Isaac moved the boat still farther forward, until his men could reach the anchor cable. A hatchet was produced and made short work of the heavy hawser; it parted and, still unnoticed by the inattentive watchmen, the frigate was free in the confined shallow water of Tavern Creek.

"Isaac! What the hell is that?" One of the men was pointing ashore and whispering frantically. A glow was building, lighting the blackness and outlining the trees. True to form, the British raiding party ashore had fired a building, likely belonging to some unco-operative farmer, and would soon be returning to their ship.

"We best be gettin' ourselves outta here, lads. I 'spect them marines'll be headed back quick as you please now they done they's dirty work. Reckon they'll be some surprised." Isaac smiled unseen in the darkness and, as the oars were shipped, steered the boat toward the shoreline and their sloop. A sharp crack, a musket shot, rang out from the deck of the frigate. And a cry.

"Alarm, alarm! Starboard side. Small boat 'eadin' off!" A watch-man on the frigate had finally looked their way.

"Row, men. They've smoked us." Isaac steered closer to shore, hoping the boat would blend in; but the light of the burning building behind them silhouetted the boat for the Royal Marines firing at them. More shots rent the night, then a crashing boom as one of the swivel guns mounted in the frigate's fighting top fired. The water around the boat was pocked with falling shot and the oarsman immediately in front of Isaac sighed and slumped over his oar.

Isaac grabbed the man by the front of his shirt and pulled him to the deck. He then took the dead man's seat and pulled his oar, his hand sticky on it from the man's blood. An explosion lit up the darkness and covering the rig of the warship briefly in it's flare.

"That's the first of 'em, lads. Keep rowing. It ought to take they's minds off'n us." Isaac was delighted to see that one of the charges they had only moments before planted on the frigate's starboard channels had done its job. The other one should be going off soon now and, as more of the British sailors and marines came on deck, someone was bound to notice that the ship was drifting with the ebbing tide. Still, the more determined of the Royal Marines maintained their fusillade of musketry and their misses pocked the water around the boat. The thump of balls hitting their hull kept the men rowing, not in a panic, but with the steady, rhythmic strokes of seasoned professionals.

Clive Billings, rowing the forward shore-side oar, suddenly screamed and dropped his oar as he clutched at his chest and shoulder. Even his normal voice sounded like a stuck door being forced; his scream penetrated the senses. His mate picked up the other oar, barely missing a stroke, and resumed pulling, handling both oars until Sam Hay, crouching in the bow, shoved the stricken Billings aside and pulled his oar. He spoke sharply to the wounded man.

"Get you aft, Clive, and take the tiller. You ain't hurt so bad as you cain't steer. Isaac's pullin' an oar. Get goin'. An' stop that hollerin'. You givin' them something to shoot at." The thought that the Royal Marines on the frigate were aiming at the sound of his voice made Clive immediately cease his "hollerin' " and stumble aft to the tiller. In his effort to remain silent, his lips formed a thin line across his face; his head swiveled back to the warship and his eyes darted wildly around, bouncing from the frigate to the dark shoreline, trying to see who had, and might again, shoot at him.

Isaac maintained the pace of their rowing while he, too, sought the source of the shot that wounded Billings. It couldn't have come from the frigate, he reasoned; the angle was wrong. Besides, the marines and sailors on the British ship, lit up brightly from the fire burning amidships, were now likely too busy to worry about the escaping Americans.

Then he heard crashing through the underbrush ashore and, ahead of them, muffled orders, and the sounds of men running, breaking branches and splashing through the shallows. As he twisted his head around to see, a muzzle flash flared dazzlingly for a second, then another, and another. The air hummed as musket balls flew close to the now desperately rowing raiders.

"Steer away! Get further from the shore." He spoke sharply to the wounded man at the tiller, and the boat swerved toward the middle of the creek. More shots came from shore; thankfully, the Marines on the frigate remained silent, still busy with the fires. Isaac also realized that the boat could well be out of their range by now. The small boat had to be getting close to the sloop and the limited sanctuary it offered.

"Isaac, larboard, man! Steer to larboard!" Tate's voice rang out over the water, and Clive Billings, his pain forgotten for the moment, pulled on the tiller. The boat responded instantly and immediately a thunderous crash filled the night. Screams and curses erupted from the trees along the shoreline. It took the men on the boat a moment to realize what had happened.

"Good job, Jake. Hit 'em again if'n you can!" Isaac bellowed at the sloop and its sole occupant who was manning the diminutive weapon mounted on the forward bulwark. The boat was suddenly alongside, and again the little flared swivel gun crashed. Fire was not returned from the shore.

The men scrambled out of the boat and onto the deck of the sloop; Isaac helped the wounded Billings aboard and then two men handed up the body of their dead shipmate. The boat was cut loose and the men went unbidden to their stations for making sail. In a trice the black sail was up and the anchor cable cut with the same hatchet used on the British cable. The light breeze filled the sail, soon augmented by the jib and stays'l, and the sloop gathered way. Biggs steered her clear of the shoreline and headed for the turn in the creek which would lead them to the Bay, the relative safety it offered, and the ability to set the tops'l. The sloop gathered speed quickly, and soon they were safely hidden in the dark of the Bay. He could still see the glow in the sky from both the burning farmhouse and the lesser fire on the English warship. And behind both, the orange and red harbingers of the sunrise.

CHAPTER TWO

"Maybe you oughtn't take on a frigate, even a little sxth-rate frigate, by your own self again, Isaac. Might be something we could do as a two-boat expedition. Sounds to me like you come pretty close to gettin' yourself caught . . . or dead." Jack Clements had arrived back at Kent Island the day after Biggs' sloop had been warped into the dock, returning without further incident, and the two, with Jake Tate and Frank Clark, were enjoying a tankard at the Barking Dog, a block from the Eastern Bay waterfront.

"Jack, that frigate didn't look 'little' to us, I'll warrant, but you're likely right; with two boats we could use the second to watch our backs. But I ain't thinkin' they's gonna be too many more chances to get alongside a frigate. Anywhere but out in the Bay the water's too thin by half for 'em. I'd think most of 'em'll stay down south of Tangier Island. Whoever that was commandin' the one I went after must've been takin' some kind o' chance, goin' into Tavern Creek like he done. 'Specially on a tide what could only be ebbin' when he was ready to get gone." He paused, took a pull at his mug of ale, and nodded at the young man next to him. " 'Twas young Jake, here, saved our arses with that swivel gun. She's old, but they ain't much I'd trade for it." He smiled at Tate, and the one-armed Marylander sat a little straighter and beamed at the praise.

"Well, I'd reckon he done that cuz he figgered wasn't no way he could sail that sloop back to Kent with but one arm and, without you and them others, that was his choice. Probably was thinkin' 'bout Miss Charity over to Frederick County pinin' away for her darlin' Chauncey." He winked at Jake, noticed the look the newly-married Bayman threw at him at the mention of his real name, and went on in the same vein. "You ain't been home more'n once since you two got married up, have you, Jake? Isaac, I'd say you ought to let this cove get along home to his bride. He's likely got some business to take care of." All three men were smiling now; Isaac and Clements at Jack's ribald humor, and Jake at the thought of spending some time yardarm-to-yardarm with his new bride. The flash of anger at Jack passed as quickly as it came.

Frank Clark sat silently, his gaze, as near as anyone could tell, shifting from Clements to Biggs to Tate as he struggled to understand the past the three men had shared. It bothered him that he would never have the close relationship, the easy camaraderie, these three enjoyed. His broad forehead furrowed and his wide set eyes alternately danced with pleasure or dimmed in consternation as events from their experiences in the Caribbean or New England were recalled. His mostly bald head was shiny with sweat, and his short pigtail bounced with each nod as he tried in vain to share the relationship his mates had with one another. Under the table, unseen, his fists clenched tightly on his legs.

"I 'spect we could drop him off in Baltimore when next we go over there. You might get a day or two if'n you step along to your in-laws'." Isaac aimed a look at Jake, whose smile broadened to split his face. The young man took a long swallow, gathering his thoughts as he did, and looked at the former bosun and his shipmate on the ill-starred *USS Chesapeake*.

"You surely are right, Jack. I could put up with a day or two at the farm — an' even with my new in-laws. Got some unfinished business with Charity. Isaac here ain't given me more'n a day at a time to spend with her since we was married up. Mayhaps I ought to just get on with it. Hear tell lots of coves headin' home; reckon they figger this war ain't goin' nowhere, an' what's the use of sendin' out small boats 'gainst the Royal Navy." His mouth smiled, but his eyes were flat; he was only half in jest.

Isaac could not accept that the young man who had been through so much might be in earnest and said hopefully, "I know you're just trying to rile me up, Jake. You know we're doin' real good here. I reckon that frigate we tangled with the other night won't be fightin' any too soon. They'll be re-riggin' the main shrouds anyway, and likely fixin' the damage the fires caused."

Biggs paused and shook his head. "I sure would like to know why that for'ard powder keg never went off. That would have really slowed 'em down. As to sendin' "small boats" out to fight — I cain't think of anything else we could be doin'. Sendin' frigates or even brigs into some of these back waters would give us the same trouble it gives the Royal Navy. We'd be runnin' aground every time we turned a bend, same as them. I'd wager it took 'em two tides, maybe more, to get that one from the other night off'n the hard. No sir, we're doin' good, and I hear that Commodore Barney's gunboats down south are doin' a fine job, 's'well." He paused, and look hard at Jake. "And you know we need you. They'll be time aplenty when this is done to sit by the fire and spoon with Miss Charity. But I will let you have a run ashore for a few days. Maybe help to put out some of them fires burnin' in your belly."

Jake's face was alight at the thought of a few days with his new bride, and his smile belied his feigned attention to his companions as his mind drifted off in that direction and the conversation swirled around him. He never had any intention of leaving Isaac and Jack and the rakish sloops. But some time exploring the delights of marriage would be a welcome respite from the risky expeditions that had occupied their time for the past three months. And he thought of Charity's tears and wails of grief when he told her shortly after their wedding that he would be leaving her to join Commodore Barney's 'private navy'. But a man's got to pull his share, and sailing was the only skill he knew, and the Bay the only place left where he could help the cause.

" . . . 'bout it Jake. Jake?" Clark touched the young man's shoulder, one eye looking questioningly at him while the other struggled to focus and finally squinted down, eliminating the image of Clements across the table. "You comin'?" Clark stood up, his barrel-shaped body looming over the slighter, one-armed figure of his friend. His large hands were no longer balled into fists, but even relaxed he appeared coiled, ready to spring at whatever was in front of him.

"Oh . . . uh . . . aye. I'm with you." Jake stood and finished in one swallow the remains of his tankard. He followed Frank to the door, and Isaac and Jack heard him say as they left, "Where're we goin', Frank?"

Jack laughed with Isaac as they watched Clark take Jake by the arm and guide him out the door of the alehouse. The dim room brightened suddenly as the door opened, letting the afternoon sun burst in, illuminating the dust particles and smoke in the air, then just as quickly darkened as Frank closed it in their wake.

"There's two good men, Isaac. I wouldn't want to be doin' this work without either one of 'em. You really gonna give Jake a run ashore, or was you just puttin' him off?"

"I said I would, and I will, I reckon. I figger the commodore'll be sending us out again in a day or two, and we can set him ashore 'cross the Bay. Maybe we ought to try a run together — see how it works out."

"Likely might keep your arse from gettin' shot up or worse were there to be another sloop to help you out — or you me." Jack nodded seriously at his friend and in his mind the matter was settled: the next time they were ordered out, it would be as a two-boat expedition. His hand moved absently to touch the gold ring in his missing ear; realizing his error, he quickly pulled his hand away and lifted his tankard for a long draught.

"Say, Isaac, join me on the sloop; I have something to show you." Jack stood, and Isaac, with a questioning look at his former shipmate, rose from his chair, finishing his ale as he did so.

As the pair approached the pier where the two sloops and a variety of other craft were tied, they each commented again on the fine job the British had done in building it, and how considerate it was of them to abandon it last summer when they left Kent Island, ultimately leaving the Bay, except for a small force left at Lynnhaven, by year's end. As they neared Clements' sloop, they could hear the deep and insistent barking of a dog — a large dog from the sound of its bark.

"That dog sounds like it's on your vessel, Jack. I never knew you had much time for animals." Isaac looked at Clements who just smiled and continued walking. The barking became more insistent.

As they came abreast of the second sloop in Commodore Barney's flotilla, Isaac could see a huge gray dog straining at a chain which connected him to the lower mast. In spite of the constriction of the rope tied around the beast's neck, his barking was undiminished, and he lunged against the chain, baring fangs and pawing at the air with great forepaws. His hackles stood up along his back, from his massive head all the way to the top of his long tail. Isaac stopped dead in his tracks.

"If that's what you wanted to show me, Jack, I'll be happy to look from here. That ain't nothin' I want to get any closer to. Why you'd want a beast like him on board I cain't imagine, 'specially since movin' with some silence is important to what we do."

"Oh, he's quiet when I tell him to be, an' he likely won't hurt you none, long as I'm right here. Come on aboard; I'll show you." And with that, Clements stepped aboard the vessel and went up to the dog which immediately became quiet. "That's a good boy, Carronade. Come on, Isaac. Lookee here; he's tame as ever could be. Just put out your hand so's he can sniff it."

"What'd you call him, Jack? Carronade? What kind of a name is that for a dog?" Isaac, while aboard the sloop, remained safely out of range of the beast's chain.

"Aye, Isaac. Carronade it is. Not much good at any kind of range, but close aboard, he's a smasher, by God." The tall good-natured captain laughed as he always did when asked to explain the dog's name, then he became more serious. "An' he's got damn fine ears; better than mine, anyway — 'specially seein's how he's still got two of 'em! He don't carry on like he done when we're close in. Just growls some when he hears something. I reckon he can smell an Englishman from a league an' more." Jack scratched the huge animal lovingly behind one floppy ear, and the dog, his eyes half closed and clearly enraptured, leaned easily against the former bosun's leg.

Isaac approached warily, his hand tentatively outstretched for the dog to sniff — or help himself to a piece of; he watched the dog's eyes, now open and alert, for an indication of which it might be. Jack spoke softly to him and Carronade smelled the proffered hand disinterestedly and looked adoringly at his master.

"Go ahead, Isaac. Pet him some. He ain't gonna hurt you. Now he knows you're a friend."

Gradually, Biggs let his hand rest on top of the dog's head and, when there was no reaction from Carronade, patted him nervously. Isaac smiled. "I sure am glad he's on our side, Jack. I'd hate to try an' get aboard this vessel if'n he didn't want me to." He withdrew his hand, clasping both behind his back. No sense in taking chances. "Where'd you find him?"

"Got him last time out, I did. Found him tied to a wagon an' left. Reckon the British raidin' party musta catched him and were takin' him aboard the brig we found down toward the lower part of Talbot County. When we run 'em off, they just left him, and I figgered he might be a good addition to my crew. Seemed to take to me right off, an' here we are." He looked at the dog and smiled. "Ain't that right, Carronade? You'd sooner be bitin' them Redcoats than . . ." He never finished the sentence, interrupted as he was by a rider on a sweat-streaked horse who stopped his dash down the pier at the sloop.

Carronade began to bark and snarl at the intruder and the rider thought better of dismounting, preferring to remain safely aboard his horse as he called out, "Cap'n Biggs? Cap'n Clements? Got a message from the Commodore for you."

CHAPTER THREE

"Looks like you ain't gonna be gettin' over to t'other side o' the Bay this time, Jake. Your young bride's just gonna have to wait a bit more. I 'spect we'll be back up this way again sooner than later, though, so don't despair yet." Isaac was grim-faced as he broke the news to the young Lothario whose face darkened as he thought of the indeterminate wait he would have before he again saw his new wife.

In the two days since the rider had brought the demand from Commodore Barney that the two sloops be in the Patuxent River as quick as ever possible, Isaac and Jack had provisioned their vessels to be self-sufficient and made their plans for departure during the period of the new moon. Since there were continuing reports of British concentrations both ashore and afloat from Sharp's Island south, and it was only in April that the Royal Navy had seized and burned sixteen and more American vessels in the same area, the American captains decided that making the run south would best be done in the dark hours, taking advantage of their black sails and hulls and easy familiarity with the shoals and passages unavailable to the larger ships they might encounter — should a dash to safety be necessary.

The two left their pier-side berths before the new moon rose in the last hours of the evening watch. Their black sails rendered them nearly invisible and their dark hulls merged with the leaden waters of Eastern Bay as they slipped away unnoticed. Isaac led the second sloop out past Kent Point and into the Chesapeake proper, hugging the shore line as Jake, his misery over not seeing

Charity now behind him, called the bottom and guided them safely past unseen hazards.

Jack and Isaac, in consultation with both Tate and Frank Clark, had decided to make the run along the Eastern Shore, feeling that the safety offered by the creeks and rivers, islands and peninsulas corrugating the coastline more than compensated for the slightly longer distance they would sail. The water was good and the northwest wind fair for the passage; with the tide helping them along, they expected to be passing Somervell's (now Solomon's) Island at the mouth of the Patuxent shortly after dawn.

The two vessels remained within shouting distance of each other, though of course, no one was shouting. The night remained clear, and with just the sliver of a new moon showing low on the Eastern horizon, quite dark. They had followed the edge of Tilghman Island south, heading for the mouth of the Choptank River when Sam Hay, on Isaac's sloop, called out quietly from the leeward shrouds.

"Isaac. Lookee there . . . comin' out of the Choptank. Ain't that a ship headin' this way? Looks like she might be brig-rigged. Take a look."

Biggs was in the rigging instantly, climbing up past Hay with the ease of a seasoned topman. Even as he reached the tops'l yard, his longglass was at his eye. After a moment of study he grabbed a halyard and slid to the deck in the tradition of the men who earned their keep in the dizzying heights of the upper masts on the tall ships.

"Bring her around. Hands to wear ship" He spoke only as loudly as was necessary to be heard and the little ship's stern smoothly crossed the wind as Isaac, with Jake calling the bottom, guided her into the shallows behind Black Walnut Point and up the back side of Tilghman Island. Their pace dropped perceptibly as they came into the lee of the point and the northwest breeze was cut in half by the tall trees which gave the point its name.

The cloak of invisibility provided by their dark hulls and sails worked both for them and against them; no one on Jack Clements' sloop noticed that their companions had worn ship and ducked behind Black Walnut Point. They proceeded to sail serenely across the mouth of the Choptank — and the unseen bow of the ship beating out of the river in the easy breeze.

"'eave to there and identify yourself." The hail from the ship provided the American's first notice of it as she loomed within easy musket range. Carronade, already alert and sniffing the air suspiciously, peered over the bulwark at the British voice. A low and menacing growl escaped his throat. Jack took the tiller and calling his men to stations for tacking, brought the sloop around smartly on a reverse course, and hard on the wind. Voices, broken in the wind, carried to them from the brig.

"Looks like . . . tacked."

"Aye, black . . . devilish 'ard . . . make out."

". . . American raid . . . bounty . . ."

Then *Heart of Oak*, the drumbeat calling the sailors and Marines to quarters, could be heard on the British ship and Jack knew he had little time before their bow chasers would be seeking the range. The shore line of Tilghman's — and the relative safety it offered — seemed awfully far.

Boom . . . crack. The wind'ard bow chaser fired. Its echo resonated off the shoreline of the island. But no splash. The shot prompted one bark that turned into a snarl from the huge dog on the sloop.

"Jack, ease her off a trifle and, when I tell you, bring her back up. They's a channel through there that I warrant them damn Royal Navy bastards won't know, and if they follow and miss it, they'll be on the hard. Ain't marked, and unless you know it, a real trial to find." Frank Clark pointed toward the end of Tilghman's Island and, while Jack could make out little of the shore line, he had complete faith in the local knowledge the waterman possessed; he eased the sloop down. And spoke quietly to his men.

"They're just guessin' where we's at, lads. Keep it quiet as a tomb and mayhaps we can slip by 'em."

As if to punctuate his words, another shot rang out from the larger vessel. This time there was a splash, well to their wind'ard. Jack smiled in the dark, and touched Clark on the shoulder, pointing at where the dim starlight made the white splash seem brighter than it was in contrast to the darkness all around them. Frank nodded and spoke softly.

"Be bringin' her up again here right quick now. Channel's just yonder. With the wind like it is, we gonna be hard on her to make it through here in one tack. Channel's maybe only a hunnert feet wide, and ain't no water out of her. Best you get someone for'ard with a leadline. An' if'n I tell you to tack, don't wait to think about it; do it." Clark, ever the taciturn waterman, emphasized the importance of his instructions just by the volume of words he spoke.

"Hands to stations for trimming sails . . . and quiet-like." Clements whispered, and sensed rather than saw that the crew were quickly in position to manage the sloop as she navigated the narrow unmarked channel in the darkness. He put his complete confidence in Clark's experience with these waters. And he shushed the still-snarling dog — to no effect.

"Now, Jack! Bring her up, high as ever she'll go." Clark's head swiveled between the end of Black Walnut Point, the bow of the little sloop, and the dim shape of the British warship still standing out to the southwest. The distance was opening, and the sloop danced through the light chop into the unseen channel, sails hauled in tight against the northwesterly breeze.

Another shot rang out from the warship and, as the crash of the gun died off, the faint splash could be heard some distance away.

"The British ain't got no idea where we are, Jack. They're firin' in the wrong direction now." Tom Walters, idle since Clements took over the tiller himself, observed brightly. In his excitement he raised his voice, even though Jack was only a few feet away. Within a few seconds, another shot rang out from the English ship.

This time, the splash was easy to hear; the ball threw up water only a boat length from the escaping sloop. And then the sounds of the brig tacking, the sails shivering, blocks rattling, and orders being shouted, floated across the water. Carronade responded to the cacophony with a single bark, then resumed his quiet, threatening growl.

"Oh my God. They musta heard us. Silence fore an' aft." Jack's whisper was hoarse with concern; armed as she was with just a swivel gun, his little ship would not be able to stand up to even a few shots from the English twelve-pounders. They had to disappear into the darkness or be crushed into matchwood.

Silently, he wondered what had happened to Isaac. He had seen or heard nothing of him since the English ship appeared. Was it his sloop the warship had been shooting at when Jack heard no splashes? Was it that there were splashes from the shots and Clements, with but one ear, had missed them. Or was he safely away? And where did he go? Had he seen the British and called out a warning to Jack which, again with impaired hearing, he had missed? No. Someone else would have heard and acted on a warning, had there been one. Isaac must have borne off quietly in the darkness, afraid that a signal to Jack would give them away. Yes, he thought, that was it. That must be it. He would see . . . *boom . . . boom.*

His concerns for Biggs and his crew became irrelevant as the water thrown up by the iron ball came aboard. He had to look to his own crew; Isaac could take care of himself, for now anyway.

"Frank," he whispered forward into the darkness. "I'm bearing off some. Got to get some speed on her. That last shot was too close. Mind your depth." Without waiting for an answer he eased the tiller to wind'ard and felt the sloop come off the wind slightly, gathering speed as she did so. The sails paid out somewhat and the little vessel heeled and leaped ahead.

Suddenly Clark was at Jack's elbow. "Jack, you're gonna put her on the hard you don't come back up. They ain't nothin' but flats out here twixt us and that point yonder." Clark's concern was evident, even in a whisper. Another shot crashed out from their pursuer. This time, the splash was to wind'ard, right about where they would have been had Jack not borne off when he did.

A hushed voice whispered the depths as the sloop continued to gain speed, now heeled over to where her lee rail was even with the black water rushing by. The hands held their collective breath, knowing for certain it was only a matter of time until they bottomed out, stranding on the shallows while the Royal Navy took their time to find them, and then pound them into kindling. Still, the sloop rushed on. The soundings showed they were getting into thin water, but Jack carried on, intent on escaping. All his senses and instincts gained over a lifetime at sea concentrated on everything around him: the water's appearance, the soundings as they were whispered aft, the dim shoreline, and the faint outline of the British ship, enhanced by the glow of her battle lanterns.

Without warning, he threw the tiller over to leeward; the hands scurried to adjust the sails and the sloop passed smoothly through stays and charged off on the other tack, accelerating and heading back towards the channel. Clark's sigh was audible and his muttered "Thank God" voiced the feelings of the entire crew. Now if they could get back into the deeper water without . . . A grinding noise followed by shouted curses and yelled commands came from behind them. The English ship had not found the channel. And the depth under the sloop was increasing.

"She's took the bottom, Jack. God alone knows how you managed to keep us off'n the hard, but I reckon they'll be busy as ever they could be for a while now. Once them soundings get back up to three fathoms an' more, we can tack back and just follow the channel back out to the Bay. Put us 'bout two miles behind where we come in, but we'll be offshore o' the British. Probably sail by 'em easy as kiss my hand." Clark, in his quiet way, was as jubilant in their narrow escape as any had ever seen him. Clements released the breath he had been holding and smiled in the darkness. Carronade offered a final deep bark and became silent. He laid down on the diminutive quarterdeck, head on his forepaws, confident that he done his job well.

CHAPTER FOUR

The thunder was continuous; one shattering crash led directly into the next and the lightning maintained an incessant brilliance from horizon to horizon. The succession of window-rattling blasts from the heavens, with their instantaneous shocks of blinding yellow light, had stopped all conversation in the ramshackle building Commodore Joshua Barney used as a temporary headquarters on the edge of a shallow and narrow tributary of the Patuxent River called St. Leonard Creek.

Isaac and Jack Clements stood by a window transfixed by the ferocity of the storm; neither, in their years at sea, had seen anything quite like this. To be sure, they had each witnessed their share and more of head-shaking weather, including thunder and lightning, rain, snow, wind and worse, but what made this so unusual was the constancy of the heavenly display. It had been going on now without interruption for an hour and more and the intensity of the rain had only increased. Neither man could see the dock and two gunboats secured there though they were only a scant pistol shot distant, and, without question, the lightning surely provided adequate illumination. Strangest of all, though, was the complete lack of wind. Not a breath. The rain poured straight down; the torrent running off the steeply-pitched roof indistinguishable from that which came directly from the heavens.

The men who remained sitting at the table suddenly stood and, without comment, picked up the table and chairs and moved them for the third time away from the expanding leak overhead. Commodore Barney again lit the fat candle in the table's center, after drying the wick in his fingers.

"Lightning's bright enough we likely don't need this." He smiled at the four men who sat with him at the table littered with water-stained charts and mugs of thick coffee.

The men from the black-hulled sloops, Biggs and Tate, Clements and Clark, had been called to a meeting with the commodore in the waning hours of daylight. Jared Talbot and Luke Cooper, two of the senior gunboat captains, had also been invited. Something over two weeks before, they were chased into the Patuxent River and more recently into the creek, along with the gunboats and barges, and now were effectively blockaded there by a brace of frigates and a seventy-four, each with its complement of attendant schooners and cutters.

The American captains reflected their commodore's black humor and so far, no one had put forth a plan to escape that had even the smallest chance of success. Isaac and Jack had left the table in frustration and had been watching the storm and talking quietly while the others, the Baymen and the gunboat skippers, continued hatching and discarding ruses by which they might fool the British into opening the river's mouth.

Now even they were silenced, as much by the noise of the storm as by their lack of ideas. Each looked up as they realized Barney was speaking.

" . . . know them raids the damn Royal Navy is doin' is aimed at getting us to engage 'em. Ever since they chased us up here from Cedar Point they been tryin' to figger out how to get to us to make a break for it. I'd reckon it's only a matter of time afore they sail right in here brazen as ever you please." He paused, a thoughtful look, then a thin smile crossed his face. "I'd rather take 'em on here in the river where we might have an edge with our shallow draft than out yonder where they got sea room." Barney looked from face to face, seeing nods of agreement around the table.

Clements turned away from the window and fixed the commodore with a hard look. His hand lightly rubbed the scar where his ear had been. "'Ceptin' for the sloops. We could outsail 'em easy as kiss my hand out in the Bay. In here, ain't much we can do to help you. Isaac an' me an' our lads been doin' some good up the Bay. Down here, we're just 'bout as useful as teats on a boar." The lanky deep waterman, for all his easy going manner and good humor, was not happy at being trapped with the gunboats in the Patuxent River. Indeed, not just the sloops and gunboats were bottled up in the narrow river, but most of Barney's squadron, including thirteen row barges and four light ketches used as fire ships, were trapped as well.

He felt Isaac touch his arm lightly and, turning back to the window, caught the warning look from his friend. Clements aimed his scowl at the downpour and drifted back a few weeks as he thought again of the events which had conspired to neutralize the flotilla and the two sloops.

After escaping the British brig at the mouth of the Choptank River, Jack had sailed south without further incident, finding the gunboats and barges anchored at the mouth of the Patuxent River just off Cedar Point. Setting his anchor offshore of them, he found the commodore in one of the gunboats and paid him a visit to report his arrival. Isaac's sloop was not in evidence.

"Where's Biggs and the other sloop?" were the first words out of Barney's mouth when Jack climbed over the rail on the gunboat.

"Last saw him off'n the Choptank in the dark hours, Commodore. Thought he'd be here afore me, seein' as how I had a little set-to with a British brig." A brief smile crossed the tall sloop captain' face as he recalled the way he left his adversary. "Left the might of the Royal Navy on the hard off Tilghman's so I'd reckon they didn't give Isaac any problem, but I got nary a thought as to where he might have got his self." The look that passed between Jack and Frank Clark indicated the concern that both men shared about their friend. Clark had been casting an eye back along their track from the north as if he expected to see Isaac's sloop break the horizon any moment.

"Damme. I need both sloops if we're to accomplish anything here. The English are building up a garrison on Tangier Island and Secretary Jones wants us to make their lives as miserable as possible; harass their ships and take the smaller ones, raid the island and whatever else we can think of." The commodore paused, removed his cocked hat and ran a hand through his still-dark hair — even at fifty-five years of age, he looked many years younger. He wiped his face and neck with a lace-trimmed handkerchief. Even before he resumed, the sweat was again freely coursing down his high forehead, beading in his bushy eyebrows, and running unchecked down the end of his long nose where it sprayed out with every word he uttered. "Hear tell they're building up a force of escaped slaves on Tangier Island and gettin' 'em riled up to fight against us. Callin' 'em *Colonial Marines.* And givin' 'em transport to Bermuda or Halifax if'n they ain't of a mind to fight.

"Your sloop, and Isaac's, will give us speed and surprise — just like you done up the Bay. Let the English think we got a lot of 'em. I'm thinkin' of putting some light cannons — maybe six- or eight-pounders — aboard and sending you out after their transports. The smaller ones, of course. Take a few of 'em and we might discourage some of the Negroes who're thinkin' on joinin' up with the Colonial Marines. My gunboats and the barges can do the rest, but I was countin' on both of them sloops."

Joshua Barney, his face flushed in anger, suffered Jack and Frank another hour of his tirade. The three stood in the mid-day sun and, while the commodore paused every so often to wipe his dripping face and neck, Jack and Frank let the sweat run freely down, soaking their shirts and gradually turning their faces red, almost as red as Commodore Barney's. Neither was particularly moved by Barney's useless ranting and, after a short spell, their minds drifted off, wondering about the whereabouts of Isaac; the commodore's words blurred and swirled around them finally blending into the background noise of the wind and the cries of the sea birds.

A cry from Clements' sloop brought a welcome end to the commodore's declamation. "Ships! Two sail in sight to the north. Headin' this way. 'Ppears they ain't but small ones." The ensuing silence was complete — and short lived.

Orders flew from the commodore's vessel and were echoed throughout the small fleet. Clements and Clark, openly joyful at the excuse to be away, jumped to the rail and into their waiting boat, encouraging the four oarsmen to pull "like the divil himself was in their wake".

Anchors were won and, to Barney's cries of "Sails and oars!", the flotilla was underway to cut off these two small vessels. Jack's sloop led the way and the oarsmen in the barges strained to augment their lateen sails and keep up. Carronade, perched in the bow of the sloop, kept up a fearsome noise, either exhorting the British to heave to or the men on the sloop to make it go faster.

Before the Americans gained the deeper water of the Bay, the British vessels passed, turning "cutting off" into a stern chase.

"Jack, that ain't jest two vessels." Clark had returned to the deck after a few minutes in the shrouds with the longglass. "Looks to me like we're chasin' a schooner and six, mayhaps seven sailin' barges." He looked astern, a dour expression crossing his face, and pointed with his chin. "Them gunboats and barges ain't gonna be much help less'n they can keep up with us. And if'n we catch the enemy up afore they get here, that little swivel gun ain't gonna be much help neither." Clements nodded at his second in command, but ordered no reduction in sail. The sloop careered down the Bay, closing with the fleeing British ships — outstripping the American gunboats and barges.

Boom. A shot rang out. "That came from the schooner; you can see the smoke. Ranging, I'd reckon, with they's stern chaser." Jack watched carefully for the splash.

"There it is. Short. And from a small bore gun, be my guess. Not much water throw'd up." Frank Clark correctly surmised that they had "a fair amount of chase left" before they'd be within the range of the light — probably six-pounder — cannon in the schooner. "Any idea what we gonna do when we catch them up, Jack?"

Boom. Another shot was fired with little change in the threat it posed to the American sloop.

"I reckon we'll just have to take our chances, Frank. Don't much take to bein' on the receivin' end of they's shot, so I 'spect we'll have to stay out of their range 'til them others catch up. May-haps we can slow 'em down a bit, though right now, I cain't think of how with just the swivel gun." Clements' good humor was fading fast, and he was beginning to think they should have stayed in the waters off Baltimore, the commodore and his orders be damned.

"Ship! They's another ship ahead! Wind'ard bow, three, maybe four leagues. Don't 'ppear she's set with sail, but she's tall." The lookout, hanging on to the windward shrouds near the mast cap, was alert and watching more than the fleeing schooner. Jack grabbed his glass and leaped into the rigging.

"A seventy-four, by my lights. Damn. We got some trouble now." He glanced astern at the gunboats straining their rigs and the men's backs to catch up. *They's still a cannon shot and more back,* he thought and trained his glass on the British schooner and beyond it, the anchored battleship. *This ain't what I signed on for. Ain't gonna take on a three-decker with that toy gun.* He peered aft again, hopeful that he would notice a difference in the position of the gunboats. Something caught his eye beyond them, and he refocused the longglass.

By God, that's Isaac. I'd bet my life on it. Cain't be more than the two of us with black sails and hulls. He part slid and part scrambled down the ratlines.

"Frank. Have look aft an' tell me what you see." He handed the bayman the glass and waited impatiently while the stocky mate adjusted the focus, squinted through it, changed eyes after a moment, then refocused.

"Looks like a black-sailed sloop to me. Got his tops'l set and makin' a fair turn of speed it 'pears. Reckon it could be young Isaac catchin' up with us." He handed the glass back to Clements and looked at him for a moment. Then he pointed forward with his chin. "What'd you see up ahead there when you was aloft?"

"That's a seventy-four up there. I'd warrant our friends here are runnin' under her guns. If my figgerin's right, Isaac's gonna get here just about the time we're all in her range. An' he don't have any idea he's sailing into a hornet's nest." He cast his eyes about the tiny quarterdeck and forward, seeking some way to warn his friend and former shipmate.

"Flags! Flags on the gunboat astern." The lookout was earning his keep today.

"What's that all about, Jack? He's just put 'em up." As Clark spoke, a gun fired on the commodore's boat.

"Must be in the book. Maybe something 'bout Isaac comin' on." Clements was thumbing through the slim volume of signals that had been designed by Barney. He looked up from time to time, licking his finger as he turned pages in the book.

"They're tacking, Jack. The gunboats're tacking; headin' back north, they are, by God. Mayhaps that commodore cove got some sense after all."

"By God you're right, Frank. Hand the tops'l, lads, then get to your stations for tacking."

Four men swarmed aloft and stepped out on the single yard. Sheets were cast off and the small tops'l was quickly drawn up and furled. Even before the topmen were back on deck, Jack threw the tiller over and the sloop spun smartly toward the shoreline, continued through the eye of the wind and back the way they'd come, close hauled and hard on the wind.

"Schooner's tacked, too. And they's a cutter comin' out from the seventy-four, looks like." Again the lookout was alert. Everyone on deck looked aft, even the man on the tiller.

"That cutter ain't gonna take no time to catch up with them. Looks like the barges didn't come about, though. I don't like runnin' when we ain't got to. I'd warrant Isaac an' us an' them two gunboats could make short work of that schooner. Cutter too, like as not." Clements looked back toward the enemy again and then forward, figuring how fast Isaac, still headed south, would close them. He picked up the signal book again, rapidly turning the pages and muttering. "They must have something in here I can use to tell the commodore what I'm thinkin'."

He handed the book to Clark, pointed to a signal and said, "Here. Use that. He'll get the idea."

The necessary flags snapped in the breeze as they were hauled up to the tops'l yardarm and Jack ordered a single shot fired to windward to get their attention. "And reload that piece with grape quick as you fire it."

The gunboat carrying the commodore luffed up, waiting for the sloop and the pursuing British vessels to catch up; Isaac's sloop closed quickly and, within a moment or two, was within a pistol shot of the other Americans. The barges continued to the north, seeking the shelter of Cedar Point and the Patuxent River.

Boom! Boom! The twenty-four-pounders on the gunboats thundered out their greeting to the on-rushing British schooner. Jack and Isaac, now within range of their swivel guns, waited until they were sure of their shot and fired almost simultaneously.

"Jack! That cutter . . . he's firin' rockets!" Frank was pointing at the small cutter, still pressing on with a vengeance. And the schooner now opened fire at what amounted to point-blank range. The air was alight with British rockets fired from the seventy-four's cutter. A hole appeared in Clements' mainsail and they could hear the crash and splintering as one of the schooner's shot found a mark in Isaac's bulwark.

A cannon roared out from the commodore's vessel, and he immediately bore off heading for the protection of the river. The two sloop captains, realizing they were outgunned, followed suit. And the cutter, rockets streaking off her deck willy-nilly, pressed on after them.

"Reckon we slowed that schooner some, Jack. Don't think he's gonna be botherin' us for a while." Frank allowed himself a small smile and pointed aft at the wallowing schooner; its mainsail was not only down, but hanging over the side. They could see sailors scrambling to get it contained as the vessel lay hove to.

"Musta been one of the gunboats' shot done that. Don't reckon even a lucky shot with them swivels woulda taken down their mains'l."

The little flotilla had gained the river mouth and the protection of Cedar Point; the British cutter fired another barrage of rockets and broke off, returning to offer assistance to the stricken schooner.

Barney led his ships deeper into the Patuxent and anchored. They could see the cutter and the schooner, once again under sail, maneuvering across the entrance to the river.

The Americans waited, and the captains were called to the gunboat to plot a strategy, as everyone else kept a wary eye on the British.

"Look there, Commodore. That vessel comin' in. It's American I'd warrant." Isaac had been keeping one eye on the mouth of the river and called everyone's attention to the tops'l schooner heading in. Suddenly, as they watched, boats put off from the two British vessels and the cutter fired rockets at the American. Then the British sailors in the boats boarded her.

"My God. They're gonna fire her. Lookee there. That's smoke already comin' outta the schooner 'midships, by all the stars. Commodore, we oughta get out there an' give 'em a hand. Chase them bastards off, by God. Ain't right settin' here safe an' sound while they burn that vessel." Jack was rightly put out by the action of the blockading ships against the unarmed American ship.

"That's just what they's hopin', Captain Clements; that we'll come rushin' out there and then they got us. No, we will wait until we can get clear without losing our ships."

"Jack, cast an eye yonder, friend. I'd reckon that might be that seventy-four we seen earlier at the mouth of the Potomac. You can make her tops over the point. And I'd guess she's sailin' this way. Commodore's right; we'd have sailed right into her guns." Isaac ran a hand through his curly hair, and wiped the sweat off his face. His frustration was matched by all aboard as they watched in silence while the American schooner burned to the waterline. And then the three-decker hove into view, its guns run out and the red coats of the Royal Marines visible in the fighting tops.

CHAPTER FIVE

"They're comin' in again! Stand by your guns and move toward the creek!" Barney's bellowed commands were easily heard throughout the flotilla in the early morning stillness. An alert lookout had spotted HMS *Loire* (38), a frigate, and a smaller brig, *Jaseur*, heading into the Patuxent in the second attempt to catch the gunboats, barges, and sloops still sheltering in the bight behind Cedar Point. They brought their barges and the schooner HMS *St. Lawrence* with them, most likely hoping their shallower drafts would find less difficulty with the tricky waters of the Patuxent.

For nearly two weeks it had been quiet; two frigates, a brig, the schooner, and the seventy-four, which had turned out to be *HMS Dragon*, maintained their vigil just off the entrance to the river, occasionally sending in small boats to harass the Americans or just to have a look. Yesterday, June seventh, the whole force moved into the mouth of the Patuxent, and Barney had responded by easing his group further into the river. He had told his captains of his plan to move into St. Leonard Creek should the need arise. Only Clements had commented, and so only Isaac could hear, "Once they get us in there, we might's well start walkin' home. Ain't no way to get out or around them in that little creek. The British can keep us bottled up long as they want — and likely with one frigate."

Isaac had nodded, silently agreeing with his older friend and former shipmate, but as he pointed out, "We ain't exactly gonna sail right outta the river, neither, Jack, with the *Dragon* and them others settin' off the point. Why, they'd turn us to matchwood in a heartbeat, I'd warrant."

And now, as the lookout had announced, here they were, coming further into the river again. Joshua Barney's gunboat led the way toward the mouth of St. Leonard Creek on the northern shore of the river, a league from their earlier anchorage inside Point Patience. The second gunboat followed and Isaac and Jack in the black sloops led the barges, keeping more to the middle of the river, a concession to their deeper drafts.

Jake Tate stood on the tiny quarterdeck of Isaac's sloop, his untied blond hair blowing in the morning breeze. He watched the British ships as they sailed around Point Patience, their topmasts moving strangely above the trees on the point and, then as they tacked to clear the shallows, joined by the hulls and lower masts.

"Isaac, lookee there. That schooner — ain't that the self-same one we tangled with out on the Bay afore they chased us in? Watch; it 'ppears to me they headin' up higher than the others. Might be she's tryin' to cut across the bar and get to the creek afore we do." Tate resumed tying his hair into a queue — a task none too easy with but one hand — as he kept a steady eye on the schooner.

"Aye, Jake. An' if'n she does, commodore's gonna have to fight his way in there. An' I'd bet he won't want to do that. Hope he sees what's actin' there."

The two watched in silence as the British schooner worked her way to weather of the slow and ungainly American gunboats, her intentions becoming increasingly clear. Isaac spoke quietly to the man at the tiller.

"Bring her up some, Sam. We got room here. Maybe we can distract 'em some." He raised his voice, calling forward. "Stand by to trim; we're hardenin' up. For'ard there: stand by with the swivel."

"Isaac! Look! She's took the ground, by God! Skipper's put her right on the hard. Must have thought he could clear that bar — or didn't know it was there. Reckon he's got some problems now. Har har!" The smile that split Jake's face and the evident pleasure he derived from the ignominy of the British schooner captain made Isaac smile.

Boom! Boom! The gunboats sailed by the stricken schooner and offered a salute to her plight. One round told; the stranded vessel's bowsprit and jibboom drooped, then fell, hanging from their rigging, and her jib and stays'l went slack. Men scurried around, trying to clear the wreckage while others tried to get a boat in the water to row out a kedge anchor.

"Reckon we ain't got to worry 'bout them for a while . . . and probably not that brig, neither." Tate was pointing to HMS *Jaseur* which had split away from the frigate and was heading as high as she could make toward the shallows and the grounded schooner. The flotilla pressed on, fighting the falling tide in the easy morning breeze. Their only consolation was the fact that the British ships, even less weatherly and of deeper draft, were fighting the same tide and light breezes. The mouth of St. Leonard Creek slowly drew closer and it was apparent to the Americans that they would reach the relative safety it offered before the British could cut them off. In time, they tacked and were inside.

Signal flags flew to the mast of the commodore's gunboat and then flapped lackadaisically in the light air. "What's that say, Isaac?" Jake called out the flags as Isaac thumbed through the flotilla's signal book trying to make sense of the commodore's orders.

"Looks like he wants us to make a line of battle, Jake." Isaac looked at the young one-armed sailor, a perplexed look on his face. "I sure don't understand this signal book nonsense. You'd think we was in the Navy or something. Them coves do this flag . . ."

"Isaac. Follow me and set your hook next to me." Jack Clements sailed across Isaac's stern heading for the far bank of the creek. The former Navy bosun and privateersman had understood the signal and was heading to a position between the gunboats and some of the barges, an anchor ready at his bow, another at his stern.

"That's what he meant, by God, Jake. Form a line across the creek. Reckon we're gonna stand an' fight, it looks like. Let's get it done, then." Isaac paused and shouted forward. "You men there, haul out the anchor cable and stand by. Stations for anchorin'. Look lively, there."

When the flotilla finally came to rest, they were formed in a line stretching from one high bank of the creek to the other. Less than a mile to their south the frigate *Loire* came to her anchor in the deeper waters of the Patuxent and launched her boats. These were joined by the British barges that had accompanied the squadron into the river and together they rowed, tentatively, into the mouth of the creek.

"Stand by . . . fire on my order . . . *FIRE!*" Barney's voice rang out clearly. The gunboats, barges, and sloops fired as one, then continued raggedly, at the approaching British boats. Some of their shots told and, with the shrieks of their wounded echoing off the high banks of the creek, the British retreated to the safety of the frigate.

"We stopped 'em, Jack. Reckon they won't be rushin' back in here right quick." Isaac called to his friend on the next boat and stepped over to the low bulwark to talk to him further. Clements followed suit.

"Isaac, I been meanin' to ask you since you showed up here two weeks ago — where'd you go that night back up toward the Choptank? Near as I could tell, you just disappeared from right in front of us. One minute you was there, then you was gone and that British brig was standin' out right for me. Commodore come after me like I was some kinda fool, not knowin' where you was when I got down here."

"Sorry, Jack. I couldn't holler at you with that brig right there. Figgered they might not have seen us yet and we just wore around and went up the back side of Tilghman's. Jake knew they was a cut there and some kinda channel 'long the shoreline. Reckon they missed us completely, lookin' at us like they was with the trees behind us. An' it was pretty dark that night, as I recollect, too. We . . ."

Jack jumped in enthusiastically. "Aye, we headed up towards Tilghman's 's'well. Clark had us in a channel off the end of the island — right there by Black Walnut Point, it was. But after the brig took the bottom, we come back out into the Bay easy as kiss my hand, only 'bout a league, maybe a bit more, from where we started. What kept you? Since I didn't hear no firin' I knew you wasn't tangling with 'em an' I figgered you'd show up down here 'bout the same time as me." All the while Jack was chatting with his friend, he patted his big dog who sat by the bulwark, his huge head resting on it. The dog's eyes were closed and he was quite obviously at peace with everyone, including Isaac, who was quite happy to have half a boat length of open water between them.

The two men continued to chat, each occasionally casting a glance toward the mouth of the creek. They could see quite clearly the masts of the British frigate, but there was no sign of the small boats and, so far, neither the brig *Jaseur* nor the schooner *St.*

Lawrence had made an appearance.

Suddenly, Carronade's eyes snapped open and he lifted his head from the bulwark. Clements smoothed the fur on the back of the dog's neck as the familiar, low, throaty growl started and Carronade swiveled his head around, finally settling on the shore about a musket shot distant. The growl changed to a snarl, then a bark.

"They's some British troops yonder, Isaac. I'd bet my life on it. Carronade ain't missed yet." Both men peered at the high shoreline looking for some movement behind the trees. A flash of red caught Isaac's attention.

"There . . . yonder just inside the tree line there. D'you see that? A red coat. . . and there's another. By the Almighty, Jack, that dog o' yours is right keen."

Others had seen the British marines as well and the commodore gave orders to "hold your fire 'til we see what's actin'."

"Lookee yonder. Flames. Them English bastards set a fire up yonder." One of the barge sailors noticed the glow before it turned into a well-defined fire. Still the commodore would not let the gunboats or barges open fire. "They's some American militia up yonder. Wouldn't do no good to fire into them. Wait'll you can see them red coats clear. 'Sides, them fires ain't hurtin' us."

"They's on t'other side too. Can see them red coats o' their'n plain as day up on the top o' the bank yonder." One of the gunboat sailors on the west side of the creek hollered out to no one in particular.

"They're just tryin' to get us out o' here, men. Hold your fire 'til you got something to shoot at." Barney's shouted orders could be well heard by both ends of his line. A musket shot rang out from the near shore and one of the bargemen screamed and fell in the water.

Immediately two twelve-pounders spoke and the men could hear the grape shot smashing through the underbrush. Barney bellowed out to "Hold your fire, damn it. Ain't nothin' to shoot at up there."

An unseen voice from one of the boats answered. "That 'nothin'' just shot me mate, damn 'em. Don't you tell us we cain't shoot." Another cannon roared and vegetation ashore fell before the onslaught. And the fire set on the eastern bank brightened.

Suddenly, the banks of the creek erupted in musket fire punctuated with the deeper *crack* of a small artillery piece. Sounds of a body of men crashing through the brush filtered down amid the cacophony of guns, and then silence. A cheer went up from the banks, first the eastern and then the western bank followed suit.

"What the hell's goin' on up there? Who's doin' all the hollerin'?" Voices rose from the anchored flotilla, its men frustrated by the tall trees and scrub growth that hampered their view of the banks. Other voices echoed the concerns up and down the line of boats.

"Hold your fire, lads. Wait'll we see what's actin' yonder." Barney was still worried about shooting into the Maryland militia unit stationed above him.

Without warning, a British marine stepped brazenly through the trees, appearing plainly to all below. "You sods in the boats! Lay down your arms and give it up. Your militia 'as run off. You've no chance of escaping or stopping . . ."

His arrogance was cut off mid-sentence by a well-aimed musket from one of the barges. The shot was followed immediately by a barrage of grape and canister from half a dozen cannon. The underbrush exploded in the fusillade and screams from the high bank spoke eloquently of the accuracy of the fire. The men in the creek were further rewarded with more sounds of men crashing willy-nilly through the underbrush. Only this time, the sailors were sure the runners were British. Excited chatter spread across the line of anchored boats. "We got 'em, by God. We done 'em some dirt."

Time passed and the men quieted down, waiting in uneasy anticipation of what the future might hold for them. Occasional nervous laughter broke the silence as the heat of the day began to build. The sun stood overhead, beating down on the men, adding to their discomfort. Some slept, others ate some of their rations, and still others stood staring, shifting their glances from the banks of the creek to the top hamper of the frigate, still clearly visible through the trees at the creek's entrance.

"Boats comin' in!" hollered one of those unable to find a patch of shade in which to lie down. No sooner were the words out of his mouth when the bright sky was streaked with white smoke trailing behind the red glow of rockets and Barney's flotilla was again under attack. This time from a barrage of Congreve rockets. Their courses were erratic and no one, including the British gunners, had any idea of where they might fly, which made them all the more dangerous.

Men leaped to their stations, instantly awake, as the rockets snaked through the air across the line of boats. Guns were run out; those with ball shot had their loads drawn and replaced with grape, not an easy task to accomplish while trying to keep one's head below the low bulwarks of the barges and gunboats. One unfortunate soul stood erect — only for a moment to see how close the enemy had gotten — and took a rocket right through his chest. He stood a moment longer, the clothes and his flesh around the wound smoking from the rocket's fire, then fell back into the arms of his mates. The startled look on his face faded as he died. A transparent wisp of smoke issued from the man's chest, and disappeared into the barely perceptible breeze.

Still unable to bring their guns to bear, Barney's flotilla remained silent; the men and officers were frustrated with their inability to defend themselves and tempers flared. Joshua Barney's voice rose above the melee. "Keep your heads down, lads. They're only tryin' to draw us out where that frigate yonder can bear on us. Them rockets'll do us little . . ."

His encouraging speech ended abruptly, cut off by a deafening explosion; one of the American barges carrying half a ton of powder and nearly seventy men blew up, raining matchwood on the others along with bits of their mates. The sudden silence was complete; even the rockets seemed to fly silently overhead. Then a cry from the eastern end of the line of anchored boats: "I got 'em. I can bear. . . FIRE, DAMN IT!"

And fire they did; not just the one or two boats which actually could bear on the rocket launching British, but the entire eastern end of the line. The thunder roared out from the carronades and long guns, spewing fire and shot, but mostly canister and grape. The British vessels withdrew, seemingly unharmed.

As the day waned and darkness fell, it became clear there would be no further attack; Barney had called his key captains to the meeting in a shed he had found ashore and appropriated for his temporary headquarters.

"I reckon he ain't real pleased with what we done. I 'spect I'm likely one of them he's gonna fire a broadside at since it was my lads what fired off all three guns at nothin'." Jared Talbot, for all his huge size and menacing looks, seemed genuinely contrite. He fixed the two deep-water men with his one eye — the other was just a scar running down his cheek to his chin — and absently cut a finger nail with the sheath knife which normally resided in the back of his trousers, almost touching the leather tied plait of hair hanging down Talbot's back. The knife, a substantial piece of steel, looked puny in the man's great paws.

Biggs and Clements nodded and kept walking up the hill toward the small cabin, not wanting to irritate this giant of a man who happened to be holding a knife. Carronade trotted silently at his master's side, occasionally pausing to sniff this tree or that, and sprinkling those he felt deserving.

It was Jake Tate, walking with Frank Clark and another gunboat captain a step behind, who spoke up. "You wasn't the onliest one, Cap'n. They was at least half a dozen, mayhaps more, what fired. I just wish the commodore'd do something to get us outta here . . . that or send us home. That would suit me just fine; I got a young bride waitin' on me up to Frederick. We sure as hell ain't doin' nothing useful settin' here takin' British fire."

The men drew abreast of the shack as the conversation ended and Barney, outside to greet them, had quite obviously heard the remark.

"Mister Tate, those ships out yonder may be keepin' us bottled up in this damn creek, but they ain't out on the Bay attackin' our ships or raidin' the coastline. So while we ain't exactly bringin' 'em to their knees, we are keepin' 'em busy. And I'd warrant that seventy-four yonder would be a trial for 'em up the Bay. Those're the things I got to think about, not whether or not you young rascals is gettin' your share of the fightin'. Now come in, sit down, and let me tell you what's actin', and what I think we might do. And Cap'n Clements, I reckon that animal might be happier stayin' outside." Barney turned and walked into the gloom of the cabin without a backward glance.

The captains and mates followed. As did Carronade, who decided at once that the corner close by the door would suit him perfectly. He stretched himself out along the wall where he could watch the room and closed his eyes.

CHAPTER SIX

"... and the militia gonna be here within a week. Likely bring a field piece or two with 'em as well." Barney was explaining the steps he had taken as part of his plan to get the flotilla out of St. Leonard Creek and, realizing that they should be listening, Isaac turned away from the storm and Jack from his recollections of the previous weeks to give the commodore their attention.

"I 'spect them bastards'll try some other tactic to get us outta the creek sooner than later and, when them militia lads get themselves down to the point, I'd warrant they'll give 'em a right warm reception. Ha!" Barney seemed quite sure of the several plans he had developed and now all that remained was for the British to try another foray into the confines of the creek, after the militia was in position.

"You men want to wait up here outta the weather, you're welcome; or go back to your vessels. And take the animal with you, if you please, should your choice be goin'."

Jack Clements, an oiled-canvas hat pulled low over his forehead, was first out of the door; without a word from his master, Carronade stood up, shook himself mightily head to tail, stretched and, without a backward glance, followed Clements into the wet night. Biggs, Tate, Clark, and the others shrugged into their tarpaulin jackets and stepped out, their shoulders hunched against the downpour.

"And remember you men, no wild firin' of your guns. You ain't independent units no longer. I'll tell you when to shoot. And at what." From the cabin door, Barney hurled a final reminder at his captains, knowing it would be passed along to the others quicker and with more impact than had he told them himself. No one had been singled out for reprimand when they arrived, contrary to Captain Talbot's suspicions. It was not Barney's style.

By dawn, the storm had passed, the wind changed, and the sun popped into a cloudless sky with little fanfare. The gunboats, barges, and sloops were warped around to keep their gun barrels pointed fair. Then the crews settled down to wait for their antagonists to make another move. The day proved to be even hotter than its predecessors and the men suffered, as much from the waiting as from the heat. Captains found busy work for their crews to do while lookouts kept wary eyes on the lofty spars of the frigate still visible over the trees.

Even the breeze was hot and did little to temper the June sun in the south Chesapeake; deck seams oozed their tar and the men drew buckets of the creek water to cool the decks, if only temporarily. As the heat built to a shimmering crescendo at midday and the crews were called to their dinners, faint music could be heard wafting through the tress. Being as far out of context as it was, it got attention, and those who had not heard it at first were *shushed* by their mates until all hands were listening intently. Then the cries went up.

"There they are!"

"They're comin' in again."

"The bastards're playin' music, for the love o' Mike!"

And indeed they were; a small squadron of boats came around the point and hove into sight, each flying flags and pennants, and the first, carrying a band in full cry. But they were beyond the range of Barney's guns, and were not themselves firing.

"Hold men . . . stand by your anchors . . . look to your matches . . . NOW! By the Almighty, FIRE!" Barney's boats opened fire at the same moment the British barges did and the crashing and roaring of the cannons and carronades was horrendous.

The air was filled with iron; the British added some rockets to the mix and a barge took one aboard, immediately starting a fire. From its neighboring vessel, an officer leaped over the bulwark and smothered the flames before they could get started; it was Commodore Barney's son who had managed to douse the fires before they reached the barge's store of powder and any more serious damage was caused.

"Up your anchors! Sails and oars! Attack! Attack!" Barney had considered his action and it appeared the British might be yielding to his fire power; at least no longer were they approaching the American line. An aggressive American move might convince whoever was in charge of the squadron of boats that there was naught to be gained by pressing home their attack.

The American sailors and captains, long held in check and eager beyond words, had their vessels underway in a trice. Many simply cut their anchor cables and rowed or sailed straight toward the wavering British line, guns firing chain, grape, and ball shot. The crews were filled with the rush of action, responding to orders with efficiency and alacrity. In moments, the entire flotilla was rushing pell mell straight at the British boats.

Barney's move worked; with a shout barely heard over the din of the battle, the orders were given and the British turned tail and ran, rowing as fast as ever they could to get under the guns of the larger ships anchored at the mouth of St. Leonard Creek. The Americans kept pace, maintaining their fire. Their enthusiasm was now fed by the desperation of the British retreat and their own barrage of cannonading. And the band was now silent, their instruments dropped in the bilges while their owners lent a hand on the oars.

As the American boats turned the point of the creek, the crews saw the schooner they had last seen on the hard a week and more before.

"Isaac! Bear off. That schooner is the *St. Lawrence*." Jake Tate standing, as was his habit in the bows of the sloop, shouted his warning back to Biggs. But the sloop pressed on, the gunboats, barges and Clements' sloop keeping pace. *St. Lawrence* opened her own fire as the Americans came into range of her six and eight pounder cannon.

The gunboats shifted their fire to the schooner at once with a devastating accuracy, while the sloops and some of the barges continued to hammer the British boats still within range. The British boats and crews were in total disarray and suffered heavily from the accurate American fire.

And the *St. Lawrence* was being overwhelmed by the shot she received. Her hull was holed in several places and her rig all ahoo; the mains'l gaff hung listlessly down, its halyards shot away and once again, her jib boom had carried away. But still she kept firing. And many of her hastily laid shots told. Several American barges and one of the gunboats felt the weight of British iron, and slowed or withdrew from the contest completely. But the damage to the British vessel had been done; in their haste to get out of the range of the American gunboats, she again took the ground, and her crew, realizing they had little recourse, abandoned the schooner.

The other American boats continued to press home their attack, both against the boats and the *St. Lawrence*. In their focused effort, none in the American vessels noticed the taller spars of the *Loire* frigate and *Jaseur* moving behind the trees on the point of St. Leonard Creek. They announced their presence with the throaty roar of eighteen- and twenty-four-pounder cannon as they hove into view and rounded up to unmask their broadsides while remaining in the deeper waters of the Patuxent.

Barney saw immediately the potential for a disaster. Indeed, even the newcomers' ranging shots were shockingly accurate. And both vessels were launching their boats; red-coated Marines could be seen clambering down the ships' sides into them. He realized that he had led his flotilla right into a trap like some rank amateur, not a veteran seasoned with action in two wars.

He looked around frantically at his boats; many were still on the attack while others were lagging behind dealing with damaged hulls and wounded crews. His voice rose above the roar of the guns, the shouts of the men and general cacophony of the engagement. Signal flags whipped to the top of his gunboat's mast, giving visually the same orders he yelled out to his men.

"Back into the creek, men. Tack around. We're outgunned here." There was little hesitation in obeying the orders and any who might have delayed had only to see the boats from both the brig and the frigate pursuing them. The high splashes from the heavier guns also added inspiration.

Suffering the loss of only two of his barges, Commodore Barney headed his boats back into the relative safety of St. Leonard Creek, pursued by the British boats showing scant freeboard, loaded as they were with Royal Marines. The *Jaseur* brig broke off her attack to take the severely wounded, grounded, and abandoned *St. Lawrence* under tow, yet again.

"Isaac! Them boats — the ones from the frigate — they look like they's gonna land over yonder." Jake had not taken his off the pursuing British small craft. "Lookee there . . . just outside o'the western point. They are, by God! They's puttin' them lobster-backs ashore!"

"Aye, I see 'em." Isaac saw the other black-hulled sloop nearby and shouted to his friend. "Jack: have a look toward the point, there. What do you 'spose they're up to now? Better pass the word over to the commodore, in case he ain't noticed." Biggs, steering his sloop up the creek with the ease of an accomplished deep water sailor, continued to watch the Royal Marines as they disembarked from the frigate's cutter and made their way up the steep embankment a half mile distant. In the back of his mind, he was conscious of voices relaying the message to Barney and, from the rear of the flotilla, a gunboat detached itself and sailed toward the landing point where the red-coated marines — there seemed to be sixty or seventy of them — continued to climb the slope from the small beach. And the American flotilla sailed slowly against the ebbing tide as they sought the relative safety of St. Leonard Creek.

Crack. A musket shot rang out, followed by another and then a whole barrage opened up. The crew of the American sloop looked wildly around trying to determine where the shots came from. Their confusion resolved itself quickly as the water around the vessel became pocked with tiny splashes. The hull thudded dully as several rounds went home.

"Get down. And trim that mains'l; I'm bringin' her up." Isaac quickly turned the sloop toward the eastern bank of the creek — away from the British small arms fire. The others nearby followed his lead. From behind them a carronade roared out, and the men of the flotilla peeked over the bulwarks of their boats in time to see the bank below the British marines as it erupted in dirt and greenery thrown up by the ball. The musket fire paused, then began anew. And again the carronade from the commodore's gunboat spoke, this time apparently loaded with grape and canister shot.

The shrubbery on top of the embankment took the brunt of the punishment, disappearing in a green cloud which rained down on the slope below. The musketry stopped as the Royal Marines moved back away from the hilltop. Gradually, the American boats came to their anchors, and the creek became quiet except for the occasional shouted comment that passed through the fleet. A single boat from the British frigate *Loire* drifted safely out of range and watched the Americans.

"We showed them bastards!"

"Commodore oughtta let us get after 'em ever' time. Teach 'em a lesson, it would, by the Almighty."

"We gonna spend the rest of the war hidin' up this damn mud hole?"

"Nice shootin', Jared. You done good with that schooner, I'd warrant."

"How many got hurt?"

"Every one still got plenty o' shot an' powder?"

A few taunts from the safety of their anchorage were tossed out at the Royal Marines, presumably still ashore on the Western side of the creek.

"You damned Redcoats couldn't hit a barn from th' inside."

"You try any more of that tactic and you'll get another taste of American iron, by God."

Eventually, it became apparent that there would be no further action, and the shouting and high-spirited comments died out of their own accord. Night settled, bringing a cooling breeze and welcome relief. Nobody noticed the *Loire's* boat pulling for the frigate around midnight.

CHAPTER SEVEN

"You got to send some o' your men to help us, by God. The damn militia run off at the first sign of them Redcoats. Prob'ly made it half way to Washington afore the Redcoats was even outta their boats."

"Aye. We're likely to be run out of our own homes and ruint, you don't help us. You're the only one around we can turn to, Commodore."

"British been all the way up to Upper Marlboro, they have. And burnin' everything they cain't carry off. Livestock stolen, warehouses burned, slaves run off. Ain't no one lifted a damn finger to stop 'em, the bastards."

It wasn't immediately clear if the agitated farmer standing toe to toe with Joshua Barney was referring to the British Marines or the American farmers and militia in his frustration.

The three-man envoy sent by their neighbors to enlist the flotilla's aid had painted a grim picture of the Royal Navy's presence up the Patuxent River. Raids from small boats, twelve in all and carrying over two hundred Royal Marines, had been carried out with chilling precision from Benedict all the way to Upper Marlboro, just as these men had explained. Barney knew from his own observation that another frigate, HMS *Narcissus* (32) had joined the blockade of the Patuxent River and St. Leonard Creek, providing the necessary boats and marines to raid most of the river front communities nearly to the point where the river became a stream. And at the same time, effectively curtailing all traffic into and out of the Patuxent River and its tributaries. With a seventy-four-gun ship of the line, two frigates, a brig, the repaired schooner *St. Lawrence*, and assorted cutters and barges it was unlikely that any captain would try the river mouth, and certainly, Joshua Barney's little flotilla would be staying put.

"You men got to understand that they's nothing — not a damn thing — that I can do to help you out. The ships them boats is from are anchored right out yonder . . . lookee, you can see the t'gallant masts of the seventy-four over the trees there. They got me penned in here sure as if they'da built a wall right 'round the creek. If'n I send my men off with you overland, the British'll be in here quicker than you can say it and burn every one of my vessels right to their waterlines. No, I'm afraid you're gonna have to depend on the militia." Joshua Barney shook his head sadly, realizing the frustration and helpless anger these men must feel. To depend on the largely-unproved local militia was tantamount to disaster.

The spokesman for the three looked hard at the commodore, searching for a break, an opening, anything that might give them a glimmer of hope for help from his sailors. The man's eyes narrowed and the silence hung in the air for a long moment. His companions fidgeted nervously, sure that their friend had overstepped the bounds of civility and likely angered their only chance at saving their farms. The spokesman stepped back a half step and spat. He looked at one of his companions.

"You was right, Samuel. These coves ain't gonna help us none, just like you thought. They's just as afraid of the damn Redcoats as the militia. I reckon them bastards could just march right into Washington if they'd a mind to and kick Mr. Madison outta the President's House an' move right in. Wouldn't no one lift a finger to stop 'em."

Barney bristled at the suggestion that he or his men were afraid of the British navy or marines.

"Look here, men. We've been fightin' 'em right here in this creek and out yonder in the Patuxent for nigh onto a month now. And afore that, we was attackin' their ships and stations up and down the Bay. Why, just a week ago we showed 'em what we was made of, and make no mistake. Chased 'em right outta the creek here and out into the river, we did. Like as not sunk one o' they's vessels and wounded more than one of the others. They'd be gone by now but for bringin' in a frigate and a brig to help 'em out. But I can tell you this: they ain't been back in here with they's boats or

Marines since then. Been right peaceful in the creek here. No sir, ain't no one afraid of 'em here, by God. And they got a seventy-four, two frigates, a brig, and who knows what else settin' out yonder 'stead o' sailing up and down the Bay harassin' our shipping."

"No, that's right, Commodore. They ain't harassin' our shipping none; they's burnin' our warehouses, stealin' our livestock an' tobacco, grabbin' our slaves, and harassin' *us*. They ain't a plantation what's within a mile of the river what ain't been raided. Cole's, Kent's, Ballard's, Magruder's — they all been hit, an' hit hard. British say they's 'rightful prizes'. 'Rightful' my arse. They's just stealin' and raidin' like damn rascally hooligans, by all that's holy." Another of the farmers had stepped up, his voice filled with contempt; a bubble of spittle formed at the corner of his mouth. Barney stood silent, his eyes holding first one and then the others in turn.His brow furrowed and he took off his hat to push a delicate hand through his hair. He turned to the apparent leader of the group.

"I 'spect a unit or more of the militia as well as some federal troops ought to be showin' here in a day or two with some field pieces and you're welcome to stay and have a word with 'em when they get here. That's the best I can offer you right now." He shook his head. "I'm real sorry, but that's the way it is." The commodore looked genuinely grieved that he was powerless to help these men and their neighbors.

"If you can be patient, when we get through them ships out yonder, I can send some barges and men up the river to help you, but they ain't no way I can get out of here now. Even Secretary Jones — he's the Secretary of the Navy up to Washington, you know — he sent a messenger down here wantin' us to pull the boats over the land out to the Bay, if you can believe that. That's how desperate he is for us to get out, and believe you me, we all — every one of my officers and men — are just as desperate. No, sir, ain't nothing I can do to help you right now." His brow creased again as he shook his head, and he shifted his gaze to the point where the top hampers of several British ships were quite visible over the trees. He smiled ruefully.

"Thinkin' on it, I'd reckon that Captain Barrie — he's in command of them ships out there and likely the boats and Marines up your way — he'd be right pleased if we came runnin' outta here to help you out. Be just what I'd want in his shoes. He cain't get us out with his cutters and barges, so he's figgered that by gettin' his marines up the river a ways and doin' some raidin' we'd go after 'em. But it ain't gonna work that way. Barrie and his Admiral — Cockburn — been chasin' me nearly a year now. They'd like nothing better than to remove the thorn in their side that we have placed there." The commodore shrugged his shoulders, at a loss for more words to offer instead of the requested assistance. He turned to walk away. And practically ran over a young sailor nervously waiting for a chance to speak.

"Commodore? Mister Biggs sent me to tell you it looks like that seventy-four — what'd he say? — the *Dragon*, I recollect — 'peared to be makin' sail. Her and some o' them others. Small craft mostly, he said. An' might be another load o' Redcoats headin' either in here or back up river." The young man — hardly more than a boy — crushed a tattered tarpaulin hat in dirty hands, shifting his bare feet in the dirt, while he stared at the commodore wide eyed. His cheek muscles worked and his gaze darted around wildly as he tried to recall if there was anything else he had been told to report.

"Is that all, sailor?" Barney questioned the nervous boy.

"Aye, sir. Reckon that's all he told me." The lad nodded, his relief at delivering his message evident. He started to back away from the group carefully, not turning around until he was half a dozen steps away, then quickly moving through the trees and down the embankment.

"So I reckon you'll be headin' up our way now, Commodore. Soon's them ships yonder get gone, like the boy said?" The first emissary had heard the whole exchange and his hope was rekindled. Barney wheeled on him, his voice cracking like a whip.

"Aye. Just as soon as the two frigates, the brig and whatever barges they left turn they's backs and hide they's eyes. You men wasn't attending what I said before; we're blockaded in here just as sure as the Navy ships like the *Constellation* are blockaded into Norfolk." He softened his voice somewhat. " 'sides, maybe now they got they's marines and small boats back, they're done with you folks up-river. You men can go home and likely not be bothered by 'em again."

"That boy said they was another boatload of 'em headin' back up the river, so I reckon we can 'spect 'em sooner than later." The citizen looked hard at the commodore, then turned and shook his head. "Come on, lads, we best be gettin' ourselves back home afore them damn Redcoats get there and we ain't got homes to get back to." Without looking behind him, he started down the narrow road carved through the trees and his companions fell into line behind him. Barney watched them for a while as they made their way single-file, their shoulders slumped, down the road, then turned and headed to the water and his boats, calling for Biggs and several other captains as he approached the shoreline.

"Get you some men and cut trees; I want a log boom rigged across the creek afore the day is out. And get a couple of twelve-pounder cannon up on that embankment to the west. If the British want to come visitin' again, we'll give something to think on, by the Almighty." Then aloud, but to himself, he added, "shoulda done that a week ago. Don't know why I didn't think of it afore now. Them coves was right; I cain't depend on the militia any more'n they can. We got to take care of our own selves."

CHAPTER EIGHT

B arney was more than a little surprised and quite delighted when eight days later, on June 22nd, 1814, Captain Samuel Miller, USMC, arrived on St. Leonard Creek with one hundred marines. He was accompanied by three long twelve pounders manned by elements of the Thirty-Sixth United States Infantry from Leonardtown. Two days later, Colonel Decius Wadsworth personally delivered from Washington two eighteen-pounders and their crews; Wadsworth was Army Commissary General of Ordinance and placed high stock in the need for Barney and his flotilla to be somewhere besides St. Leonard Creek.

Isaac, Jack Clements, and Jared Talbot met for a full day with Barney and Wadsworth, hatching a plan to break the flotilla out of the Creek and do some damage to the British ships in the process. They met in the leaky shack the commodore referred to as his "headquarters" and the atmosphere in the diminutive building quickly became thick with tobacco smoke from the cheroots and pipe used by the gunboat captain and Colonel Wadsworth, respectively.

As the deep-water men stepped outside, Isaac wiped his eyes and remarked to Clements, "I never seen a room fill up with smoke so fast — neither ashore nor afloat. Them two must be usin' green leaves to burn!"

The former Navy bosun smiled and nodded. "Aye, Isaac. Even that hog pen yonder smells better'n the tobacky them coves is usin'." He referred to the collection of food animals — mostly hogs — which the commodore had secured from local farms for the use of the flotilla. They were penned near the building and on a hot airless day, the air near the pen seemed to shimmer with a malodorous mixture of the pigs, sheep, chickens, and their various leavings. Not to mention the rotting food scraps thrown into the area to supplement the animals' regular diet. The butcher had set up shop near at hand and the spoils of his labors added to the fetid atmosphere hanging at nose level around the headquarters area.

"Ain't no wonder the commodore don't spend much time up here." Isaac shook his head. "Thought it was on account of his wantin' to be on the boats. Reckon not. Guess we better get ourselves back in there."

Clements and Biggs turned away from their view of the creek and the boats still anchored below them. They were no longer extended in a line across the water; the log boom the men had rigged across the entrance had been effective in dissuading the British small boats from visiting. That or the two manned twelve pounder cannon in plain sight on the embankment above the western shore of St. Leonard Creek.

". . . set, then. Guns are to be in place and ready soon's Keyser's infantry gets here. Oughtta be this very night, I'm thinkin' based on what the major told me afore I left the Capital." Wadsworth was referring to Major George Keyser who was supposed to be on the march with his Thirty-eighth Infantry from Annapolis. They had sailed there from Baltimore the day before on the order of Colonel Wadsworth.

"Wouldn't wait on them coves, were it me, Commodore. More'n thirty miles down from Annapolis. They ain't gonna march that in a day and be in any shape to fight the next." Jared Talbot had been disappointed before by the land units the flotilla had counted on and spoke, he knew, for the other barge and gunboat skippers. Best they just use what they've got and get on with it.

Wadsworth fairly bristled at the suggestion his orders would not be carried out. "Captain, Major Keyser is a professional — a United States Army officer — and his infantrymen are army soldiers, not militia. If he said he's comin', he'll be here. And as to fightin', well, you just be damn good and sure your sailors can do your own part. You ain't got to worry none about the Army bein' in this scrap — and on time."

Talbot said nothing, but glanced at the two sloop captains. His one-eyed look gave each a pretty good insight as to his feelings on the subject. The other men, seeking to avoid a possible confrontation, stood, and the meeting was over.

But not the day — or night. Some of the newly-arrived long guns, soldiers, and Marines were put in position on the western shore of the creek where they could fire into the Patuxent, augmenting the two cannon Barney had emplaced the week before. Others were set to fire along the shore of the Patuxent, and the infantry were dug in behind the artillery. Still other cannon were dug in on the eastern shore of the Creek where they would be able to fire into British ships moving up the Patuxent toward the Creek. Wadsworth's twelve-pounders were sited on the reverse slope of the hill with the hope they would be virtually invisible to the British; they were, but unfortunately, the British were also invisible to them, causing them, when called to action, to fire blind. And Keyser's troops did arrive from Annapolis in time, getting themselves quickly and professionally into position for the opening salvo.

Which occurred as eight bells, signaling the start of the morning watch, sounded the next morning. The two frigates, *Loire* and *Narcissus*, were caught unawares and heavily damaged by the initial cannonading. The British were unable to elevate their cannon sufficiently to return the American fire, but they recovered and launched a rocket boat which immediately fired on the hilltop. While the frigates' gunners struggled to fire back, the ships' crews were busy trying to get out of range.

But they soon had more problems than the American shore guns; Barney's gunboats and barges were racing down the creek under sails and oars and managed to get to within four hundred yards of the already wounded frigates. The American boats opened fire and chaos ensued.

Barney noted with pride that iron shot was falling with accuracy around the British frigates. But so was it also falling around the barges. He knew for certain that the frigates had not yet fired a shot and, horror-stricken, realized what was happening.

"My God Almighty. Wadsworth's shot is falling short. Get that boat overboard and get in there. Tell him to cease firing." Barney looked wildly around for someone to send. The smoke around the American boats was so thick that there was no chance of

Wadsworth seeing signal flags, even had Barney raised them.

Suddenly, as if on command, the majority of the American shore fire stopped of its own accord. "Ain't got time to deal with that now. Thank the Lord he's seen us and stopped." He raised his voice, now hoarse and cracking from the acrid smoke and his own shouting. "Keep firin' at them frigates, men. We're hurtin' 'em.'"

"Commodore! That boat's settin' Marines ashore yonder. You want we should get over there?" Talbot's rumbling bass voice cut through the noise and confusion of the battle like an approaching thunder squall, even though he was several boat lengths away. The gunboat captain was paying attention to more than just the frigates.

"Keyser or one of them ashore gonna have to handle 'em. I can spare not a single boat. Keep firin' men. We're going to carry the day!" Barney was delighted with the efforts of his gunners and the damage they were inflicting on the two frigates. He whooped his encouragement, his joy and enthusiasm at the Americans' success overcoming his normally reserved demeanor.

And then the frigates began firing back. If they couldn't elevate their guns far enough to hit the shore positions, the boats close at hand — barely a musket shot distant — were another story entirely. Both British ships turned their attention to the barges and gunboats and the Americans received a heavy weight of British metal.

Splinters flew as round shot smashed into the boats bulwarks and sides; the masts of two went overboard, their shrouds shot away, dragging the boats to leeward. The screams of the wounded and the shouts of the now confused American sailors penetrated the din of battle. How quickly the tide had turned.

Barney, realizing he had lost his shore support, was in a quandary. He had but one choice if he were to save his flotilla and men. He climbed halfway up the wind'ard ratlines on his gunboat and shouted as loud as his scorched throat would allow. "Captains: separate yourselves. Don't bunch up. Be ready to pull back, should we need to."

His voice carried to the nearby barges and the order was passed along to the others. Isaac and Jack Clements, on the flank of the action, had maintained some room to maneuver and saw a change in the battle, and the error the commodore was about to make. Both turned almost as one to their quartermasters, signal books in hand, and ordered a series of flags which they hoped would communicate to Barney their discovery.

"Hay: get them flags up. Look lively, man. Commodore's about to pull back. Jack," Isaac bellowed across the water to his friend. "Bear off and follow me. We got us an opening."

Barney saw the flags whipping in sloops' rigging. He looked around, and a smile, unseen by but a few close by, crossed his face. He saw quickly what the alert sloop captains had seen, but due to his different perspective, had initially missed. He shouted again at the boats near at hand. "They're pullin' back, men. We got 'em on the run. Looks like they's headin' back down the river. Keep firin'."

Gradually, the frigates withdrew to the shelter of Point Patience, and Barney led the undamaged units of his flotilla out into the Patuxent. The British saw, but were powerless to stop him; they needed to tend to their own badly-damaged ships.

With a fair but light wind, though fighting the tide, Barney and the flotilla didn't stop until they reached Benedict, fifteen miles and more up river. The sloops led the way and the row barges and gunboats followed along. As the town hove into view, Isaac spoke to Tate.

"You don't reckon them coves is expecting us, do you Jake? Looks like they turned out all hands to greet us."

"I'd say we might have a problem, Isaac. That looks like militia, to me. A hatfull of 'em, too, it 'pears."

Isaac glanced aloft at the truck of his mast, allowing himself a small smile when he saw the Stars and Stripes waving limply in the light breeze. "Reckon they'll be some relieved — mayhaps even happy — when they figger out who we are."

A boat pulled out from the shore, obviously making for the black sloop. As it drew near, a figure stood up in the stern sheets, steadying himself on the shoulder of an oarsman.

"We thought you was the British. Been told they's headin' up river. Mighty glad to see you flying that flag, Cap'n. Might you be part of Commodore Barney's flotilla?"

"Aye, that we are and far as I know, the British are still down off St. Leonard Creek or Point Patience. And ain't but a few ships o' sail at that." Isaac stood on the bulwark, his hand resting lightly on the larboard leg of the backstay. "Come aboard, if you care to. Commodore ought to be showin' up right quick, be my guess."

And he did, in fact, show up within the hour; his gunboat anchored close aboard the sloop, and a few of the local dignitaries were rowed out to visit with him. As was Decius Wadsworth, the Army colonel who provided artillery to assist the flotilla in making its escape from St. Leonard Creek. He remained after the townsmen had taken their leave and, that night, after the men had eaten their fill for supper, the commodore called his captains onto his gunboat.

As Jack Clements came alongside the gunboat in what he jokingly referred to as his 'gig', Barney glared down at him, an order ready on his lips to leave the big dog in the boat; the dog was not in evidence, and the Commodore allowed himself a secret smile. *That damn dog is discomfitin' at best, by all that's holy.*

The others followed quickly and they all stood or leaned under the canvas Barney had had rigged over the deck of his vessel in an effort to provide some shelter from the heat of the sun. Even with only the last rays of the setting sun shining on them, the temperature under the awning rose quickly, but except for a quick pat with his handkerchief, Barney seemed not to notice or acknowledge it. He began by praising the men lavishly for their performances and gunnery skills, and he thanked Colonel Wadsworth, who acknowledged his words with the slightest inclination of his head. "Perhaps, Colonel, you would care to tell my captains of your travails ashore and how we might be of help to you now, if you find you need our assistance?"

"I'd reckon to give a quick sketch of the battle from our view point, Commodore, but I doubt it'll make any of your men sit up an' take notice. Pretty ugly, it was, but I ain't going to cast disrespect on any of my officers, as I don't yet have all the particulars from them. But, the fact is, someone in the infantry unit decided on a retreat afore even a single man was killed — or even wounded. The Royal Navy was trying to get around to our rear, rowing their barges up the Creek after you men had got out. Before I knew it, I was left with only enough men to work one gun, which I had turned to the rear, hoping to keep their damn barges in check.

"After a bit, I reckon we did 'em some dirt, on account of they were gettin' themselves underway and retiring down the river. But I found I was left with no alternative but to spike the guns that remained to prevent them from being useful to the enemy, should they get hold of them. I should add that the infantry, even in retreat, acquitted themselves with honor, leaving the field as they did in perfect order, though without my instruction. And they did return when I was able to halt them and bring them back. Course, the fightin' was all but done by then." The Colonel paused, wiped the sweat from his face and neck, and removed his jacket. His account had obviously provided him with some discomfort.

He leaned back against the bulwark again, and added, "I do hope that given our lack of preparation, the excessive fatigue the men experienced, and the heat of the day, we will not be judged too harshly; after all, we did achieve the release of your flotilla. I have not determined how much damage we inflicted on the enemy as I was not in a position to judge the fall of our shot, being enfiladed as I was behind a rise. From the haste of his retreat, however, one might infer it was considerable."

"It damn near was 'considerable' to our boats, Colonel. Your shot from where you was set behind that rise was fallin' short by a hundred and more yards; your men couldn't see us, but it was only by the Grace of God none of my boats was sunk by American guns. Don't know what caused you to stop firin' but, by the Almighty, I was right glad of it." Joshua Barney hid none of his disdain for the land units — whether under Colonel Wadsworth or anyone else. "But we're pleased to be out of that creek and, for your help in that endeavor, I thank your, Sir." The commodore smiled thinly at the Army officer, who had the good grace to appear ill at ease.

Barney quickly moved the conversation to other aspects of the battle, and then he began to ruminate on what they had left behind.

"I have no idea what Miller and Keyser's doin', or even if they're still fightin' the Marines who came ashore from the *Loire*." Barney paused, then he nodded, almost to himself as though he had just reached a decision. "Isaac, you'll take your sloop down river and find out what's actin' with 'em. And salvage what you can from the two gunboats we' left behind. Put everything else to the torch; no point in lettin' them damn Redcoats have anything what might help 'em." He added, as an afterthought, "and scuttle them two, after you burn 'em."

"Aye, Commodore, we can do that. We'll get out on the tide in the morning." Isaac's relief at not being sent right out was clear; he was looking forward to a full night's sleep for himself and his crew.

"And you'll take the surgeon with you. Might be them Army coves at St. Leonard be needin' his services and I reckon he'll be finishing up with our men any time now. Plumm's his name, Jeremiah Plumm. Does his doctorin' here abouts 'round Benedict. Local coves seem to think he knows his business. So far, I cain't disagree; I watched him take the leg off'n one of our men what took a fair-sized splinter in the action this morning. Did it quick as I ever seen it done and claims the cove'll live. Didn't think the wound would turn putrid at all. Course, bein' ashore, he ain't got any of the same problems the surgeons at sea got, but I reckon that acts to our favor."

Barney nodded his head in silent affirmation of his decision to send the surgeon down river to St. Leonard Creek. Several lanterns had been lit by a seaman as the dusk grew into full dark, and the yellow lamplight flickered and shone on the commodore's sweat-beaded face. As if he had suddenly noticed the heat, he stood and gestured to his guests. "You men got things to tend to, I'd warrant. Best you get on with 'em. We'll be here a few days at least." And he left.

CHAPTER NINE

E ven as the sun broke the horizon the next morning, Jake burst into Isaac's diminutive cabin. "Isaac: they's some cove lookin' for you topside. I ain't never seen a wild man, but I'd reckon to recognize one now, seein' that one yonder. An' he's got a white eye!" Tate was clearly in awe of the stranger waiting on the sloop's deck for Isaac. The one-armed sailor hung back a trifle as he accompanied the captain topside to greet the fellow.

"You are the captain? I was expecting a man of greater years. Indeed, the commodore gave me to understand . . ." The man's voice was a combination of the howling of a dog who didn't quite make it over the fence and the sound of a rasp on hardwood. Listeners frequently winced on hearing his first words. He was quite tall — maybe something over six feet, Isaac thought as he craned his neck to look up into the man's face. Which was frightening in its own right; high cheekbones gave way to a black beard shot with white. Presiding over it was a long pointed nose, its length emphasized by the sunken eyes and bushy brows. A great shock of black hair, also shot with white, hung unbound to the man's shoulders, but on the top of his head, the hair seemed to have a will of its own, pointing in all directions. He did not wear a hat.

Isaac, for all that he tried, was unable to take his gaze from the man's left eye; it was, as Jake had foretold, white. There was no black pupil nor any ring of color. And the rest of the eye was spidered with red veins.

Biggs noticed that the other eye appeared quite normal and had fixed him with a hard gaze. Isaac thought, with an unseen smile, that the eye appeared to be looking through a hole in a plank, so deep was it set in the man's face.

Finally, Isaac was able to find his voice. "I am the captain. Isaac Biggs, sir, at your service. And you are . . .?" He let his voice trail off, a questioning look in his own eyes.

"Mr. Plumm," the wild man stated, as if it should have been obvious. "Jeremiah Plumm, surgeon and practitioner of the art of restoring the balance among the humors of mankind. I collect I am to take passage on your . . .". He paused, looking around the deck as if seeking a word suitable to his impression of the sloop, and continued, albeit disdainfully. " . . . vessel down to St. Leonard to offer what succor I can to the American troops recently engaged in mortal combat with the Royal Marines." The voice did not appear to fit the appearance of Mr. Plumm. *He should have a deep voice — like it was comin' outta the grave. Aye, that would be more fittin'*, Isaac thought.

"Well, I'm pleased to have you aboard, sir. We'll be gettin' underway just as soon's the tide turns. Wind's fair now and buildin', it is. Might get a taste of some weather as the day develops. Reckon be about another hour an' more afore we're ready to get loose of the dock. If you got dunnage to get aboard, I'd be pleased to send a man with you to help, should you need it." Isaac smiled and offered his hand to the surgeon. He was surprised at the strength of the grip from this man of the healing arts.

"I'll be taking my leave then, sir. And a man to fetch my belongings would be most welcome. You may expect my return in one hour's time, I should think." He pulled a large gold watch from the pocket of his black vest and consulted it at length. Then Plumm turned on his heel and, without a backward glance, raised first one long black clad leg over the bulwark and then the other. He paused for a moment, then dropped to the dock and strode off, assuming the sailor assigned to help him would follow. Isaac had had his sloop moved to the dock after the commodore's meeting last night in anticipation of loading some stores.

After assigning Sam Hay to accompany Jeremiah Plumm and watching while the stocky sailor hurried in his rolling gait down the dock, Isaac turned to Jake. The one-armed Bayman was struggling to contain his mirth and, when Isaac faced him with a smile, he gave up and burst out in full-throated laughter.

Tate drew himself up as high as his five-and-a-half-foot stature would allow and pushed his hand backward through his blond hair. He pitched his voice to mimic the doctor. " 'I am Jeremiah Plumm, surgeon and practitioner of the art of restoring the balance among the humors of mankind.' Isaac, I ain't never heard nothing like that cove afore. What'd you make of him?" It was an effort to get the words out between fits of laughter.

Isaac, also laughing, shook his head. "Not in all my life have I seen the likes of that afore! I reckon we's stuck with him, though. Commodore told me we was takin' him back to the creek, so I'd warrant we'll be doin' just that. Prob'ly oughta be makin' some space for him and his gear below."

He noticed that the other men on deck were enjoying a laugh at the medico's expense; one of them had ruffled his hair so it stood out from his head and was strutting around the deck in a poor imitation of Plumm. Another — Isaac saw it was Clive Billings — had managed to get his already noisesome voice into a close rendition of the doctor's and was entertaining his messmates with a running commentary on how he might go about 'restoring the balance in the humors of mankind'. Apparently, thought Isaac, the shoulder wound Billings suffered in Tavern Creek six weeks and more back was no longer a distraction for him. Isaac watched them for a moment, amused. Then he became serious.

"All right you men, get on with your work there. Ain't time to be prancin' around and skylarkin'. We got a pair of six-pounders to get aboard and shot and powder for them and the swivel. Look lively, now." His words were sharp; his tone was not. But the men returned to their work with a will.

He turned to Jake. "I'm going to see 'bout them cannon. And maybe find us another swivel for the stern. You keep the watch here and have someone rig a piece of canvas or something below for the good doctor. Cain't have a man of his stripe livin' out in the open with us common coves!" He smiled broadly at the mental image and climbed quickly over the bulwark to the dock.

Commodore Barney, standing on the shore just off the dock, was waiting for him.

"Isaac, I'd guess we're lookin' at a spell of some weather comin' in right smartly. Best you get you gone quick as ever possible. Wind's fair now, and I'd reckon the tide'll be turning fair in a trice."

Barney paused and looked beyond his sloop captain at the black-hulled vessel tugging none too gently at her lines as the river's chop flowed by her sleek sides. He watched the men preparing for sea and saw a double whip being rigged at the single yard on the mast.

"You fixin' to take on some heavy dunnage, Isaac? Doc Plumm told me he was just bringin' his doctorin' box."

"Aye, Commodore. I got a pair of six-pounders we found and I'm going to rig 'em larboard and starboard. Might try to find me another swivel gun into the bargain. But never you fear, sir, I seen the weather makin' up and I'll be on my way quick as you please. An' quick as the worthy Mr. Plumm returns with his stores." Now Isaac paused, his brow furrowed some as he thought how to put the question on his mind to the commodore.

"Anything you might want to be tellin' me 'bout him, by the by, Commodore? I ain't never run into anything or anyone quite like him afore." Isaac looked hopefully at the older man.

"Well, Isaac, Jeremiah Plumm's somewhat of an odd cove, I'd reckon." He smiled and said, "But I guess you got that far your own self. As a doc, he ain't bad at all, I'm told. Heard he cut his teeth in the War for Independence and saved a host of men from bein' heaved over the standin' part o' the foresheet. Been takin' care of folks up both sides of the Patuxent since afore the turn of century and I ain't heard no one say a bad word about him." Barney paused, then added almost to himself, "Course, any what might complain likely ain't got a breath left in 'em . . .

"And he's had a look at the dozen an' more what got hurt yesterday in that scrap and reckons every man Jack of 'em save, o' course Brown — he's the one what had his leg took — will be returned to duty quick as you please. And for that, I'm grateful. So I'd warrant Miller and Keyser and their men back at St. Leonard might be glad of his help, once you get him down there. Assuming they's any of 'em left."

Barney's ominous codicil caused Isaac to raise his eyebrows, a move which did not go unnoticed by his superior. He hastened to correct the young New Englander's misconception.

"Oh, I ain't thinkin' they all been killed off, Isaac; I was thinkin' they mighta headed back to Washington or Baltimore — less'n o' course they's still scrappin' with the Royal Marines. Har har." Barney's rarely heard laugh sounded more like a flogging sail than someone laughing, but the smile on his face made apparent his mood.

Isaac continued his quest ashore and shortly returned to the sloop with not only the promised pair of cannon being dragged down the dock behind him, but also with two men carrying a swivel gun, bigger by half than the one already mounted on the sloop's bow bulwark. Jack Clements brought up the rear of the procession. He was carrying a seabag. Before he was halfway down the dock, a large dark blur rounded the corner and galloped down the pier; Carronade joined his master, a short piece of frayed rope hanging from around his neck.

"Hope you ain't got a problem with another hand — or paw — Isaac. Seems like Carronade ain't takin' to bein' left in our wake." The former Navy bosun beamed at his dog and then at Isaac.

"Reckon he can come along, Jack, long as he don't take a hankerin' to any of the lads. You fed him recently?"

"That won't be no worry, Isaac. You ain't got no Englishmen aboard, do you?"

Isaac shook his head — whether in dismay or silent resignation Jack couldn't tell — and stepped over the rail. He organized a crew to hoist the six-pounders aboard his sloop while Jack — and the dog — supervised the operation from the dock. As the last gun was wrestled into position at the larboard bulwark and its tackle properly secured, a wagon drawn by a pair of mules stopped at the head of the pier.

"Let's get all hands out to that wagon. It's got our powder and shot aboard. Step lively now. Anybody seen the doctor?"

A round of "no's" responded and Biggs looked at his fellow sloop captain. "Wait'll you see this cove, Jack. What a strange bird. Just don't laugh; I'd warrant he wouldn't take real kindly to any mockery. But Barney says he's some fine medico and it's possible them marines and soldiers may be in sore need of some doctorin'." Under his breath he added, "Hope he don't got a problem with your pet."

As the final cask of black powder was handed onto the deck, Carronade, who had been slouching against the mast, looked alert and barked his deep resonating bark once. All eyes turned to the dog and then to where he was looking. Jeremiah Plumm strode purposefully down the dock, Sam Hay behind him, staggering under a huge box.

"Mister Biggs: I sincerely hope I have not delayed your departure. I was detained by a difficulty with one of the men whose leg I removed yesterday. Unlucky cove had the bad fortune to develop a bit of putrefaction. Had to bleed him and re-dress the wound with . . . hello! What's this? Is that beast a dog or what?" Plumm took a step backwards.

Carronade remained forward, his eyes never leaving the stranger. The hair on his neck and back bristled and he gave voice to a low, barely audible growl. Jack Clements looked at him and then the doctor.

"Why, that's just Carronade, Doctor. He's a dog, by my lights, and a fine one at that. Hates the British, he does, and suffers no nonsense from nobody. Here, let me introduce you to him." He started forward.

"You can stay right there, sir. And the cur as well." Plumm took a step backward. "I'd warrant that beast won't take kindly to me — few do. Is it going on the boat?"

"Aye, *he's* goin' and you'll be glad to have him, we run into any British Marines down there. Worth three men in a fight, I'd warrant. But I doubt he'd give you cause for concern."

"Just the same, sir, I'll maintain my distance if you don't mind. And who might you be, if I may inquire?"

Isaac stepped forward and gestured at the one-eared captain. "Doc, this here's Jack Clements, skipper of the other sloop — the one just down the shore there. Bein' how we got a bunch of his men to man the extra guns we put aboard, we figgered he'd be a good hand to sign on as well. Sailed together, we did, on a privateer down to the Indies, and a fairer hand layin' a gun or managin' a vessel you couldn't find."

"Glad to make your acquaintance, sir. And may I inquire as to what happened to your ear. That's as fine a bit of stitchin' as ever I've seen."

'You two'll have plenty of time to yarn after we're full and by, you don't mind. But for now, we got to get the barky headed south. Weather ain't lookin' too promisin' and we've lost more'n an hour of this tide." Isaac raised his voice. "Stations for makin' sail and gettin' underway, lads, and smartly."

Suddenly the sloop was a hive of activity; hands manned halyards for the stays'l and main while others stepped to the lines holding the sloop land-bound. The vessel tugged more violently at her lines as the surface of the river became more roiled in the growing wind. Isaac stepped to the tiller and nodded at the men forward. The stays'l rose smartly up the forestay, flapping wildly as the wind caught it.

"Let go the lines. Sheet in the stays'l, lively now. Stand by the main. Hands aloft to the tops'l yard." Isaac pushed the tiller over and the sloop, suddenly freed from her tethers, bore away from the dock into the mainstream of the Patuxent River. "Main halyard, heave. Cast off the sheet." Biggs waited until the mains'l was all the way up, its gaff swaying drunkenly as the sail flogged, then shouted above the rising wind, "Peak her up and sheet her home, lads."

The black-hulled sloop leaned her shoulder into the chop on the river and heeled over as the wind filled the big sail. She picked up speed quickly and, keeping his course in the middle of the waterway, Isaac guided his vessel back down the river, back to the hornet's nest they had left only the day previous. He noted, in the back of his mind, Mr. Plumm's wide-eyed, but silent, reaction to the unusual black-dyed sails as they filled and drew nicely over the sloop's black hull.

CHAPTER TEN

The sky had turned the color of burnished pewter; there was no twilight, and uncharacteristically, the wind continued to increase as the scant light gave up its struggle and became night. The tide had begun its flood, causing the chop in the river to steepen and the now moaning wind blew the tops off the waves. The black sloop made a fine turn of speed, even shortened down to a reefed mains'l and single jib. The square tops'l had been first reefed and then finally furled on its yard as Isaac saw his sloop was being overpowered by the increasing wind. Spray flew over the bows, as the sharp prow cut through the incoming tide.

Carronade, at what he considered his post in the sloop's bow, was soaked, but undeterred in his determination to see what might be ahead. The rest of the crew, save the lookouts, who were changed every hour, remained aft or below. Mr. Plumm stood just off the quarterdeck, deep in conversation with Jake Tate and Jack Clements. He had earlier been cautioned to remain clear of the captain's domain.

"Did he really say 'Don't give up the ship' as he is credited with saying? You know that has become the battle cry for the American Navy on the fresh water. And I am told, by one who was there I should mention, that Oliver Perry had the ships of his squadron on Lake Erie fly flags with the words emblazoned on them during his heroic battle there. And you may know that his flagship was indeed named for the late Captain Lawrence. Of course, it was nearly lost and he moved bag and baggage *during the fight* to another — the *Niagara*, I believe it was." Plumm was seemingly well-informed and both the deepwater man and the blond-haired Bayman nodded and made appreciative grunts for this news.

Quite animated, Plumm had been quizzing the two for most of the afternoon about their wounds, and the devastating loss of USS *Chesapeake* to Broke's HMS *Shannon* the year before and the death of Captain Lawrence.

Especially interested, he was, in the skill of the British naval surgeon who patched up the two Americans. He examined their scars in the failing light, turning Jack's head this way and that to better see the work done where once he had had an ear. Tate and the former bosun had become embarrassed by the attention and turned the subject to their incarceration in Halifax.

"So you spent time in Melville Island, did you? I've heard, second hand, mind you, that it was a hell hole of the first water. But you coves are the first who've actually been there that I've come across. Surely, with your most serious wounds, they must have had you in hospital for some time after bringing you ashore from their frigate?"

"Not on your life. We was marched right into the compound with all the other coves from the *Chesapeake* frigate. Some was wounded worse than us, by my lights, and . . ." Clements turned to the former topman. "Remember ol' Tim Connoughy, Jake?" He received a nod and continued. "They marched him with the three or four other British tars we had aboard across the neck of land from Halifax. Damn near bled to death, the way Robert Coleman told it. Put him in the hospital at Melville Island, they did, and it wasn't for a month an' more that we seen him again. Had a cutlass or a splinter wound in his leg, as I recollect, and I reckon his mates had to carry him the last half league to the prison, 'cordin' to Coleman. Coleman was Royal Navy what we picked up in the Indies back in the year '12 off'n a prize. Decided, he did, he'd rather fight on American ships 'stead o' gettin' flogged every time some Royal Navy captain took a mind to show who was in charge. Connoughy the same, 'ceptin' he was an Irisher."

"And where are these turncoat British tars now? Hanged, I'd warrant, eh?"

"Not by a long shot, sir. Last Jake an' I seen 'em, they was marchin' off toward Sacketts Harbor from Boston to join up with the freshwater coves fightin' up to the lakes. Along with a hundred or so others whose services wasn't needed in a navy blockaded into port by them damn English ships. We all got out of Melville at the same time. Isaac there," Jack pointed with his chin at the New Englander at the sloop's tiller, " 'long with some coves from a privateer outta Salem, come got us out. Salem — that's up to Massachusetts." Clements and Tate both smiled in the darkness at the recollection of their escape from the prison and Halifax Harbor.

After several hours of listening to Plumm, Jake decided he'd had more than he could manage. "Isaac, you want me to spell you a while on the tiller? Give you a chance to get you some vittles, too." He winked at his former shipmate, still held by the persistent medico, and headed aft to relieve Biggs.

The rain, which had been falling in a half-hearted, sullen drizzle, now poured down with renewed vigor and those on deck could hear the distant rattle and thump of thunder well to the east. Biggs came out of the scuttle dressed in his oiled tarpaulin hat and a canvas coat. He had the remnants of a ship's biscuit in his hand which he sheltered under his coat as he stepped out into the wet.

"I'd warrant we gonna get us a wind shift here any time now, Isaac. Reckon it'll be comin' in outta the east." Jake greeted his captain as the New Englander stepped onto the quarterdeck.

"Aye, and by my figurin' I'd guess we still got maybe a couple of leagues to go afore we can expect to see the opening of the creek. Less'n we go right by without never seein' it 't'all. Ha." His laugh sounded hollow and insincere. "This surely has gotten to be a dirty night. Cain't make out much of anything yonder. Ease her over to the larboard some, Jake. Let's get us a trifle closer to that shore; see if'n we can make out anything along there."

The sloop hardened up some, sails were trimmed, and her speed diminished as her hull showed more of itself to the strong flood tide. Lightning began to streak the sky in sporadic flashes, not yet close enough to their position to offer any help in defining the shoreline. The wind began to shift, coming more around to the bow as Jake had predicted. And the rain came down harder. Isaac put his hand on Jake's shoulder and pointed with his other one.

"That look like something burnin' to you, Jake?. See . . . yonder there . . . looks like something on fire in there."

"Aye. Might be a house or something. Sure ain't a cookfire. But could be a bunch of trees what got struck by the lightning too." Jake squinted through the rain. There was definitely something afire not far from the shoreline.

The two watched as the sloop went by; soon it was only a dim glow astern and then gone completely.

"Well, either it's too far astern to see, or the rain put out whatever it was what was burnin'." Isaac shrugged and turned to watch forward as the black sloop continued on her wet course to the south.

In short order, a dark smudge developed into the shoreline about a cable's length distant and, in a brilliant flash of lightning, the trees on the banks lining the river were suddenly displayed in stark silhouette against the sky. The darkness made them appear a good deal closer than they actually were. Jake eased the tiller over a trifle and the sloop bore off, away from the hazards of the shoreline. The lightning flashed again, accompanied by a resonating crash of thunder.

"Jake — did I imagine that or did you see it too?" Isaac stared at the shore seemingly close off their larboard bow.

"I seen trees and, I guess, the shoreline . . . and I think I mighta seen the creek opening 'bout half a point off the larboard bow. What was you . . ." The next crash of thunder and simultaneous double-forked streak of bright yellow lightning drowned out the rest of his words. Then he was pointing with his good arm, holding the tiller against his leg, and shouting. "There, I seen it too, Isaac. A boat yonder right along the shore. And by the Almighty, she looked to be headin' same way we are. Did you see it again?" From for'ard, the two heard the distinct deep throated bark which confirmed their sighting.

"Aye, I seen it. From the look I got, she looked to be cutter rigged and shortened way down. Gotta be British; ain't no one else 'ceptin' us 'round here. And Jack's dog seems to think it's them, too." He paused, peering through the darkness and rain. Then he turned back to the young Bayman. "I'll take the tiller. Get you for'ard and get a couple of the lads to load that swivel gun. Keep the canvas over her 'til we're closer, and I ain't got to tell you, keep the powder dry. And no shoutin'. No point in lettin' 'em know our whereabouts, in case they ain't yet seen us."

In the next flash of lightning, they saw that the cutter had altered her course and, having hardened up, was running for the Creek entrance.

"Action stations. Hands to action stations. Trim her, lads, I'm bringin' her up some." Isaac had to raise his voice to be heard in the bows over the storm. He knew the only reason the British cutter had seen them was the lightning; he could do nothing about that, but he also knew that absent the lightning, his black sails and hull made him even more invisible than they were to him. He steered the sloop toward where he perceived the entrance to the creek lay and kept her driving through the foul night, hoping the British sailors would assume he had not seen them.

A flash of lightning and the immediate overhead crash of thunder. "Stand by the swivel, lads. And get the larboard six pounder run out. Next flash of lightning, you men on the swivel let 'em have it!"

"FIRE!" Jack Clements had assumed command of the gun and the order was barely out of his mouth when, with a sharp crack, the small gun spoke. And its report disappeared in the deep *boom* of next clap of thunder. "Load grape." Isaac heard Jack's words, whipped aft by the wind, even before the echo of the gun had faded

The next flash of lightning revealed their target within a pistol shot and unscathed; a small gun — apparently a four-pounder — was mounted in the bows and as he watched it, Isaac saw a tongue of fire issue from the muzzle. The sharp report followed a split second later. And a splash just for'ard of the sloop's bowsprit spoke eloquently of the marksmanship of the British gunner.

Crack! The sloop's swivel gun returned the shot and shrieks of pain came down on the wind from the cutter. A cheer went up on the American sloop.

"Don't start celebratin' yet, lads. They ain't struck or dead; they's just hurt some. Give 'em another." Isaac watched carefully, waiting for the next flash of lightning to determine the condition of the enemy boat.

Boom! He ducked involuntarily, then chastised himself when he realized it was thunder, not the four-pounder. *Crack!* Now the British gun spoke, and the sloop shuddered as the ball found its mark amidships, midway between wind and water. In the next flash of lightning, he saw the cutter bearing off, trying to cross his bow and rake the sloop — as much as one gun could. He pulled the tiller over and bore off to parallel the other boat.

"Fire, Jack; keep it up! You can't miss. She's barely a biscuit toss away. You lads amidships — put a ball into her." Isaac shouted his encouragement to his crew. He heard the swivel fire followed a heartbeat later by the six-pounder; the cutter returned their fire. Another thump and shudder from the sloop told of a British hit — this time for'ard.

The sounds of a scuffle came aft on the wind. "Damn it, man . . . Outta the . . . here . . . aft . . ." Words, disembodied in the darkness and indistinct in the wind, and almost continuous thunder, carried to the quarterdeck, along with Carronade's barking.

"What's goin' on, there? Keep that gun firin'." Isaac bellowed into the wind and was rewarded with the sharp crack of the swivel. This time, he heard cries from the cutter and no answering fire. In the next flash of lightning, he saw the cutter had borne up and was in stays, her heavily reefed sail flogging itself to rags, and a gap had opened in her starboard side aft where there should have been solid wood. The top half of her mast was gone and, in the image frozen in his mind by the lightning, he saw men struggling to regain control of the boat.

"Stand by to board, lads. I'm takin' her alongside. Grab up your cutlasses and half pikes." Isaac's bellow fed the already blooded mind-set that pervaded the sloop and the rail was quickly lined with as rum a bunch of cut-throats as ever sailed.

The chop on the river and the pitch-black night were of no help in his effort to lay the sloop alongside the British cutter. But Isaac's seamanship and natural ability, with a little help from strong American hands and a pair of grapnels, put his vessel side by side with the enemy, and quickly they were lashed together. The sounds of grinding — wood on wood — as the waves worked the two hulls against each other was intermingled with the cries of both British and American voices. But, other than some of his crew straddling the sloop's bulwark, no move was made to board the British boat.

"Isaac, boarding ain't gonna answer; ain't room yonder for any more'n what's there. Likely sink 'em. 'Sides, they already struck." Jack Clements' high spirits were evident, even over the still howling wind. "I reckon bringin' a few aboard the sloop and puttin' one or two of ours aboard them might serve 'til we get 'em ashore in the Creek."

As Isaac approached the waist where the cutter was secured, he saw Jack and a Royal Navy lieutenant conferring, their faces reflecting the flickering light of a bull's eye lantern held by a British sailor. The officer's waistcoat showed a blotch of red spreading under the handkerchief he held against his side. The rain blurred the scene but a more miserable crew would be hard to imagine, soaked, bloody, and defeated. There was nothing animated in the conversation between Jack and the lieutenant, save for their sudden moves to counter the bouncing and rocking of the two vessels.

"Let's get 'em secured aft and make for the creek, Jack. We're both bein' blown to leeward which we're gonna have to make up. Put your men aboard." Already eight of the Royal Navy seamen had clambered over the bulwark onto the sloop and stood between several heavily-armed American sailors who watched them much like a wolf might watch a cornered cow. Carronade sat tensely next to his master, alternating his gaze between the crew still in the British cutter and those on deck. His almost constant growl could be heard only by those close aboard the huge animal. Jeremiah Plumm made his way aft and Isaac noticed in the flickering light from the lamp he held that his face, above his beard, was bruised. He had no time to worry about the doctor now.

"Jake: take the tiller and get her underway; let's get into the Creek and sort this out there." Isaac also said, but to himself, *Give me time to figger out what to do with these coves. God Almighty, I surely don't need prisoners right now!*

The sloop, its prize in tow, bore away, then tacked laying a course that would take them into the mouth of St. Leonard Creek.

CHAPTER ELEVEN

"You know, Isaac, I was thinkin' we was mighty lucky last night; the frigate them lads is off'n mighta been settin' here waitin' on the cutter to come back. We'd a been caught all aback, were they there." Clements stood with Isaac and Jake Tate on the western shore of the creek just inside its mouth.

The sloop and the British cutter were anchored in water barely deep enough to float them and the pale morning light showed two groups of men standing and squatting on the diminutive beach at the edge of the trees; the Americans were armed with muskets and cutlasses. Someone had made a fire and the smell of breakfast mingled with the wood smoke and the heavy, dank smell of wet earth and vegetation which clung to the bordering woods like a cloak. From the black sloop, the sounds of hammering and sawing could be heard; repairs to the vessel were obviously proceeding apace.

They watched absently while Jeremiah Plumm examined again each of the wounded Royal Navy sailors. Most of the men had been treated when first the two vessels came to their anchors and, according to the medico, none of the wounds were life-threatening. The British lieutenant had received the worst of them and was under a makeshift sailcloth tent slightly separated from his crew. Plumm seemed thorough in his inspection, Isaac thought. The bruise the doctor sported on his face again piqued Isaac's curiosity. He reminded himself to ask Clements about it.

"Aye, Jack. But they weren't and here we are." Isaac nodded

at his friend and allowed the trace of a smile to form. It was gone as quickly as it appeared and the young New Englander continued. "Now we got to figger out what to do with 'em. I figgered to burn the cutter when we burn the barges and all that we can't salvage of our equipment, but I ain't got a thought as to what to do with these coves, 'specially the ones what're hurt." Isaac looked around at the forty and more Royal Navy sailors sprawling on the sand and scrub vegetation.

Jake studied Isaac for a moment, his brow furrowed as he put his thoughts into words. "I doubt whatever ship they's off'n gonna wait long past four bells for 'em to come back. They mighta figgered they'd run into the creek during the weather last night, but I'd reckon they'll be lookin' for 'em right quick now that storm's moved through. 'Cordin' to one I spoke to, they's off'n a sixth-rate frigate just come in yesterday. They was sent out to help themselves to vittles from any ashore what had 'em." He paused, shifting his gaze to the British sailors sprawled on the shoreline. "And I'd warrant they was the ones what set that fire we seen last night, Isaac. Frigate's anchored, the cove said, down to Point Patience with them others." It was rare for Tate to offer an opinion, but when he did, he was frequently right on the mark.

Jake's comment seemed to remind Isaac of his responsibilities. "I got to talk to some o' these coves; find out what they're about. The commodore'd keelhaul me with my own guts he ever found out we had all these Royal Navy lads here and I didn't get nothin' from 'em."

Isaac paused and looked around. He turned to his one-armed mate. "Jake, get you some vittles and then take a few of the lads in the small boat across the creek yonder. Take a glass with you and see what's actin' with them frigates. You can see right plain from the top of the hill right across from here." Isaac looked at the mottled gray sky, tinged with the pale light of clearing, and then out toward the Patuxent. It was still choppy, but with the turn of the tide just before dawn, it was already showing signs of flattening out. "I don't reckon we'll have any more weather for a while, but don't tarry; get you over there and back quick as ever you please. An' if you see any of them army coves, tell 'em to stand fast." He finished and watched as Jake stepped over to the fire for his breakfast, then turned to Clements.

"I meant to ask you last night, Jack, what happened up by the gun for'ard when we was after the cutter? Sounded like you was havin' a set-to with someone."

Clements lowered his voice and turned to face Biggs. "Aye, indeed I was. I ain't figgered out yet if the doc was just gettin' in the way on account of his wantin' to see what was actin' — or if'n he was trying to stop us from firin'. He mighta lost his balance in the way the barky was tossin' around, but he grabbed onto the swivel and spun her around just as we was about to fire into the cutter. Damn close to firin' right aft, we was. Almost seemed like . . . well, I ain't gonna say he was trying to stop us firin', but it mighta seemed like that to some.' He paused, lost for the moment in thought as he absently fingered the scar that had replaced his ear. "Now I'm thinkin' on it, aye, I'd warrant that's 'xactly what he was about."

Clements normally cheery face was serious and his eyes flicked around, settling on Plumm as the medico emerged from the tent sheltering the Royal Navy lieutenant. The doctor shot a glance at Clements and Biggs as he moved away from the tent. There was little warmth in his eye. Jack added, his voice even lower. "And I reckon it was me give him that black eye when I suggested he'd be more comfortable aft." The thought brought a fleeting smile to Clements' face.

Isaac smiled at his friend's choice of words, then became serious again. "Hmph. I wondered 'bout that. Let's keep an eye on him. Commodore mentioned to me they was a lot of British sympathizers — Federalists — in these parts — kinda like up to New England last year. Hearin' what you're telling me, it wouldn't surprise me none if ol' Doc Plumm was one of 'em. But I'd be surprised if he would intentionally do something to hurt us. He's a right cove, 'cordin' to Barney. Been around the river since the War of Independence, he said."

Isaac started for the Royal Navy lieutenant's tent. "Might as well see what that cove has to say for himself. Want to join me?"

The two lifted the flap and ducked inside. The light filtering through the dirty canvas bathed everything it touched in a mottled gray pallor — especially the young man lying on the make-shift pallet. It made him look a good deal worse than he likely was. The man's hairless upper body was bared, save for the bandage Plumm had carefully wrapped around his ribcage. From the blood still seeping through the fresh dressing, it was apparent that his wound was serious, perhaps life-threatening. The top of his britches was stained brown from the blood, now dried, that had flowed down them before the doctor patched him up. In repose, the lieutenant looked even younger than he had last night and Isaac surmised he was likely the junior officer on whatever ship he called home.

"Good morning, Lieutenant. I collect the good doctor has taken adequate care of your needs?" Isaac greeted the man, who looked at his visitors then away. "Reckon we might have a few things to talk about. An' I ain't figgered out yet what to do with you — whether to bring you back with me or send you back to . . .". Biggs left his sentence hanging, hopeful that the young man would finish it.

"His Majesty's frigate *Favorite*. That would be a right proper gesture on your part, sir. And . . ." He stopped and, realizing his error, looked away again. When the young officer had looked directly at Isaac, dried streaks on his cheek spoke of his pain — from his wound or from being captured in what was likely his first "command".

"Anchored inside Point Patience, I'd warrant, with them others?" Clements spoke softly, almost gently. And waited.

"Aye. I reckon you could see 'er right clear, should you 'ave a look. And who are you and why ever should you care what ship I'm from?"

"What does your cap'n plan on doin', now he's got here too late to help out his mates on *Loire* and *Jaseur*? Ain't much actin' down this way now."

The youngster flared. "You damn Yankees just wait. Wait 'til the rest of the fleet shows up. Then you'll see what's actin' down this way . . . and more, by God. Cap'n Burns says we're going to teach you upstarts a lesson once and for all. I'd warrant you rascals are part of that hooligan navy with Joshua Barney we've heard so much about. 'Uncatchable', indeed. As soon as the other ships get here from Bermuda, we'll settle your accounts, right quick; count on it." Now the lieutenant, breathless from the exertion of his outburst, stared at his captors with as hard a look as he could manage. Jack and Isaac looked at each other.

The smile on Jack's face quickly disappeared as he realized that their identity as Barney's men had not been a guess on the young officer's part; he had heard it from someone during the night or this morning.

"Mayhaps we might work out something with your cap'n to send you and your men — leastways, thems what's wounded — back to *Favorite*. I might be able to send a boat out under a flag of truce with a letter if'n you was to give me something in return." Biggs left the idea hanging and turning from the wounded man, walked out of the tent without another word. Jack followed closely behind. Suddenly Biggs stopped, causing Jack to scramble to avoid a collision, and retraced his steps.

"Did you say your captain's name was 'Burns'?"

"Aye. Captain Joseph Burns."

"In his thirties, speaks soft, 'bout as tall as that cove what was just in here with me, but some stouter?"

"Aye, that's 'im. 'ow'd you know about Cap'n Burns? What are you, a deserter? I've 'eard about sailors runnin' 'ere in America. Not a one 'as run off'n *Favorite*, though, 'ere or anywhere, I 'ear, since Cap'n Burns took 'er over."

"I sailed in the Royal Navy near two years back afore the war started; sailed with Mister Burns — I mean *Cap'n* Burns. On *Orpheus*, it was." Isaac turned suddenly and, bending, stepped out into the brightening day.

"What was that about, Isaac? You went back in there so sudden I didn't even know you was gone. You ain't really plannin' on lettin' them go, are you? What would that serve?"

"You heard him mention a Cap'n Burns, Jack? Burns was first lieutenant on *Orhpeus*, the fifth-rate frigate I was on in the Indies. Fact is, he's the one that pressed me off'n *Anne* back in the year ten. He escaped off'n *Glory* when we was in Haiti. You remember, Jack; he jumped right over the side and swum for it. Cap'n Smalley was right tore up when he found out I was the one let Burns escape. I know you recollect the cove — you was second on *Glory* when you captured them two British prizes — merchantmen they was — we was sailin' to Antigua."

Jack stared at his friend. Then broke into a smile at the memory of the privateer. "Aye, I do recollect the cove. Some pompous ass he was when he come aboard *Glory*, as I recall — stormin' an' struttin' around like some damn peacock what got strung by a hornet. I heard about him jumpin' over the rail in Port au Prince, but I'd already gone ashore when you . . . But I can picture Smalley's face when you told him. He was sore wantin' to get that cove back to the States. But he ain't got no bearin' on us, now, cap'n or no."

Clements looked wistfully again toward the fire. He repeated his earlier question. "What are you going to do with them prisoners, Isaac? You really ain't gonna let 'em go, are you?"

"I ain't figgered out what to do with 'em, yet Jack. But I ain't gonna take 'em back to Benedict with us. They's more of them than us. Be easy for 'em to take over the sloop should they get a mind to on the way back up river. But I'd surely like to find out more about what that youngster was sayin' in there. Reckon the commodore'd like to know, 's'well. Less'n, o' course, he was just blowin' to try and shake us.

"For now, though, let's get us some breakfast and then I'm gonna take some of the lads up the hill and see what's left of the Army. I'd appreciate it if'n you an' Carronade kept your eyes on things here. 'specially the good Doctor." Isaac had noticed that all hands seemed to give the big dog a wide berth — even the Americans.

The twinkle had returned to Clements' eyes and he fondly patted his dog, who had remained outside the tent but came and sat by his master once the two men stepped back into the growing light. Carronade stood eagerly as the men started toward the tantalizing odors of food.

"Aye, and with great pleasure. Though I don't reckon any of them coves'll try anything just yet. Their cutter's pretty busted up and they's too many of our lads on the sloop. Don't figger any'd want to tangle with Carronade, neither. All this talk's made me some sharp-set. Time for vittles." Without waiting for an answer, Jack, the big dog at his heel, stepped quickly down the beach toward the fine smells that promised breakfast. Isaac followed, and gratefully took the offered mug of coffee from Hay.

CHAPTER TWELVE

S tanding on the top of the bluff overlooking the mouth of St. Leonard Creek, Isaac and his handful of men surveyed the scene of the recent battle — short-lived, though it had been — between the American Marines and the British. Some of the artillery pieces had been overturned and articles of clothing and packs strewn around spoke of the fury of the battle and the heat of the late June day.

Well, I can sure see how come Colonel Wadsworth couldn't see where he was shootin'. Isaac had squatted down behind the berm where some of the cannon were still sited. The waters of the Patuxent were completely hidden by the hill and the trees. Wadsworth had indeed been shooting blind. *Lucky for us, I reckon, he didn't hit the gunboats, firin' like that.*

Sam Hay and Clive Billings were investigating several artillery pieces. Clive's distinct voice brought Isaac out of his reverie. "This here gun ain't been spiked. Fire as good as ever it would, I'd reckon."

"Check them others, you two. If'n we cain't get 'em down to the water and onto the sloop, we'll have to spike 'em where they stand." He glanced around the wooded area where several artillery pieces were evident. One was turned to fire toward the back of the creek and Isaac recalled the colonel's comments about the Royal Navy trying to get behind the gun emplacements with their barges. A furnace for heating the shot sat in a small dirt enclosure surrounded by other accouterments left behind.

"Silence fore 'n' aft! Get you down behind them trees, lads. Sounds like someone's comin' this way." Biggs saw his men instantly unsling their muskets and crouch behind convenient trees and cannon. They watched silently, waiting as the sounds of men moving none too carefully through the woods got louder and louder.

"Hold! Avast and lay down them guns." Isaac stood, his musket leveled at the leader of the small group as he emerged into the clearing. The American sailors also stood, muskets at the ready.

"Who the hell are you? And what do you think you're about, pointing them guns at us? Do we look like Royal-damn-Marines to you? These coats is blue, by all that's holy." One of the newcomers, apparently the leader, took exception at having been surprised by this rag-tag bunch. And he did not lay down his weapon.

"Who are you coves and what are you lookin' to find hereabouts?" Isaac would not be put off.

"We are members of the Maryland Militia, sent here by Captain Carberry to recover them artillery pieces and anything else 'at's here. Now who the hell are you? And I ain't gonna ask you again."

"Part of Barney's flotilla. We was sent back to see if'n you coves needed any help. And get our own equipment we left up the creek yonder. Brought a medico with us, should you got any what's wounded. Figgered to spike these guns if'n we couldn't get 'em down the hill to the boat."

Both sides lowered their guns and the militiamen stepped forward, clearly out of sorts at finding the sailors here. One was openly hostile, pushing a sailor out of his path, uttering an oath as he did so.

". . . wasn't for you bastards, none of this woulda happened. Damn Britishers ain't got no interest in Calvert County or the river. Just lookin' to get you damn sailor-boys an' your boats. Tore up half the country side 'round here, they did, stole the food stocks, burned or stole the tobacky outta the warehouses, run off the slaves. An' now they's settin' out yonder just waitin' for the chance to catch Barney's flotilla. What the devil have you to come into the Patuxent fer, anyway?" A chorus of "aye's" indicated that the man spoke for his mates and probably for most of the citizens of the county. Isaac was fairly caught aback by the venomous attack. He'd had no idea the vitriol aimed by the locals at Barney's men was so widespread.

"Well, we're gone outta your creek now and back only long enough to get our belongin's and take care of a couple o' gunboats got left behind. An' we didn't — none of us — want any part of bein' holed up here." He turned to his sailors. "We'll leave these guns to the soldiers, lads; let them carry 'em off. Let's get us back down to the water and get about what we was sent for. No tellin' how long afore the Royal Navy down off Point Patience decides to have a look into the creek." And without further comment, the flotillamen clambered down the hill behind their captain, to the beach where Jake Tate had just returned from his foray to the other side.

"They's there, Isaac. Counted three frigates — one of 'em's smaller than the others, mebbe twenty-two or twenty-four guns — and a brig. Schooner's there too. Reckon it's the selfsame one we tangled with. Looks like they's a powerful lot of knottin' and splicin' goin' on, ceptin' on the little frigate. A few boats — barges mostly — either anchored with 'em or strung out alongside. Don't seem like they's fixin' to go anywhere real quick. Fact is, one o' the frigates got his foretopmast struck down. Mighta took a hit the other day."

"That's a good report, Jake. Don't sound like they's real worried about they's men here yet. Sooner or later, though, they're likely to send a boat out to have a look for 'em." Isaac looked around and saw Clements standing up to his waist in the water near the sloop. Carronade paced up and down the water's edge, never taking his eyes off the former bosun.

"Jack, what's actin' with the boat? They got them planks replaced yet? We need to get up the creek right quick."

"Aye, Isaac. Just about done, they are." Jack waded back toward shore, to the obvious delight of the big dog.

"We'll leave half the men here to keep an eye on our prisoners. Leave 'em the rowboat, 's'well. The rest get aboard the sloop soon's the job's done, and get up to where we left the gunboats and the rest. Likely take the rest of the day to load the spars and whatever else we find an' burn the boats."

Isaac's orders set off a flurry of activity and soon the sloop was sailing quietly up the creek, manned by half a dozen flotillamen, Jake and Isaac. Several were still finishing up the repair work, but the sloop, to Isaac's pleasure, was sea-worthy. Clements, the dog, and the other half of the sloop's augmented crew, all well-armed, were left on the beach, as was Jeremiah Plumm.

The doctor watched the sloop as she made her way up the creek. His patients had all been treated and, save for the lieutenant, none had life-threatening wounds. And all by now knew the identity of their captors. Plumm was certain that word would get to the Royal Navy before the day was out that a vessel and several dozen flotillamen were back in St. Leonard Creek; he just had not yet determined how to accomplish it. He was sure that Clements and that damn dog would hamper any plan he might make, but hopeful that he would be able to get one seaman out of the makeshift camp.

He continued making his rounds of the British sailors, accompanied by a young man, a boy really, who carried a few instruments and a pouch of medicines. With frequent and furtive glances at the more attentive American sailors and Jack Clements, he looked for a Royal Navyman who might slip out of the camp unnoticed and either swim out to the anchored ships or somehow signal them from the shore just down the coast.

Jack and Sam Hay, also left behind, chatted at the water's edge; Carronade had lain down on the sand, his back to the water, and watched the sailors moving about the area. Suddenly the dog sat up, his ears alert. The movement made the two Americans look beyond the dog and they watched as the doctor stood, patted one seaman affectionately on the shoulder, and made his way into the lieutenant's tent. The boy followed.

"What's happenin' with them, do you s'pose? Seems that Doc Plumm is bein' real attentive to our guests, Sam. Some of them Britishers don't look that bad hurt to me, 'ceptin' the lieutenant. I'd warrant that cove won't make another day, being gut shot with a chunk of grape like he was." Jack touched Hay's elbow and nodded toward the tent.

The two men moved closer to the makeshift shelter and stood where they could make out the voices of Plumm and the young lieutenant. The hushed tones that filtered out sounded strained, filled with urgency, but the two Americans could make out only a few of the words.

". . . Pennington said. . . could. . . likely. . . word. . . ship. . ."

". . . barge. . . matchwood. . . dark. . ."

"What'd you make of that, Sam? Sounds to me like them bastards is plannin' somethin'. I thought that Plumm cove was more 'n he seemed. I'd wager a month's pay — ain't much, thinkin' on it — that he's figgerin' a way to get our prisoners out of here. Isaac said we ought to watch him; he sure was right."

"Aye, get 'em out or maybe somehow get a boat from one of

them ships yonder in to catch us. Be a real feather in they's cap were they able to catch one o' Barney's boats and a bunch o' his men." Sam used the same barely audible tone Clements had used. The two moved away from the tent just as Plumm emerged, cast them a dark look, and made his way to a fallen tree where he sat down as far from the big gray dog as he could get. His temporary loblolly boy followed, then wandered down to the water's edge and began idly to pitch stones into the water.

Gradually, a quiet, relaxed atmosphere descended on the camp; the Americans and unhurt British sailors sitting together, yarning and comparing notes, while others slept. All sought what shade they could find from the summer sun. Several of the Americans had decided to make the repairs to the British cutter and the sounds of their hammering and sawing broke the tranquillity. The heat built steadily as the day wore on and more and more of the men, both British and American, became less animated in their conversation; it simply took too much effort — even to talk — and with little now to occupy themselves, most slept.

At midday, a makeshift dinner was served out and Jeremiah Plumm again made his rounds. When he emerged from the lieutenant's tent, the final stop on his tour of the wounded, he walked directly to Jack Clements who was sitting on a driftwood log eating some ill-prepared lobscouse, while he shared off-soundings stories with Sam Hay. The medico stood, looking down on the two sailors.

"With this heat, I think it might be salubrious for the men to have a swim, those who want to. Cool them down some. Of course, the wounded would have to stay put — and someone to watch them, but the others might find it a pleasant diversion. Unless you have something for them to do after they eat. And what is this . . . this . . . mess you're feeding them? It is certainly beyond the capabilities of my palate. I'd warrant it can't be healthy — even for a strong, well person — to swallow this . . ."

"Doc, they's gettin' fed same as everyone, wounded and healthy alike. It's what we got and 'til Isaac gets back with the sloop and, hopefully, some of the vittles we left ashore a few days back, it's all we got. So eat it if'n you want, or not, but quit your carpin'. As to the men havin' a swim, I got no objection. Might be I could use some 'salubrious' my own self." Clements returned to his meal and, after fixing the former bosun with his one-eyed glare for a moment, Plumm backed away, returning to his log on the opposite side of the clearing.

In spite of the doctor's complaints about the food, there was little left; even the wounded British sailors were happy to fill their bellies. Carronade sat anxiously by the fire, hoping. And the men went swimming.

They cavorted around the shallows of the creek like children, splashing each other, the men working to repair the shot damage to the British cutter, and those who remained ashore. Some who could swim, ventured further out and the cries and laughter of the sailors, American and British, filled the afternoon air. Nobody noticed one swimmer who ventured further out into the creek and, indeed, made it all the way to the far shore.

After a scant supper of ship's biscuit and peas, the two crews settled down to await the setting of the sun and the anticipated relief from the heat. A gentle breeze stirred the trees above them and rippled the waters of the creek. As the night sucked the daylight out of the sky, dry lightning could be seen, lighting the distant sky with sheets of brilliance from beyond the horizon. A glow in the sky to the northeast told the Americans that Isaac had fired the hulks of the two gunboats Barney had left behind.

Jack and Sam Hay kept a watch on the group, with occasional glances up the creek. Each carried a musket and had a cutlass slung over his shoulder. A lantern near their feet made a pool of yellow light which only a few yards out faded to black, unable to compete with the profound darkness. Other lanterns cast similar puddles of light, making weird shadows as the men moved around the camp.

"Jack, have a listen, there. Don't that sound like a boat movin' through the water? Can't get a direction on her, though. Could be comin' from the river easy as the creek."

"Aye, likely to be Isaac comin' back from burnin' them two gunboats we left. Hope he didn't run into any troubles. An' got us some vittles."

The two listened intently, trying to determine the source of the sound. Jack walked a ways down the beach heading for the Patuxent, his head cocked favoring his good ear. Carronade moved silently at his side, as if sensing that he should be hearing something too. Suddenly, the dog turned and bolted back up the beach, reaching the camp and continuing along the edge of the water, further into the creek. Jack laughed and reversed his own course, realizing that the dog had heard and identified the American sloop.

"Sam, that'll be Isaac, more 'n likely. Have a few of the lads bear a hand there and stand by, case it ain't, but I cain't fathom who else it might be from that direction."

Sure enough, the sloop's barely visible form appeared, first as a dark smudge, then solidifying into the familiar sleek, rakish hull and rig. She ghosted into the shallows, rounded up and dropped an anchor with hardly a sound. As the sloop drifted back toward the shoreline, Jack could see that her decks were cluttered with spars, cordage and oars. A large mound of indeterminate form took up much of the foredeck, and even in the dark, he could see that the men aboard were moving with difficulty around the cluttered deck. The sloop settled to her anchor and soft splashes were the only indications that the crew, led by Isaac, had dropped into the water and were wading ashore. Clements met his captain at the water's edge.

"I collect you had no problems, Isaac? Didn't meet any Royal Marines hangin' about? Appears you found a good stock of spars and what-have-you. Come to any plan on the course we'll take with these prisoners? How 'bout vittles; find any we could use?"

Isaac laughed. "Ease her up some, Jack. First off, any problems here? I heard from one of the locals we talked to up the creek that the Royal Navy been pokin' around the creek a few times since we left. 'Course, I had more troubles with the locals — they was hard on it, strippin' everything they could off'n both boats. Already had spars loaded on a wagon, and was fixin' to add some powder an' shot when we got there. I can tell you, they was none too happy to see us sail in and tie on alongside! None too friendly, any of 'em. Sounded like I was talkin' to them militiamen — or they's kin!" Isaac laughed ruefully, then continued.

"I guess they ain't many 'round here what favors Barney's flotilla. Most of 'em figgers we're the reason the British ships are in the Patuxent. Never mind that Washington City, Annapolis, and Baltimore are less than a day's march from up the river a ways." Isaac paused, peered through the darkness at the camp and the pockets of conversation among the Americans as the sailors caught up on each other's activities. "I reckon you had no trouble here. Doc Plumm behave himself? Where is he, still treatin' the lieutenant?"

"I ain't seen him much since supper, Isaac. We ain't exactly cozy, him an' me. He's kinda kept his distance and I sure ain't gone lookin' for him. Cove seems more at ease with them damn British prisoners than ever he does with his own."

"Mayhaps them prisoners is his own, Jack. He do anything what caught your attention while we was gone?"

"Well, he spent a lot of time in the tent with the lieutenant. Sam an' me heard 'em one time — we was right outside; couldn't catch much of what they was sayin' but it didn't sound real good to either me or Sam. Somethin' 'bout a 'barge', an' the 'dark', an' what we thought mighta been 'matchwood'. Didn't make much sense to either of us, but that's about all we could make out. Plumm didn't seem none to happy to see us standin' around by the tent when he come out, neither." Clements shook his head, unseen in the dark. "But what're we gonna do with the prisoners, Isaac. More I thought about it today, the more I don't like takin' 'em with us back to Benedict. 'sides, folks there'd likely let 'em go if'n they's as fond of the British as Plumm is."

"That's what I was thinkin', too, Jack. Figgered to leave 'em here. Right where they's settin'. But we'll burn the cutter afore we go. Don't want to make it too easy for 'em. Figgered to take the lieutenant with us, bein' how's he's cruel hurt, an' the Doc can keep an eye on him while we head back. If'n he lives long enough Barney can have a chat with him. Mayhaps find out more'n we been able to."

"Some of the men fixed up the cutter, Isaac. Mostly for want of something to do, I reckon. Likely good as new, by God! Might want to take 'er with us 'stead o' burnin' her. Could tow her right behind the sloop. Even could put a couple of men in her an' sail her back. Don't seem right to burn a perfectly good boat."

"Aye, we'll do that, then. Just tow the cutter astern. Maybe put the doc and the lieutenant in her." Isaac laughed at the thought of the doctor in the cutter; his frustration at being in a position to escape, but with his lack of seamanship and the incapacitated British officer, unable to, would be palpable. "Aye, that's exactly what we'll do. Let's see about gettin' the lads aboard and make preparations to get underweigh."

The two moved up the beach, rallying the American sailors while they continued their conversation.

CHAPTER THIRTEEN

"Sounds like a boat, Isaac. You can hear the oars scrapin' on the gun'ls. Someone's tryin' to be quiet, but whatever they's doin' don't answer." Tate, leaning on the swivel gun forward, was alert as always.

"Silence there. All hands stand fast!" Isaac's whispered command was probably more forceful than had he shouted. Instantly, the final loading of the sloop halted and the hands remained stationary. Even Carronade stopped his pacing on the beach and sat down, his ears cocked as he too listened intently. The British sailors, certainly not helping with the loading, but not yet informed that they were to remain behind, moved toward the water's edge. One of them picked up a lantern and swung it back and forth, its yellow light reflecting off the ripples in the Creek and creating dancing highlights further out from the shore.

"Put that damn lantern out." Jack's hoarse whisper cut through the silence. It had no effect.

"Over 'ere. . . 'ere we are, lads." The British voice from the shore was soon joined by others and the quiet night was filled with their shouts.

"Man your guns, lads. Hands to action stations. Clear away that cordage there. Get the swivels loaded. Run out the side guns." Isaac moved through the sloop giving orders and inspiring his men to faster action. It was plain to any now that a British row-barge was about to engage them.

Guess they finally missed their shipmates, Isaac thought as he helped pull spare spars from the gunboats to one side so the little six-pounder cannon could be manned. He could not have known about the young sailor who had swum across the mouth of the Creek and made his way along the shore to Point Patience.

Boom! A roar and a six-foot tongue of flame leaped out of the bowchaser on the row-barge. The cries from the beach told the story; their range was long. They had unknowingly fired right into their own seamen lining the shore.

"Get the rest of the men aboard, Jack. Get the cutter secured astern." The doctor and his Royal Navy patient had already been installed in the cutter, with the explanation that they would be more comfortable there, and there would be no one to disturb the wounded officer. Most of the supplies and implements off-loaded the night before had been reloaded and anything that hadn't would be left.

The remaining American sailors were quick to clamber aboard, the sloop's black sail was raised by willing hands, and the anchor was won quickly. She paid off on a tack that would clear the mouth of the creek, but at the same time, exposed her side to the approaching barge. Black hull and black sails made her little more than a dark shadow on the inky water.

"To larboard! To larboard! Bear off! They're gonna get away!" The British sailors — those that could — were running down the beach shouting directions at their mates in the barge. They would take no chance that the Royal Navy would make the same mistake and overshoot their target again.

Boom! Another shot rang out, and the splash was close enough to wet the deck of the fleeing sloop. "Jack, lay that larboard six-pounder at the muzzle flash. Try a shot when she bears." Isaac alternated his gaze from trying to see where the shoreline bent around to the northwest, indicating the opening to the Patuxent and the British barge. He could hear willing hands levering the cannon around to make it bear more aft. Then it roared out a sharp crash and a sheet of blinding yellow fire.

The splash was ahead of the barge, but close. "Bring her aft, some, Jack. I'll bring the barky up a trifle." Isaac cried out even as he pushed the sloop's tiller down.

Boom! The British gun fired. The men amidships ducked instinctively as the ball whined over their heads, through the big mainsail and on to splash to leeward.

Crash. Jack's six-pounder spoke again. This time, the Americans were rewarded with the satisfying *thump* of the ball striking wood and followed by a sharp scream. Then silence.

"Sounded right good, Jack. Hit 'em again." Isaac yelled encouragement to his gunners. And the sloop cleared the entrance to St. Leonard Creek. "Make it quick; I'm gonna bear off."

Instantly, the little gun shot out its flame and sharp report, and the sloop eased her course into the broader, deeper waters of the Patuxent. And the British barge responded.

Boom! This time the British ball found wood, but in the cutter astern of the sloop. A startled cry went up from the smaller vessel. Isaac recognized the high raspy voice of Jeremiah Plumm. Again the barge fired, its gunner satisfied that they had found their target, and again, the formerly British cutter took the punishment.

Within a few moments, Isaac could feel the pull of the cutter on its tow rope; it had to be taking water now. Barely able to see it through the darkness, Isaac was sure the little boat astern looked lower in the water. He thought quickly.

"Billlings there! Cut it loose! Quick man. Use the hatchet." Billings, manning the swivel gun at the stern, wasted no time; the hatchet swung into the sloop's taffrail and through the hempen line that tethered the cutter to them. Freed from the drag astern, the sloop leaped ahead as if thrilled to be shed of her burden. She danced away, her black sails and hull merging with the night, as her sharp bow cut cleanly through the black water of the Patuxent River.

Boom, boom! The British gunners, unaware they had the wrong target, continued to pound the defenseless cutter, now drifting in the slight chop of the Patuxent River. The Americans, their own guns quiet, watched as a light appeared — a lantern held aloft — in the cutter. Its glow showed the boat low in the water, wallowing and helpless. A cry rose from the standing figure. The men on the sloop recognized Jeremiah Plumm's voice, even though they could not make out his words.

Crack! The high pitched report of a musket echoed across the water and the light fell, accompanied by a shriek in the same voice. Then darkness closed in again.

"What the hell was that, Isaac? Sounded like a musket shot from the barge to me." Tate, standing beside Isaac leaned forward, straining to see through the darkness.

"Aye. That's exactly what it was, Jake. And I'd reckon that wasn't the lieutenant standing up there holding that lantern. Looks like ol' Jeremiah Plumm might be gonna be needin' his own services about now. By the time them bastards figger out they shot the wrong boat, we'll be safely away. Kinda too bad we can't bring Plumm and that lieutenant back to the commodore, but I reckon we got all we was gonna get from the officer and I doubt the doctor would give up much. Guess Barney's gonna have to take our word for what's actin' with the Royal Navy."

Sailing against the tide, but with the breeze fair from the Bay, the sloop made Benedict just before a clear summer day began to dawn. Even before it was light, Isaac and his men could see the gunboats and row barges had left; the anchorage was empty as was the single dock that the sloop had left only two days previously. Isaac maneuvered the sloop expertly into it and, once the sails were secured, went ashore to find out where the flotilla had gone. Jake Tate accompanied him.

"Jake, I been thinkin'. Back in April or May I reckon it was, when I told you you could trot yourself up to Frederick and see your bride." Jake nodded and smiled hopefully. "Well, looks like we're gonna be here for a while and now would likely be as good a time as any to get that done. 'Sides, no tellin' . . ." Isaac fairly jumped as his words were cut off by the *whoop* the young sailor let out.

"You mean right now, Isaac? Or just sometime while we're tied up here in Benedict?" The smile had been replaced by an earnest seriousness that was uncharacteristic of this veteran of a major frigate action and Melville Island. But the smile returned in a trice when he heard Biggs, somewhat taken aback by the '*whoop*', utter "Right now. Get what you need from the sloop and get gone."

His smile matched that of his friend, but faded as he told the one-armed sailor, "You'll have to find us when you get back. No tellin' where we'll be, but I'd warrant it'll be further up-river than Benedict."

Jake, standing still, but leaning toward the sloop so anxious was he to be away, nodded. "When you figger you'll need me back aboard, Isaac? Don't know how far we are from Frederick here, but I figger it'll take me more 'n a couple of days to make it there. And back."

"Let's see. Nigh on to Independence Day, ain't it? Well, you be back by the end of the month. That oughta give you time enough to re-acquaint yourself with Miss Charity, I'd warrant."

"Thank you, thank you. I surely will be back. You can count on me, and thank you." The words were barely out of Jake's mouth before he was gone, running back to the sloop for his dunnage. His *whoops* caused the few people out to look at him strangely. Indeed, there was precious little to *whoop* about these days, what with the British fleet likely to appear anytime, food scarce, and the militia about as useful as a pitchfork in a sinking boat.

Biggs went on toward the square and a coffee house where he was sure he would find the information he sought. He smiled in spite of himself, so infectious was Tate's joy.

A silence fell over the group of men in the coffee house when Isaac entered; all looked his way, studied him for a moment and, deciding he was not a threat to them, resumed their conversations. A grizzled soul, his beard and hair awry, his clothes soiled, and a knife in his belt, continued to watch him and finally spoke. His expression did not invite Isaac to join him — or even step closer.

"You lookin' for somebody, boy?" The voice was a rumble from deep in his chest.

"Aye, I am," said Isaac walking toward the man, a smile ready. "I was hopin' you or somebody hereabouts might tell me of the commodore's flotilla. And where they might have got to."

"They ain't here," came the rumble. "Left on the tide yesterday after the commodore headed off to Washington City. On horseback." Still the dour expression continued, showing no warmth or invitation to the young captain. Isaac stopped where he was.

"Well, I didn't pass them comin' up the river, so I reckon they musta headed further up?" Isaac was still smiling, but the bearded face continued hard, showing no hint of friendliness toward him.

"Reckon they scampered when they heard that Royal Navy cove, Cap'n Barrie, and his ships was headin' up from the Bay. Now I 'spose we gonna have to depend on the militia. Ha!" There was no mirth in the laugh. "Them gunboats is all the damn Royal Navy is after and, with Barney runnin' further up the river ever' time they get close, all he's doin' is bringin' trouble to us an' them others what want to be left out o' this damn mess."

"But Barrie and his ships are anchored at Point Patience, down south of St. Leonard Creek. I seen 'em there yesterday with my own eyes." Isaac really hadn't, but Tate had, and that was good enough, he supposed.

"Well, ain't what we heard. They'll be along right quick, you mark my words, boy. An' if you're one o' Barney's lads, you better chase your arse outta here an' go find him. You people brought nothin' but trouble hereabouts." And the old man turned his attention back to his coffee, gripping the chipped discolored mug with two hands and, without lifting it off the table, slurped it noisily. The conversation was over, Isaac realized, but at least he got a little information. And he found that the folks here were just as opposed to the war and the American forces — or at least the flotilla — as they were further down the Patuxent.

Without further talk, Biggs left the establishment and, blinking as he emerged into the bright sunlight, thought about his next move. As he stood on the grass, it occurred to him how like his native Marblehead it looked: the trees in full leaf, some flowers someone had planted, grass, and a monument to some forgotten event nearby. It had a tranquil feeling to it and Isaac lingered for a while, remembering his New England home, his parents, and the last time he visited them.

It seemed long ago, but was in fact only eight or nine months back; he had stopped by to tell his parents, Charles and Liza Biggs, of his adventures with Captain Rogers on the privateer *General Washington* and of his plans to head back to Baltimore to find a ship.

He smiled to himself as he thought of his mother's fine meal, salted liberally with the concern she shared with his father about his plans for the future. Hadn't daring to enter the Northwest Arm and Melville Island up to Nova Scotia been enough excitement for him? Why would he want to go seeking a fight when things had finally quieted down in Massachusetts, thanks to the British ships sailing off and on the coastline? Why, that was just as silly as running off to New York and the fresh water fleets being built there, like his former shipmates — those nice British boys, Coleman and Conoughy — had done. Isaac had tried to explain to his mother that the two didn't "run off" to the freshwater; they had been sent by the Navy, of which they were still a part. It did no good, as she merely asked him in a voice filled with quiet concern "and who is sending you to the Chesapeake, Isaac?"

His father had tried half-heartedly to help, adding that they should be proud of the lad for wanting to help his country, but Mother would have none of it. She was, like most of her New England contemporaries, dead set against this craziness of 'Mister Madison's war'. And on top of that, she worried about her 'boy' deliberately putting himself in harm's way. Isaac had left their home on a less-than-pleasant note and a frown began to form as he recalled their warnings that "nothing good will come of this nonsense. Better you stay here and out of it."

"My goodness! You certainly seem serious. And on such a pretty day." So lost in his thoughts had Isaac been that he failed to notice the young woman who had walked right up to him. And was now addressing him.

"Oh, excuse me, ma'am. I guess I was daydreamin'. Didn't see you 'til you spoke." Isaac, caught completely off guard, was flustered; his experience with the fairer sex was limited indeed. Suddenly, so suddenly in fact that the young lady started, Isaac remembered his manners and snatched the weathered canvas hat off his head. He twisted and turned it self-consciously in his hands.

"Well! That's certainly something a girl wants to hear, that she just blended into the background!" The young woman flounced her skirts and turned away, as if preparing to take her departure.

"I'm sorry, ma'am. That's not what I meant at all. It's just that, well, I was thinkin' on something else, and you, well, it was my fault. I just didn't see you comin'." This was not going well at all. "Please don't run off, ma'am. My name is Isaac Biggs. I'm from up to New England, Marblehead. That's in Massachusetts."

"And I am Sarah Thomas. I am from right here in Benedict. My father is Colonel Thomas, in charge of the militia here. What would a Massachusetts man find to do here in Benedict, if I may inquire?" She had turned around and now faced Isaac from three feet away.

He studied her guardedly, not sure of what he should be doing or saying. She was of his height, so she was able to look directly into his eyes, which she did with an unflinching stare. Her hair, what he could see of it under her bonnet, was as black as night and shiny as a just-tarred shroud on a Royal Navy man of war. Pale skin, almost luminescent, with a full-lipped mouth, small nose slightly turned up, and eyes; oh, those eyes! They were big and dark and penetrating. Isaac thought they could look right inside him. It was somewhat unsettling. Her dress was of a medium blue and her straw bonnet was tied under her chin with a light blue ribbon. She carried a basket in her left hand. Empty, he noticed.

"Well . . . I'm . . . that is . . ." Isaac couldn't put two words together. He took a breath and tried again. "I'mIsaaccBiggsguessI-toldyouthatalready." This wasn't getting any easier. Another breath, slower this time. "I'm on that sloop at the pier, there. Part of Commodore Barney's flotilla. They was here couple of days ago." That was better. He smiled hopefully.

"That must be very dangerous work. I heard about your terrible battle with the Royal Navy a few days ago down river. St. Leonard Creek, I believe they said. I hope there weren't too many of your friends hurt in it. It must have been frightful. Were you scared?" Her expression became open and her eyes got bigger, Isaac noticed.

"No, ma'am. None of my crew got hurt in that, but some of the other boats had a few killed and some others was cruel wounded. Doc Plumm took care of 'em when we got here — to Benedict." Isaac found he could actually carry on a conversation with this striking young woman, as long as he didn't look too hard at her; when he did that, his brain got all confused, like the sea in a sudden change of wind.

"Yes," she said, her expression changing to a frown. "I know Doctor Plumm. A good doctor, I'm told, but I fear his loyalties never changed from the days of the War of Independence; he was surgeon on a British ship, you know. That is, I am led to believe, where he learned his medicine. And he's one of those who feel we shouldn't be taking up arms against the British after all they've done for us. What with trade and commerce and things that I am not supposed to understand. I am told repeatedly that I am wrong — or that I should stay out of it — but I think it's high time we removed ourselves from under the Royal thumb. I can tell you, that opinion is held in little regard by most here." She looked intently at Isaac, who involuntarily took a step backwards.

"I've noticed that most of the folks here and down toward St. Leonard seem to wish we — or at least they — was out of it. Been told that a lot. But we're in it now and got to see it through. That's what we need to do. Aye. Finish it, and get them dam . . . — 'scuse me, ma'am — get them ships out of our waters so we can get back to our own business. Ain't likely they'll leave 'til we beat 'em — and beat 'em good." Isaac had not consciously thought about his feelings toward the Royal Navy since he escaped from *Orpheus*, but it felt good to say it out loud. Actually, he thought, just talking to this black-haired young lady with the piercing eyes felt good. He smiled, in spite of himself.

"What do you find so amusing, Isaac Biggs of Marblehead, Massachusetts? The fact that I have an opinion, or that I am not afraid to voice it? I suspect you're thinking 'what an outspoken girl she is', right?"

Isaac recovered quickly. "Oh no, ma'am. It weren't that at all. Just smiling at the thought of sending the British packin' back across the ocean. That was all." The smile was gone.

Now Sarah Thomas was smiling. "I must be on about my chores. One must get to the shops early nowadays as there is so little on the shelves. I am told it's because the British have stolen or burned most of our stocks of food and goods. Will you be staying here in Benedict for a while?" The implication to Isaac was that she'd like to see him again.

"Well, I reckon I got to get back aboard the sloop and get about findin' the commodore. Don't know for sure where he got off to, but I aim to try up the river further. Would you like to see the sloop?" That last just kind of slipped out. He really didn't mean to be forward, but he was thinking that he didn't want her to disappear right now. And the words just came without any conscious thought.

"Why that would be nice; yes, I'd love to see your — what did you call it, a sloop?" She turned toward the dock, just a short walk away.

Isaac, delighted, but again caught all aback by her willingness to continue to be in his company, took a moment to realize she'd agreed, and had to take a couple of fast steps to put himself beside her.

Together they walked down the street, Isaac still twisting his hat with both hands, to the pier. Rounding the corner of a building, Sarah saw the sloop and exclaimed, "Oh what a beautiful boat! But it's painted black. How extraordinary!"

"Aye, she is that, Miss Sarah. That's so she cain't be seen real good in the dark. Her sails is black, too." Isaac was getting back on familiar ground and was more comfortable talking about his boat as long as he didn't dwell on the fact that he was talking about it to a beautiful woman. He went on. "And she's fast on top of it. With a fair breeze and a press of canvas set, ain't much on the Bay what can catch her. Raised hell — 'scuse me, again, ma'am — I mean to say, we've raised the devil with the Royal Navy up the Bay some. Ain't done so much since we got down this way, though. Spent most of the time trapped in . . . well, I guess you ain't interested in that."

They arrived at the end of the dock and Sarah stepped right up to the bulwark, ready to peer over it. She drew back quickly when the large gray head of Carronade appeared over the rail, directly in front of her.

"Oh my goodness! What a huge animal. Is he yours?"

"Oh no, Miss Sarah. He belongs to Jack Clements. He's skipper of the sistership to this one . . . I mean Jack is, not the dog. His name's Carronade — the dog, that is."

She laughed, her face alight with pleasure at Isaac's obvious discomfort. "Can we go on the boat? Does your captain allow you to have visitors?"

As Isaac was about to answer the question, Sam Hay appeared from below and, seeing Isaac had returned, stepped to the bulwark. He did not miss seeing Isaac's companion.

"Uh. . . Cap'n, while you was gone, some cove come by the barky and said the commodore'd headed up to some place called Lower Marlboro. Left word, he did, we was 'sposed to get along up there quick as ever we could. G'morning, ma'am." Hay removed his shabby worn hat when he addressed Sarah.

Before Isaac could respond, Sarah voiced her surprise at this revelation. "He called you 'captain'. You didn't mention you were the captain of this boat, Isaac. And here I thought you . . . well, never you mind what I thought." She turned back to the bulwark where Carronade was resting his head. The dog had not taken his eyes off Sarah; it appeared that even he was smitten with the young lady. Reaching out a delicate hand, she patted the huge animal and, seeing that he didn't seem to mind, scratched his ear.

Isaac was stunned; no one had ever approached Carronade so casually and with so much confidence. The dog closed his eyes and almost smiled. "Ain't no one ever got away with that afore, save Jack, Miss Sarah. Looks like he took to you right off.

"Sam, this here's Miss Thomas; her father is colonel in charge of the local militia hereabouts. Miss Sarah, this cove is Sam Hay, one of my sailors, and a fair hand with the guns." The sailor stood straighter and beamed at being presented to the girl. He made his bow and the smile broadened, but he said nothing. "Sam, go get a box or something to help Miss Sarah get aboard. Cain't ask a lady to climb over the bulwark, now."

Before the sailor could move, Sarah stepped onto the waterway outside of the bulwark and sitting down on the top of it, swung her legs over and slipped onto the deck right beside Carronade. Isaac was speechless. So was Hay.

Laughing at their shocked expressions, Sarah said, "Just because I'm a girl doesn't mean I'm helpless, you know. Now, Isaac, are you going to show me around your boat?" She scratched the dog unconcernedly.

The deepwater sailor jumped aboard and was quickly in control of himself. He turned to Sam Hay. "Get the men out and prepare to make sail, Sam. I'll show Miss Thomas around topside." He turned to the young woman. "We'll start for'ard, Miss Sarah, if that's all right with you." He was rewarded with a smile.

She followed Isaac toward the rakish bowsprit and Carronade followed her, not willing to give up the affection she had shown him. Isaac stopped upon reaching the eyes of the boat and began to explain the elements of the sloop, including the lethal little swivel gun perched on the rail. She was suitably impressed and said as much. Isaac colored at the compliment, but continued the tour, working his way aft.

The crew of the sloop began to appear on deck, the word having been passed quickly that there was a most attractive young woman aboard. As each went by — and each found an excuse to do so — he tipped his hat, smiled and muttered a suitable greeting. Except Clive Billings. Obviously taken with the girl's beauty, he tipped his hat, turned, and tripped over a sheet block. He fell backwards landing full length at his captain's feet.

"Here, now, Billings. Get on with your duties. We'll be gettin' the barky underweigh quick as ever you please. No time for sky-larkin'." Isaac worked hard to control his laughter at Billing's discomfort. The red-faced seaman, all his bravado and gallantry evaporated, scrambled to his feet and hastened to the bow where he busied himself taking the harbor furl off the stays'l. He cast furtive glances at Sarah, hoping she would look at him and smile. The sudden slump of his shoulders when she continued aft with Isaac spoke eloquently of a disappointment that knew no bounds.

When the pair reached the quarterdeck, they found Jack Clements waiting there. Carronade, still close aboard to Sarah, made no move to join his master. After the introductions were made, Jack commented on the dog's behavior.

"Ain't that I've known him all that long, Miss Sarah, but in the time I have, I ain't never seen Carronade take to someone like he's took to you. You surely have charmed him." Clements smiled and reached toward the dog. He was rewarded with a low growl and withdrew his hand.

"Now, Carronade, I must be getting along. You stay here and be nice to Mister Clements. After all, he's the one who rescued you from the nasty British soldiers." The big dog looked at her with sad eyes as if he had understood her words. She turned to Isaac. "Thank you kindly for showing me your wonderful boat — excuse me — sloop. I know you have to be on your way to find your commodore, but I do hope you'll be passing by here again?" It was a question.

"I ain't got no idea, Miss Sarah, but I surely do hope so. Fact is, I'd like that just fine my own self." He led her to the bulwark amidships where a box had been set on either side to aid her departure. She stepped daintily onto it, over the rail, and on to the one on the dock.

"I shall watch for your . . . sloop, Isaac. Please don't disappoint me."

Biggs was again tongue-tied and mumbled something about "being back right soon . . ." and turning, he ordered hands to stations for making sail. The sloop slipped away from the dock, her black sails filling to the easy breeze, and headed up river. Isaac watched the dock with furtive glances and was more than pleased to see that Sarah Thomas watched them until they turned a bend in the river.

CHAPTER FOURTEEN

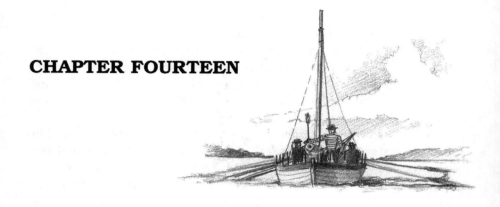

"That's about the whole of it, Commodore. Ain't too much more to tell, 'ceptin' the folks down to Benedict ain't real friendly towards us. Kind of got the impression they blame us for all of the grief and problems they got with the British. Just like the folks down to St. Leonard. And the militias." Isaac finished his report to Barney in the Cabin of the black sloop anchored in the narrows off Lower Marlboro. Jared Talbot, Jack Clements and Luke Cooper, skipper of Barney's flagship sat around the table in the small cabin and had listened to the whole tale.

"So you think Plumm is either dead or captured by the British?" Barney asked quietly.

"Well, he might have got killed by them in the row-barge, but if'n he didn't, I'd reckon he ain't their prisoner; he likely went over willingly. Seemed to Jack and me to favor them more'n us. We ain't figgered out how the British officers knew to send that barge into the creek, but I'd warrant that the good doctor had something to do with it. Jack says he never left the camp while I was takin' care o' them two gunboats, but it ain't beyond the pale that he figgered out how to send someone." Clements nodded in silent affirmation of Isaac's statement. Biggs continued. "And a person in Benedict told me he learned his doctorin' in the Royal Navy durin' the War of Independence, not the American Navy." Isaac was a little vague about who the 'person in Benedict' might have been, but colored slightly as he thought about who it was. In fact, he had thought of little else until he began his report to Barney.

Barney's face gave little away, but he accepted the report on Plumm without comment, save a brief sigh at its conclusion. Then he got to the business at hand.

"As most of you men know, I just got back from Washington. Met with General Winder, Secretary Jones, and Mr. Monroe — he's the Secretary of State, you know; there's mixed ideas about what the British are thinkin'. Some favor them attackin' at Annapolis and some others think it's gonna be Baltimore from overland. I think they're gonna try and take Washington. It ain't but a short march from the river. And if I were gonna attack Baltimore, I reckon I'd likely do it from the water. Be easier by half than tryin' to march that distance — 'specially in this blasted heat." Barney looked at his top captains, seeking some indication of their concurrence. Most nodded silently at his words.

"I read in a newspaper while I was in the Capital an account of what they's already callin' the "Battle of St. Leonard Creek". Seems the cove who wrote the story didn't have much use for the federal troops what come down there to help us get out of the Creek and even went so far as to question the ability of the government at defendin' the folks here-abouts. Told how the British Navy had been raidin' and stealin' food, tobacco, and slaves from over on the Potomac just like they been doin' here on the Patuxent. Said they was only here on account of lookin' for us, and that we was to blame for most of the problems the folks is havin'. More specifical, I guess, me. Seemed to follow right along the same course as what we been hearin' since last May — from most of the people here. Well, I got a job to do and, by God, we're gonna get it done. And damn them what's against us." The commodore had gotten himself quite worked up with his tirade; he paused, calming himself, then wiped his brow with a handkerchief. He began anew, in a quieter voice.

"Jared, I want you to pick a score or so of men and get yourself to Baltimore — you'll have to make it overland, since you ain't likely to just sail out of the river here. There are fourteen and more gunboats there, and if the British decide to try for Baltimore like some in Washington think, we're gonna need them gunboats ready whether they come over land or from the water. If it turns out I'm right, or Secretary Jones is right and they attack Annapolis, we'll get word to you and you can rejoin us — wherever we are. And if they attack Baltimore, me and the rest of the lads can get there in a day." Talbot nodded, pleased at being given this big responsibility. Barney went on.

"As to the rest of us, we'll be gettin' the flotilla underway again, and movin' up to Nottingham. That's a town what the militia has left alone — reckon they heard the British was comin' and ran back to Washington." The scorn in Barney's voice reinforced his low regard for the local land units assigned to protect the riverfront towns. "There's a narrowin' of the river there, even more than here, and we can hold that just like we held in St. Leonard Creek. It'll be easier to get messages to and from Secretary Jones from there as well. An' I understand that Colonel Wadsworth is bringin' his troops up to Benedict just in case the enemy tries to move up the river along the shore." Isaac's eyes snapped to the commodore's, the only indication that Benedict might be more than just another river town.

After swinging to their anchors for the night, a night when some of the sailors and officers went ashore only to find an attitude consistent with that of the other towns the flotilla had visited, the gunboats, barges and sloops won their anchors and sailed further up the Patuxent. Clements, with the big dog and the half dozen men who had augmented Isaac's crew, was back aboard his own sloop — Frank Clark having sailed her to Lower Marlboro in Jack's absence — and Isaac was back to his regular crew less, of course, Jake Tate who, Isaac reckoned, was enjoying the company of his new wife in Frederick. Likely her family less so.

The vessels had not been in Nottingham two full days when a breathless messenger arrived on a lathered horse seeking the commodore.

"They's comin', by God, and eight hunnert strong! You gotta get down there and help, for the love of God!" The boy panted out the words in barely understandable gasps as soon as he had been brought to Barney.

"Haul small there, lad. Who's comin' eight hundred strong? And where? Slow down, catch your breath. Another minute or two ain't gonna make a big difference."

"Benedict. The Royal Navy is landin' eight hunnert strong at Benedict. Probably gettin' there now. Colonel Thomas sent me to fetch you." The lad had calmed down, but was still consumed with the urgency of his mission.

"Damn them militia coves! They run at the sight of a red coat and cuss at me for bringin' the British into the river, but I'm the first one they call when they need help. Where's Colonel Wadsworth? He's supposed to be in Benedict already. Can not his troops deal with . . . no, I reckon not, seein' as how half of 'em run at St. Leonard." Barney darkened and fumed at the messenger and any within earshot. He paced along the shoreline where the boy had found him.

Finally he shook his head in frustration. How could he refuse? He turned to one of his sailors loitering nearby.

"Run and find any of the men what's ashore and get 'em back aboard the boats. Then find Cap'n Cooper and the others and tell 'em we'll be leavin' forthwith." He turned to the rudimentary pier and spied his cutter making ready to pull back to the gunboat. "Avast there! Stay at the dock. I shall be with you in a trice," he shouted.

The boat back-watered and once again made fast a line to the dock. The sailor hurried off to find the crews. The messenger from Benedict, wide-eyed at the activity he had started, stood rooted to the ground until Barney spoke to him.

"You gonna ride that horse back or sail down there with me?"

"I . . . uh . . . well, sir . . . I don't rightly know what I'm s'posed to do. The colonel didn't tell me no more 'an get up here an' find you." He looked around as if the answer would be found on the faces of the few people who had gathered to witness the commotion.

"Well make up your mind, lad. If the Royal Marines are landing at Benedict now, I surely ain't got time to wait whilst you figure out what to do." Barney, having made his decision, was anxious to get going and engage the enemy. Little would be gained by waiting now.

"If'n it's all right with you, sir, I'll take the ride in your boat. I reckon the horse oughta be fine here for a spell." To himself he added, *Might be safer than just ridin' into a fight on top of it.*

"Then get you down to that boat there, lad. Soon's the crews are aboard the barges and gunboats, we'll be headin' down river with all haste."

Without waiting for an answer or the boy, the commodore strode purposefully down the shoreline and out the dock. His boots rang hollowly on the planking. A hand helped him into the cutter and Barney settled himself in the sternsheets for the short pull to his gunboat. The boy ran down the dock and leaped into the bow of the cutter as it pulled away. He crouched in the very bows, panting, the sweat running freely from his face.

Throughout the anchorage, shouts of "Stations for makin' sail, lads" could be heard as Barney's orders to "Get underweigh" were delivered. Flags snapped at mastheads and gaffs, reinforcing the spoken word. Boats pulled between the barges and gunboats returning crews and officers. The air filled with the sounds of blocks squeaking, sails flogging, capstans turning to haul anchors from the river bottom, and men shouting and cursing as they prepared cannon, vessels, and themselves for the eagerly anticipated battle. Filtering through the melee was the resonant voice of Carronade as he encouraged sailors on Jack's sloop and the gunboats nearby to make haste.

"Sails and oars, lads; sails and oars!" Barney's voice rang out across the water and his instructions were repeated boat to boat by voice and flag. The barges and gunboats sprouted great oars from their sides, and willing backs bent to the task of augmenting the gentle breeze. The sloops, with their big mains'ls, stays'ls and jibs bellied out, quickly set their square tops'ls to keep pace with the armada as it tore down the Patuxent toward Benedict — and the arriving British.

Isaac paced his sloop's deck nervously; *what the devil was goin' on down there? How could the British get there that quick and with eight hundred marines? What was the militia doing? Were the townspeople involved? What would their reception be this time? And finally, what was Miss Sarah doing? Was she all right? What if . . .* He refused to let himself think that way. Of course she would be just fine.

Oh my God. What am I doin' thinkin' that way? I hardly know the girl. Sure, she's pretty to look at and she seems to have a spark and I do like talkin' to her, even if it confuses me sometimes. An' she has been on my mind for the past few days an' more. I ain't never felt like this afore. Even that gal down to Nassau — what was her name? Oh yes, Becca. She surely didn't make me feel like this. What's goin' on with me? Isaac had gripped the bulwark with such force that he suddenly realized that his hands hurt. He let go and moved to the quarterdeck where Sam Hay was at the tiller.

Looking across the fifty yards of water separating the two black-sailed sloops, he saw Clements pacing his own quarterdeck and Carronade standing at his post in the bows. The gunboats and barges were keeping pace, the cadence of their stroke floated over the water just behind the dip of their oars. The bright early summer sun glinted and sparkled as it struck the wet blades and the evenly spaced white patches on the water dazzled the eyes with their brilliance. A fine sight they made, indeed. Suddenly, something he saw on a nearby gunboat — it was Jared Talbot's but without the big one-eyed Bayman — called his mind to the task at hand.

"Billings, get the muskets and cutlasses topside and stacked. You there, Jackson, get powder and shot on deck." He turned to the helmsman. "Sam, get them guns loaded. I'll take her while you do. Load the swivels with grape or canister and ball shot for the cannon. The Lord alone knows what we're likely to find when we get there, but bein' ready'll answer best." He stepped over and put his hand on the big tiller, smiling as he felt the tug and surge of the sloop's speed on her rudder.

"What a sweet sailing vessel she is, by God. And pretty as a sprightly girl. Just like Miss Sarah. Must make quite a sight, all of us sailin' like this. Put fear into the hearts of any Royal Navy cove to see this, it would." He mused out loud, safely out of earshot of any of his crew.

"What was that, Isaac? Sorry, I didn't catch your words." The gray-bearded sailor loading and checking the stern-mounted swivel gun paused and looked up from his work, squinting at the captain.

"Oh, wasn't nothin'. Just talkin' to my own self, I was." Isaac was surprised that he had missed the oldest member of the sloop's crew, who must have walked right by him on his way to the gun. And equally surprised he had spoken aloud. *What's the matter with me? Where's my head gotten to?* This time he made sure he was only thinking the words; his lips formed a thin line across his face and his brow furrowed in consternation. He didn't completely understand this change that had come over him — and just since he was in Benedict.

CHAPTER FIFTEEN

"It sure don't look like the British come up by ship, by God! You see anything lookin' like a Royal Navy man o' war, Isaac?" Jack's shout was the first sound any of them heard after rounding the bend just above Benedict. The crews had become thoughtfully silent as their destination — and an uncertain future — neared. Clements' sloop was a little ahead of the rest of the flotilla, followed closely by Isaac's, and the scarred deepwater man was standing in the bow of his vessel next to the big dog. Carronade was alert, but silent, adding credence to his master's words.

As they approached the town landing, the crews standing ready at their guns with slow matches lit, the flotillamen saw no sign of a British invasion — or of anything else. All remained quite serene; there seemed to be few townspeople visible and the ones the men could see appeared to be in no distress.

The sloops luffed their sails as the gunboats drew closer. Barney ordered anchors out, but at short stay and rigged with spring lines to turn the vessels and bring guns to bear should it be necessary. Then he called for his cutter to be lowered.

Isaac, his longglass at his eye, watched the commodore as he made his way up the dock. The town green was visible beyond the buildings at the head of the dock and Isaac's mind flashed to an image of Sarah Thomas in her blue dress and bonnet. Their conversation ran through his mind and he watched himself and the girl walk from the green to the dock. He smiled as he saw her hoist herself aboard the sloop without assistance, and become instant friends with that monster dog of Jack's.

The commodore disappeared around the corner of a building, but Isaac barely noticed; a figure in a pale green frock was moving down the dock. He brought the glass back to his eye and refocused it. As the green dress sharpened and the face above it snapped into view, Isaac felt his mouth go dry.

"Hay, Billings: get the boat in the water. Lively now. I'm goin' ashore." Isaac was moving toward the vessel's waist as he spoke and fussed impatiently, issuing superfluous instructions, as the little boat was swung out and splashed alongside. The men cast furtive glances at their skipper as they worked, muttering among themselves about his strange manner. Barely had his boat smacked down when Isaac was over the rail and in it, ordering two of his crew in to row him ashore.

"Say, Isaac. Ain't that your lady friend what was here when we come up from the Creek?" Jack's voice boomed out over the water and Biggs looked at the other black sloop to see his friend standing on the bulwark amidships with a longglass in his hand. With his other hand he held lightly onto the starboard main shroud. A grin, larger by half than his normal cheery smile, split his face as he alternated his gaze between his love-struck mate and the pretty girl who now stood at the end of the pier, her hands on her hips. The young Marblehead sailor colored at Clements' observation, but said nothing. The two seamen grinned, realizing at last the reason for their captain's haste and his fussing.

His boat bumped alongside the high dock, made even higher by the low tide in the river, and Isaac shinnied up a piling to climb onto the rough boards of the pier. As he raised himself up from his hands and knees, he heard the rustle of cloth moved by the breeze. Looking up, he saw the light green of Sarah's skirt and above that, her wonderful face wreathed in that radiant black hair; she was standing right in front of him!

As he scrambled to his feet, her eyes followed his movement and met his gaze with a slight smile on her lips and a twinkle in her eyes.

"I . . . uh . . . good morning, Miss Sarah. I surely didn't expect to see you again so . . . that is to say . . . uh . . . I wasn't 'spectin' that we'd be comin' back . . . uh. . ."

"Well. That's a fine greeting! And I am glad to see you again, too, Isaac. I heard the flotilla might be returning to Benedict soon, but I surely didn't think it would be *this* soon. And with all the boats . . . uh, excuse me, sloops. What a delightful surprise!"

"Aye, ma'am. It surely is a nice surprise. For me too. But they's not all sloops, Miss Sarah; ain't but two of 'em sloops. Mine and that other black one yonder. That's Jack Clements' sloop. He's the one what owns the big dog what took to you afore." He seemed to have found his voice again. But he couldn't get out the words he wanted. The girl stepped in again to rescue him.

"Oh, I do remember the dog well. And Mister Clements. But he was sailing with you when last you were here, was he not?"

"Oh, aye. That he was. And I'm mighty glad to see you here, Miss Sarah." There, he'd got it out. Finally. "But someone — said it was Colonel Thomas, he did — sent a messenger to Commodore Barney up to Nottingham. Said the British was landin' eight hundred Marines here in Benedict. Don't look to me like they's any Redcoats 'round, that I can see."

"I can't understand why Father would send for the commodore. There have been no British soldiers anywhere near Benedict for some weeks now. But you're here and I am so glad. Had I known how quickly you would respond, I would have sent for you myself!" An impish smile on her lips and a sparkle in her eyes reinforced her words.

Isaac colored again, his face reddening beneath the weathered tan, but he smiled broadly at the compliment from the pretty young woman. And followed close aboard as she turned and strolled slowly up the dock toward the town. The pair carried on quietly, enjoying each other's company in silence. As they reached the green where they had met, Isaac's thoughts swirled and filled with their meeting; it had been only a few days ago, but already he felt that he had known this striking girl forever.

"Would you like to meet Father?" she asked suddenly. "Then you could inquire yourself about the message you received in Nottingham." Sarah looked searchingly at him.

"Well, I . . . umm . . . that is . . . it ain't for me to question . . . uh . . . I reckon the commodore's likely doin' that very thing. He's already went off to find . . . well, I don't know who he went to find, but someone what can sort this all out for him. And the message we got weren't 'xactly for me, neither." Isaac was caught off-guard again.

"But surely he doesn't know where Father might be; I do. I am sure your commodore would be pleased to have your insight to the problem, should one indeed exist."

"I'd be right pleased to meet your father, Miss Sarah, but I surely wouldn't want to be takin' Commodore Barney's wind on this; he likely wouldn't take real kindly to it."

"Well, then, you certainly shall meet him and should the subject come up, you can inquire yourself. What you do with the knowledge will be up to you." She turned and strode purposefully across the green with Isaac again making all sail to catch up to her.

A short walk from the green, the pair stopped in front of a well-appointed, two-story house surrounded by tall trees. A short brick path led from the street to steps leading to a half-round porch and the front door. The four windows on the ground floor were open wide, as was the centered door. Upstairs, three windows in dormers were likewise open, and Isaac could see curtains billowing in the breeze. *Hmm*, he thought as he studied what he assumed was the home of Sarah's father. *Curtains. Houses this fancy in Marblehead only belong to important folks.* He remembered seeing the Crowninshield home in Salem a year and more back; it was only a little bigger than this and he recalled seeing curtains there, too. The house in Salem was also "built lapstrake" as Isaac recalled, not knowing the proper name for clapboards. And the Crowninshields were among the most important — and well-set — families in Salem. This cove must surely be more than just a colonel of the militia.

"You live here, Miss Sarah?" Isaac was uncertain now on how to proceed. He hesitated as she started up the brick path.

"Oh no, silly. This is Mister Summers' home; he's head of the Benedict Citizens' Committee and I believe Father said he was going to be meeting with him this day to determine what should be done with our Militia. In the event the British do, in fact, come. And I've been told that there are some federal soldiers expected any day now. I'd imagine they're likely talking on that as well." She waited while Isaac continued to struggle with her impetuous desire to interrupt this obviously important meeting.

"Uh . . . well . . . Miss Sarah. I don't think we ought to just barge in there. They got more important things they's thinkin' on than us. Mayhaps we'd better wait a spell, 'til they get done." Biggs remained on the street, as Sarah somewhat less than patiently, waited a few steps beyond on the walk.

"Oh, do come with me, Isaac. Father will be glad to meet you and I'm sure that they must be finishing quickly. They've been talking for quite some time now. Surely there can't be *that* much of importance to discuss."

As they continued to debate the merits of interrupting the august personages of the Head of the Citizens' Committee, Colonel of the Militia, and who knew who else, figures appeared at the doorway of the home. Sarah caught Isaac's glance as it shifted to a point beyond her and turned back to the house.

"Oh, Father, there you are! We were just about to come and get you. Are you quite done with your meeting?" The girl seemed, to Isaac at least, to float up the walk toward the three men now standing on the steps. As they watched, a fourth appeared in the doorway and emerged into the bright daylight. It was Joshua Barney.

"Well, Sarah. How nice to see you and how pretty you look in that green dress." One of the figures detached itself from the group and stepped off the porch onto the first step. He was dressed in gray trousers, a white shirt with a gray waistcoat and no jacket — a concession to the Chesapeake summer, no doubt. Sarah gave him a brief hug. Isaac watched from the street, unable to hear their words, but assumed she was greeting her father. Further conversation and a curtsy indicated her introductions to the other men.

"Isaac. Come here and meet Mister Summers. And my father." The young woman's words were not to be ignored and, even though he was sure he did not belong there with those obviously important men, he took a few tentative steps toward the house and the group waiting for him on the porch.

"Isaac, this is my godfather, Mister Summers, and this is my father, Colonel Thomas. This gentleman is Colonel Wadsworth and I believe you know Commodore Barney. Gentlemen, this is Captain Isaac Biggs, of Marblehead, Massachusetts, and commander of a beautiful black sloop anchored in our river." Sarah's smile was echoed along with suitable greetings from three of the men; Joshua Barney merely nodded.

Isaac crumpled his hat in one hand while he shook hands with each of the local dignitaries. Colonel Wadsworth shook Isaac's hand saying, "I remember you from down at St. Leonard Creek and, then after the flotilla got freed, right here in Benedict. On the commodore's gunboat, it was." He turned to Colonel Thomas and Summers. "This young man and another commanding a similar vessel were most helpful in getting the commodore's flotilla out of

St. Leonard Creek. A fine sailorman he is."

Isaac blushed at the compliment and crushed his hat tighter in his fist. Wadsworth now addressed Biggs. "Did you enjoy success on your return to the creek, Captain? The commodore ain't mentioned anything but that you went and was back with the spars and powder you was sent to fetch."

"Aye, sir. We got it done just fine. Took a small prize — a cutter from the Sixth Rate *Favorite* — but lost her in a scrap with a British row-barge."

"Did not Doctor Plumm accompany you on this voyage, young man?" This from Sarah's godfather.

Isaac looked at the group, settling his gaze on Joshua Barney. He received a barely perceptible nod from the commodore.

"Aye, that he did, sir. Accompanied us down to the creek to offer his services to any of the army or militia coves what might be needin' 'em after the fightin'. But we took a prize, as I mentioned, Sir, and they was some of them British sailors what got wounded in the takin' so he spent his time doctorin' them. And their lieutenant was cruel hurt — gut shot with grape, beggin' your pardon, Miss Sarah — and he needed Doc Plumm's help more'n the others." He paused in his narrative, again casting a glance at Barney.

"Go on, Isaac. You might as well tell 'em the whole of it." The commodore prodded the sloop captain.

Isaac took a breath, not sure how to explain the doctor's absence, then plunged forward. "We was bringin' out our prize an' Mister Plumm and the English lieutenant was in the cutter, bein' towed astern the sloop. It was dark as pitch, bein' as how the row-barge attacked us durin' the middle watch, and they was shootin' at what I reckon they thought was the sloop. But it weren't; it was the cutter astern of us and it got cruel wounded. Likely holed, it were. I reckon the doctor and the lieutenant was either killed or taken by 'em to one o' the British men o' war layin' off Point Patience." He stopped his tale short of expounding on the doctor's traitorous behavior.

"A real pity, that. We'll surely miss his skills hereabouts. Been here long as most of us can remember." Colonel Thomas was examining Isaac carefully. It was apparent that either Sarah had mentioned him or that he had noticed the way his daughter acted around the sailor and he took the young man's measure. Slowly.

Isaac felt like a butterfly on a pin in one of those cases he had seen once. He twisted his hat and shuffled his feet. "I. . . uh . . . I best be gettin' back aboard, Miss Sarah. A pleasure to meet you gentlemen." He nodded to each and then to the commodore. "Sir? Will we be gettin' underweigh directly?"

Before the man could answer, Sarah put her hand on Isaac's arm and addressed her father. "Father, you never asked why we were here. Isaac wanted to know why the messenger . . ."

Oh, Lord, Miss Sarah, not now. Don't say no more! Isaac thought as he heard the girl heading off on this tack. He glanced at Barney. A slight smile played at the corners of the commodore's mouth; *No help there,* Isaac thought. And Sarah continued.

". . . eight hundred strong and landing here." She looked earnestly at her father.

"Commodore Barney and I have already been over that ground, young lady, and I seem to recollect we've had conversations in the past about you bein' caught up with things that don't concern you. And should the commodore want to discuss the matter with Captain Biggs, I expect he will. Why don't you finish doin' them errands you was about and leave the menfolk to handle this." Colonel Thomas had drawn himself up to his full six feet of height and the words he spoke were accompanied by a look that would brook no nonsense. Sarah seemed not to notice.

"Come, Isaac. I will walk you back to the dock. I do hope your little boat has waited to carry you back out to the . . . sloop. Oh, how silly of me; of course they will wait, you're their captain." With hardly a glance at her father or any other, she turned and floated gracefully back down the walk to the street.

The deepwater man, again in what he perceived to be water beyond his depth, looked questioningly at his commodore; he received a shrug in response to his unasked question. And nodding silently again at each of the others in turn, followed the girl to the street.

He heard someone, he thought it might have been Colonel Thomas or possibly Mr. Summers, say "He's got his hands full with that one, by God. Poor lad'll never figure out what hit him." Then laughter.

As he hurried to catch up with Sarah, Isaac felt the color rise up his neck at the comment. A fluke of wind brought him the parting words of the men as they said their goodbyes and he sensed that Barney would soon be heading to the dock behind him. He came abreast of the girl who had slowed her pace. He didn't know quite what to say — or even if he should say anything. Sarah solved his problem for him.

"I told you my father — and most of the other men in town — think I meddle in what they claim as their private domain. But I think I have a right to know what is happening around here. Particularly if the British are indeed coming up the river. We will all have to deal with that event if — or perhaps I should say, when, since most think they're after your boats and you are here — it occurs. And we are all — men and women alike — suffering the same privations since the British began stealing our foods and supplies. Oh! I get so vexed at Father sometimes. It's almost as if he doesn't want me to think for myself!" She stamped her foot raising a small cloud of dust in the dry dirt road.

Isaac was caught aback by the outburst; this was a side of this pretty young woman he had not before seen. Obviously she is smart, he thought as he struggled to come up with some words to mollify her before he returned to the sloop. He didn't have time.

"You probably agree with them, being a man, don't you Isaac?" She stopped and looked intently at him from a disturbingly close distance, still miffed at her father's rebuke. "You must think I'm a complete fool, but let me tell you, the ones who are the fools are the ones who would welcome the British to Benedict."

"No, ma'am, Miss Sarah. . . I mean, aye, that's right. . . about the ones welcoming the British. And no, I surely don't think you are a fool, or anything close to one. In fact, I think you are right smart." He smiled, hopefully. He cast about in his mind for something else to say that would cause her to change course. He needn't have worried. As quickly as it appeared, her anger was gone and she looked at him and smiled.

"Why, thank you, Isaac. That's a most pleasant compliment. I think you are 'right smart' as well. Do you think you'll have to sail back up to Nottingham at once?" She looked over his shoulder at the figure moving briskly toward them. "Oh, here comes your commodore — Barney, if I remember correctly. Perchance he will tell us."

Before Isaac could say a word, she stepped right up to Barney and when he stopped and doffed his hat, she did in fact ask him.

"Oh, Commodore. Are you planning to sail immediately? If not, Father and I would like you and Captain Biggs to join us for supper this evening. Should you have time, of course, from your many duties." She curtsied sweetly and looked at the man with an eager and earnest face.

"Well, Miss Thomas, I believe we will not be leaving until the morning tide. And I thank you most kindly for your delightful invitation to sup with you and the colonel. Unfortunately, my duties will prevent me from joining you, but I am sure that Captain Biggs would be most pleased to." Barney smiled and looked at Isaac. The young man's face was a panoply of expression; confusion, switching from horror at the pluck of the girl to delight at the opportunity of spending more time with her and then to embarrassment at Barney's involvement.

Isaac broke into a tentative smile again. "Aye. I would be. Uh . . . that is, Commodore, if'n you ain't got nothin' you need me an' the lads to get done while we're here."

"No, Isaac. I believe we can spare you to join this lovely young miss and her father at supper." Barney turned and made his way to the end of the pier where his boat had been waiting since the late morning when he came ashore. He didn't break into a smile until he was nearly to the boat. Isaac and Sarah watched as he was rowed out to the gunboat.

"You can help me with some shopping, Isaac, and then we'll go home. You can visit with Father whilst I prepare the meal."

"I probably oughta be gettin' back aboard for a spell, Miss Sarah, and check on a few things. If you could let me know . . ."

"Oh, yes. Men don't help with shopping, do they?" She chided him, but the old anger was gone. "You may meet me on the green at a half four, if that would suit you." Her dark eyes sparkled.

"Aye, one bell in the first dog watch, on the green. I'll be there, Miss Sarah, and glad to be." He made his bow and turned, walking down the dock with a lightness in his step. The grin was still on his face when he stepped aboard the sloop.

CHAPTER SIXTEEN

The back room of the ale house was all but empty at this early hour of the day; a few early starters and a single hang-over from the previous evening's clientele occupied two tables in the dim room.

"Aye, this'll do fine. Just clear out these coves and be sure the door is kept closed. We could be here all morning and for your trouble — and loss of business," Joshua Barney shot a glance at the two men working on tall mugs of ale and the passed-out drunk in the corner — "I'll arrange for us all to take dinner here at midday. And of course, we'll require coffee as soon as my guests arrive."

The publican bowed slightly from the waist, pleased that Barney had chosen the River Rose as the place for this important meeting, but at the same time annoyed as it would appear to put him in sympathy with the man who most saw as the root of all their troubles. But the extra money during a normally quiet morning would offset his neighbors' scorn.

While the owner rousted the drunk from his torpor and invited the other two men to take a table in the front room, Barney strode outside to await his guests, recoiling from the brightness and heat that had already built, though it was barely nine o'clock. This July had been one of the hottest he ever recalled and, contrary to his habit of always being properly attired, he stripped off his jacket, folded it carefully, and draped it over his arm. A large maple tree at the corner of the building provided him some shade and he stood resolutely under it as he considered the events of the week that had passed since the flotilla had returned to Nottingham from it's wild goose chase.

On July fifteenth, only a day after their return, Barney had received word that five warships and two transports showing British colors had arrived at the mouth of the Patuxent. His informant had been unclear as to the size or weight of metal of the warships, but seemed not to waver in his story of their arrival. Nonetheless, Barney, remembering his rush to Benedict, remained skeptical. Should the report prove correct, there would be a sizable fleet now gathered at Point Patience.

A report he received just three days later added some veracity; several British ships — again size and configuration unknown — had landed troops at God's Grace Point, moved inland to Huntingtown and burned the tobacco warehouse there. Unfortunately, the fire had gotten out of control and the entire town had burned to ashes.

Finally, Captain Nourse of the HMS *Severn* had accompanied Royal Marines and sailors to Prince Frederick, the seat of Calvert County, and had personally overseen the burning of the courthouse there. They had again landed at God's Grace Point. Most vexing, but not in the least surprising to Commodore Barney, was the fact that a large militia force had been present in the county seat, but not a shot had been fired. That had been on July nineteenth.

And now, Brigadier General William Winder had sent a message that he would be in Nottingham this morning and desired a meeting with Barney and his senior staff. Barney had smiled at that, as he had exactly no staff, senior or otherwise. He would include some of his skippers, he decided, and had notified Jack Clements, Luke Cooper, and Isaac Biggs. He wished he had not sent Jared Talbot to Baltimore; his insights and direct manner of speaking them would have been useful.

Looking down the road with its clinging haze of dust, he saw the three captains striding toward the River Rose. They all three had the rolling gait that marked them immediately as sailors. To his dismay, he also saw Clements' huge dog trotting along behind his master. *Haven't seen that beast in a while,* he thought as he watched the trio and the dog move easily through the dust, leaving an even larger cloud of the road dirt in their wake. *And I surely ain't missed him, neither.* He moved to intercept them before they gained the door.

"I 'spect that beast of your'n ain't likely to be all that welcome in there, Captain Clements. Perhaps he'd be happier settin' out here. There's a patch of shade yonder where you can leave him."

Jack looked at the commodore, then the 'patch of shade yonder', and then the dog who was panting just beyond the men near the door to the ale house, waiting expectantly for it to be opened. "Don't reckon he's likely to bother anyone, Commodore. And I think he might be wantin' a pan of water. Hot ain't in it out here, and gonna get hotter quicker 'an not." Jack smiled and stepped past his senior into the tavern, holding the door for his grateful dog. They disappeared into the gloom inside and the door closed behind them.

"Damme! He's done it again! That rascal just don't get it. I don't like that beast one bit. Damn thing makes me uncomfortable just bein' around." Barney fussed at the two captains whose efforts at controlling their mirth were largely ineffective.

"Commodore, who's this Winder cove what wants to meet with us? What's he comin' here to Nottingham for?" Luke Cooper, the captain of Barney's flagship was known for his directness. He and Isaac waited while the commodore thought for a moment; Barney drew a breath and faced his captain.

"What he is, Captain Cooper, is the man placed in charge of the army in the District of Columbia, Maryland and even down to Virginia. And the one who's gonna be responsible for directin' the troops when the British attack — wherever that might be."

"Aye, but does he know anything? Some o' the coves we've come across running the militia ain't got no idea what they's doin'."

"Well, he got the appointment on account of his uncle, I'm told by them what claim to know, and I understand he's a better lawyer than general. Heard he's even been captured once — 'bout a year back, up toward Niagra, I believe — but he's what we got and he's comin' here to see if'n we cain't figure a way to . . ."

Before he could finish the sentence, a coach drawn by a pair of dappled horses rounded a corner behind the tavern and slowed, rolling to a stop opposite the three men. The cloud of dust they had created roiled around them; Barney put a handkerchief to his face while the others just turned away.

In a moment, the door opened and a stout man in full military rig stepped down somewhat stiffly. Isaac and Luke Cooper turned back and watched as Barney strode forward, his hand extended in greeting. The general doffed his hat, ignoring the commodore's hand, and Barney quickly recovered and did the same.

Hmmmm, thought Isaac. This cove's sure got his sails full. He nudged Cooper with his elbow and shot a quick glance at him. Cooper smiled thinly. They watched the general and their commodore chat for a few minutes by the still open door of the coach. Then Barney gently steered the army man over to where his captains waited.

Isaac had a moment to take the man's measure while the pair approached. Medium height, stout, and somewhat bandy-legged; hair brown but showing signs of gray and worn touching his collar in the current style. Winder's face was narrow, with a sharp nose topped with necessarily close-set eyes. He seemed to Isaac to be a very serious man. And then Barney was introducing him.

"A pleasure, I'm sure, Captain." Isaac noticed that even while Winder spoke to him, he was looking elsewhere. No doffing of hats or shaking hands. Biggs made the appropriate response, unheard, and Winder moved toward the door with Barney hurrying along in his wake. The other two cast glances at each other and followed.

Once inside, Winder again doffed his hat and looked around for someone to take it. When no one stepped forward, he brushed his handkerchief across a corner of a nearby table, set the hat carefully on it, and looked critically around the room.

A few tables and chairs had been pushed more or less together while the remainder of them seemed to be randomly placed. The warm breeze that blew in when the door opened had disturbed the dust that floated in from the street; the particles swirled in the beams of sunlight streaming in from the east-facing windows. The room smelled faintly of spirits, tobacco and sweat, but the general and the sailors barely noticed. Bits of white clay from the tavern's assortment of pipes littered the floor and crunched under foot as the men moved to a table. Winder settled himself in a chair with his back to the east wall. It required that any who looked at him would be looking into the sun — at least for a while.

Jack Clements was duly introduced while Barney looked furtively around the room and wondered silently — and hopefully — what had happened to the dog; he was nowhere in evidence. The commodore took a seat and motioned his captains to do the same.

"Commodore, I asked you and your staff to meet with me to discuss the situation both here and in Washington, and to inform you of the enemy's next move," Winder blandly opened the meeting.

Barney raised his eyebrows at this statement; the other three merely squinted at the general.

"As you undoubtedly are aware, there have been several additions to the fleet anchored down river — near Patience's Point, I believe it is. Somewhat close to the mouth of the river."

"Point Patience, I think you mean, General. A league and more in from the Bay." Barney spoke quietly, but Winder went on as if he had said not a word.

"It is expected that they will sail their ships as far up the Patuxent as they can and then disembark Marines and sailors who will then march overland to attack Annapolis. After that I cannot say where they will go, but Baltimore would, I expect, answer nicely for them."

The general was about to continue with his forecast of the British movements when there was a knock on the door and, upon direction, the River Rose's owner appeared with a tray of cups and a pitcher of coffee. A moment or two later, the man was gone. While Joshua Barney poured out the coffee, Winder, annoyed at the disturbance, cast a scathing look first at the publican's back and then at Barney; scowling, he continued his assessment of the enemy's plan.

"As you all are also likely aware, Admiral Cockburn, who is apparently in charge of the Royal Navy forces here in the Chesapeake, has been conducting raids up and down the Potomac similar to the ones Captains Nourse and Barrie have been carrying out on the Patuxent. It is my belief that those raids are purely diversionary in nature and designed to make us think that the capital city is their intended target. Of course, there are military fortifications along the Potomac which are restricting their movements; for the moment, anyway, they have remained below St. Clements Creek." Winder paused in his monologue and looked around the table. The light haloed behind him, giving him a glow that, to the sailors staring wide-eyed at him, was unnerving.

"General, meaning no disrespect, sir, how can you possibly be sure of what you are telling us? Do you have an agent in Cockburn's employ, or have you captured a British officer who shared that knowledge with you? And I believe that Cockburn's superior, the man actually in charge on the Bay, is an Admiral Sir Alexander Cochrane." Barney had trouble hiding his disdain for the haphazard assessment of the enemy's strength as well as his incredulity at the confidence Winder had placed in his own idea of the British plan. Barney was equally sure the British target would be Washington and no other. Several, including Navy Secretary Jones, agreed, but there were others who thought, like Winder, that Annapolis would be first, and still more who thought Baltimore a likely target.

Barney's tone caused Winder's eyebrows to shoot up, and his own tone reflected the beginnings of outrage. "Of course not! I have studied their movements carefully and after consulting with my staff, have deduced that what I have outlined for you is the only possible course they have to follow. Do you not agree?"

"Well, actually, General, no; I surely do not. With every respect. I have every reason to believe that they are after my flotilla and will go to whatever lengths necessary to destroy it. After that, I am firmly of the opinion that they will attack Washington." Barney fixed Winder with a look that had caused sailors to blanch. Because of his angle to the window, the sunlight had no effect on him. He continued, "I surely hope that you are not positioning units of the army and militia based on your idea . . ."

Winder stood suddenly, interrupting the commodore with a voice like a cannon shot. "I most certainly am. It is the only possible way to prevent a disaster. I have already instructed Wadsworth and Thomas to take up positions on the Annapolis road so as to strengthen the militia there. They should be nearly there by now. And I am ordering you to move your units . . ."

Now Barney leaped to his feet; his expression changing from horror to outrage. His face reddened quite suddenly and a vein stood out in high relief on his neck. His voice was low and threatening, more distrubing than had he shouted his response.

"General, I take my orders only from Secretary Jones. I am not part of your Army nor is the flotilla connected in any way with any militia. You will not give me orders of any nature."

The two men, each among the most senior in their fields, stood nearly nose to nosem glaring at each other. Winder had a trickle of spittle running from a small bubble that had formed in the corner of his mouth. Barney's eyes were squinted down and his left eyebrow twitched, a sign of extreme agitation only a few of his officers had ever witnessed.

Isaac was speechless. Jack and Luke Cooper merely looked at

one another and tried to maintain the expected level of solemnity; it was an effort. In the silence, the sailors heard movement from a corner of the room and soft footfalls.

Turning, they all saw Carronade walking easily from the corner where his sleep had been disturbed by the outburst. Out of the corner of his eye, the general saw not a large dog, but a gray creature of sizable proportions floating through swirling dust motes and heading directly for him. Its open mouth revealed large shiny teeth, and a long pink tongue lolled from the outboard side.

Horrified, Winder tore his eyes away from the apparition and sputtered, "Great Scott! What in the name of all that's holy is that? And what is it doing in here?"

"That's just ol' Carronade, General. He's just a dog. No reason he should be layin' outside in all this heat when they's a cool spot in here and a pan of water for him." Clements smiled at Winder and reached out a hand to the animal. It still appeared to the general that he was heading right for him.

He backed up, knocking over his chair in the process and stumbled, but caught himself before he fell. Carronade sat panting next to Jack and looked disinterestedly at the retreating general. Clements continued to smile disarmingly, his hand on the beast's head, while Isaac and Luke were straining to control themselves. Even Commodore Barney unsuccessfully tried to suppress a smile. He moved back a step and directed his smile at the still sputtering Brigadier General.

"General, if we can get this conversation back on course, I reckon we might accomplish something. No point in shouting into each other's face like a couple of liquored up tars in some alley. As to the dog, he is perfectly safe and I'm sure that Captain Clements," he nodded at Jack, "would be pleased to maintain some level of control over him. Please sit down and let us talk like gentlemen."

Winder sputtered, but sat as Barney had suggested, keeping a wary eye on Jack's dog.

And so the meeting continued on a more civilized basis. Barney disagreed with most of the general's plans as much as he disagreed with the general's ideas of the British targets, certainly as much as General Winder disagreed with Barney's thoughts. The only area in which there was an eventual meeting of the minds was that the British were determined to capture or, barring that, destroy, the gunboats, barges, and sloops of Barney's flotilla.

When he realized that this meeting would lead nowhere, the commodore suggested that his captains' attendance would no longer be necessary and the three men, with Carronade, left the River Rose for the sweltering heat of a late July morning in southern Maryland.

"Well, I reckon the high point of that get-together was when the gen'ral met Carronade. I thought he was gonna back right out through the window — leastways, 'til he fell over the chair," Clements laughed to his mates.

"Aye. Even the commodore was grinnin' like a dog with a mouthful o' bees. An' he hates that dog o' your'n Jack." Luke Cooper's normally taciturn face split into a smile as he recalled the scene. "Jared ain't gonna believe this one. Too bad he's settin' on his arse up to Baltimore waiting on the Royal Navy to show up. Commodore sure seems almighty sure they's goin' after the Capital." Cooper was back to his serious self again, the incident in the tavern now well astern. He likely would drag it out again to share with his mate Jared Talbot when they met up, but for now, it was not the time for laughing and skylarking.

Isaac spoke for the first time since the meeting began. "I reckon what the commodore said about the British bein' after us was likely right. Only a matter of time 'til they sail up the river and get after us. And we ain't got no place to go but further in. Too bad we didn't try for the Bay when we got out of St. Leonard Creek. We mighta been . . ."

"Aye, Isaac, but then we'da never made Benedict." Clements looked at his fellow deep-waterman and winked. "And by the by, you ain't never told me nothin' about your dinner with the sweet young Miss Sarah and her Colonel Daddy. You been silent as a clam 'bout that." Jack looked earnestly at Biggs, but the twinkle in his eyes said it all.

"Well, Jack, it was right pleasant. Sarah met me at the green there in the middle of town just like she said she would and we walked to her father's house. It wasn't near as grand as that one where Mister Summers lives, but it was right nice. Her father remembered me from the meetin' that morning and we set and talked about the war an' my time in the Royal Navy while Sarah fixed up a fine supper. Better'n peas and biscuits, I'll tell you!" He looked at Clements earnestly.

"Aye, I'd warrant it were, Isaac. But I'd reckon if she'd afixed you weevily hard tack and wormy salt horse you'd a thought it splendid." Jack's normally cheerful face beamed at Biggs.

Isaac was not deterred in the slightest. "Oh, I ain't so sure on that, Jack; it was a mighty fine meal. And they had wine and something like a plum pudding after. Splendid it was, I'm tellin' you. The colonel told me 'bout the militia and that they met up with Colonel Wadsworth. I told him we ain't had such a good relationship with the militia folks we met up with so far, but he said his militia was different. And they'd fight if'n they got the chance. Said Wadsworth had a lot of men camped right behind Benedict, he did. And just waitin' on the Royal Marines to show up. Course, now they's likely up on the Annapolis road, 'cordin' to the gen'ral."

"Aye, I can surely believe that. You seen what Wadsworth's troops done down to St. Leonard Creek; why they run off afore the Redcoats even landed. They'll fight indeed!" Luke Cooper had been listening to Isaac's story and interjected his feelings on the militia. Most of the sailors agreed with him and had little faith in the Army or the militia.

"So what happened after supper, Isaac?" Jack prodded his friend. "You ain't told me nothin' real important yet." The grin broadened.

"Well, Jack. There ain't much to tell. She and I sat for a spell and talked about the flotilla and what I done afore joinin' Barney. Told her about you bein' up to Melville Island after fightin' with Cap'n Lawrence on the *Chesapeake* and me bein' on the *Gen'l Washington*. Told her I was in the Royal Navy, too. She was interested in that. An' she asked me about what happened to Doc Plumm. Told her we reckoned he was more likely to help the British than us. She just nodded her head at that — almost like she already knew it.

"After a time, she walked with me back to the dock. It was right nice, I'll tell you, Jack. She's something special, I think. And I surely do enjoy bein' in her company. Makes me feel good, the way she looks at me. Sometimes though, she looks at me with them eyes of hers and I can't even think. Everything just goes right out of my head, it does. Feels like a big wave broke over me when she does it."

Isaac's mind drifted back to that wonderful evening and he smiled secretly as he recalled the way Sarah had taken his hand as they walked and then lightly brushed his cheek with her lips as they parted. He tripped on a brick left in the road and barely noticed. His mates did, however, and Luke nudged Clements with his elbow and smiled.

"You sound mighty sweet on this girl, Isaac. Watch you ain't out over your head. Water can get real tricky when you get yourself into it far enough. Be just like a landsman takin' command of a vessel when the weather turns ugly. You mind my words." Jack words were ominous, but his voice still had the usual smile in it. "How did her mother take to you, Isaac. Was she . . ."

"Her mother's gone, Jack. Passed on, I reckon, a couple years back from the fever. She said Doc Plumm couldn't do nothing but give her laudanum to ease her passin'. I . . . she told me she's been takin' care of her father ever since. Likely why she's as headstrong as she is. But I like the way she is." The young seaman smiled at his mate as they arrived at the end of the dock and found a boat waiting for them.

CHAPTER SEVENTEEN

Nottingham, Maryland

My dear Sir:

I had the honor of receiving your instructions delivered on board on the 27th instant by messenger regarding the feasibility of moving the Flotilla overland from Queen Anne's on the Patuxent River to the South River, and thence by that river to the defense of Annapolis, should such become necessary in the event of an attack by British forces at that city.

To that end, I have sent a boat and surveyors to the location directed to determine the potential and requirements for such an undertaking. The vessel has only just returned and I herewith offer the following report.

The depth of water at that point in the Patuxent River is such that only the shallower draft barges might actually reach beyond Queen Anne's and would necessitate leaving the gunboats and sloops further down river at a point some distance from the town. There is a place where they might be taken onto the land and thence to the road where the Flotilla would again be complete, meeting up with the afore-mentioned barges.

In order to move fourteen vessels overland from Queen Anne's or the lower point of withdrawal, there would exist the following requirements:

   450 draft horses
   64 wagons of sufficient weight capacity
   56 pair of dray wheels
   150 teamsters

Noting the apparent paucity of both horses and

wagons available in this area, I respectfully submit that this proposal, while not without merit, would face overwhelming logistical problems. In addition, the traitorous populace resident in this area would likely betray our activities to the enemy, putting the entire Flotilla and men at some considerable risk, esp. during the landing and launching of our vessels.

Should your decision be to carry out this plan, I would need only one day to effect it and, should the necessary horses &c be available, authorization from your Office to appropriate said horses, wagons, &c would be most welcome. As the banks on the riverside at Queen Anne's are not as daunting as those at St. Leonard Creek, it would be possible to move the vessels to the road with due alacrity.

When I met with Gen'l Winder this week past, I was given to understand that his opinion, which was voiced in strong terms, was that the location of the next British attack would fall at Annapolis, a view with which I disagree most strenuously. As I have mentioned to you and Secretary Monroe, it is my feeling that Washington City is at some peril from attack and that it will come overland from this location or further south at Benedict.

To that end, I respectfully request that the Flotilla be maintained here at Nottingham, being in a position to delay any movement of the enemy fleet beyond this point and thus giving time to prepare a defense of the Capital City. I can do naught but suggest that the enemy would be unlikely to leave this town untouched as the riches of the area would be most attractive to them.

I shall continue to observe the movements of the enemy with all the resources at my disposal and I shall provide timely reports to your Office giving any particulars concerning their movement. I and my Flotilla stand ready to act in concert with your wishes and as circumstances may dictate. I have the honor to be, Sir, your most humble servant,

Joshua Barney   July 30th, 1814
Commodore

CHAPTER EIGHTEEN

"Get your men together, Isaac, and take your sloop down to the Bay. I need to know what's actin' down there. I get reports daily about more ships comin' in with more and more soldiers. Then I get a report they're sailin' up the river toward Benedict. Ain't a single damn one of 'em I can believe less'n I find out myself what's right or not."

Commodore Barney stood on the shore with several of his captains as the pink and orange tinged fingers of dawn splayed out over the cloudless eastern sky, bathing the river and surrounds in a warm, gentle glow. Another day with the promise of uncomfortable heat.

The furrows in Barney's brow spoke silently of his dilemma; he trusted no one nor any of the information provided by the local citizenry. He was concerned and frustrated by both the inadequacy of his intelligence and his inability to fight his flotilla. At least he could find out for himself what the enemy was up to. Whether he would then be in a position to fight remained to be seen.

"Aye, sir. I'll take Jack with me and a few of his men. They answered right fine when we was down to the creek last month. And I still got them extra guns I found in Benedict." Isaac was frustrated by inactivity as well and, while he enjoyed the occasional visit the flotilla made to Benedict, it was not the same as engaging the enemy. He turned and headed for the short pier and the small boat which had brought him ashore.

"And don't get yourself caught, Isaac. I need you and that sloop back here quick as ever you can make it." Barney fired off the warning and the young New Englander waved a hand in response.

Isaac was about to step into his boat when he heard a horse's hoofs beating on the dry, hard-packed dirt road. *Another messenger from Washington, I'll warrant. And probably with some other hair-brained orders for us — move the flotilla overland to Washington!* he smiled ruefully to himself as he sat down and pushed off.

"Hold on, Isaac!" Jake Tate's voice caused him to stop and look back toward the shore. Sure enough, there was the one-armed seaman sitting astride a chestnut mare as she picked her way down the pier.

Tate jumped off her back, pulled a tie from the saddle, and yanked down his scant seabag from where it had been secured behind him. Throwing the bag over his shoulder, he turned the horse over to a handy flotilla sailor and strode purposefully to the end of the dock. A grin split his face as Isaac gave an order for the boat to return for him.

"Well, Jake. Glad to see you made it back. I collect all was well in Frederick — and with your bride?"

"Aye, Just fine, it were. And it was right nice bein' with Charity for a spell. But I'll tell you, she put up a real fuss when I told her I had to get back down here. I'da been here yesterday, was you all in Benedict; went there first, then had to double back up here. Some cove down there told me you all was hunkered down waitin' for the Royal Navy to attack." He looked around at the gunboats and barges anchored in the stream. There was no unusual activity visible. "Don't look like 'hunkered down' to me."

"No, we ain't seen hide nor hair of 'em since Jack and I sailed back down to the Creek — right after you headed north, it was. Took us a prize, we did. But then we lost it in another scrap with 'em. Jack and I'll tell you all about it while we're sailin'." Isaac's smile made it clear to the young man that his return was timely and most welcome.

The boat stopped by Clements' sloop to let Jack know he and some of his men were needed, and then went on to the other sloop. All the while Jake kept up a steady stream of chatter about homey matters, his time picnicking with his wife, and his complete disregard for her family. They still felt the war a complete waste of time, a great expense with little to gain, and a major disruption of their commerce with England. Isaac felt a little pang of jealousy at Tate's "homey" stories. He could picture himself alternately visiting with his own parents and picnicking with Sarah Thomas.

Jake spat over the side as they approached the side of the sloop. "And Charity's daddy — he thinks the banks are about to shut down on account of the war. Said if that happens, the whole country ain't gonna last long. 'Can not do business anywhere, Chauncey, my boy, without the availability of credit and banking services.' " Jake did a fair impression of Charity's Federalist father.

Then he switched back to his own voice. "Won't even call me 'Jake,' by God, Isaac. Says if my mama wanted me called 'Jake' she wouldn'ta named me Chauncey. Ain't that som'pin?" He went on, again assuming the role of Charity's father. " 'Why, the whole system's going to fall apart. And it won't matter a lick if a body is engaged in commerce or the military; no one will be able to accomplish a thing without the banks. Shows a complete lack of confidence in the action of Mister Madison's government, by God. At least by those who matter!' "

Jake heaved his bag over the sloop's bulwark and climbing after it, looked at his friend and captain. "What's that mean, Isaac? I cain't reckon that the whole country gonna quit just on account of the banks not workin'. I never had much use for 'em anyway."

"Jake, I ain't got any idea. Don't bother with that side of things too much my own self, neither. But I can tell you this: less'n us and the militia can stop the British afore they get to Washington, it won't make a lick of difference. They won't be no government or banks to worry about. Now let's see about gettin' the barky underway." He turned towards Clements' sloop, some fifty yards to weather, and raised his voice. "Heave out an' up there, Jack. Commodore wants us down there an' back afore winter." He got a hard look and an impatient wave from Clements.

Within an hour and, on a fair tide, the black sloop was headed down river sailing on an easy reach with all sails billowing out in the growing morning breeze. Isaac knew from having been in the area now for some months that the breeze would likely fail him by mid-day and wanted to get as much distance under his keel before then as possible.

Jack had joined Isaac and Jake on the quarterdeck; Carronade, unwilling to be left behind, stood at his post in the bow of the sloop, maintaining a lookout. By noon time, when dinner was brought out along with the ever-present ration of grog, the two deepwater men had brought Jake current with the goings-on of the flotilla and of their own adventures with the British at St. Leonard Creek. And Jack, with lavish embellishment, had filled him in on Sarah Thomas, to Isaac's chagrin.

"It ain't that way at all, Jake. Ain't no 'romance bloomin' like Jack said nor anything else. She's just a right nice girl who ain't thinkin' like most 'round here. She wants the British gone and done with. 'Sides, her father's a colonel in the Militia." Jake noticed that as Isaac spoke, the color on his face had deepened and he remembered the chiding he took himself over Charity a year and a half back — from Jack, Robert Coleman and Tim Conoughy, and later from Isaac Biggs. He smiled.

"Aye, Isaac. I know exactly what you're sayin'. Felt the same way about a girl my own self, once." The grin broadened.

"Well, there you are, then. You know exactly what I mean." Isaac's tan still showed traces of red.

"Aye, I surely do. Yes, sir." He repeated. "And I married her — and damn glad she'd have me." Jake laughed and Jack slapped the young New Englander on the back.

"It's just like I been tellin' the lads, Isaac. You got yourself hooked just as sure as one o' them dumb Cod fishes you tol' me about up to New England."

The hilarity on the quarterdeck caused some of the crew to look up from the work they were doing: checking the locks on the cannons amidships and moving shot and powder into place by each gun. Carronade, disinterested in the antics of his master and the others, continued to watch the water ahead, his fur ruffling in the cooling breeze.

As the sloop swept by Benedict, still with a fair breeze, Isaac caught himself glancing at the dock as it passed a cable's length away. No sign of anybody there. But then no one knew they were coming, so why would anyone be there to watch them go by. He also caught the looks and nudges his crew passed among themselves as they passed. He forced himself to look away and studied intently the set of the tops'l. Then they were by. And on to somewhere short of Point Patience where they could catch a glimpse of the British fleet.

With supper time passed and the crew fed, Isaac eased the sloop toward the southern shore and put Sam Hay on the starboard channel with a leadline. He found that by following the corrugations in the shoreline he could maintain sufficient depth under his keel, while at the same time, minimize his vulnerability to the frigates of the Royal Navy, which he presumed were still anchored inside of Point Patience. At least he hoped they were.

"Jack, you remember that little spit of land what come out the far side just above St. Leonard Creek?" A pause and, after receiving a nod from Clements, he continued. "I think duckin' in behind there oughtta answer just about right. We'll take a few of the lads ashore and have a look over to Point Patience from the hill there."

"Why not just get the barky into the creek? Be closer and we know the water there."

"Aye, and them coves off'n the frigates do as well. Wouldn't do at all to have one of them cutters or a barge come nosin' around while we was in the Creek. Commodore'd be real unhappy if'n we didn't come back with his information." Isaac smiled and added, "And we come close once to gettin' ourselves caught in there. That's enough for me."

As darkness fell the sloop, her black topsides and sails a darker smudge on the deeply-shadowed shoreline, coasted to a stop and gently lowered an anchor into the shallow waters short of Point Patience and on the other side of the river. Both cannons and both swivel guns were loaded and slow matches were lit and resting in sand buckets. The cannon both had firing locks, but Isaac and Jack had seen too many failures of the sometimes balky locks and felt more secure with the old reliable slow match. At least a body could see that would work.

Jake and Jack Clements took four men — all but Jake and Clive Billings from Jack's crew — and rowed ashore. They took a nightglass Isaac had borrowed from the commodore and, as Isaac watched, straining his eyes to see them in the darkness, they disappeared into the undergrowth. The man they left behind pulled the boat into the overhanging branches where it was all but invisible from the sloop and, Isaac hoped, from any passing vessel.

Shoulda gone with 'em. This waitin's harder than what they're doin', I'd warrant. Isaac paced the full length of his sloop, followed at each turn by Carronade. The dog periodically stood with his forepaws on the shoreside bulwark, his ears pricked up listening for any sign of his master — or anything else. Isaac was glad of the big dog's company.

As a quarter moon rose into the eastern sky, Isaac stopped his pacing long enough to look around and decide that his sloop was still unlikely to be seen from the river and, hopefully, there was no one ashore to notice.

"Reckon we'll be all right here for a while, Carronade. Don't expect they's no one ashore what cares about us. Probably think we're just British sailors come in for water or something anyway. An' from out yonder," Isaac threw a thumb over his shoulder toward the middle of the river, "I'd warrant even you'd have a hard time seein' us." The dog cocked his head quizzically at Isaac's words and sat down. His long tongue lolled from the side of his mouth as he panted in the unrelieved heat of the day.

The young New Englander leaned on the bulwark at the quarterdeck, his chin in his hands, and watched the moon as it made its slow ascent across the night sky. Without warning, Sarah Thomas's face popped into his mind; he smiled silently into the darkness, recalling for the hundredth time their stroll to the dock after supper with her father and how she had taken his hand as they walked. And then kissed him. Oh, yes, a chaste kiss to be sure, but a kiss all the same. He wished he had had the courage to kiss her back; next time, by the Almighty, he would, and no mistake there. Actually, he decided, it wasn't that he lacked the courage, but more that she had caught him unawares and then danced off into the darkness before he could recover his senses. Aye, that was most surely it. He heard again her every word in her sweet voice and saw her eyes flashing at him when she was vexed over something. And saw her eyes looking right into the center of his soul. Mercy! Even thinking about it addled his brain!

So he didn't hear the boat bearing Jack, Jake, and the others until Carronade *woofed* quietly.

"What's the matter, boy? You hear something?" He looked at the dog and saw him at the bulwark again peering intently at the water. "Oh, Jack, it's you. I didn't even hear you comin' out. What did you discover?"

"Better you be gettin' ready to sail, Isaac. We're gonna have visitors any time now. Seen 'em comin' up river just about to pass the point yonder. Don't reckon they've seen us yet, but soon's they turn the point . . ."

Boom! Boom! By the second shot, Isaac caught the muzzle flash from the British row-barge as it turned into the little cove where the sloop was anchored. *Boom!* Another shot and the splash not a biscuit toss away.

"Slip the anchor! Leave the boat! Get that stays'l up. Main halyard, haul! Jack, give Jake a hand with that larboard side gun. Here . . . a couple of you lads lend a hand with it." Orders flew and Isaac's well-trained crew moved silently and efficiently to get the sloop underway and into the main part of the river. The scant breeze was fair, but Isaac realized he would be fighting the ebbing tide. Well, so, by God, were the British!

Boom! The barge fired again and Isaac saw the water turn white almost exactly where they had been anchored. The moonlight starkly highlighted the splash from the shot, making it whiter than it likely was.

"I'd reckon they's firin' a twelve-pounder, by God, Isaac. Bear off a trifle so's I can get this beauty to bear and we'll give 'em a taste of American iron." Even in dire straights, the cheerfulness was there in Jack's voice. Isaac could picture him grinning as he sighted down the barrel of their own little six-pounder and he knew it put the crew at ease.

Crash! Now the sloop answered. The sharp report of the aft swivel gun immediately echoed the deeper voice of the six-pounder and sent a double handful of musket shot, bits of iron, and scraps of chain skimming across the water.

"Got her loaded with canister, now, Isaac. Bring the barky back down again so's I can bear." Jack still had the grin in his voice, but now there was also a sense of urgency.

Crash! The six-pounder spoke again, and this time the Americans were rewarded with the sound of splintering wood and shouts from the barge.

"Jack! Change sides. I'm bringin' her about. Hands to sail handling stations. Stand by to tack." Isaac pushed the long tiller down, and the sloop responded swiftly, passing her bow smoothly through the eye of the wind and onto the other tack. They were making forward progress, but losing ground to leeward as the tide worked at cross purposes to their need.

Boom! The English gun thundered again, and Isaac could see from the muzzle flash that the Royal Navy barge wasn't any closer than it had been. But their aim was getting better; a hole appeared in the aft edge of the mains'l.

That ain't gonna help none. Isaac thought, as he heard the whining passage of the twelve-pounder's ball, and saw the perfectly round silvery gap where the moonlight shone through the rent in the black sail. "Jack, you gotta do better. Them coves is got the range pretty close. . ."

Another British shot cut off his words, and the thud and screech of rending wood added credence to his estimation of the enemy's accuracy. Splinters flew from the bulwark and the mast.

"Somebody get a look at the mast. Make sure it'll hold up. We're dead if'n it don't, so step . . ."

His words disappeared again in the crash of their own gun, now double shotted; Clements had laid his barrel on the muzzle flash, and this time, he was right on the mark! An explosion from the barge rewarded the American crew, then screams and splashes.

"Musta got the powder, Jack. Nice shootin'! And not a moment too soon, I'd warrant. I ain't so sure we coulda took another one of them balls aboard." Biggs pulled out the nightglass and studied the barge, some three hundred yards distant and dropping behind. She was low in the water and flames flickered low on the deck. "Looks like they lost they's taste for the game, lads. A good night's work, by all that's holy." He looked forward again. "What's the report on the mast, there? How much did we lose on it?"

"Looks like it ain't too bad, Isaac; took a piece size o' my fist outta the front side. Have it braced up quick as . . . hello. . . what's this? Jack! It don't look like your dog done too good. Better get up here and have a look." The unseen voice from forward sounded concerned; Jack flew from the gun, followed by Jake.

"Oh, my God, Carronade. What happened to you boy? Here, lay down. Somebody get me some cloth. Get a lantern up here. Move, damn it." Even from the quarterdeck. Isaac could hear the hurt in Jack's voice, and sensed rather than saw, the hands moving to do his bidding.

The sloop was out of danger for the present; the breeze had not gained strength to speak of, but Isaac thought the tide might be getting ready to go slack then turn fair. Probably just before dawn, he thought. For now, they were making progress, slowly, but in the right direction, and an occasional look astern through the nightglass showed an empty river. He became aware of another form on the quarterdeck and peered into the dark.

"Oh, Jake. Didn't smoke you right off. Everything quiet for'ard?"

"Aye. I can take her for a while, Isaac, you want to get some rest. Reckon that Sam and his crew got the mast patched up good enough to get us home and the bulwark ain't no problem. Ain't pretty, but won't hurt us none. Looks like the only casualty was Jack's dog."

Isaac gratefully relinquished the tiller. "Glad none of the men got 'emsleves hurt none. Where's Jack? I oughtta see what's actin' with him."

Leaving the one-armed seaman with the tiller, Isaac made his way forward to where Jake had told him Jack was sitting with Carronade.

"How's he doin', Jack? Carronade seems like too tough a dog to get laid low by anything them British bastards could manage." He sat down on the hatch next to where his friend was gently stroking the big gray animal.

"I 'spect he'll be fine in time, Isaac. I think I got all the splinter outta his hide. Took a fair sized piece of the bulwark there into his stern end. Looks like he's lost some blood, but I think I got that mostly stopped. Never wrapped a bandage 'round a dog afore. Some different from a man. But I think he'll be comin' round just fine. Kinda wish ol' Doc Plumm was still around so's he coulda had a look-see. Maybe give him some laudanum for the pain."

"Jack, he wouldn'ta got close enough to him to see anything. He was scared to death of Carronade. Reckon that ol' dog was quicker to pick up Plumm's British side than we were. Remember how he sat there growling at him when first he come aboard up to Benedict?"

"Aye. That I surely do." The smile was back in Jack's voice. Isaac saw him move his hand to Carronade's head. "You're gonna be all right, my friend, and we'll get you a chance to even the score, by God!"

Jack's words were greeted by a weak thump of the animal's tail on the sloop's deck. And the one-eared former bosun smiled unseen into the dark night.

CHAPTER NINETEEN

"Seven frigates and a pair of seventy-fours, you say? That's surely a fair-sized squadron they's a-building — but hardly surprising. But no transports. That's odd. If they was gonna march to Washington — or anywhere else over land — I reckon they'd need all the soldiers they could muster. Them frigates and seventy-fours got Marines, but not enough by half to manage a full-scale assault." Barney received the report from Biggs and Clements with little comment. Then he curtly dismissed the two from the gunboat.

"He sure was in an all-fired rush to get us out of there, Isaac. What do you s'pose is on is mind?" The pair were headed back to their respective sloops for some much needed sleep after their all-night sail back to rejoin the flotilla. Fortunately, they had had only to sail as far as Benedict, as Barney had moved the entire group down from Nottingham only that day. As Isaac's sloop had rounded the bend in the river downstream of Benedict, Jake saw that the river was choked with gunboats and barges, and the commodore's gunboat, his blue pendant waving listlessly from the mast truck, was secured to the pier.

Isaac rounded his vessel into the wind, finding a comfortable anchorage with room to swing, and dropped his spare anchor. He made a mental note to see about getting a replacement for the one they had left down river. Apparently, the commodore had noted their return as a hoist had been run up on his gunboat even before their sails were furled. The flags hung limply in the barely-moving air, but Isaac could read his sloop's number and "Captain repair aboard," which he did, accompanied by Jack.

Carronade, still hurting from his splinter wound, remained

aboard the sloop resting comfortably on the fo'c'sle under a small awning that Jack, with Jake's help, had rigged from an old stays'l. Isaac's crew, augmented by a handful of Clements' men, quickly put the sloop to rights and those that weren't needed for the repairs to the battle damage found places to lay up out of the intense sun and went immediately to sleep.

While the two captains were rowed back to the sloop, Isaac considered Jack's question. Finally he spoke. "I reckon he's likely firing off another letter to Secretary Jones and any other what'll listen telling 'em what we found. He's right sure they're gonna come up here, then march to Washington."

"I'd be inclined to agree with that, my own self; why would they be layin' up down here if they was gonna go after Annapolis? With these light breezes, that's a day's sail from here. And close-hauled on top of it. But they gotta be waitin' on something down there. With the seven frigates they got, an' the smaller vessels, they surely got enough weight of metal to take anything ashore — leastways up this far, they do."

"Aye, reckon you're right, Jack. But that's for the commodore to figger out. As for me, I'm gonna get me into a cot quick as ever you please and sleep. Feel like I ain't slept in a week, by all that's holy. You're welcome to the boat, you want to get back to your vessel — or you can stay right here. And Carronade's welcome long as he wants." With that, Isaac swung over the bulwark, and disappeared down the scuttle.

Jack walked forward, picking his way over and around sleeping sailors, and sat beside his dog. He got a lethargic thump of the long tail in response to his patting Carronade's big head. The bandage on the dog's hindquarters showed no fresh blood; Clements smiled and leaned back against the bulwark. He was instantly asleep.

Isaac had been right on the mark with his comment about the commodore; a messenger had immediately been dispatched on horseback with the report Isaac had brought. Try as he might, Barney could come up with no other likely plan of the British attack. Regardless of Winder, Monore, and all those other Washington politicians, Annapolis just didn't answer; the attack had to be against the capital. Perhaps this additional intelligence would aid Secretary Jones in his effort to convince his colleagues that Barney and he were most likely right about Washington.

The flotilla remained in Benedict for over a week, to Isaac's delight. He managed to visit Sarah frequently, providing Clements and Tate with further proof of their convictions. By the time they returned to Nottingham in mid-August, even Isaac knew he was in love. But there were now more important considerations occupying all their minds.

On August eighteenth, Barney received a report from Thomas Swann, a trusted friend who had been assigned to watch the Bay from Point Lookout at the mouth of the Potomac, that "they was comin', and it looked like the whole Royal Navy was in the Bay." Indeed, the hastily-written report indicated that a further seven frigates, seven transports, one sixty-four-gun ship and three brigs were headed for the mouth of the Patuxent. They were accompanied by sloops, bomb-ships, fire-ketches, a few schooners and dispatch boats, and covered an area extending over two miles in length. A total of forty-six sail had been counted. An exceedingly impressive display of the might of the Royal Navy.

This information was immediately forwarded to Washington with all dispatch, but before it had even reached the Capital, more reports were arriving in Nottingham that the fleet was underway from Point Patience, and heading up river. Then on August twentieth, Barney was visited by Sarah Thomas.

"It is truly delightful to see you again, Miss Thomas," he greeted the pretty young woman as she stepped aboard his flagship. "I expect you ain't come all this way from Benedict to visit an aging commodore. I will send for Captain Biggs at once. Please make yourself comfortable."

"Thank you most kindly, sir. However, I did indeed come to see you and to inform you that the British are even now anchored off Benedict and are landing marines, soldiers, and sailors. A General Ross commands the Army though Admiral Cockburn, I am told, is personally in charge of the invasion and has been heard to boast that he would be 'dining in Washington on Sunday!'." Her wide-eyed sincerity told Barney all he needed to know about the veracity of her report. He sent a messenger for Isaac and another to Washington with the news in a sharply worded dispatch.

Isaac, when he came ashore in response to the commodore's summons, was surprised and pleased to see Sarah, but horrified at the thought of her alone in Benedict. "Sarah, you cain't go back there. You'll be in too much danger with all them Royal Marines runnin' around. Why don't you just stay here in Nottingham 'til they's gone on their way? Commodore Barney thinks they's gonna be marchin' right quick into Washington." They walked toward an inn where he hoped she would remain and where she had left the borrowed horse she rode to warn them.

"Isaac, I can not remain here; I have promised Father that I would help with the wounded should there be a battle in Benedict. I shall be taking a room in my godfather's home — the one I am sure you recollect where you met Father for the first time. In any case, I doubt that the British would harm a woman; there have been no reports of such action since they arrived in our river. Do not worry, dear, I shall be quite safe. Besides, if indeed they are truly marching to Washington, they can ill-afford to remain long in Benedict."

As they reached the inn, Sarah took up the reins of her horse, which, Isaac noted, was rigged with one of those saddles women favored which kept both their legs on the same side of the animal. She stepped onto a mounting block and, leaning over to kiss Isaac, slipped. He caught her, and held her in his arms for a moment longer than necessary. And she, he noticed, seemed reluctant to remove her arms from around his neck.

Setting her aright and back on the block, he took her hand as she planted herself gracefully on the horse and arranged her skirts over the horns of the saddle. Her smile lit her whole face and she looked at the young man with her irresistible eyes; yet her confident words only temporarily stilled his worries. She became serious again.

"Now let go of my hand, Isaac, so that I may return. And do not worry about me; worry instead that you will safely escape with the flotilla and return to me when this . . . disagreeable business is finished." She flashed her smile and those eyes at him and, helpless to do otherwise, he reluctantly relinquished her hand. She dug a spur into the horse's flank and waved to him as though she had not a care in the world as she galloped down the dirt street.

Isaac returned to the river and the boats to find a bustle of frantic activity; sailors and officers were shouting across the water to one another and he could see harbor furls being removed. A string of signals flew from the commodore's gunboat and were repeated at each of the other gunboats and barges. A boat waited for him at the dock.

"We're takin' the vessels up to Queen Anne's, Isaac. Ol' Barney's not gonna get us captured if'n he can help it. S'posed to make all sail and get up there quick as ever we can." Jake met him when he came aboard the sloop and was clearly excited by the promise of some action — even evasive action.

Jack's crewmen and Carronade returned to Clements' sloop, their places on Isaac's boat taken by men from the gunboats lost in St. Leonard Creek. With Carronade at his post in the bow, the two sloops made sail for Queen Anne's — and who knew what else.

"Startin' to shoal up, Isaac. Keep her in the middle or we're gonna be on the hard afore you know it." Sam Hay was swinging the leadline from the larboard channel; the alarm in his voice amplified the gravity of his reports on the soundings. Isaac hardened up some and the sloop eased closer to the middle of the narrowing river.

He could see shore birds standing in the shallows, their long legs moving gracefully as they lifted each foot clear of the water to work the bottom with long bills, searching out tasty morsels to satisfy their constant hunger. They seemed to Isaac much further into the river than they had only a few short miles to the south and yet the water came up no higher on their legs.

"Pig Point comin' up to starboard, Isaac; looks like a bar comin' pretty far out from the shore." Tate stood in the bows, as was his habit, and called back to Biggs who had personally taken over the tiller.

"Aye, I got it. Sam keep that lead workin'; no tellin' what we're gonna find for water here."

Practically before the words were out of his mouth, Isaac felt the sloop jerk and scrape under his feet. He threw the tiller over and bellowed to his crew.

"Trim the mains'l flat, lads; we're takin' the bottom. Sheet home the stays'l."

The vessel's momentum allowed her to respond to the rudder; she carried across the shoal and worked to weather with reduced draft thanks to her sharper angle of heel. Isaac kept the sails trimmed tightly to maintain the boat's slant and pressed on. The hands stopped whatever tasks they had been doing and held their collective breaths; this would not be a good place to put her aground — she would quickly become an easy target for even the most insignificant British boat to take at its leisure. The leadline showed thinner and thinner water and the sloop's wake described a convoluted course as Isaac struggled to find a way around the bar.

SCRAAAAAPE! Their forward motion stopped with a lurch and, in spite of their best efforts and all the tricks the Baymen could muster to free her, the sloop remained hard aground.

"Sam, better get a signal up. Let them others know we've found the bottom here. Tell 'em to anchor below us." He raised his voice and called forward. "Clive: draw the shot outta the swivel for'ard there and fire a half load o' powder when them flags get aloft."

As the gunboats, led by Clements' black-hulled sloop, came around Pig Point, the little gun fired with a dispirited *craack*, and the captains saw immediately Isaac's plight. They each rounded up and dropped their anchors in water barely sufficient to float them, forming an almost straight line down the center of the river. Isaac ordered his boat launched and had himself rowed to the commodore's gunboat.

"I ain't took soundings ahead of us yet, no, sir, but I don't reckon they's much deeper water beyond the Point. Been showin' shallower and shallower right up to where we struck." Isaac shook his head in response to Barney's question and looked beyond his sloop. The river narrowed appreciably and the vegetation was growing well out from the banks.

Within minutes, flags broke from the flagship signaling "Captains repair aboard." Isaac remained and soon was joined by some dozen and more gunboat and barge captains and, of course, Jack Clements. Carronade, still sore from his wound, remained on the sloop.

With the August sun beating down mercilessly and all hands sweating profusely, Barney addressed his senior officers on the deck of the gunboat under the canvas awning his crew had hastily rigged after coming to anchor.

"You men have done splendidly, you may rest assured. But now Washington, in the person of Secretary Jones, has ordered me to leave the vessels and get to the Capital. With most of our men. I believe you are looking at the final resting place of our flotilla; my orders are to burn each and every one of them, spike the guns and destroy anything that might be of use to the enemy if the British appear in these waters. They must not get our boats, no matter the cost. And I think it is only a question of *when* the British show up;

there is little doubt in my mind that they will indeed.

"I will lead the majority of our men overland to Washington tomorrow. In the meantime, you will prepare your vessels with powder charges and fuses set so that those who remain behind can quickly set them alight."

"Who's gonna take care o' that little detail, Commodore?" Luke Cooper, never one to hold back a question, took a step forward from the group. While he waited for the commodore's answer, he hauled a dirty blue handkerchief the size of a tops'l from his hip pocket and mopped his dripping face and neck.

"I propose leaving Captain Biggs in charge of the flotilla, with two or three men on each vessel. Slow matches will be kept burning and, on his signal, the vessels will be fired. The men and Captain Biggs will then retire to the shore and make their way overland to join the rest of us. Most likely on the road to Washington.

"Since we know the British troops are even now marching through Benedict with the announced intent of attacking the Capital, we will be felling trees across the road, burning bridges, and doing anything we can to hamper their movement. As I plan on taking four or five cannon with me to Washington, we will be moving slower than I'd like. It is likely that we will be little further than Upper Marlboro when you find us, Isaac, but find us you must. I caution you not to delay; the very moment you see any sign of a British approach, you must fire the fleet."

Isaac nodded soberly. What a way to end the career of his sleek black sloop, not to mention the gunboats and barges that had performed so well during their many encounters with the enemy. And now he and all his fellows were to be afoot and very probably fighting the British ashore. Not what he had had in mind last winter when he, Jack, and Jake signed on. No sir, not at all.

Throughout the balance of the afternoon and into the evening the crews toiled in the oppressive heat, preparing their boats for destruction and removing onto the shore anything that might prove useful. Three twelve-pounders and two eighteen-pounders were man-handled to the shore at the cost of several crushed hands and strained backs. The heat was beyond oppressive. One of the men compared it to walking through the steam coming from a kettle over a hot fire, except it didn't just stay in one place; it was everywhere. Evening brought little respite from it, and even after dark the air remained thick — almost palpable. It slowed everyone down, especially those unfortunates who had to go below; it was so unbearably hot in the holds and living quarters that few men could spend more than a few moments there. Dry lightning lit the western sky as the darkness became complete. Powder kegs were fused and rigged in key locations; trains of powder connected them and lengths of slow match led topside. The remaining guns were spiked, rendering them useless to the British in the event they tried to salvage them from the burned and scuttled fleet.

By the start of the middle watch, the crews fell exhausted on deck, enjoying the cooling of the scant breeze on their bare chests and heads. Even as tired as all were, few slept; the thought of burning the flotilla and the likelihood of fighting ashore against crack British Marines made sleep impossible. Even the lowest sea-man understood that Napoleon's defeat by the English — heard by all in June — would mean the cream of the British fighting men, battled-hardened veterans who had served under the Duke of Wellington, would be coming to America, and no one harbored any delusions about the outcome of a militia unit meeting those troops.

Towards dawn, a few had found consolation in deep dream-less sleep only to be awakened by the others preparing to leave the vessels.

"Isaac, you mind yourself, now. Don't forget to light the fuses *afore* you head for the beach. We'll see you right quick, I'm thinkin' — you and Jake. Good luck to you, lad." Clements passed close by in his boat and Isaac looked down at him. His two oarsmen rested on their oars and, even at this early hour, the sweat streamed off their faces.

"You mind your own self, Jack. Good luck to you too. And take care o' that dog. Don't worry none about Jake and me; we'll catch up to you quick as ever you please." The young New Englander leaned on the bulwark of his sloop acting as though he had not a care in the world as he chatted with his friend. Carronade, he noticed with a smile, seemed nearly healed and Jack had reduced his bandage to the minimum. The dog stood in the bow of the boat, shifting his glance between his master and Isaac, while his tail described slow circles in the morning haze. With a part of his mind, Biggs wondered if ever he'd see his old shipmate — or the dog, to whom he had grown quite attached — again.

Jack's boat pulled on and, joined by a dozen and more, made

for the far river bank. The men spilled out and began picking up the weapons, supplies, and personal items they had put ashore during the night. Five teams rigged lines to the cannon hidden in the brush and, clapping on, dragged the ponderous guns into the forest. Isaac and Jake, along with as many as four men on each of the other vessels watched as, one by one, Commodore Barney and their flotilla mates disappeared into the undergrowth and headed through the trees for Washington.

"You reckon the English'll sail up here, Isaac, or walk?" Jake was leaning against the bulwark next to his captain. The early morning silence was eerie; not a sound save the few birds calling in the trees. The normal motion of the boat would cause the rigging to creak and even a light breeze would whisper as it brushed past the spars and lines of the sloop. The boat was still aground and the breeze non-existent, making it feel all the hotter.

"I 'spect they'll come up here in barges or cutters; water's too thin by half for anything much bigger. If'n they decide to walk up, we might have a little problem gettin' ashore after we fire the boats." Isaac paused, thinking, for a moment. "' Specially if'n they come up both sides. They could just set on the banks and take they's time about killin' us, I reckon."

Isaac's dark comment provoked no further conversation for a while. The sobering thought of meeting the crack British troops ashore — or riflemen in the tree line targeting the sailors as they tried to get ashore from the burning boats — caused both Jake and Isaac, as well as the two sailors who had heard the comment, to withdraw into themselves. The images they held in sharp relief in their minds were unappealing and there didn't appear to be a solution to the problem — at least none that either Isaac or Jake could produce.

The men on the other boats were equally quiet, perhaps pondering equally unanswerable questions. Or perhaps saddened by the inevitable scuttling and burning of these little ships. No sailor ever wanted to see his ship, no matter how ugly, crank, or insignificant, sunk or burned. Many of the flotillamen had been with Barney and the gunboats since they were built; they were Baymen who knew these waters and most of the inlets and creeks with an intimacy gained over a lifetime of fishing and trading on and in them. Fighting the British answered just fine for them, but from ships and boats, not ashore. And the waiting was taking its toll.

"Say, Isaac, why not set the fires and get while we got the chance? No need to wait on the damn British 'til they's ready to climb over the transom," one of the flotillamen called to Isaac from a nearby barge.

"Commodore said wait 'til we see 'em comin' and that's what I aim to do. Just rest easy and wait for my signal. We'll get ashore all right. And keep a sharp lookout." Biggs knew Barney was counting on him to follow his orders, but he wished he felt the confidence he had just voiced, and that he knew Joshua Barney had placed in him.

CHAPTER TWENTY

"Looks like they's comin' Isaac. Look yonder through them trees there." Jake handed Isaac the longglass through which he had been peering intently.

Biggs took the proffered telescope and raised it to his eye. The late morning sun dazzled the water, but even with the glare all he needed was a glance; a cutter was indeed visible nearly a league distant, propelled by a dozen oarsmen. A tall figure with gold epaulettes stood in the sternsheets. The glare of the sun, now well above the trees, bathed the boat and its crew in its harsh light and glanced off the gold braid on the officer's uniform, glinting almost white in the effulgence. A slight shift in the glass brought into focus four larger boats — barges, they appeared to be — behind the cutter. And behind them, he could see quite clearly through the trees, the top hamper of a small brig anchored in the bend of the river south of Pig Point. Aye, comin' indeed, by the Almighty!

"Looks like the admiral himself come for a look, Jake. And he brought some friends along, too. Make the signal." Isaac spoke quietly, the droop of his shoulders silently echoing the resignation in his voice.

The prepared flags rose to the masthead of the sloop and, within a scant moment, he and Jake could see plumes of smoke rising from many of the vessels. Quite apparently, none were eager to stay and see what happened. Several men were already scrambling over the sides of the gunboats into boats secured alongside.

"Best get them fuses lit, Jake, and then let's get us gone. They ain't gonna be long gettin' here." Isaac held a smoldering slow match and had already started forward as he spoke; Jake picked up another and moved to the aft scuttle where a length of powder-impregnated cord showed above the lip. The other two sailors from Isaac's crew disappeared below to perform their part in this sad duty.

They met at the boat tied off amidships and dropped into it. Sam Hay and his crew mate took the oars while Jake in the bow and Isaac at the tiller in the stern pushed them away from the black sloop — for the last time. They could see the bow of the English cutter as it rounded the point, and the men pulled hard for the shoreline, joined by a dozen other small boats, each occupied by three or four men. The barges following were not yet visible, but Isaac was certain they had not stopped.

As they climbed the short bank into the scrub oak and pine, Isaac made sure each of the men was accounted for. Then he turned for a last look at his sloop and the other vessels of Barney's flotilla. Each had a satisfying but sad plume of smoke rising from the deck, and several showed flames already licking at the masts and rigging.

The cutter was now within a cannon shot from the nearest gunboat and, on a faintly heard order, its oarsmen rested on their oars. Isaac, and Jake who had joined him, knew that Admiral Cockburn could plainly see Barney's blue pendant lifting in the heat-generated breeze. And the fires consuming their targets.

With breath-taking impact, an explosion wracked the air. So intense was it that the men on the shore could feel the concussion on their chests. It was followed quickly by others as flames reached the magazines and, within minutes, the entire fleet was burning, the outline of each vessel shimmering in the flames and smoke.

The cutter backed away from the intensifying heat and the likelihood of further explosions. Its crew and the admiral watched, mesmerized, as his nemesis on the lower Bay and particularly on the Patuxent, was destroyed before their very eyes. Ironically, it was exactly what the British had been trying to accomplish for six months and more and here the Americans had done it for them. Isaac noticed the slump of Cockburn's shoulders as the admiral witnessed the conflagration; it was apparent to the Americans that he took no satisfaction from it.

As Isaac, Jake and the other American seamen watched, Admiral Cockburn, still standing in the stern, doffed his hat in a silent salute to his adversary, wiped his sweating brow, and gave his crew the order to turn about. They met the row barges which had been rowed the nine miles up from Nottingham and now would be rowed back in the crushing heat of an August day on the upper Patuxent. The Americans disappeared into the trees.

They had gone barely a mile along the river bank when a sailor from the rear of the line ran forward and tapped Isaac on the shoulder.

"Sounds like they might be so'jers comin' up the shore, Isaac. Astern of us . . . mebbe a cannon shot back, but no more." Even the whisper carried the urgency of the message and Isaac held up his hand to stop the procession.

He held his finger to his lips and the signal was passed to the rear quickly; the silence was complete. Not a bird, an insect, or even the breeze made a sound. He and all the men strained to hear. After all, a body of British Marines coming through the forest would most likely make a pretty good ruckus. After a moment or two, he grabbed Jake Tate and, putting his mouth close to the sailor's ear, whispered to him. Then he signaled the column forward, gesturing his men to continued silence.

Jake stepped off the trail — if the serpentine and overgrown path could be so dignified — and squatted down to wait, nodding to each of the sailors as they passed. He held a pistol in his left hand, and another was tucked into the top of his canvas trousers. A cutlass rested in a strap hanging from his shoulder.

Long minutes passed and the last of the flotillamen had disappeared from sight. The birds again sang and insects buzzed. There was still not a breath of a breeze and small flying insects annoyed the waiting seaman as they flew into his face and crawled down the neck of his jersey. With but one arm, and an unwillingness to release his grip of the pistol, Jake let them be, occasionally shaking his head sharply when the cloud became unbearable. Barely noticing the rivulets of sweat that coursed down his face, neck, and back, he waited — and listened.

To nothing, damn it. Ain't no one out there and here I sit lettin' Isaac and them get further and further away while I'm gettin' my own self chewed up by these damn flies. If these woods are full of Royal Marines, they're quieter than I figgered they could be — or they ain't here. Tate had started to stand when he heard — or rather didn't hear the sound. The birds had stopped their constant warbling. He listened harder and then he had it; faint to be certain, but there it was — the sound of men moving none too carefully through the scrub and undergrowth. But it seemed they were some distance inland. He figured there would be little risk in having a look.

I cain't see nothin' from here. Gotta move some. He stood and as silently as he could, made his way inland from his stand along the river. The sound he had heard grew louder. Then through the scrub and trees he caught a flash of light — a reflection off something shiny, perhaps a bayonet or buckle. Whatever it was, he knew it wasn't anything that grew in the woods. He stopped and waited.

His patience was rewarded when, through a break in the trees a long musket shot away, he saw the column of Royal Marines. They carried huge packs and muskets with fixed bayonets. Their tall hats, red jackets, and white trousers offered them no camouflage, and he could see quite clearly each individual as he passed. They weren't close enough to make out their faces but, from the way they marched and from the look of their uniforms, the heat had and would continue to take its toll on them. Many seemed to stagger, and most showed dark stains on their red jackets where the sweat had soaked through. All walked stooped over and were quite obviously exhausted. From their direction of march, Jake realized they weren't after the flotillamen at all; they were heading for Washington. And at a pace quite extraordinary in this strength-sapping heat.

He waited, watching silently as the haggard, exhausted soldiers went past. Then he melted back into the forest and made for the river bank and the path to catch up with Isaac.

He moved quietly, as much to avoid attracting the attention of the British — even though they were probably further away than when he first had seen them — as to see if he could sneak up on the rear of the flotillamen without being caught. Without warning, he saw the familiar blue jacket of one of Barney's sailors through the trees ahead; they had not been crashing through the underbrush as he had thought, but then, neither was he and he knew they had not heard his approach.

He stepped along a little faster and got within an arm's length of the last man in the column. Either the man was deaf, daydreaming as he marched, or too busy dealing with the flies and the August heat but, no matter the distraction, he very nearly came out of his shoes so startled was he when Jake touched his shoulder.

"You damn fool! I coulda shot you easy as kiss my hand," the sailor hissed at his "attacker." Not surprisingly, he was edgy. Jake just smiled at him, put his finger to his lips and moved further up the line of men. The next several got the same treatment with much the same result, excepting that the final one — the one who ended Jake's little game — cried out and wheeled with a cutlass at his presumed enemy. Jake ducked the blow and his smile remained in place.

Now the others in the rear of the column were aware that he had returned and was having sport at their expense. Isaac called quietly from the front of the line.

"Whatever is goin' on back there, stop. Silence fore 'n' aft, you men. You're makin' noise enough to wake the dead, let alone tell the enemy where we're at."

Jake stepped along to the front and when he reached Isaac's side, he was laughing silently.

"You shoulda seen them poor coves jump when I come up behind 'em, Isaac. They like as not come right outta they's shoes!"

"Aye, I reckon you likely made few friends back there. What did you discover?" Isaac was not amused. He was perhaps even more edgy than his men, equally out of his element marching like a militiaman through the forest, and concerned about finding Barney and the rest of the flotillamen before another day had passed. There was also the matter of a column of Royal Marines coming up astern. He looked back down the line behind Tate as he waited for Jake's answer, as if expecting to see his men in hand to hand combat with the enemy at any instant.

"They's not comin' this way, Isaac. Reckon they's headin' for Washington, just like the commodore said they was. I seen 'em and they's bore off some from our track and headin' inland some. They's totin' full packs and more on top of it and some're draggin' cannon — three I seen, but mighta been more. Little ones, though, not more 'an three- or six-pounders. They're movin' at a pace that'll likely put 'em in Washington sooner than later, I'd warrant, but from the look of 'em, I wouldn't worry too much about them bein' ready to fight; they looked some wore out. Them heavy uniforms and carrying the packs they got in this heat gonna do 'em in faster than anything we could do to 'em. If they's headin' off to take the Capital . . . well, I reckon a bunch o' women could turn 'em around the way they looked when I seen 'em."

"Jake, one of the things I learned — in fact I learned it from the Royal Navy — is never to underestimate your enemy. Just 'cause they don't look like they want to fight don't mean they can't — or won't. Be a dangerous mistake to make. But I'm right glad they ain't comin' this way. Even with 'em wore down, I doubt we could take 'em if we got into a scrap. Ain't none of us here know anything 'bout fightin' on land. Hope the commodore's got a plan on what we're s'posed to do, 'cause I surely don't." The furrows in Isaac's brow deepened and tiny rivulets of sweat poured out of his hair line and down his face. He wiped the salty moisture out of his eyes with his already-soaked sleeve and trudged on, not willing to take a break or slow the pace.

By what, under normal circumstances, would have been supper time for the sweaty, drained and foot-sore Americans, Isaac noticed that the trees were thinning and beyond them, to their left, cultivated fields were visible. He called to Jake Tate.

"How about you have a look 'bout a cannon shot to larboard, Jake. Mayhaps some ahead of us 's well. I'd reckon we're comin' to that town the commodore told me he'd meet us up in . . . Upper Marlboro, I recollect he said it were. Looks like we're gettin' into a more settled area here. Don't tarry in gettin' back, neither. The lads are likely real sharp set, bein's how none of us got any dinner and I'd warrant it's past supper time by now 's well. If'n that's the town comin' up, we'll lay up there and get us some vittles." Isaac patted the young Marylander on his shoulder and handed him his pistol, which Tate stuck into the top of his trousers as he moved to carry out Isaac's orders.

As an afterthought, Isaac called after the departing sailor, "And no skylarkin' when you come back. I'd warrant the men wouldn't likely take too kindly to any more of your humor!"

Tate waved his hand without looking back, but Isaac knew his one-armed friend was smiling.

Within one turn of the glass, Jake was back, sweating even harder than the others, and out of breath. He matched Isaac's pace while he caught his wind and then smiled at his captain.

"You done right good, Isaac. I saw the wheel marks of them cannon the commodore's draggin' and mebbe a league ahead of us they's what looks like it oughta be a town. Cannon tracks lead right toward it. He musta been inland of us some and . . ."

Craack! A shot rang out on the flotillamen's back trail. It was immediately answered by another and then another. Isaac and his men moved into thicker bushes toward the river — now barely a stream — and crouched down, listening.

"That didn't sound all that close, Isaac. And I'd bet a pretty good distance astern. Might be them Redcoats I was watchin' earlier. Wonder what's actin'."

"I ain't got no idea, Jake. But I can tell you I ain't interested one bit in gettin' into a scrap with 'em now or even later, for that matter." He stopped, listening, then stood up. He peered intently through the underbrush and scrub trees, a scowl across his face. "Whatever it were, sounds like it's done with. You hear anything?" He looked questioningly at his second in command, who was now standing as well.

"Not a thing, Isaac. And sounds like the birds're chirping again too. They wouldn't be if'n they was something out there." Jake cocked his head, and looked into the forest. After a moment he spoke again. "Wish ol' Carronade was with us 'stead of Jack and the commodore. He'd let us know right quick what was goin' on yonder. Leastways if'n it was the British."

"Well, he ain't and it sounds quiet enough out there now. Let's get movin' and hope that'll be Upper Marlboro ahead of us'n — and that the rest of the men're there." Isaac wiped a grimy hand across his sweat-streaked face and made up his mind. Jake saw his friend's jaw muscles clenching and then he turned away. Without a look back, Biggs stepped off and angled his course inland and further up the river.

CHAPTER TWENTY-ONE

Dear Sarah:

I hope this letter finds you safe and unharmed. You have barely been out of my thoughts since you rode off on your horse from Nottingham a week and some back and I have been praying you did what you said you would and stayed away from the British soldiers. After what they done at Hampton to the folks — and the women — I have been miserable just thinking they might be doing the same at Benedict.

I guess you must have heard by now — or at least you will by the time this finds you — that the British got into to the Capital without no hardship save the heat and set fire to most of the buildings there. All I can say is that I am right glad I am not a soldier. Going everywhere on foot and fighting on the land is not my pleasure and I hope I can get back to sea before too long. But I'm getting ahead of myself here. So much has happened I got to start at the beginning to tell you about it.

When the flotilla left Nottingham — it seems a long time back, but it wasn't but a week — the commodore had us sail as far up the river as we could float the vessels and then he took most of the men and a few cannon and marched off to Washington. I reckon it was on the orders of Mr. Jones. He's the Secretary of the Navy, as you might know. Anyway, he left me and some others on the boats with orders to burn them should the British show up, which they did the same day he left. I can tell you, it was some hard setting fires and powder kegs on that fine black sloop you remember. But we did and on all the other vessels as well and so I guess we kept the British from getting them. Admiral Cockburn his own self come up in a cutter and seen them burning. Reckon he rowed all the way back to Nottingham right quick after that.

We marched — about forty or fifty of us it was — further up the river and caught up with the commodore just after dark the same day. Jack Clements — you remember him, I reckon; he's the one owns that dog what took to you, Carronade — was there with the men and Luke Cooper and the cannons. Commodore Barney had already rode out to Washington on a borrowed horse and we was supposed to follow quick as ever we might. Which was that same night after we got us some vittles. A long few days it were, I can tell you. We was bone-tired by the time we fetched up at the marine barracks right at the Navy yard by the bridge across the Eastern Branch of the Potomac River. And the commodore was there too.

He had us set the guns we brought and some others he found there along the shore to defend the bridge since, he told us, the enemy was coming that way and would likely try to get into Washington by that route. That was according to General Winder who I met not long ago in Nottingham.

We was waiting there when who but President Madison himself, along with a cove Jack said was called Jim Monroe and some others, come along and told the commodore to get us moved, guns and all, to Bladensburg. Which we done quick as ever you please.

It was some march; I can never remember being that hot, even in the Indies. Men was dropping from the heat and even the horses was falling down — dead when they hit the ground. The lads was some tired already and that march like enough broke us completely. We was still a mile and more off when some Marine officer what was sent by the commodore rode up and told us to hurry, that we was needed now. We could hear the firing so we knew pretty well what was acting. Sarah, I'm telling you, we had to run the last mile and more dragging the cannons. It was killing us all faster than any enemy action I ever faced. But we made it and set up where we was told by the commodore who had rode ahead of us to see where was the enemy. Turns out the British was already coming in from the other side and headed right for us. Right down the main road into Bladensburg. We could hear the shooting right easy — cannons and muskets — and not real far off.

There was a bridge right in front of us and we knew the British would be coming over it. Commodore Barney told us we was all that was between them and the Capital if the militia units didn't hold them. Well, it was looking like the militia wasn't doing nothing but backing up. Must have been hundreds of them what come over that bridge and another further up the river. They didn't look like they'd been in a fight. Wasn't none of them even scratched that we could see as they run by us. And running they was.

Pretty soon, the commodore, who's on the far side of the bridge on his horse, waved his sword and hollered, "Here they come, boys. Hold your fire 'til I tell you." It got real quiet on our side of the bridge and we waited. We couldn't see them yet, but we could hear them marching right down the main road there just like they was on parade. Drums beating and all. Cannons and the artillery pieces we had was loaded with grape and canister shot and the matches was lit. Then Barney come charging across that bridge like the devil hisself was on his heels. He wheeled his horse around and told us to get ready. Well, Sarah, I can tell you, we was already ready — had been for a while. Then around the corner on the far side comes the first Redcoats. Marched almost up to the bridge and halted. Stood there looking at us like they seen something they don't expect. I reckon they could see our guns aimed right down the bridge and set up on the banks of the river right across in front of them. Commodore talked real quiet to us; I was in charge of a eighteen-pounder right along side of him and a Captain Miller of the Marines had a crew manning another piece on his other side. Jack was next to me.

That dog of his was growling and snarling for all he was worth. You likely recall he don't much take to the British. I don't reckon the dog was scared — seemed more like he was just mad — but I can tell you, I sure was. And hot. Well, we all was hot.

After a minute and more, the enemy started to move and head for the bridge. "Fire, lads!" cried the commodore and we did. Give them two barrels of grape right into they's faces. And some of Captain Miller's riflemen opened fire right along side of us. Their commander had his horse shot out from under him and some of the sailors who wasn't manning cannon run after the enemy soldiers what turned tail. They was shouting "Board them!" to each other. Reckon it was all they knew, being seamen.

Well, I can tell you, we cleared that bridge quick as ever you please. Wasn't a red coat to be seen, 'cepting the ones on the dead Royal Marines. Then they formed up again and tried to get across again and we give it to them again, same as the first time, and again, they fell back. Of course, they was shooting back each time and we had a dozen or so men killed or wounded — some cruel. Captain Miller lost a fair number of his Marines as well. Three times they done it afore they quit and moved over to our right. Commodore called it 'flanking' us. But Luke Copper was there with a couple of twelve-pounders and beat them back same as we did. They lost a passel of they's soldiers, dead and wounded. There was some army men — not militia I was told — up on a rise beyond Luke's battery, and we figured they'd be a big help if the British tried to get through on that end.

The British had some sharp-shooters — Marines, I'd warrant, same as they use in the fighting tops of they's ships at sea — laying in the grass and hiding in the trees shooting at us. Shot Commodore Barney's horse dead right with him still aboard. But the senior British commander got his horse shot right quick after that. Then they started coming across hard on the right end. Luke couldn't fire his guns fast enough to hold them off and over they come. We figured the Army coves up on the hill would bear a hand when they seen we wasn't holding them, but they fired a few rounds of musket and run off. And our teamsters — the ones driving our ammunition wagons — run right with them. Left us holding a sack full of nothing, they did. Close enough to out of shot and powder as to not matter and none in sight. Nothing but Redcoats cutting right through us. Luke got hisself shot dead and some of his men. A fair number of them manning the guns got sore wounded or killed, but the sailors what had been acting like soldiers took over they's places on the guns to keep them firing 'til they run out of powder. Then Barney caught a ball in his thigh. Cruel hurt, he was, and losing blood quick as I ever saw. Reckon he saw we was done for, cause he ordered us to retire after spiking our guns. Some of us tried to help him, but he made us leave him under a tree and get away so as not to be taken by the British. It was real hard leaving him there, but he told us the British would take care of him and their doctor would fix him up fine. We headed back towards Washington right ahead of the British soldiers. We was still some scared with them chasing after us, but I reckon most of us was angry on top of it. Oh, Sarah, if only them soldiers hadn't run off like they done.

Jack and I watched from a distance off and seen Admiral Cockburn, the same one what watched the gunboats burn, talking to the commodore along with some other cove with gold braid and high rank. We found out later it was none other than General Ross, the head of the whole British army!

Well, Sarah, the ones of us what was left from the flotilla marched — well, maybe marching don't answer, but we moved right quick-like — back the way we'd just come, back into Washington. The Redcoats chased us for a while, but then I reckon the heat got to them same as us. We had men dropping from it all through our ranks — some of them dead on the spot. After a few miles, the lads in the rear passed the word up the enemy wasn't in sight no more and we slowed down some. Even rested for a bit afore we got into the city.

Sarah, I can tell you I was some stunned when we got

there; wasn't a soul to be seen! It was like the whole city was a ghost-ship. Nary a body anywhere and the buildings and streets empty. Doors stood open and it seemed like a lot of people's belongings was just layin' about everywhere — in the streets, outside homes and shops, all over the place. We finally found some cove — Tingey, I think his name was, a captain — at the Navy Yard. His clerk had pretty well emptied most of the arms and munitions and took them out of the city and he had a few men ready to torch the vessels and buildings there in the yard. Said he'd been ordered to do that to keep the British from getting them. Just like the commodore had us do to the flotilla over to Pig Point. We heard the enemy had entered the city sometime after supper and the captain, well, he just set off the fires and powder charges all over the Yard. They was a frigate there — a fine looking one almost done building called the USS *Essex* — and a smaller ship, USS *Argus*, a sloop of war what went up in the flames. A real pity it were, Sarah, to see them fine vessels burning afore they ever got to sea. When we put the torch to the rope walk close by the Navy Yard, it made a blaze like I never seen afore. Flames must have reached high as the frigate's main t'gallant pole. And hot. There was one ship in the Navy Yard we couldn't get to take the fire; the *New York* frigate — she was built back during the time we was fighting the Frenchies — right around 1800, somebody told me. From a distance, she looked right pretty setting there, but close up, she was as rotten and waterlogged as any I ever seen. Probably why she wouldn't burn; she was just too wet in all her timbers.

The night hadn't cooled off the air even a little and, with the fires that was burning, the whole place was like being in a oven. And we could see the flames from the other part of the city from the fires the British set. We saw later that they had burnt most of the new buildings — some, like the Capitol building, wasn't even finished. Reckon they torched the President's house as well. Some of the folks said that Admiral Cockburn and his officers went in first and ate a meal right there in the President's dining room! Can you believe that?!

After the new day dawned, the British just kept going, burning everything they hadn't got around to the night before. They even set more fires in the Navy Yard and finished ruining what we hadn't done already. They kept it up all the day long until about midway through the afternoon watch — must of been near 3:00. There was an explosion like I never heard afore. Shook the buildings and the ground as well. We found out later it was the powder stored in the magazine on Greenleaf's Point, over by Long Bridge and, when it went off, it killed a passel of Redcoats. Can't say I'm sorry about that!

About the same time, a storm come through the city like the hurricanes they have in the Indies. Dark as night it were, quick as anything I ever saw, and rain. Rain coming down so hard you couldn't see anything, and then the wind come so strong a man couldn't even walk. Put out most of the fires that still burned. And then after a bit, the rain quit and the wind died off. Cooled the air some which was a relief. Everything was turned to mud — all the streets was running water and sticky, sucking mud. Just walking was a trial, I can tell you.

We could see the camp fires of the British army all night long, burning all around the city. Some of the folks which had come back into Washington was saying the Redcoats was going to start it all up again the next morning and finish what they started, but when the morning come, they was gone! Completely. Nothing left but some of they's wounded which was being taken care of by an American doctor.

Word come to us still at the Navy Yard — or what was left of it — to pack up our slops and get us to Baltimore quick as ever we could get there. We didn't even drag the guns along since it would slow us down too much. We went back through Bladensburg just this morning and I never seen such a sight. Dead Redcoats and more than a few wounded laying all over the roads and fields. Reckon we did some damage to them when we met them there, but it weren't enough to stop them. Some slaves was out digging graves for them and some others was picking up the wounded ones to take care of them. What a horror it was, Sarah. I never seen such a mess even in ship actions when I was in the Royal Navy. I reckon the butcher's bill for that fight was bigger than anyone figured.

I got to stop this now and try to get some sleep. We're about halfway to Baltimore and ain't seen hide nor hair of the British, so I don't know what we'll do when we get there. I was told to take the men and find Commodore Rogers and he'd tell us what to do. Sure hope it don't have to be fighting on the land again. I seen enough of that to last me the rest of my life!

I hope you are staying safe and the war ain't touched you or your kin. I will post this quick as I can and hope I can get back there to Benedict to see you sooner than later.

Yrs. faithfully,

Isaac Biggs   August 28, 1814

CHAPTER TWENTY-TWO

"Take your men and put 'em aboard the gunboats you'll find here and here." Josiah Eldridge pointed a long manicured finger at different locations on the map he had spread out on the barrel of a cannon while Isaac and Jack looked on. "Until Commodore Rodgers and Captain Porter return from Washington, you'll have to report to Jared Talbot — he's got a passel of men and a dozen and more gunboats on both sides of McHenry. I 'spect he'll be found in Ridgley's Cove with more 'an a few of his vessels. Leastways, that's where I'd start lookin' for him."

The pinch-faced civilian wiped a hand across his sweating face and tried ineffectively to dry his now-dripping hand on his dirty trousers. His shirt was soaked and stained both from the constant sweat and the dirt and mud being moved onto the revetment. It was apparent to the sailors that he took his job most seriously. He squinted at the two captains and raised his brows questioningly to insure their understanding. Both nodded and smiled at the news that their friend was here and then looked out from Federal Hill to orient themselves with the positions on the map. Eldridge cast a glance over Clements' shoulder to assure himself that the big dog still showed no interest in him; indeed Carronade had found a patch of shade next to another cannon and was sound asleep, snoring softly.

The flotillamen had had less success in finding shade but had, to a man, collapsed, exhausted from their forced march and the once-again overwhelming heat. Isaac and Jack had led their sailors into Baltimore and, after almost a day lost to their attempt to find "competent authority," had found Josiah Eldridge in a redoubt atop a hill overlooking the city. He seemed to be knowledgeable and apparently had some authority. He had introduced himself to the sailors as a member of the Committee of Vigilance and Safety.

Secretary Jones had instructed Isaac to find either David Porter or John Rodgers; both, it turned out, were still in Washington dealing with the British retreat on the Potomac River. The redoubt was one of many surrounding the city and part of a defense perimeter thrown up and reinforced after the word of Washington's collapse had reached Baltimore. Both the military and the city fathers were determined that *their* city would not fall, reflecting the feelings of not only the locals but the general populace as well. Mayor Edward Johnson had helped establish the Committee of Vigilance and Safety, the successor to the Committee of Supply, formed in 1813. Its function had been the defense of the city of Baltimore and its newly-formed stepchild was designed to augment and assist with the extraordinary measures necessary if the city was to survive the anticipated invasion by the British.

Manpower was provided at the request of the Committee to complete and increase the modest number of entrenchments designed to protect the city from invasion — unlike its sister city to the south. During the British move on Washington, daily news of the enemy's progress was monitored carefully in Baltimore; the militia drilled more frequently and in greater number. There were further stimuli to the preparation.

Indeed, the federal government, after the enemy had withdrawn, had quickly taken a firm hold in the Capital, sent troops under both Rodgers and Porter to deal with the British ships and marines still on the Potomac, and reshuffled the top of the military hierarchy, naming James Monroe as acting Secretary of War. General Armstrong, who had bungled the job so thoroughly, was sent in disgrace to his home in New York state.

"You figger the militia gonna stand and fight, sir, or run off like they done in Washington?" Jack had little interest in participating in another rout. "We heard the folks is already talking about the 'Bladensburg Races' acause the damn militia *and* the army run off so fast when the Royal Marines showed up."

"It seems to me, Captain . . . Clements, isn't it?" Eldridge paused, leaning back against the dirt wall surrounding them and, getting a nod from the one-eared sailor, continued, "The folks here as well as the military units from elsewhere in Maryland and Virginia have gotten some iron in their backbones after hearing what happened in the Capital. I have had no trouble — no trouble at all — in finding sufficient troop strength to man the defensive positions around the city. Additional men are being sent from as far away as Virginia and I am told that the recruiting offices are overwhelmed with volunteers.

"Commodore Perry will be here with his men along with Commodores Rodgers and Porter from Washington — in a few days, I should think — as soon as they have routed the enemy from the Potomac. I have heard they have with them several hundred sailors from the campaigns on the freshwater as well as some of Porter's crew from his ill-fated but successful cruise into the Pacific on the *Essex* frigate.

"Perry, I have been told, will take responsibility for the naval forces in the harbor. He actually is ordered to the command of USS *Java*, a frigate of forty-four guns, but she is not yet ready for sea. In fact, her battery is now positioned on several important points around the harbor. Yes, indeed, I am hopeful that the enemy will find a quite different attitude when they arrive in Baltimore."

"Aye, I've heard the folks has finally gotten they's dander up. Saw a newspaper already calling the attack on Washington 'a second-rate buccaneering expedition' that was right spiteful and served no useful purpose for the British. 'Specially since they didn't even stay there after they took the city. Reckon it mighta been just what was needed to get the citizens to help out, though. Mayhaps it had the opposite effect than what the damn British thought it would." Jack was as tired as the rest of the military at the pervasive attitude that ranged from antipathy to hostility on the part of most of the populace. Their cooperation would be a welcome change indeed.

Isaac looked up from the map he had been studying and after a lengthy survey of the waterfront and those approaches to the city that were visible from their hill, he spoke. "Anybody got an idea 'bout when the enemy is expected to come here, Mr. Eldridge?"

"I know you're concerned about how much time we have to establish the defenses of the city, Captain Biggs, but quite frankly, I have no idea when they might show up. I heard just this morning that they have returned to their ships in Benedict and are headed back down the Patuxent River. That would likely have been yesterday or perhaps the day before.

"But I have heard nothing about them leaving from the Potomac River. In fact, it was just yesterday I was informed that Captain Porter was maintaining a heavy barrage on the British ships from the new fort at White House, Virginia. What effect they have had is not known, but I would think it likely ain't something the British would relish. What will they do next? I am afraid I know not, sir." The hot, sweaty, and grimy civilian paused, shifting his glance between the two captains and the waterfront below them.

He noticed that some workers had stopped their toils to have a smoke and his face clouded. His glance at Biggs and Clements made it apparent that he had no more time for the flotillamen and already his mind was solving other, more pressing, problems. After a moment, he continued. "I can assure you, however, that we will be quite ready whenever they do show up and give them a reception they'll not soon forget. Now, if you have no further questions, I must see to other matters." Without waiting for a response, he turned and strode purposefully away toward the men once again shoveling dirt onto the end of the embankment.

"Well, I reckon we might as well go find these gunboats he was talkin' about. Looks like Jared and his men are down there with 'em, just like they's s'posed to be. Come on, Carronade. Get your lazy arse up; they's no time for sleepin' now."

The dog opened one eye and looked at his master. He got up slowly, stretched, shook, and then sat down, his pink tongue lolling from the side of his mouth. Isaac roused the sailors and met with less success, but eventually all hands, man and beast, started down the hill toward the harbor.

"You reckon they's 'spectin' the gunboats to take on the Royal Navy, Isaac? Seems like a right tall order, you ask me. And that cove said the *Java* frigate ain't ready or even manned yet on top of it." Neither Jake Tate nor Jack's second in command, Frank Clark, had been privy to all that passed between their captains and Eldridge, but Isaac had told the men the good news that they would be back on their beloved gunboats — different ones to be sure, but gunboats all the same. The men — all of them — had certainly had enough of this land fighting and marching to and fro like soldiers. And most looked forward to seeing their old shipmate again. Jake and Frank Clark walked down the hill toward the waterfront alongside Jack and Isaac; Carronade trotted a step astern of his master.

"Knowing what they showed up with in the Patuxent, Jake, I'd be real surprised if that was they's plan. But I reckon we'll find out more when we meet up with Jared. I been wonderin' just what they got here in the way of vessels. I sure would like to get my hands on another sloop like them ones we had 'til a couple of weeks ago, eh, Jack?"

Clements smiled, recalling the cooler days and familiar motion under his feet, as he trod through the muddy back streets of Baltimore. The four lapsed into silence, each deep in his own thoughts, ranging from their good fortune at surviving, first, the best of the Royal Marines at Bladensburg and then the destruction of the Capital, to what the future held.

Isaac's mind ran through the words of the pinch-faced, middle-aged civilian, Mr. Eldridge, recalling that he had mentioned that the British had, only a few days back, passed again through Benedict.

What did they do to the local populace? What had they done to the town and the pretty little grassy square in its center — the one where he had first met Sarah. And Sarah? What had happened to her? Was she safe? He knew in his heart that she had most likely not remained safely hidden away in her house or that of her godfather; it would not have answered for a girl of her stripe. And like as not, had there been any action, she would surely have been helping with the wounded . . . or worse. Isaac shuddered at the thought.

With her feelings about proving herself to the men of Benedict, most especially her father, it was not beyond belief that she might even have been a participant in any fighting that took place. An image flashed into his mind, unbidden, of her with a musket, soiled and grimy with the dirt of battle. She crouched in the scant cover offered by a rail fence, resting an uncocked musket on its top. She was in her blue dress, with her straw bonnet pushed back and hanging from the silk ribbon tied 'round her neck. Both were stained and torn. A lock of hair, a raven's wing, fell down the side of her sweat-soaked and powder-stained face. Without conscious thought, she pushed the offending strand back over her head.

She pulled back the lock to cock it, aimed the musket and fired at the approaching Redcoats, her body shuddering with the shock of the recoil. One fell, and she stood to celebrate her triumph as a mate of the fallen Marine fired. Isaac shook his head and closed his eyes. He had stopped walking and put a hand out on a post to steady himself.

No. No, that would not answer. She cain't be shootin'. Likely helpin' with the wounded. Aye, that was more like it. He opened his eyes again and pictured her wrapping bandages and helping the other women consoling and comforting the fallen militiamen. He again walked, focused on the image in his brain.

"Isaac, where the hell are you going? Eldridge said to go off to starboard when we got here. Where's your head at, lad?" Clements grabbed Biggs' elbow and steered him to the right and down a street which appeared to lead to the water.

"Uh, sorry, Jack. I guess I was thinkin' on something else. Aye, you're right again. This is likely the way we should be goin'." Isaac smiled at his friend, thankful for the interruption in his reverie.

"You men, there. Stop! Who are you?" A harsh voice shouted from astern of the leaders and they stopped and turned to see a bearded figure heading for them from an alley. He appeared to be in uniform — or at least, parts of a uniform— and was filthy. His unkempt beard and wild hair were soaked in sweat as was the shirt he wore. Torn canvas trousers, equally filthy, marked him as a sailor. Or one who once had been a sailor. In one huge paw he carried a musket — at full cock, they saw — and a cutlass hung from a leather belt slung over his shoulder. A great shock of white hair fell down to his shoulders, unbound and greasy.

"Sent to find Jared Talbot and the gunboats . . . by Mr. Eldridge." Isaac stopped and, by necessity, so did his men. He, Clements, and Jake Tate studied the figure as he continued toward them.

They noticed that the weapon was still held loosely in his left hand, but his right now rested in the hilt of the cutlass. The man made his way through the opening which appeared in the ranks quite naturally before him. Both Tate and Clements noticed more than a few noses wrinkling as he passed; Isaac's eyes remained fixed on the apparition.

"Eldridge sent you down here — his own self?" The man stopped inches in front of Isaac; his two companions stepped back without thought, but Isaac stood his ground. His nose wrinkled some, but he stood fast. Carronade watched the man closely, almost sitting, but tense and ready to leap should he feel it necessary.

"Aye, that he did. Said we was to find Talbot and wait on Commodore Perry to show up. Who might you be?"

The man's hand tightened on the cutlass and he continued to stare at Isaac. He looked him over unabashedly, from the top of his sweat-streaked head with its curly dark hair plastered down to it to the worn leather shoes, still covered with mud from their march out of Washington on rain-soaked streets. Isaac waited and unflinchingly returned the stare, aware that, on his flanks, both Clements and Jake had taken a grip on their own cutlasses. He heard a hint of a growl from the dog.

Apparently satisfied with what he saw, the man spoke. "I can take you to Captain Talbot. But if you ain't what you say . . ." The wild-looking fellow shook his head and turned. Isaac, Jack and Jake released the breaths they had unconsciously been holding and looked at one another as their guard and, hopefully, their guide stepped off toward the waterfront. Only once did he scowl back at them to ensure that Biggs and his sailors were following. After a moment of hesitation, they did.

And in a few minutes — less than a mile away — they saw the masts of the gunboats anchored along the water's edge. As the remnants of Joshua Barney's flotillamen reached the pier, Isaac and Jack heard a familiar voice bellowing from a building on their starboard hand.

"Clements! That you? And Biggs! Reckon the rumors we heard wasn't true after all. But how'd you get here? Ain't been no boats come in here in the last day an' more. Been waitin' on a couple of my lads to get back from the Eastern Shore." Jared Talbot's huge form stepped out of the open front of a waterfront stall and lumbered toward the four men, a smile covering his scarred face. The familiar knife hung in its sheath at his back and the plaited hair slapped his grimy shirt just above his rope-tied trousers as he walked toward them.

"Jared, you old dog. You just been settin' here on your arse while we been doin' all the work down to the Patuxent. You must be bored to death." Isaac grasped his fellow captain's great paw and pumped it. Talbot shook hands with each of the men he knew and welcomed them to Baltimore. "Glad that Crazy Bill found you — and didn't do nothin' hurtful to you. He sometimes does; don't mean no harm, but forgets where he's at from time to time. Got hisself head shot in the War for Independence and been carryin' a little luff in his sails ever since. Here, let your lads have a look around the cove — it's called Ridgely's Cove, by the way — and come in here out of the sun for a glass. You can catch me up on what's actin' down to Washington." Talbot reached down and scratched the big dog on the back of his head and, ever hopeful of more, Carronade paced beside his old acquaintance as they marched into the shack.

'Crazy' Bill followed them in bringing up the rear. And then, quite without warning or word, he turned about and set sail for the street. Jared watched him go, shaking his head.

"Poor bastard. Found him wandering around the waterfront when we first got here. Seemed to latch on to me right off and kinda been following me around since. He's like as not back where you lads found him, guarding the street. Been doin' that ever since he heard us talkin' 'bout the British invadin' Baltimore! Reckon he fancies hisself a lookout." Talbot sat and signaled the publican for a round of ales.

Jack and Jake had followed Isaac and Jared into the stall of what turned out to be a rudimentary alehouse. Carronade welcomed the shade and thirstily drank the pan of water Jack put down for him. Frank Clark, Jack's mate on the sloop, figured to sit a while as long as Jake was.

When all the new arrivals had found chairs, the big gunboat captain smiled ruefully at them. "So you couldn't stop them damn Redcoats afore they got themselves to the capital, eh, lads? Sounded up here like they done run ever' damn soul — soldiers an' politicians both — right outta the city. Had they's run of anywhere they wanted to go. Heard, too, they burned more'n half the city down. Couldn'ta been that bad, right men?" Jared wrapped his huge hands around a partially-drunk tankard of ale and took a long draught while he waited for confirmation that the rumors were nothing more than exaggerations.

"Aye, Jared. Bad as that and more. Militia and army run off damn near afore the politicians done it. Most never even fired a shot. They just seen them damn red coats comin' down the road and high-tailed it for the hills of Virginia. British marched in and set every public building afire right off. Waited 'til the next day and fired the ones they missed. But for the rain squall — more like an Indies hurricane, it were — what come through, the whole damn city woulda likely burned to ashes. Then they up and left. Heard they marched right back to Benedict and they's ships." Jack paused long enough to take a big swallow of his own tankard, then continued.

"Heard they was a bunch of ships headin' back down the Potomac, but one of them Commodores — Porter, wasn't it, Isaac? — was firin' on 'em as they left. Don't know that that'll do any good, but mayhaps he'll get one or two of they's frigates. Be that many fewer what can raise Cain over to the Eastern Shore and the rest of the Bay — or here, I reckon." He wiped his sleeve across his mouth, then drank again.

"What have you and your lads here been doin', Jared?" Isaac was trying to figure out where he and the almost three hundred men he brought were going to fit in.

"Well, Isaac. The Committee's got itself a plan for the defense of the city. Reckon Porter and Rodgers had a hand in figgerin' it out since they's a passel of gunboats and sailors gonna figger into it. The men you brung sure gonna come in handy, I'd warrant. I got shore side batteries and such what gotta be manned and I'd wager a fair piece of change the commodore's gonna want to move a few more of the boats over to Fells Point." Talbot stopped, as though suddenly realizing that something was wrong.

"Isaac, where in hell is Commodore Barney? It just dawned on me he ain't here."

"Commodore got hisself shot by some Royal Marine at Bladensburg, Jared." Seeing the horrified look on his friend's face, he hurried on. "Not shot dead. It was just a leg wound. Cruel hurt he was, though, and lost more 'an a little blood. He made us leave him when the British was comin' on hard, figgerin' they wouldn't hurt him none, just take him prisoner."

Jack picked up the story. "Isaac an' me watched that admiral — Cockburn, right, Isaac?" Getting a nod, he continued. "Him and the head of the whole army, Ross it were, come and took him prisoner personally and when we left, they was loadin' Barney on a litter. I reckon to take him to a hospital or a doctor. If he lives, I reckon he'll be fine right quick. Might even turn up here. I know that'd be his want, if'n he's able." Clements smiled lopsidedly. "Bein's how Luke got hisself killed in the same action, reckon young Isaac here's in charge of the flotilla. Leastways, 'til we got here and found you."

"I'm right sorry to hear that Luke's gone, Jack. He was a fine man and a damn good skipper. A good friend too." Jared raised his tankard in silent and solemn tribute to his friend and the newcomers followed suit.

After a swallow and a thoughtful pause, Talbot continued filling in the newcomers on the preparations for a British invasion at Baltimore. Suddenly he stopped his narrative and, getting up, walked to the fireplace. He rooted around in the cold ashes for a moment and found a serviceable lump of charcoal. "This'll answer." he muttered as he made his way back to the table. Using the charcoal, he quickly drew a map on the tabletop, saying as he did so, "Lookee here, lads."

"We got gunboats set here in Ridgley's what we'll move right across to Fort Covington across the way, yonder." He pointed out the door of the alehouse to a structure on the far side of the cove. "As I said afore, I reckon they'll want to put some others of 'em over to Fells Point; I got more 'an I need here. Afore he headed over to Washington, Rodgers had the townspeople start building entrenchments and settin' batteries above the city up on Federal Hill and here to the east . . . and here, along the waterfront. And of course, there's Fort McHenry on Whetstone Point. They got some pretty heavy artillery and some naval guns there, and they's a good man in charge, a Major Armistead. That fort's a stout-built structure — reckon it could take more'n a few balls without much notice." Talbot paused, drank, and went on with a smile. "And I hear he's got damn near a thousand hands behind the walls — regulars and volunteers."

Isaac looked at the rudimentary, but quite accurate, map Jared had drawn. "Reckon that fort is 'bout all what's between the Bay and the city, so if the British plan on comin' ashore, they'll likely have to get past 'em there. Seems like the folks here got this planned out pretty good."

"Aye. But who . . ." Talbot never finished the thought. He was interrupted by a cry from the quay wall.

"Boat! Boat comin' in, Jared. Looks like Jones and Andrews in number twenty-seven — and they's some shot up."

The men stood as one, tankards falling unnoticed as the unsteady table was jostled, pushed their way through the narrow door, and ran to the waterfront.

CHAPTER
TWENTY-THREE

"Looks like you lads mighta bit off more'n you could chew, Jones. Who'd you tangle with over there?" Jared, like his late friend Luke Cooper, was never one to mince words.

"It were the *Menelaus* frigate, Jared. An' Tom Morris an' his lads're still over there. Sent me in to tell you what's actin' and mebbe get some help." Captain Jones stepped onto the quay wall as the gunboat's sails came down, hiding holes in both, fore and aft. A bloody bandage was tied around his upper arm and smears of red remained on the side of his face where he had hastily wiped away the blood from a scalp wound. He looked back at his battered boat and shook his head.

"They was settin' right there in Fairlee Creek, swingin' to they's hook like they owned the whole damn place. Didn't even have a lookout posted. That was a couple . . . no, three days ago. We seen 'em and Tom and me just sailed in there in the dark of the night. Reckon most of the bastards was ashore burnin' farms." He paused and shifted the cutlass hanging from his shoulder. "Heard they got John Waltham's place — "Skidmore" he called it. Burned every damn thing on it, buildings, storage sheds, even the wheat standing in the fields. We could see the fires from the creek and I reckon the sailors what was still on the frigate was watchin' it to boot, 'cause we sailed right up pretty as you please, an' fired a few rounds of chain and some grape into 'em. Some surprised they was, I can tell you!" The wounded man's eyes sparkled as he recalled the audacious attack, then quickly grew serious as he recounted what happened next.

"They musta found enough men to run out a few guns even in they's confused state. 'Cause quicker'n anyone of us ever expected it, they was firin' back. Used mostly grape, I'd warrant. Tom took a load of it into his hull but got hisself over toward the shoreline where either they couldn't see him no more, or didn't care, seein' as how they had me lookin' like easy pickin's. We took some shot through the sails and into the hull 's'well, but the wind was up and, since they was to they's anchor, we was able to get clear afore they done any real serious damage to the boat. Had one killed and one asides me what got hisself hurt some."

He looked back into the boat where some of his crew were lifting one of their number into willing hands ashore. "Whaley, it were. Took a piece of grape through his belly an' a splinter in the leg. Lost a lot of blood, but if they's a medico 'round here, reckon he'll live."

"Where's Andrews?" Jared peered into the boat in the rapidly failing last light of the day and then looked at his junior captain.

"He was the one killed, I'm sorry to tell. Took a chunk of British grape right full into the face. Wasn't hardly enough left of his . . . well, reckon he died pretty quick. Buried him ashore the next morning, we did." Jones shook his head again, recalling the devastating turn of events.

"You was some crazy, sailin' in there and firin' on a frigate. You was just askin' for trouble. What happened to Tom and his boat?" Jared's one eye squinted down at Jones and his face clenched as his anger — and color — rose.

"Well, we got us outta the creek and round the point some. Didn't figger they'd follow, bein's how they was anchored with most of they's crew ashore. An' they didn't. Tom and me fetched up on the shoreline some to the north of the creek's mouth and spent the rest of the night knottin' an' splicin' our riggin' and pluggin' the holes in the boats. They's a big farm right there an' some militia was camped there on top of it. Figgered if they was more trouble, them soldier-boys might lend a hand.

"We talked to one of 'em. Tol' us they was more soldiers just inland a bit — at Belle Air it were — an' they was just waitin' to get them damn Royal Marines ashore where they's colonel, a cove named Reed, if'n I recall rightly, was waitin' to give 'em what-fer." He stopped and looked around, suddenly noticing the throng of men standing around the quay in the growing gloom. His gaze took in Isaac and Jack standing close behind Talbot, and then

Chapter Twenty-Three

Jack's dog, sitting at his side.

"Who're all these coves, Jared? You recruitin' locals to help out? An' what about that beast settin' yonder — he gonna sail with us?"

"Never mind about them for now, Jones. Tell me the rest of the story. What happened after you got your boats mended?" Jared couldn't afford to lose a boat, especially now, and needed to know when Morris would be back . . . or if. His scowl and sharp words put Jones back on course and the gunboat captain picked up his story again.

"Well, like I was sayin', them militia coves was strainin' at they's lines to get a whack at the enemy, an' Tom, he spoke up an' tol' that militia soldier 'Why, them Redcoats is just 'round the point yonder, burnin' farms and raisin' Cain right there. Damn near under your nose, they are.' An' the soldier, he says, 'Well, we cain't go after 'em 'til Colonel Reed says to. Reckon we'll get the chance; yes sir, I reckon we surely will!' Tom an' me, we just went back to our knottin' an' splicin' an' didn't pay that cove no more mind. Just like all them militia coves, I reckon. Only ones doin' anything to help out with this damn mess is the Navy and us flotillamen." He looked again at the sea of faces around. "Jared, why don't we finish this in the tavern there. I'm in powerful need of a pint o' something; reckon it'll ease the pain of this arm, it will." He rubbed the dirty, blood-stained bandage thoughtfully as he looked beyond the huge commander — now in charge of the flotilla — and eyed thirstily the welcoming light of the still-empty alehouse.

"Aye, we can do that. Forgot for the moment about your wound." Jared softened some and turned to make his way back to the makeshift tavern. Isaac, Jack, and Carronade followed. Jake and Frank Clark remained on the quay with most of the other men, lending a hand as the work began, putting the gunboat to rights.

"Like I was sayin', Jared." Jones again picked up his tale after finding a stool and taking a long draught from the tankard placed before him. "A day later, we was put mostly to rights again and then she come — the *Menelaus* frigate, I mean, sailin' outta the creek under her tops'ls and a stays'l or two. Reckon they didn't see us, on account of we was behind a little rise, and they turned to the south. Likely figgered they chased us off for good. Well, they was wrong! We made sail and went right after 'em, we did. Eased our way out toward the middle of the Bay and come up behind 'em. Tom an' me both fired into they's quartergallery an' then bore off under they's stern. Figgered on hittin' they's rudder post. That's the weakest place on them frigates, you know," he added unnecessarily. "Wind was fair outta the nor'east, an' we thought we might be able to make the damn ship chase us over to this side. Ceptin' they was headin' somewhere right purposeful, they was, an' when we bore up astern of 'em again, they kept right on headin' sou'west just like they been. Fired a couple of stern-chasers at us. Got a lucky hit on my boat what raised some splinters and stove in the bulwark aft there, like you seen, and tore up the sails a trifle more. Missed ol' Tom clean, they done." He paused in his tale to take another long pull at the ale.

"So where's Morris and the other gunboat, Jones? You ain't tol' me much of any use, 'ceptin' they's a frigate out yonder doin' what they been doin' for a year now — burnin' farms and crops. That an' that you an' Morris ain't got much sense — takin' on a frigate, for God's sake! What was goin' on in your minds I can only imagine! Guess you thought you was gonna be the first gunboats ever to take a frigate as a prize! Commodore Barney was here, he'da had you flogged by now and likely locked up. Now," Jared paused and looked right at the gunboat skipper, hard-eyed and ugly. "Where in hell is Tom Morris and Gunboat Forty-Three?"

"Honest to God, Jared, right now I ain't got any idea; he sent me in to tell you what was actin' and said he be along soon's he found out what the damn frigate was up to. He could be here tonight yet or more likely tomorrow or the next day, be my guess." Jones had finally come to the realization that Talbot was fast losing patience with him. Contrition filled his voice as he realized that their actions had been not only dangerous, but stupid as well. But the longer he thought on it, the more his regret over the attempt on the frigate eased itself into anger — both at himself and Tom Morris. He was none too pleased with Jared Talbot at dressing him down in front of the men, either.

Figuring that his absence might save his hide — at least for the moment — he stood suddenly, rocking the little table. The color was up in the back of his neck and his hands made tight fists as he struggled to control his temper. He didn't take to the hard-edged questioning from Talbot — even if Talbot was his commander. "Gotta see to the boat. Reckon I tol' you everything I could tell. Tom'll have to tell you what he done when he shows up." His voice quavered slightly as he tried to maintain a neutral tone. Without so much as a glance back, the gunboat skipper strode into the night and made his way to the quay, pushing angrily through the stragglers of the flotillamen who had been pressing closer to hear what they might. He muttered curses aimed with equal rancor at Jared Talbot and Tom Morris.

It was two full days and into the third when Tom Morris sailed easily into the anchorage in Ridgely's Cove, rounded up, and brought his vessel to anchor as smartly as anyone had seen. It wasn't until after his boat had been lowered and was pulling for the pier that someone commented, "Will you have a look at the larboard bow, there! He musta took some heavy iron in there, chewed up like he is."

Of course, every pair of eyes that weren't otherwise engaged squinted into the morning light reflecting brightly off the water. Soon a crowd of men, eager for some good news, gathered at the landing point and began shouting questions at the skipper — who mostly ignored them.

By the time the boat had landed, Talbot had been found and was waiting on the pier for Captain Morris' report — and news of what was "actin' on the Bay." Isaac and Jake, who were both currently unemployed, stood near at hand. Isaac looked hard at the young Tom Morris.

A nice looking cove, he thought. *Seems like he might be some smart. Eyes peerin' out of a too-thin face, takin' in everyone and everything . . . seems to be lookin' everywhere at once. Them eyebrows pokin' up in the middle make him look kinda surprised-like. Or like he knows something no one else does,* Isaac decided. *Must be on account of he wasn't expectin' a reception like this. Or mayhaps, he beat that frigate Jones and his lads was tellin' us about a few days ago. An' he ain't any older 'an me, neither."*

". . . ashore there they was. One of my lads heard 'em talkin' 'bout chasin' the militia clear across the Eastern shore, all the way into the Atlantic! Well, I can tell you, they got 'emselves some kinda surprise, they done, by God. Reckon they'd heard 'bout Colonel Reed's men there at Belle Air and was fixin' to teach 'em a thing or two. 'Ceptin' Reed an' his men wasn't at Belle Air, they was waitin' for the British to come ashore over toward Chestertown." Morris' eyes sparkled as recalled the sight of the *Menelaus* frigate anchoring in the last glimmer of light on August 30th right off the shore opposite William Raisin's farm, Chantilly.

"We was practically within cannon-shot of 'em, but kinda round the point so they couldn't see anything more'n our mast, an' I reckon they lost that in the trees soon as the sun set. 'Bout an hour after full dark, the moon come up bright as you please and there they was, puttin' sailors an' marine into they's boats and headin' ashore. All whispers and muffled oars, they was. They was sneakin' in to take the farm and run off the militia, I reckon. Wasn't long afore they had the soldiers ashore — whole mess of 'em, probably over a hunnert, seemed like — and they started movin' inland. Left the Raisin's farm alone, likely figgerin' to burn it on the way back." Morris paused and looked around at the large and still growing group of sailors, including Captain Jones and several of his crew, who seemed to be hanging on his every word. The new arrival smiled, enjoying his momentary celebrity.

"Well, me an' some of the lads followed along. We didn't have a plan, just figgered to stay out of sight and mayhaps warn the militia if'n we got the chance to get ahead of 'em. Hadn't gone more'n a half mile inland when up ahead, they's shots, then the sound of runnin' horses. Then we heard more shots, comin' from the direction the horses run, and pretty quick, cannon shots. Well, any thought them Marines had of surprisin' anyone was gone then; don't reckon they wasn't anyone within a league an' more what wasn't alert an' ready for 'em.

"They commenced marchin' quick-time right down the middle of the road then and it wasn't long afore they took fire from some of the advance warning posts Colonel Reed had set out. When the riflemen in them outposts started backin' up, the British followed 'em into a place called Caulk's fields an' right into the middle of the biggest damn artillery bombardment you ever seen! They was grape and canister flyin', and musta been a couple o' companies of riflemen firin' right into them Redcoats. We seen some red-coated cove carrryin' a bunch of staffs — musta been for them rockets they's so fond of — but he caught a round early on an' we never seen a rocket used. Good thing, too, I'll warrant; mighta come out different if'n they'd a-fired them Congreves." Again, Morris paused, letting his audience digest what they had so far.

"Them damn-fool Royal Marines charged right into the face of that heavy fire — they was either damn well-trained or plumb stupid, you ask me — and was fallin' like leaves in a gale. This cove, Sir Peter Parker — he was their leader and been around the Bay on the *Menelaus* for a year an' more, I heard — took a shot. We saw him go down, but in the fightin' and confusion and the dark, I couldn't make out what happened next."

The silence that surrounded the gunboat captain was complete. Even the harbor sounds and the hustle and bustle of a city fortifying for an attack seemed to be momentarily suspended, waiting for Morris to finish his story. He looked around the eager faces, making them wait, still savoring the moment. So far unimpressed, Jared brought him back to reality quickly.

"How'd you get your boat shot up, Tom? Was that the same action Jones was in when you two thought you'd take on a thirty-eight-gun frigate?"

"Naw, Jared. I'm gettin' to that." The smile had left his face and without it, Isaac thought, it looked more drawn and severe. "We got that other damage fixed up right quick next day. Didn't Jones tell you 'bout that?" A nod from Talbot brought a quick smile to Morris' face, which faded just as quickly as he thought about what happened next.

"So like I was sayin', the British just don't know when to haul they's wind and head out. What'd they do after gettin' they's commander shot and half they's men hurt or killed? They charged again. Only this time, the militia was in an even stronger position and whoever was leadin' the British musta decided then that followin' these coves from one position to the next, an' each one stronger than the one afore, was right dumb, and he ordered 'em to withdraw." Someone in the group made a ribald comment at this, but Morris ignored it and went on.

"They done it so fast they left a fair number of they's dead and wounded right where they fell, they did. And a passel of muskets, pistols, and cutlasses. Militia chased 'em a bit, then let 'em run off. Nearly got ourselves caught when they run by us, but since we didn't, it don't signify. The Marines scurried back to the shore and they's boats. We got our own selves back to the gunboat and figgered to give 'em a bigger headache than the one they already got from the militia." Morris's easy, matter-of-fact delivery and his almost smiling look put one in mind of someone talking about nothing more consequential than the weather, not a life and death encounter with a vastly superior force.

"Planned to hit 'em as they was loadin' they's troops an' what wounded they had — mayhaps take out a few of they's boats into the bargain — but the wind was dyin' to a whisper and by the time we got out there, they was already settin' tops'ls and winnin' they's anchor.

"Reckon either they seen us comin' or was just ready, not wantin' to get caught short again like they done ashore. But they got off a few lucky shots from they's stern-chasers and that's what you seen yonder, on the larboard bow. Carson an' Scott was close to cut in half by the ball, an' I reckon, the splinters. Dead afore they hit the deck, they was, and the larboard six-pounder blown to smithereens.

"We bore off, an' they headed south down the Bay, settin' courses and stays'ls as they went. Goin' like hell, they was, and the devil take the hindermost. That was yesterday morning. We kinda took our time comin' back with the bow shot up like it were. Didn't want to take more water aboard than we could pump out, so we didn't turn North Point 'til first light this morning. Spoke a schooner comin' in just now — said he seen 'em anchored off Kent Island." Morris looked around again at the faces of his fellow flotillamen; he saw disappointment and heard mutterings from various quarters.

"Thought he was gonna tell us he took the frigate!"

"Aye. An' all he done was got his boat and men shot up."

"Maybe we oughtta get our own selves out yonder and have a crack at them Royal Navy bastards."

"Aye. Gonna have to, we want to fight. Don't figger 'em to come in here; be right stupid of 'em to think they could just sail in, tip they's hat, and take the city."

"That's a fact, mate. This ain't Washington, by God."

CHAPTER
TWENTY-FOUR

Several days after his gunboats returned, and while the men were engaged in patching them up and strengthening the fortifications around Ridgeley's Cove, Jared Talbot sailed across the harbor to Fells Point, passing Fort McHenry to larboard. Jack, his dog, Isaac and Jake Tate accompanied the flotilla commander.

"That sure is some big fort, Jared. Them walls don't look like they was nothin' what could get through 'em." Tate's eyes were wide at the sight; never had he seen anything quite so impressive. "Looks like they got guns set up outside the walls as well. See there, Isaac. You can see 'em pokin' out through them dirt mounds." He nudged his friend and pointed. "Don't reckon I'd want to be out there firin' them outboard guns. Too exposed by half for me. Course I don't reckon I'd be much use on any gun crew with but one arm." This last was spoken quietly, almost under his breath.

As he had described, there were indeed what appeared to the men to be thirty-six-pounders in emplacements in a high embankment before the ramparts of the fort. And the ramparts themselves fairly bristled with smaller guns — likely eighteen-pounders, they decided — as the little sloop Talbot used sailed easily by, throwing up spray from the light chop only to have it whisked away by the fresh breeze. The fifteen-star flag flew from a tall mast just inside the massive walls. Except for Jared, who had seen the fort countless times and, in fact, been through it more than once with Major

Armistead, the Fort's commander, all hands on the little sloop were rapt with the imposing structure.

"I reckon you coves can see it ain't just a wall with some cannon set on it; that fort is built in the shape of a star. See there, you can see some of the points pokin' out right 'round the whole end here. They ain't gonna be much what can get past that place, I'll tell you!" Talbot gestured at the high stone and masonry walls that did indeed resemble the shape of a star.

He eased the sloop up some, making the big mains'l shiver as the wind fluked further to the east. Slowed, he turned his eyes to the impressive structure on which Baltimore depended for its protection. He had to raise his voice to be heard over the flogging of the mains'l. "The guns facin' toward Fells can reach over there easy as kiss my hand and, on the other side, they likely could hit anything tryin' to get into Ridgely's Cove, I'd warrant. And there's a pair of smaller forts — more like batteries — just round there." He pointed again to the north, back the way they had come. "You seen 'em when we cleared the point outta Ridgely's. That first one — the one with the high brick walls and the barracks building — was what they're callin' Fort Covington." He paused, seeing a questioning look on Jake's face and anticipated the question. "Aye, Jake, that's the one you seen from the cove, and further in 'tween that one and McHenry is Babcock. That's only a little fellow — reckon they've only got six or so guns in her, but they's all pointin' into the harbor so, whatever the lads at McHenry cain't fire on, they can. Pretty smart settin' up like that, you ask me." Jared smiled at his mates, pulled the tiller over to make the sloop bear off some, and sent the little boat again flying through the harbor.

Everywhere they looked the American seamen saw a bustle of activity; gangs of men digging redoubts, dragging guns large and small to strategic locations along the waterfront, and noticeable numbers of troops in uniform drilling — marching and countermarching — to the shouted orders of their commanders. They were impressed.

"What a difference from them poor souls down to Washington, eh, Isaac? Why these folks here look as though they might actually fight if the British show up. And seein' what's goin' on yonder, I, for one, surely hope they do. Might be a right fine scrap!" Jack Clements' smile grew broader as he watched the preparations ashore. He scratched the head of his big dog who was leaning contentedly against the bulwark of the sloop completely unmindful of the motion and the spray. Carronade seemed less interested than his human counterparts in the activity on the beach and was quite happy just being with Jack and Isaac.

As they rounded the end of Whetstone Point and its huge fort, they could see similar hustle and bustle on Fells Point and a small fleet of gunboats moored along the shoreline. Isaac noticed them first.

"Them gunboats yonder — they yours too, Jared?"

"Reckon so, Isaac, now that the commodore's not here. Them gunboats, and the ones back at Ridgely's, is about all the ships available to fight from the water. And I for one ain't lookin' forward to goin' up against what I hear the Royal Navy's got out on the Bay. Commodore Rodgers told me afore he run off to Washington that we was it should the British try to sail into the harbor. Course, I reckon the shore guns'll be some help." The big man smiled ruefully as he thought of even a fleet of gunboats taking on the might of the British Chesapeake Squadron.

"What about them yonder, Jared? Looks to me like a couple of frigates 'long the shore there just outside the gunboats. I reckon they'd be able to help out — not that we'd need 'em!" Jake pointed out what indeed appeared to be several large men-of-war as well as a couple of sloops tied alongside a pier at Fells Point. He smiled at his remark, as if hearing it pointed up its obvious bravado. He returned his arm to its resting place on the bulwark and looked expectantly at Talbot.

"Aye, need 'em indeed! That one closer in — that's the frigate *Java*. The one Commodore Perry's takin' command of when she's done buildin' and fittin' out. Only problem with her is that on account of her not bein' finished, they never put her guns aboard. No, sir, they got them spread all over the city — and manned by sailors. So she's not gonna be much help if'n it comes to that. An' I don't reckon Perry'll do anything to change that when he finally gets hisself back here. Rodgers himself had a bunch of them guns set up on the hill above the city. Said the only ones he trusted to man 'em proper was his sailors and the ones come with Perry from New York. Them two smaller ones on the next pier are the navy sloops *Ontario* and *Erie*. They're done building and fittin' out, but they ain't goin' nowhere real soon." Jared stopped talking as he watched the shoreline for a place to land his sloop.

"Isaac: you wanna get yourself forward there and standby with a line. Looks like a spot we can tie up right yonder at that dock there. Jack, you can get ready to hand the mains'l when I tell you, and Jake, you handle the stern line." Assignments for landing made, Talbot concentrated on working the sloop through the heavy traffic of rowboats, small sloops, and a good-sized merchant brig heading out. All of the small boats were loaded either with men or materiel; some had large stacks of boxes and baskets piled so high on their decks as to cause concern over their stability. Jake commented on the merchantman.

"I surely hope that cove knows what he's headin' for out yonder. I don't reckon he'll make it much past the point without runnin' afoul of some Royal Navy vessel. What the hell do you s'pose he's thinkin', Jared?"

"I don't reckon he's gonna . . . mind your head there, I'm comin' 'round now . . . like I was sayin', I don't figger he's plannin' on leavin' the Patapsco. Probably headin' out to Sparrows or North Point with some o' the Army's gear. That or figgerin' to run up toward the Elk River and get himself outta the way for when the fightin' starts." He directed his full attention on the landing and, with a skill born of a lifetime of handling vessels large and small, brought the little sloop easily alongside the dock, giving the orders to drop sails and heave the lines just as she coasted in, gently nudging the pilings.

"You lads can sail with me anytime; that was right fine. Don't know what I expected what with you gents bein' captains an' not used to actually handlin' lines an' doin' sailors' work!" He winked at Jake, a broad grin splitting his face.

"Hey, Jack. Lookee there. Ain't that the self-same pier we come into back in the year '12 — you remember — on the *Glory*." Isaac was hauling down the sloop's jib, but looking beyond it to the next dock now three deep with gunboats secured alongside. What had caught his attention was the four or five privateers also moored there. They were the same sharp-built schooners that had given Fells Point the reputation of being a "nest of pirates," according to the English press.

Clements stopped putting gaskets on the furled mains'l long enough to look where his friend was pointing. "Aye, I reckon it is, Isaac. An' there's the Anchor an' Owl Coffee House, right over yonder. You 'member, Isaac. That's the place where Cap'n Smalley and them others met with the owners when we come in to settle up our prize shares." Seeing the privateers, apparently suffering from the blockade just as were the merchant vessels and Navy men-of-war, Jack got a distant look in his eyes as he recalled the day, sitting on the foredeck of the private armed vessel *Glory*, he made the decision to join the "frigate navy and do some real fightin'."

"They's sure been a lot of water pass under the keel since then, by God, Isaac. And it ain't been two years yet. Seems like a lot longer than that — gettin' sent into that damned *Chesapeake* frigate and bein' caught up by the Royal Navy and locked away in that pest hole on Melville Island. Makes me wonder what them other coves is up to. You remember, Robert and Tim, an' ol' Sam Johnson . . . and Mr. Blanchard. Wonder what become o' him? Wonder if'n he ever got hisself promoted to lieutenant." Clements voice trailed off and his eyes took on a far away look; he was deep within himself as he recalled some of the men he sailed and fought the British with in *Chesapeake* just a year and more previous.

Jared, helping him with the sail, didn't interrupt and finished securing the big sail alone. After he saw the former bosun shake his head and look around him as though he were suddenly aware of his surroundings, Talbot jumped with surprising ease and grace up to the pier deck and turned back to the sloop. "You lads comin' with me, or are you just gonna set there and take your ease?"

"Aye, Jared. We're with you. Where're we goin'?" Isaac clambered up to the pier with less grace than his acting commodore, but Talbot had over a foot of height on the former topman. Scooping up the big dog with a strength well-hidden in his lanky frame, Jack pushed Carronade up and followed him immediately. Jared stuck out a hand and pulled Tate up from where he had been standing on the sloop's main boom. The dog waited, taking the opportunity to cast a look of unfeigned indignation at his master over the way he had been unceremoniously boosted onto the pier.

"Reckon the tide'll be in some by the time we get back. Won't be such a climb for you little coves!" Jared couldn't resist the opportunity and the remark was taken in stride by his smaller companions as they set off toward the head of the harbor, Carronade trotting along in their wake leaving startled looks and retreating citizens astern.

The waterfront was packed; men in a variety of uniforms and men whose clothes indicated they were clearly unused to physical labor worked and sweated side by side with dock workers, white and black, and sailors. Masters worked alongside of their slaves. Horses pulled carts loaded with boxes and crates, many marked as ammunition. Some ladies — obviously from a higher social strata than might be expected by their current employment — prepared food and drink, while others helped hand it out to the sweating workers.

"Seems like they's all lending a hand, here. And looks like they's glad to do it." Isaac and Jake stopped to allow a heavy cart pulled by a pair of mules to cross in front of them, and Jake looked around, impressed by the effort.

"Aye, these folks shoulda been down to Washington. Reckon it mighta come out some different, by the Almighty!"

Jared stopped alongside his fellow captains. "Every now and again they's a British ship what puts its bowsprit into the mouth of the river; seems to inspire the folks to lend a hand here. Course, havin' all that militia showin' up from everywhere under the sun helps give 'em some confidence. Makes 'em think they got a chance even if the damn British show up like they done down to Washington. And I reckon they do, by God; I reckon they do."

The four continued up the road along the wharf side, stopping frequently to give way to carts, wagons, and drilling soldiers. At one point, they passed an open area and heard clearly the cry "Board 'em, lads. Board!" Responding to the orders was a force of about one hundred seamen, clutching muskets and running across the field. Their bare feet kicked up clouds of choking dust which, once in the air, stuck to their sweating bodies and cloaked them in layers of red dirt.

"Those sailors yonder? They'll likely be Commodore Rodgers men — or mayhaps Perry's. Since they ain't no vessel for 'em to ship on, the Committee of Vigilance and Safety assigned 'em to train and act like army or militia coves. Reckon they're right glad it ain't a permanent assignment!" Jared chuckled, both at the ill-fortune of the sailors drilling and his own good fortune for having a fleet of gunboats to occupy his time.

Suddenly, a clamor went up behind the flotillamen. A mounted civilian, forcing his way through the throngs of people, was bellowing for them to "Clear the way!" As he drew abreast, Jack put his hand on the horse's bridle and looked up at the rider. "What's your hurry? These folks is doin' they's best to get ready to fight the enemy — maybe save your arse, should it come to that. You got no call to push 'em around and ride through 'em like you're doin'."

"Leggo my bridle, you damn fool. I got to get word to Commodore Rodgers that the damn Royal Navy is showin' at the mouth of the river. They's more 'an a couple of ships this time — and big ones on top of it. Now stand outta the way!" He kicked out viciously at Jack's midsection. The seaman stepped back, allowing the booted foot to flail at the air, and let go of the bridle; the messenger rode off, spurring his horse into a gallop as the road in front cleared. The men watched as the horse and rider disappeared around the corner of a large building.

"I don't know what that cove's so worked up about; the damn British been showin' up out there with one ship or another for a month an' more now. Ain't like it's something new. An' I'd reckon that Commodore Rodgers, if'n he's back by now, likely knows all about it. He's set up a whole run of signal towers and people to man 'em all the way from here down to the Potomac. Been reports bein' brought in every day by the folks live over on the Bay. Firin' 'alert' guns and lightin' fires to let the people know where the ships is passin'." Talbot was stepping along now as though he had suddenly decided on a destination and the men, especially Jake and Isaac, almost had to run to keep up with his long-legged strides.

Jack Clements, sweating freely as he maintained Jared's pace, spoke between gulps of the dust-laden air. "I ain't seen anyone in a panic, Jared. These folks ain't actin' like they was gonna have the fight of their lives facin' 'em any minute now; no sir: they're goin' about their business like this was what they done every day. Not like them ones down to Washington. My Gawd! Them ones, what they was of 'em left by the time the British showed up, was runnin' every which way they might. Didn't have no idea what was actin' or what they oughtta be doin'. Just plain scared and showin' it!" Clements shook his head in disgust as he recalled the horror of the British Marines marching into the Capitol unopposed, buildings and homes left abandoned as the citizenry fled in abject terror.

"Aye, Jack. These folks here? Why they's full disgusted with the way their 'cousins' down to the Capital behaved. 'Shameful' they're callin' it. Militia units and volunteers from all around the area started showin' up here soon's the word reached us of what had happened in Washington. Had plenty of people, just didn't have no one to lead 'em — least 'til Commodore Rodgers and Cap'n Perry showed up. And they come with more'n five hundred sailors. Rodgers is the one, though. He's the one what figgered out how to defend the city. You lads're gonna meet him right quick, I 'spect." Jared never slowed the pace and soon conversation became next to impossible for the shorter-legged sailors; they gasped and panted and struggled to keep up. Even Clements became silent, needing all his breath to stay alongside Talbot. The heat was again oppressive, with little breeze and a palpable humidity; the sky had become white, the sun just a bright spot in the high overcast.

The road they followed took them up a hill and the sweating, dust-covered sailors were greeted by even dirtier, hotter men — some stripped to the waist — wrestling long guns into firing positions on platforms behind the embankment that had quite obviously been hand built. The guns already emplaced pointed to the east rather than toward the water, and caused Clements, when he had caught his breath, to comment.

"Somebody must be 'spectin' trouble from the shore side, the way these guns is pointin'." He turned and looked out over the landscape and saw little but a few houses and the Philadelphia Road disappearing into the shimmering heat.

"Aye, that's exactly what Commodore Rodgers had 'em set up for. He ain't as sure as some that the Brits'll only attack from the water side; he figgers it'd be just as easy for 'em to come down from yonder with army or marine units. Oh . . . there's the commodore right over there. Come on, lads. I'll introduce you to him." Jared, not the least out of breath from their walk, but sweating and grime covered like the others, turned and strode to the far end of the redoubt where John Rodgers was directing a group of sailors in the mounting of a long eighteen-pounder. He ignored the approaching group, maintaining his focus on the task at hand. The four new arrivals stood silently and watched as the barrel of the cannon, suspended from a crude but effective lifting frame, was gently lowered into position and Rodgers, standing behind it, sighted down its length. Satisfied, he stood erect and greeted the flotilla commander.

"New men, Captain Talbot? We surely can use all hands for what I reckon is comin', by the Almighty!" All of a sudden, Rodgers noticed the huge gray dog who had found a tiny patch of shade. He had sat down to wait for the men, his tongue lolling from his open mouth.

"Hell's bells! Where'd that beast come from? I never seen a dog — I collect he *is* a dog — that big!"

"Oh that's just Cap'n Clements' dog, Commodore. He seems to go everywhere with Clements, scarin' folks what don't know him. He ain't a bad beast and he ain't got no love 't'all for the damn British." Talbot pointed at Jack as he spoke; the dog remained motionless and completely unconcerned with the attention. Rodgers walked over to him and, after letting the dog have a sniff of his hand, patted his head and spoke quietly to him.

"Commodore, these here men're from the gunboats down to the Patuxent. Just got here a week ago from Washington. Cap'n Isaac Biggs and this razee cove here, he's Jake Tate, part of Isaac's crew from his sloop. And you met Cap'n Jack Clements already."

The commodore returned his attention to the men in time to see Tate smile at Jared's comparing his lost arm to a cut-down warship. Jake extended his left hand to the commodore. Each of the others shook hands with Rodgers in turn and, while he wiped his dripping face with a piece of dirty cloth, the commodore questioned each about their backgrounds — the dog, for the moment, forgotten.

The men noticed that of all the workers at the site, sailors included, Rodgers was the only one who maintained some form of uniform; his shirt, though sodden and filthy, remained buttoned and his britches were still tight around his knees. His white stockings were torn and grimy, and his shoes were covered with dirt. His blue jacket, with its gold epaulettes shining dully in the flat light, was draped over the barrel of a nearby eighteen-pounder. He sized up the men before him with hard, though bleary, eyes.

"A sloop, eh? You wouldn't be the skipper of the black-hulled sloop I was hearin' about some months back, would you? Made quite a noise, that one did; even heard about it up to Philadelphia." He addressed Jack Clements, who beamed at the recognition.

"Aye. And black sails as well. That'd be me — and Isaac here. I reckon we made pests of ourselves to the Royal Navy. I'd warrant they was some glad to hear they was burned with the commodore's gunboats just afore Washington." Jack's eyes crinkled with his smile. "Isaac here, he seen that Royal Navy admiral — what was his name, Isaac? Oh, right, Cockburn, it was — sit there in a cutter and watch the whole damn flotilla go up in flames. But they was fired by us, not them." The smile was gone as Clements recalled the tragedy of the lost gunboats and their handy little sloops.

"Well, you surely was helpin' the cause with them. And for that, I thankee most kindly. We could use a few of those sloops now." Rodgers scratched his chin thoughtfully and looked at Talbot. "You know, I reckon there might still be a right handy vessel available. Cove named Ferguson over at Fells had one he offered to me afore I went down to Washington. When you get back down there, Jared, look him up and see if he still wants to hire it out. Be right useful to have something that can swim well for carryin' messages and checkin' on the progress the enemy is makin' towards the city."

"Well, Isaac, if'n that vessel's still around, I reckon that puts an answer on what you'll be doin' — and Jack too. You can decide who'll skipper, but with the men we got available, I don't imagine it'll be a problem finding a few bodies to fill out a crew for you." Talbot looked back at the man responsible for the defense of the city. "What you figger we gonna do with the gunboats, Commodore? I still got twenty an' more of 'em 'tween Fells and Ridgely's Coves. And crews to man 'em, even with half my men mannin' guns at McHenry. And that shot and powder you had sent down to us is all loaded aboard and ready to go."

"We likely won't need all of 'em, Jared. But I want 'em standing ready on both sides of McHenry to support the batteries there. And while I'm thinkin' on it, you're going to have to send some men — likely forty-five or fifty should answer — up to the battery at Fort Covington. Something's laid most of Addison's men low and I understand that even Captain Addison is sick as well. That battery could be real helpful if the enemy tries to get past McHenry." Rodgers paused, thinking. He cast a glance down the hill toward the harbor and suddenly slapped his leg with his open hand.

"Oh yes. It almost slipped my mind. On the Fells Point side, I want you to rig a boom — one just like is on the west side of the fort — between Whetstone Point and Fells. You may not have the time to make it as perfect or fancy as that one, but we need something that'll answer there. You'll need to have a gunboat tend it on account of it's real likely that there'll be a need to get some vessels out from time to time." While he spoke, Rodgers had diagrammed in the dirt how he wanted the boom rigged. His eyes pierced the acting commodore of the flotilla and, seeing the big sailor nod, he went on. "Anything else you think might answer down there, go ahead and do. Use my authority if'n you need it."

He looked at the other three. "It was a pleasure to meet you lads and I can only wish you good luck now. Send a runner up here if you find that sloop of Ferguson's, to let me know. I imagine I'll find a use for it — and you — afore this mess is done with." Without further comment, Rodgers gave Carronade a welcome scratch on his ears and returned his attention to the gun platforms; the interview was over.

Jared called after him. "By the bye, Commodore. Something else you might be wantin' to know; one of my gunboats come in the other day with some news of a scrap over to the Eastern Shore — somewhere near Tolchester, I recollect. Had quite a fight with the militia over there, and got sent packin, they done, by God! Just a week an' more ago it were, I'd reckon."

"Aye, on Caulk's farm." Rodgers looked at Talbot and again wiped his forehead. "Heard about it myself. Lord Peter Parker got himself killed, I heard, into the bargain. I surely won't be sorry to have him gone from these waters! Been raidin' and destroyin' farms and crops all up and down the Eastern Shore. He even sailed the *Menelaus* right up to North Point not a month ago. Didn't land, but had a cutter out sailin' right around the point. But that fight you heard about — that was nothin' but a diversionary effort. Tryin' to make us think they were going to attack in force, I'd warrant. That and keep the militia over there busy. Don't signify, I'd wager; they'll be comin' here — not over yonder." He turned his attention again to the waiting laborers.

Suddenly, Rodgers whirled around and called to Talbot. "Say, Jared, where's Commodore Barney got to? He down at the waterfront with the gunboats? Tell that ornery old dog I send my compliments on a fine job over to Bladensburg. Wasn't for him and his lads I reckon the enemy woulda marched into the capital even easier than they done. His sailors and Marines were the only force that inflicted any casualties on 'em afore they got to Washington."

"The commodore caught a bullet at that very fight, Commodore. 'Cordin' to these men what was with him there, he lost a fair share of his blood and was took prisoner by the Royal Marines. Admiral Cockburn and General Ross theirselves took him. Reckon he's either dead or in some British ship as a prisoner by now."

Rodgers made a sour face, shook his head, and muttering "Damn! We're losin' good men all too often in this scrap," turned back to the work force as they made ready to lift another cannon barrel into position.

Talbot looked at the sky, studying the change for a moment. "Look's like they's gonna be some weather comin' in sooner than later, lads. Let's get us back down to the Point and find that sloop the commodore was talkin' about."

Indeed, the sky had gone from the bright white of the morning to a dull pewter color; the beginnings of puffy white clouds were showing to the northwest and the day seemed even more oppressive than it had. As they started down the back side of the gun emplacement, a rider, who had quite obviously come some distance, reined his lathered horse to an abrupt halt and jumped off, handing the reins to Isaac without a look back. He ran up the hill and made straight for Rodgers.

"Heave to a moment, lads. Let's see what this is all about." Talbot stopped and walked halfway back up the embankment, while Isaac, a startled look still in place, remained holding the horse he had been handed so unceremoniously. Carronade, who had left his shady spot to join Jack and the others, sat down again, watching the horse which was pawing the ground nervously and keeping his own weather eye on the dog.

It was only a minute of two before Jared was back and, stopping briefly where his men stood, said only, "I'll tell you on the way down. Let's make sail."

The four walked at Talbot's pace — easier going downhill for Isaac and Jake — in silence for some time, as Jared digested what he had heard. The men knew better than to badger him; he would tell them what he had found out when he was ready. Occasionally they heard him mutter "Damn!" and they noticed that his good eye continually darted toward the harbor and beyond as they made their way through the still-busy gangs of men preparing gun batteries, redoubts, and various other defenses to forestall an invasion.

Without preamble and, in a quiet voice, Talbot spoke. "Word is, they's fifty and more ships less'n a days sail down the Bay. That cove what rode in was from the alert tower just south of Annapolis. Less'n the breeze quits all together — or comes in more from the north — Rodgers figgers they'll be at the mouth of the Patapsco by noon on the eleventh. By Gawd! That's only two days from now. Lookouts said a few smaller vessels — he didn't know what they was — sailed by last night, so it's right likely they'll be out there by now even. I'd warrant they'll be scouts, lookin' for a likely spot to land they's troops — if landin' is what they got in mind.

"Commodore's sent a messenger down to some gen'l named Stricker what's got three thousand and more men — infantry, I collect — down on the Philadelphia Road. Told 'em to get underway toward North Point." Talbot smacked a fist into his open palm. "Damn! I reckon this thing is just about ready to . . ." He didn't finish.

"Troops ashore at North Point! They's here, by God. Grab up your weapons!" A black man was running hard up the hill and shouting the warning to all within earshot as he passed.

"They couldn't be landing already. There wasn't nothin' but some small vessels spotted. Wasn't big enough to carry any troops, by God," Jared called after the running man, but he never even broke his stride. "We better get ourselves down there quick as ever we can." And he picked up the pace; again Isaac and Jake had to trot to keep up.

CHAPTER TWENTY-FIVE

A t Fells Point confusion reigned supreme. Without question, the panicked messenger had already passed through the crowds still furiously engaged in fortifying the waterfront and, in some quarters, the pace had been increased tenfold, while in others, men — and women — stood in groups shouting at one another, gesticulating wildly, and casting nervous glances toward the mouth of the harbor, as though they expected momentarily to see the entire British fleet sailing hell bent for Baltimore with guns blazing.

The four sailors pushed their way through the throngs, stepping over crates left where they landed when the word of the enemy's arrival had reached those moving them. Those who didn't move immediately did so quickly once they spotted Carronade. Jared was glad to see that most of his gunboats were crewed; shot and powder had been brought on deck and the guns released from their confinement along the bulwarks. Telling his companions to wait for him, he ran over to one of the vessels and gave instructions to its captain. Only a few of his words made it through the din of the confused throngs on the pier, but it was clear that he was passing on the orders from the commodore.

". . . and rig it with chains and control lines so it can be hauled back if need be."

In an apparent response to an unheard question, he said, "Aye, use spare masts, trees, spars . . . whatever you can find. And get it done now!" He started to leave, then turned with a further comment. "And be sure you rig it inshore of the boats. We may need to get underway quick-like, and waitin' for someone to open the boom won't answer." He stepped back up to the pier, confident his men would carry out his instructions quickly and properly. They were flotillamen, after all!

"Jared, if the commodore's concerned about the British comin' right in here, why not put a few of them merchants across there in front of the boom? Anchor 'em fore 'n' aft and run lines bow to stern right through there." Isaac pointed at the widest part of the opening between Fells Point — actually a little beyond Fells Point — and the tip of Whetstone Point with its star-shaped fort. Jack added his own thought.

"Aye, Jared. A right fine idea from young Isaac. And while they is tryin' to figger a way through the anchored ships, that gun battery yonder can pound 'em into matchwood." Clements' eyes were brighter than his usual good humor made them as he thought of the hammering that would be offered to any vessel unfortunate enough to be stopped in front of the Lazaretto Battery and within range of the long eighteen-pounders in McHenry.

Talbot looked at the dozen and more merchant vessels — mostly brigs, but a few larger and several smaller coasting schooners — tied to the quay and anchored just offshore. They had been trapped in the blockade and their long idleness was evident; rigging was slack and paint peeled from the sides and spars.

It was one in particular — leaning against the quaywall at a drunken angle, clearly sinking at the dock — that gave him an idea. Her yards hung all ahoo; her sails drooped from the gaskets, and the absence of any sign of tar on her rig gave abundant testimony to her forced captivity and apparent abandonment. He scratched his beard and thought about the suggestion. But only for a moment.

"Aye, that would answer handily. But we'll sink 'em. Water's not deep enough there to cover 'em completely and ain't no one gonna sail through there with half a dozen hulks settin' on the bottom. Good idea, lads."

As he set off to implement his plan, the first drops of rain splattered into the dusty ground and instantly disappeared into the dry dirt, leaving only a wet spot as the mark of their passing. The drops were large and widely spaced, but a glance at the sky told any who looked that this was barely the beginning. The puffy white clouds that had been superimposed on the pewter sky to the northwest now towered aloft and had spread over much of the northern sky. The stillness and oppressive air that fed the damp heat of scant minutes ago was replaced with a gentle but cooling breeze that the seamen knew would grow into a half gale in no time at all. Lightning was beginning to streak the darkening sky, shooting from one cloud to another and, occasionally, down to the ground well to the north of the city. Over the noise of the preparations for an invasion one could pick up the distant and threatening rumble of thunder. It sounded like gunfire far out to sea and some of the milling throng who heard it — the more skittish of the citizens of Baltimore — cried out that the firing had already begun. They were 'shushed' quickly by their more level-headed comrades.

Shortly, the rain began to fall in earnest. The large drops quickly gave way to closely-spaced, smaller ones which increased in intensity and stung the skin where the growing wind whipped the rain horizontal.

At first, it had felt good — cooling overheated bodies, washing off the dust and dirt from their labors — then the air cooled, the rain and wind intensified and many, suddenly cold, and long-exhausted and aching from their labors, sought refuge in the nearby buildings and vessels. Some of the younger men, however, continued pushing crates and bales into position, unconcerned with the rising storm.

Isaac, Jake, and Jack stepped into the doorway of a warehouse and watched as the harbor became first riffled and pocked with raindrops, then stirred to small waves as the wind increased. As the rain became a torrent, the rising waves were beat down and the surface of the harbor took on the appearance of a boiling cauldron. The vessels secured to the pier and the quay leaned shoreward as the wind grew and pushed steadily against their rigs; smaller boats bobbed against the pilings and stones, tugging at their lines with a ferocity matched only by the intensity of the storm.

"Carronade! Get your arse in here, you fool! Get outta the storm." Jack, from the shelter of the building, saw the big animal sitting unconcerned on the quay where the men had last been. His head was lifted into the wind and his nose worked, smelling the clean air. His fur was soaked already, the water running down his back in rivulets. His eyes were closed against the ferocity of the driving rain, his only concession to the storm.

When he heard Jack calling him, he looked around at the men

sheltering in the open doorway; he pricked up his ears at the sound, but remained sitting in the now muddy street.

"Probably feels right good — that cool rain — I'd warrant. He was some hot when we climbed up to where the commodore was at." Jake smiled at his friend and looked back at Carronade, who had resumed his earlier posture.

The driving rain and lashing wind continued for half a glass and, by the time it had abated, all the workers had sought whatever shelter they could find. However, within minutes of the storm's passing, most were again outside, shifting the bales and crates, loading the carts and wagons, and tending to the preparations for the defense of their city. The flotillamen were now ashore, seeking spars, rope, and chain, already at work constructing the boom which, ultimately, would be stretched across the water to Whetstone Point.

Jared appeared from another building; his boots made sucking noises as he splashed through the morass left by the rain, and he was trailed by a gaunt, grizzled man wearing an unbuttoned black coat and a well-worn porkpie hat. The sullen remnants of the rain dripped off the brim and, unnoticed, down the man's neck. His face was covered by a scraggly gray beard which reached well below the frayed collar of his none-too-clean shirt. His dangling wrists stuck out of his sleeves like yardarms protruding from their brailed canvas.

"This here's Mister Ferguson, gents. He said the offer he made to Commodore Rodgers still stands. Sloop's right over to the next pier, and seems in fine shape. Said we could take her soon's we're ready to." Jared turned to Mr. Ferguson, whose head had been bobbing in agreement like a bird seeking worms from the morning soil. "This here's Isaac Biggs and Jack Clements; likely one of 'em'll be cap'n of your vessel — leastways 'til the Royal Navy gets sent packin'!"

Isaac took the proffered hand, noting it felt like taking hold of a bundle of sticks; he looked at Mr. Ferguson and was momentarily taken aback by the expressionless, sunken, staring eyes looking back at him, ringed with dark smudges and topped with bushy gray brows that ran in one continuous line across the man's weathered brow. The men moved off to the pier where the sloop was moored, as Jared gave orders to some men to begin moving the merchant vessels into the void off the pier. The sullen drizzle continued from the low clouds, while to the southeast the men could see the back side of the storm which was now thrashing the mouth of the Patapsco and North Point.

The sloop was indeed a handy little vessel; her hull and decks seemed well-caulked. Her bowsprit poked up into the wet sky at a rakish angle and both a jib and a flying jib were neatly secured to it. The rigging looked well-tarred and taut; obviously, this was not one of those which had suffered forced confinement.

Must be right quick since she's likely been sailed right through the blockade. Probably be able to outrun most of what's out there, Isaac thought as he studied the lines of the little sloop. Aloud he said, "I'd warrant this'll answer just fine, Jared." Isaac's seaman's eye had taken in the whole vessel quickly, sizing up her sailing abilities and seaworthiness in a glance. "Won't take more'n a handful to manage her — even if the weather pipes up. Reckon Jack and Jake an' me, 'long with one or two others could handle her just right." Clements and Tate nodded their agreement.

"All right then, Mister Ferguson. You made yourself a deal. I reckon Commodore Rodgers'll see to your fee quick as ever he might — soon's I let him know we've come to terms. Why don't you show Cap'n Biggs and the others through her while I see to a few other chores I got to take care of.

"Isaac, when you are ready, you lads can bring her over to Ridgley's and I'll grab a couple of lads off'n one of the gunboats to help me bring my vessel around. Shouldn't be more'n a half a glass behind you." With that, Talbot strode off back the way they'd come, and Isaac, Clements, and Tate stepped aboard the sloop with Mr. Ferguson.

By the time the sloop was anchored off the quay at the gunboat docks in Ridgley's Cove, the weather had eased; the rain was stopped entirely and, while the sky remained leaden and the wind easterly, there was no sign of any immediate threat from the heavens. The gunboats bobbed gently to their anchor rodes or were secured to the pier; the men busily prepared the vessels for what most of them now assumed would be an invasion by the British Chesapeake fleet. Hammering and shouting carried well past the entrance to the cove. The comments and bravado that floated over the dark water indicated that these crews also had heard of both the British ships that had appeared at the mouth of the river and those that were sailing up from the south. The men welcomed the challenge, frustrated by their forced idleness.

As Isaac and his short crew rowed ashore from the sloop, they could see two well-dressed gentlemen standing on the quay, deep in conversation.

"Them two must be lost, bein' they's down here. Mayhaps they's wantin' to sign into one of the gunboats! What d'ya think about that, Isaac?" Jake laughed at the incongruity of such fine gentlemen mixing with the likes of the gunboat sailors who populated the docks of Ridgley's Cove.

"Aye. They look like they belong over to Fells Point with them other dandies. Helpin' load wagons and jackassin' crates around." Clements studied the pair for a moment as their boat approached the stone steps on the quaywall.

"Would one of you gentlemen be Captain Jared Talbot, by any chance?" the taller of the two men called out as the boat carrying the trio — and Carronade — bumped gently against the steps and was secured with a short length of hemp. Led by the big dog, who leaped ashore with sure-footed grace, the men stepped out of the boat and made their way up the slippery, weed-covered stair.

Jack watched, amused, as Carronade's head cleared the top of the steps and the two men stepped quickly out of his path. The dog stood looking down at his master and the others; his tail, throwing little droplets of water from their recent drenching, described circles in the still-wet air. He paid little heed to the well-dressed men who by now had given him noticeable searoom.

"Not on your life, mate. He oughtta be 'long right quick though. Shouldn't be more 'an . . ." Jack, the first onto the quay, didn't finish his thought. Jake, just stepping out of the boat, pointed toward Whetstone Point and the vessel just coming into view around its seaward end.

"Ain't that Jared's boat just turnin' the Fort now? Sure looks like her."

Isaac turned and looked; they all did. "Aye," he agreed. "Reckon that'd be him right yonder." He looked at the two gentlemen whose glances shifted back and forth between the dog and the new arrivals. "Who might you gents be, if'n I might ask?"

"My name is Skinner — Colonel John Skinner." The taller of the two, the one who had earlier inquired as to the identity of Jared Talbot, extended his hand to Isaac. He kept a wary eye on Jack's dog. "I am the Prisoner of War Exchange Agent here in Baltimore.

And this is Mister Frank Key, of Georgetown. He is a lawyer in that city. He — and I — need transportation out to the British fleet."

His comment, offered quite off-handedly, caught the men's attention. Seeing their surprised looks, he quickly went on to explain. His manner continued to be matter-of-fact, as though seeking transport to the enemy fleet was a daily occurrence.

"He has been engaged by friends of Doctor William Beanes of Upper Marlboro to secure the good doctor's release from the English. He, by all accounts, is being held on Admiral Cochrane's flagship, HMS *Tonnant*. Why, we have little idea, but Mister Key and I must meet with the admiral and effect his parole. Both he and I agree that sailing into the enemy fleet would be less hazardous in a vessel which could not be mistaken for a warship. I was told that Captain Talbot had such a vessel here in Ridgley's Cove and, it would appear, have mistaken your sloop for his." Colonel Skinner, having completed his explanation, fell silent and watched as what he now knew was Talbot's sloop made for her berth on the pier. Covertly, he tried to keep an eye on the dog as well.

Isaac, also watching, responded. "Likely he'll be happy to oblige you, Colonel, but you'll have to put your question to him. I ain't in charge here."

"Colonel, you seem some nervous about ol' Carronade there. Less'n you're British, you ain't got no cause for worry from him. He ain't likely to bother you at all. Don't much take to anything British, though." Jack was absently scratching the big dog's head as the dog closed his eyes and leaned against his master's hip. The colonel didn't appear to be completely convinced, but smiled thinly at Clements' effort to put him at ease.

CHAPTER TWENTY-SIX

B y the time Colonel Skinner and Lawyer Key had reiterated their need to Jared, their tankards had been emptied and refilled. The ale house was quite full and more than a little noisy; now that most of the work on the gunboats was completed, the flotillamen had found the establishment a convenient place to gather and swap stories. Naturally, the volume of conversation rose with the volume of ale consumed, and the colonel, at the end of his story, had been forced to shout just to compete with the boisterous sailors.

"Well, it's a certainty we ain't gonna send you out there in a gunboat; don't reckon you'd last a minute without you bein' blown to matchwood soon's they spotted you — even with a truce flag a-flyin'. Them coves out there likely seen more 'an a few of 'em out on the Bay over the last year and more! An' it's a good bet they'd take a truce flag as a ruse. So I reckon you're gonna have to use either my vessel or the one Isaac just brought in." Talbot thought for a moment, then looked at Biggs and Jack. "How'd you feel 'bout sailin' out to the British fleet, Isaac? I don't 'spect they'd be likely to fire on your sloop quick-like — long as you had that white flag showin'. Be right plain she's not armed inta the bargain. Might even be able to get some idea of what's actin' with 'em. That would be right useful to Commodore Rodgers if'n you can get back in here and tell him afore the British show up."

"I can surely sail out there, Jared. Ain't a problem in that. But what makes these fine gentlemen so sure the Brits'll just let us sail right up to 'em, tip our hats, and sail away with the good doctor? I sure don't have any wish to wind up in the Royal Navy again! Once was enough for me!"

"My thoughts exactly, Isaac. I ain't got no plan on spendin' time up to Melville Island again. Was right about this time last year you got us out of that hell-hole, by the Almighty. Ain't that so, Jake?" Clements' normally cheery grin had been replaced by a dour expression at the recollection of their experiences after the *Chesapeake* disaster.

Tate just shook his head; his right sleeve, tied off with a piece of tarred hemp, provided ample testimony to his own feelings about spending time in a British prison.

"The English have a reputation of being fair-minded, particularly when it comes to prisoner exchange, and I would be most surprised should they not honor the flag of truce the vessel will be displaying." Key spoke up for the first time. "I witnessed their actions at Bladensburg, and I can assure you, they were most honorable in their treatment of any who were captured; civilians who were not involved were, for the most part, left alone as well." He paused. "Except for Doctor Beanes, that is. I can not for the life of me, understand why they felt it necessary to take him prisoner. He was not only treating Americans who fell at Bladensburg, but many of the British soldiers — and officers — as well. And the enemy used his home as a headquarters for their march on our capital. Their refusing to leave him to his task doesn't answer. No, sir, doesn't answer at all!"

"And you figger that just acause you show up on their doorstep, hat in hand, and askin' nice and proper, they're gonna just doff they's hats and turn him over to you and Colonel Skinner here. You got one of their officers to trade for him? Don't reckon they'd be much likely to make an exchange without they get somethin' into the bargain." Talbot remained skeptical of the outcome of the mission — one in which he was being asked to risk a vessel and crew.

The agent for prisoner exchange answered his concern. "As a matter of fact, Captain Talbot, we do have several British officers in our custody. Some were left behind, wounded at Bladensburg, and others fell, apparently from the heat, on their march out of the capital, and were left in Upper Marlboro — originally under the care of Doctor Beanes. Since most have fully — or nearly so — recovered from their various ordeals, I would expect they would be right glad to have some of them returned. So in answer to your question, no. We are most assuredly not going out to them empty-handed." Satisfied that he had successfully removed any doubts from Talbot's mind, Skinner sat back, finished his ale, and smiled at the flotilla commander.

"Well, that does put a little different slant on the wind most likely. How about it, Isaac? You reckon you could get these coves out there and not get you own self took back into the Royal Navy?"

Isaac nodded and glanced at Jack and his one-armed mate. Both offered nearly imperceptible nods of agreement. Carronade remained sleeping next to Jack, oblivious to the noise in the tavern, the conversation, and its implications.

"You mentioned you was at Bladensburg, Mister Key. Were you part of a militia unit there, or what?" Isaac focused on the lawyer with a look of innocent curiosity. Jake smiled inwardly, suspecting what was coming.

"As a matter of fact, Captain Biggs, I was assisting — in a civilian capacity — General Walter Smith's First Columbian Brigade. We consisted of over one thousand volunteers and militiamen and, while we were desperately short of both muskets and flints, many of our men fought and acquitted themselves honorably. When we finally had the opportunity to fight, that is." Key shook his head at his recollection of the confusion that had reigned supreme during the time immediately preceding the confrontation at Bladensburg. "We had been positioned at the Eastern Branch bridge in Washington by General Winder when his orders were countermanded by Secretary Monroe and the men were marched straight to Bladensburg.

"General Smith and I rode ahead to survey the fields and map the deployments of the units already there. But the battle had begun; advance units of the enemy's forces were already engaged with our army, under direct command of General Winder — who was quite obviously retreating under the assault." Key scowled and continued. "Many of our soldiers cut and run as soon as they took sight of the British regulars marching toward them. They were concerned about the well-being of their families outside of Bladensburg — some say rightly so — and felt their responsibility was to be with them. Others did stand and fight, but with the paucity of muskets, flints, and ball, were unable to hold for long against the apparently overwhelming force opposing them. One can not imagine the strength of the enemy at that battle without having experienced it first-hand." Key shook his head and made a sweeping gesture with both hands.

"General Smith and I were called back to Washington and reached there — I went to Georgetown, to my offices there, to safeguard my papers and personal property — shortly before the British marched into the city. By that time, most all had left and there was naught to do save move to safer ground."

"Aye, Mister Key. Isaac and Jake and me was there, right at the bridge outside of the village. Fact was, the men of Commodore Barney's flotilla was about the only ones what stood they's ground and fought. Wasn't 'til the teamsters run off with our ammunition wagons — followin' close on the heels of the militia and most of the army coves — and we was down to our last barrel of powder that the commodore ordered us to fall back. And he was shot, though some say not mortal, and we had to leave him to the mercy of the British. So, aye, sir. You can bet your boots that we knowed what was actin' there. And the way the militia performed they's duty." Clements fairly spat out his final words, his disgust at the rout ringing in the ears of the lawyer and agent for prisoner exchange.

The latter spoke up quickly, attempting to disarm a situation that had all the earmarks of undermining their quest for Doctor Beanes' release. "You lads were in Barney's flotilla? Down on the Patuxent? Why, the capture of those vessels was the very reason the British came so far up the river. You fine fellows and your gunboats surely had the British tied up in knots, by God! They risked a great deal by sailing into the Patuxent to destroy that fleet.

"Of course, had they not already been so close, they would never have marched on Washington. I know that from the very lips of General Ross himself, with whom I spoke concerning an exchange only a few days after they left the capital city. It was Admiral Cockburn, second-in-command of the naval forces, who convinced General Ross to march on to Washington. But they did not capture and burn the flotilla, and for that we are thankful, you may be assured."

"No, Colonel, it surely weren't them what burned the vessels; we done it our own selves! On the commodore's orders, and just to keep them bastards from capturing 'em — and . . ." Isaac was cut off by Clements who had jumped to his feet. He raised his voice substantially above the din to ensure the two gentlemen could miss none of his words.

"Heave to there! You tryin' to tell us it was Barney's — and us'n's — fault what made the damn British go burn down Washington? That just acause we let 'em chase us up the river? Is that what you're sayin'? First you try an' tell us the militia at Bladensburg was actin' good and proper, and now this? If'n you coves're hangin' on to them ideas, why, you can march right outta here quick as ever you like. Barney's men was the only ones what stood and fought after all them, what was s'posed to, run . . ." Jack started sputtering, he was so vexed. Both Skinner and Key remained seated, but clearly this was not going the way they had hoped. And suddenly the ale house seemed awfully quiet. Tate noticed more than a few flotillamen studying them intently.

Talbot had put a restraining hand on Jack's arm. "Ease her up there some, Jack. These coves ain't accusin' the flotilla — or the commodore — of setting the enemy on Washington. They know that ain't the fact at all. But I reckon everybody 'tween here and there knows full well about Bladensburg. The militia run off so fast the folks is callin' it the 'Bladensburg Races', by the Almighty. Ain't nothin' gonna change that." He studied both Key and Skinner with a look that had made grown men whimper; his hand had eased around behind his back. "Now let's us just all settle down and get back to the business of gettin' you gents out to the British fleet."

Clements sat as ordered and the noise in the ale house immediately returned to the level it had attained prior to Jack's outburst; the sailors realized there would be no fight — no excitement — and returned to their own shouted conversations while Talbot returned both his hands to the table and his tankard.

"I reckon we could get underway tonight — or first light tomorrow — if that'd suit, Colonel. I'd like to get some stores aboard, but I think we might get that done afore dark tonight with some help from the others." Isaac looked at Talbot for confirmation and received a nod of concurrence.

"That would answer splendidly, Captain Biggs. The sooner the better, as far as we are concerned. And let me apologize for any misunderstanding that might have been the fault of either Mister Key or myself; there was no intent to suggest that the British attack on our capital was even remotely the fault of your excellent flotilla — or Commodore Barney. The very fact that you all held out so long — and caused them so much trouble — speaks eloquently of the bravery of you fine men and your leader. And I am sure, should the need arise here in Baltimore, Captain Talbot's gunboats will sail to the fore and meet the enemy with equal fortitude and resolve." Skinner looked from Isaac to Jack smiling his acquiescence. And the matter was over.

However, as Isaac stood to take his leave, he noticed Jack had lost his easy smile and continued to scowl at the lawyer. "Come on, Jack. We got things to take care of afore we get underway."

The young New Englander led his companions and Carronade out to the still-muddy street and Jared could hear him issuing instructions of preparation as they moved to the quaywall.

"You men got yourself one fine skipper there in that young man; I only knowed him a short while afore Commodore Barney sent me up here in case the British come here 'stead of Washington, but what I seen — and heard from some what know him better — tells me they ain't much he can't get done." Jared shifted in his chair and called for more ale for himself and his guests. He tipped his chair back, balancing it on its two back legs and spoke just loud enough to be heard over the din.

"He spent nigh onto two years in the Royal Navy — pressed he was, off'n an American merchant sailin' in the Indies. Topman, and a right fine one into the bargain. Sailed with a Cap'n Rogers outta Salem in a privateer brig last year and had a fair run o' luck.

"He was involved in some kind of rescue of American prisoners-of-war up to Halifax, I'm told — and so was Jack Clements and that one-armed cove, Tate — but none of 'em talk much about that. Way I heard it, Clements and Tate was in the prison and Biggs went and got 'em out. Never did smoke the way he done it, but I know the story's likely true — or mostly so. Took some doing, I can tell you, sailing in there and getting them men out. So I reckon you gents got the right lads to carry you out there. Feel bad they ain't goin' armed, but I reckon you're right enough about the Royal Navy bein' less likely to shoot at a vessel what's unarmed."

"I believe I have heard of the Captain Rogers you mentioned, from Salem. Asa Rogers is his name and he is — or was — one of the leading citizens and ship owners in that city. Converted his best vessel for privateering at the outbreak of the war, unlike most of the others in New England who preferred to continue trading with the British in spite of the hostilities. I was slightly involved with one of his friends — or perhaps a competitor from Salem — a George Crowninshield it was — who sought and received a letter of truce from President Madison to reclaim the body of James Lawrence and his first lieutenant. . ." Here Skinner paused and thought for a moment as his fingers drummed the table absently. "Ludlow! August or Augustus Ludlow. Don't quite recollect the man's Christian name, but assuredly Ludlow was his family name. He was the first on the *Chesapeake* with Captain Lawrence when the British took her off Cape Ann. Just over a year ago, I think. Yes, now I recall exactly; it was the first of June last year. Terrible tragedy, that. What a dreadful loss. Folks're still talking about it now — even down here on the Bay. "

"Aye," Talbot acknowledged, nodding his head sadly. "That story kinda took the wind outta our sails down here for a bit. But then folks got they's dander up and tried to fight back figgerin' to try and even the score some, I'd reckon. British navy then was takin' ships right here in the Bay and raidin' and gen'lly raisin' Cain up an' down the whole length. Eastern Shore, mostly, but they didn't miss much. Then they up and left — August or September, I think it were — and we thought we'd 'em run out! Course, they was back. Showed up in April and started raidin' and burin' like they'd never quit!" He spat on the floor and grunted an expletive neither of the men caught.

"This then, assuming they do, in fact, attack Baltimore, will surely be the penultimate test of our resolve. I should think that should the British be successful here in Baltimore we would have little recourse but to capitulate. Especially after they proved the facility with which they virtually obliterated our Capital." Key, seeking validation for his idea, looked questioningly at Jared who only stared back at him, slack-jawed. Skinner, sensing a need for translation, jumped in to avoid further difficulties with the flotillamen.

"I think you are quite right, Frank. Unless we can drive the enemy away here — and I do think they will certainly attack Baltimore, and very soon — they will likely realize that we can not stand up to their might and will take more of our cities and then work their way inland. Not just in New York on the lakes there, but further west toward the frontier where some of the earlier fights took place. Truly we are sunk if that happens."

Talbot, now with some understanding of what the Georgetown lawyer had meant, nodded in agreement and stood.

"You gents will have to 'scuse me now. I got to see about a few things yonder." Without further comment, or waiting for agreement, he left the agent for prisoner exchange and the lawyer sitting in the still-boisterous ale house.

CHAPTER
TWENTY-SEVEN

U nder a darkening sky, made even darker by the threatening clouds scudding through it, the handy little sloop recently acquired by Talbot's flotilla won its anchor and headed for North Point, with Jake Tate's steady hand on the tiller. Isaac stood close by while Jack Clements, assuming the role of first mate, supervised Frank Clark, Sam Hay, and Clive Billings as they set, first the stays'l, and then the flying jib. They all recalled what Isaac, only moments before they embarked their passengers, had expressed to them.

"We got no time to tarry here lads; haste in gettin' out there and back is the orders. These coves got to get they's business done and we got to get our own selves back here afore the damn British start they's fightin'. No telling what'll be actin' then. So don't make problems for us; we'll have plenty of 'em if'n we're caught out there with the whole fleet when they're attackin' Baltimore."

"Who are these coves, Isaac, that they's so important as we got to carry 'em yonder — into the middle of the British fleet?" Clive Billings, his distinctive voice grating as usual, was quick to question their commission. Isaac and Jack tried patiently to explain — again — what they were doing, and Billings moved off to stow the gear and provisions so recently brought aboard, grumbling, but doing his work quickly and properly. The other men merely nodded at the explanation and set about taking care of the myriad details necessary to prepare the vessel.

When Skinner and Key were rowed out to the sloop, they both stopped on deck before they had been shown below to stow their personal gear and surveyed their new surroundings.

"John, I am most assuredly not a seaman, but this vessel . . . it's certainly not of significance. Do you think it will answer? We may have to travel beyond the mouth of the harbor to find Admiral Cochrane's flagship. This weather certainly doesn't appear to be improving. Are you comfortable with it?" Key spoke quietly to Colonel Skinner as he took in the fifty-foot long deck of the sloop, her tall mast and the diminutive deck house.

"I don't imagine that Captain Talbot would have sent us out in this ship unless he was confident of both the ship and the crew. I am not a sailor either, but I suspect that with Captain Biggs and his crew we will be taken where we need to go to find *Tonnant* and brought back in safety. We should perhaps concern ourselves with how we will approach the admiral when we do find him." Skinner was more used to dealing with the military — even seamen — than was the lawyer, and led his companion below, following the sailor who showed them the way.

The two emerged from the cramped space they would share as the sloop responded to the fresh breeze and pushed her shoulder into the chop of the outer harbor.

"I collect you have brought the flag you mentioned — the truce flag?" Isaac spoke to Skinner as the passengers stepped aft onto the tiny quarterdeck.

"Indeed we have, Captain. It is downstairs with my bona fides and other papers. Do you want it now?" Key answered the query quickly before the agent for prisoner exchange could utter a word.

"I think on a vessel they call it 'below', Frank. It would likely be appropriate to hand it over to Captain Biggs now so he can hoist it when he deems necessary." Skinner cast a glance at Isaac and received a nod of concurrence. Without further talk, Frank Key, the attorney from Georgetown, went quickly back 'downstairs' to fetch the white flag.

As the sloop came within sight of Sparrows Point, the men could see several men-of-war anchored in the stream off North Point; a pair of frigates and two smaller vessels. British battle colors flew at the truck of each.

"Ain't none of them big enough to be a flagship, Isaac. I'd reckon the admiral would likely be on at least a two-decker — mayhaps even a second-rater. And they surely ain't none of them yonder." Jack Clements stood at the midships rail with a longglass to his eye. Key and Skinner were close at hand and looked questioningly at one another as the former bosun spoke.

"Aye, looks that way to me, too, Jack." Isaac nodded at his friend and turned to Tate at the helm. "Let her come off a point or two, Jake. We'll bear off some and head more southerly. See if we can find the rest of the ships comin' in."

By the time it was full dark, the rain had again started, first as a desultory drizzle and then, more steadily. The wind had eased some, but remained easterly, pushing the sloop down the Bay toward the oncoming British battle fleet. A scant meal of dried peas and ship's biscuit was prepared and eaten, though with little relish by the normally shore-bound passengers. Only Key commented and was ignored by all. Isaac offered him an extra tumbler of wine or beer which he thought might make the meal more palatable to the lawyer. Key accepted it with alacrity.

"I got some lights — I think — showin' broad on the bow, Isaac. Fact is, when I can see 'em, they pretty well cover the whole horizon. Looks like a passel of ships." Hay was perched halfway up the windward rigging, his hand sheltering his eyes from the rain running unnoticed down the back of his soaked tarpaulin jacket. When he turned to shout down to the quarterdeck, Isaac could see the water droplets glistening in the man's beard, reflecting the dim light from the lamp rigged amidships.

"Well, that'll likely be what we're lookin' for, Sam. Keep an eye on 'em. How far off do you s'pose they might be?" Biggs would normally have climbed aloft to have a look for himself, but only he and Hay were on deck at this point, midway through the middle watch, and there was no one to whom he could turn over the tiller.

"I'm guessin' maybe five leagues — maybe more. I'm only seein' lights, and in this damned weather I cain't even see the horizon — let alone rigs and hulls." Hay let fly a string of curses as his bare foot slipped on the ratlines as he made his way up another few steps.

"I don't reckon I want to sail into the fleet in the dark, Sam. They won't see the flag and some cove thinkin' to make a name for hisself'll likely fire on us. Come on down here and get Clive and

Chapter Twenty-Seven

Frank out; we'll shorten down some and let them come to us."

By dawn — or more aptly, a general brightening of the sky from black to gray — the sloop was off the mouth of the West River, sailing on an easy reach under reduced sail toward the largest of the British ships, barely nothing more than ghostly images emerging from a rain storm at the mouth of Eastern Bay. The bulk of the fleet was spread across the Bay, tacking up toward the Patapsco River and Baltimore. Jack Clements had called Isaac out of a well-deserved sleep and the captain stood alone at the bow studying the impressive display of the Royal Navy's might. Even Carronade, unwilling to be left in Baltimore, had abandoned his normal post in the bow for the relative dryness of the deckhouse, much to the chagrin of the two passengers, who had yet to become accustomed to his company. His presence at the top of the ladder from below had necessitated their stepping over him when they came topside, a move requiring some care so as not to wake to beast.

"This light easterly gonna slow them down some. Reckon they're tacking all the way 'cross the Bay. They ain't gonna be gettin' to North Point much afore dark tonight, I'd warrant." Jack joined his friend and captain at the foot of the bowsprit and smiled tiredly. "Headin' to the far shore, they'll be givin' up damn near what they make goin' on the other tack. Less'n the wind backs around some, they got a long, slow ride."

"Aye, Jack. You're right about that. Let's get that reef out and see about findin' Cochrane's ship. I'd guess it'd be that two-decker there — the one about three back from the lead. Better get that white flag up now that it's light. Wouldn't want 'em to start shootin' at us." Biggs joined his first mate as they moved aft where Tate was once again on the helm.

"You see that bigger one out there, Jake? The two-decker? Let's make for that one. More'n likely that'll have the admiral aboard. I looked for a pendant at the masthead but in this light I cain't see if he's showin' one or not."

Gradually the sloop, a large piece of white bunting flapping lazily at the masthead, closed with the fleet. The Americans could feel the British longglasses trained on them and could imagine the conversations taking place aboard each of the vessels about this brazen little sloop sailing defiantly into the midst of their battle fleet.

"What do you s'pose they's thinkin', Isaac?" Jake, relieved at the helm by Isaac, was balancing the longglass on the wind'ard shroud, steadying it with his hand, and spoke without removing it from his eye. "Don't look like they got any guns run out. Probably figgerin' we ain't worth the powder and iron!"

"I'd imagine they're more 'an a little curious as to our intentions and perhaps even who we might be, young man." Colonel Skinner, Key at his elbow, had joined the group and answered before Biggs could take a breath. Jake kept looking through the glass. "Lookee there, that biggest one — what'd you call her, Isaac, a third-rate? — she's just put up a flag hoist of some kind. What do you s'pose that means?"

Before any could answer his question, Jake called out again. "Isaac! They's tackin'! The whole damn fleet of 'em. Headin' this way now they are, by God!"

And they were indeed. All aboard the sloop could see that with the unaided eye and, clearly, the fleet was now closing the sloop at a greatly increased rate, even given the light breeze.

"Well, Mister Key, Colonel Skinner: reckon you'll be wantin' to get your papers and such in order. We'll be standin' in to 'em quicker 'an kiss my hand now. And I can see that blue pendant flyin' on the two-decker. Reckon that'd be *Tonnant*, Cochrane's ship. Eighty guns would be my guess." Biggs voice was flat, without emotion, but his mind was in turmoil — jumping from thoughts of previous encounters with the Royal Navy to what he saw at Melville Island, back to his forced service aboard a Royal Navy frigate and the floggings and other injustices he witnessed, to Sarah Thomas, to his parents' admonition against 'running off to the Chesapeake Bay' to seek danger again.

Then a sharply-etched image of Sarah overshadowed the other thoughts and, in spite of his best efforts to refocus his tired brain, remained there as clearly as though she were standing alongside him. She wore the same straw bonnet tied with the blue ribbon and the pale blue dress she had worn when last he'd seen her, galloping her horse down the road back to Benedict after warning Commodore Barney of the British landing in that town.

Snippets of conversations flitted through his mind — their dinner with her father that warm night in Benedict, and the brief but wonderful kisses they'd shared; stolen moments of privacy in the middle of a war.

Wonder what's actin' with her now, Isaac thought, recognizing the futility of putting the girl back into the recesses of his mind. *Reckon she's likely back to some kind of normal life now the Redcoats've left down there. Hope she's all right and takin' care of herself . . . sure would be nice to see her again . . . wonder if her daddy's home yet — or alive. Reckon if'n he got hisself killed afore Washington, her godfather's takin' care of her . . . no . . . I don't reckon she needs nobody to take care of her . . . she's likely still rilin' up all the men there with her opinions . . . gotta get myself back there when this mess gets itself played out.* He smiled, unseen.

Without warning the earlier image he had of her — fighting and firing a musket at the British troops — appeared. *Oh lordy! What if'n she's gone and got herself killed or something. I don't reckon I could handle that. No, Isaac. You cain't let yourself think on that. Keep your mind on what's actin' right here and now. That's the whole British fleet there in front of you and you likely oughta pay it some mind.* He shook his head and forced himself to study their present situation.

It was rapidly becoming demanding. They were within a cannon shot of the flagship and, with the glass, Isaac could see several officers studying his vessel with their own glasses. The sloop had passed astern of two frigates that had watched it go by with scarcely a look. The white bunting at the masthead seemed to be doing its job!

"What is your plan, Captain? If you don't mind my inquiring, that is." Skinner had appeared at Biggs' side and was watching the eighty-gun *Tonnant* loom large as she grew closer. Key had remained amidships, but even from there, Isaac could see his eyes get big as the obvious might of the enemy surrounded them. Before he could answer Colonel Skinner's question, a voice boomed out over the water, sounding tinny from the speaking trumpet held by an officer part-way up the mizzen rigging.

"Boat there! Ahoy! What is your intention?"

"You got one of those trumpets aboard, Captain?" Skinner looked expectantly at Isaac. Jake appeared at the man's side with one in his hand and offered it to the colonel.

"I am Colonel John Skinner, Agent for Prisoner Exchange. I would like to come aboard and speak with your Admiral Cochrane, should he be available. The admiral knows me. Please offer my compliments and ask if he will see me." Skinner, the well-worn speaking trumpet at his mouth, fairly bellowed his response.

The man in the two-decker's rigging waved in acknowledgment and climbed down. After a hasty consultation with others on the ship's quarterdeck, he disappeared below. Shortly he returned and, as the Americans watched, again climbed the mizzen ratlines and raised the trumpet.

"Boat ahoy. Colonel: Admiral Cochrane says come alongside. He would be pleased to wait on you." Even as the officer spoke, the great ship began to change course slightly and men swarmed aloft to clew up some sails and back others to slow her, allowing the tiny American vessel to approach. And approach they did. The Americans could plainly hear the orders being issued to heave to the British vessel. The bosun's whistle and harsh commands brought back memories to the young New Englander. But at least they had replaced the unnerving image he had had of Sarah.

As Isaac swung the sloop around to make his landing along the warship's massive side, he kept his mind focused completely on the task at hand. However, as the huge ship got closer and her side loomed high above the diminutive sloop, he became aware that his hands were clammy and that a trickle of moisture was making its way down his face and on down his neck. It was not the continuing drizzle making him uncomfortable.

The Americans could plainly see the battens fixed to the towering side of the British vessel — a vessel whose sides were pierced on two decks for the barrels of her eighty guns. It was small comfort that the gunports were closed and no cannon, save the stern chasers on the poop, were visible. Red-coated marines were in evidence, however, and the crew of the sloop could plainly see them aiming muskets at the Americans from the spar deck as well as the fighting tops. Isaac noticed that both Clements and Jake Tate were showing signs of their own discomfort at being this close to the Royal Navy. Carronade issued forth with a low, deep-throated growl, somehow recognizing the ships for what they were. Jack patted him and spoke softly to the dog, but the growl continued.

Without warning, the whole of Isaac's life in the Royal Navy flooded into his head: the terror he had felt when he and his mates were pressed from the bark *Anne*; the excitement and fear that had overcome him when faced with his first encounter with a French naval squadron; his first taste of a real sea battle between equals; the floggings; his friends in the Royal Navy — Robert Coleman and Tim Conoughy, Jack Toppan, and the others. And young Michael

Tyler who had leaped overboard to his death rather than face an unmerciful and undeserved flogging. Now, here he was again about to secure his vessel alongside one of the finest of the Royal Navy — and his was completely unarmed, not that it would have made a difference at this point.

The sloop came into the lee of *Tonnant*'s tall side and her sails were at once all a-luff, the two-decker as effectively blocking the wind as would a headland. As Isaac guided his vessel, now coasting slowly without wind, along the side of the warship, man ropes dropped down on either side of the battens and a heavier length of hemp was thrown accurately onto the little vessel's foredeck. Billings and Frank Clark grabbed it quickly and made it fast to the bits there and the sloop was secured alongside. Carronade, his forepaws on the sloop's low bulwark and his tail unmoving, increased the intensity of his menacing growl. Isaac noticed that a fair number of the dog's teeth showed at the side of his mouth and the fur on his back formed a ridge from his neck to his tail.

Isaac and Jake craned their necks to stare up at the break in the bulwark of the British ship; several officers stood there, along with a few marines and some sailors. It seemed nearly as far away as the top of the sloop's mast, but both men knew well that it likely was not that high.

Jack Clements and Sam Hay had released the main halyard and were gathering the sail along the boom as it slid down the mast. The other two, forward, were handing the jibs. Within minutes, the sloop, her sails furled, was rocking easily under the side of the larger ship. With no need to stand at the tiller, Isaac stepped into the waist and spoke with Colonel Skinner and the Georgetown attorney.

"How long you figger you're likely to be, Colonel? I can stay here alongside if you think it'll be quick, or sail nearby *Tonnant* 'til you signal me to come get you and Mister Key if'n you're gonna be a while."

"I have no idea, Captain. Hopefully, we shall see the admiral promptly and, with luck, he will acquiesce to the release of Doctor Beanes without undue argument. Should that be the case, we will likely only be a short while and will return directly so that we might sail straight back to Baltimore. But we shall have to see what the British have in mind." Skinner, his papers in a leather case tucked under his arm, had a hand on the manrope and was already lifting a foot onto the lowest batten. Key looked anxious to get on with the task at hand, alternating his glance between Isaac and the lofty deck of the man-of-war.

As the crew of the sloop watched the two men scramble up the side, they heard a voice shout down to them from the deck.

"You there, the American captain. Have your men come aboard, if you please, and you as well. We shall trail your vessel astern. The captain is anxious to get underway as quick as ever possible."

Here was a turn of events none of the American sailors had anticipated; were they to be taken prisoner, or just held until the negotiations between Skinner, Key, and the admiral were completed? Jack and Isaac exchanged looks and Isaac noticed that, not for the first time since they had set out on this commission, Jack had lost his easy-going and seemingly ever-present grin. Almost without hesitation he called back up to the British officer. And Isaac noticed that the annyoing trickle of sweat had again begun to track down his back, in spite of the comfortable temperature.

"If'n you want us, you're gonna have to lower a sling. Got a big dog here what we ain't gonna leave aboard." Quietly he spoke to Isaac. "That oughtta give 'em something to think on for a moment or two. What do you figger them bastards want with us, Isaac? Capturing this sloop sure wouldn't signify to 'em and a handful of American sailors ain't likely to turn they's heads." Jack stopped and suddenly smiled his impish grin again. "Less'n some cove up there recognized you as a former Royal Navy tar and wants you back!"

"Oh lordy, Jack. Don't even joke about that. I ain't real comfortable with this right now, my own self. But I don't see where we got any choice in it. Hell's bells!" The young American captain spat over the side, then shook his head in resignation. "Let's get ourselves up there afore them Redcoats decide we's takin' too long." Biggs motioned to Hay and the others to get up the side and followed them up. Jack waited on the sloop until the officer yelled down to him.

"You will 'ave to leave the dog on your vessel as we have no desire to have 'im aboard. This is a ship of 'is Britannic Majesty's Navy, not some damnable kennel for your filthy Jonathan dogs. Now you, sir, will get your self aboard quick as ever you might, should you know what's good for you." More quietly, but audible to all around him, he added, "Damn Jonathans. 'is dog, indeed! Can you imagine the arrogance! Ought to just 'ave a Marine shoot the miserable cur, by God!"

Jack patted the dog and left him to his own devices, following the officer's instructions to "get yourself aboard quick as ever you might." Biggs was still making his way up the tall side. No sooner had Jack left the deck of the diminutive vessel than the sailors on the warship began paying out the line attached to the sloop's bow, easing her back down the side and, ultimately, astern. Carronade, Jack noticed from his perch on *Tonnant's* side, moved forward as the sloop drifted back and was now standing in the eyes of the little vessel, his forepaws on the butt of the bowsprit. Jack wondered idly if he was still growling.

The topmen in the rigging dropped courses while the heavers on deck of Cochrane's flagship hauled the yards around to catch the still-light breeze, and she was underway again, heading across the Bay toward Baltimore. The two-decker now occupied a position in the middle of the fleet instead of in the van where she had been — or nearly so — when she hove to to receive the Americans.

As Isaac Biggs, former Royal Navy topman, stepped through the bulwark gate onto the deck he staggered slightly and quickly caught himself with a hand on the hammock netting. Waves of familiar sights and sounds washed over him. He found himself glancing aloft at the men still occupied with the tops'ls and courses. They were higher by far than on the *Orpheus* frigate, with more men on each yard. Isaac watched for a moment, remembering, as the Royal Navy topmen worked their way along the spars, releasing the brails to allow the sails to unfurl.

"These lads seem to know well they's business — as I reckon they should, bein's how they's in the flagship," Isaac muttered to himself.

"How's that, Isaac? Didn't catch that. You got to speak into the side what's got the ear, remember? And these coves are wantin' to close up the bulwark, there." Clements came up behind his friend and playfully pushed him out of the way of the boarding area. His eyes made a quick circuit of the deck — as far as he could see — and took it all in; the red-coated marines, the crowds of sailors hauling on halyards, sheets, and braces, the carronades fore and aft and, through the gangways on the spardeck, the twenty-four-pounder cannon that lined the sides and, he knew, the sides of the deck below the one he could see.

It was an impressive amount of fire power.

Clements had only seen one British warship close up and he had been in no position then to make a study of *Shannon*'s gun-deck beyond noticing a few elements that had caught his eye. He looked aft toward the raised poop and saw the rail lined with blue coats trimmed in gold over sparkling white knee breeches. Most wore swords while others wore the dirk allowed to midshipmen.

"Isaac! They ain't even at quarters! Damn arrogant . . ." He was interrupted by an uninspiring figure approaching from aft who raised his voice in an unsuccessful attempt at command.

"You men: stand out of the way, there! You may remain for'ard of the break of the poop and off the quarterdeck. And do not wander about. Someone will come and deal with you when I know the captain's pleasure." The nasal, youthful British voice dripped with arrogance and disdain. Flashes of white on the young man's uniform jacket, along with the dirk carried at his side, identified him as a midshipman. His pocked face and smallish eyes set over a sharp nose gave him a look that did not command trust or even obedience, but none of Isaac's crew thought to question him.

Isaac and Jack just looked at the man, neither trusting their voices to respond. The other Americans all mumbled "Aye" and stayed where they were, standing against the bulwark behind the hammock netting.

"Jack, you thinkin' on your time in *Shannon*? This oughta look some familiar, I'd reckon." Isaac was still looking around the mighty ship, as awestruck as a landsman. He recalled seeing the seventy-fours in English Harbor some years ago and how impressed he'd been with their size; while *Tonnant* was not as big physically, she carried a greater weight of metal and surely more sailors and marines.

He looked at the faces he could see, hoping not to recognize any of the crew or officers. He barely heard Clements' response to his comment.

"The *Shannon* frigate, aye. Course them coves aboard that one wasn't quite so warm and friendly! Wasn't real keen on any of us havin' a look around, as I recollect, neither." Jack's grin was back; he seemed comfortable with their situation now that he knew they weren't about to be marched down to the orlop deck as prisoners.

"Isaac, what do you figger they's gonna do with us?" Jake was none too comfortable being here on the deck of this huge British vessel. He also had a memory — albeit slightly fuzzy — of spending some time on *Shannon* in a hammock drifting in and out of consciousness from the laudanum he'd been given to ease the pain of his just-amputated arm. Absently, he rubbed the stump of his arm as he looked around, still gaping at the magnitude of Admiral Cochrane's flagship.

When Isaac turned to respond to his friend, he noticed that Jake, too, was sweating and seemed unable to stand still. He shuffled his feet and shifted his weight from one to the other, unsure of what was in store for all of them. Biggs tried to ease his mind as much as he could. He smiled and Clements responded to the young man's concerns.

"They's likely gonna just let us stand here and wait on the colonel and Mister Key, I reckon. Don't nobody seem to payin' any mind to us, Jake. 'sides, what would they be wantin' with the likes of us — a one-eared bosun and a one-armed topman?"

Tate managed a thin smile, but it faded quickly. Frank Clark and Sam Hay were clearly in awe of their surroundings; even Clive Billings was, for once, silent as his gaze took in the lofty rig and the crowds of men who seemed to be everywhere he looked.

"Crew's gonna be piped to dinner right quick, you lot. Should you be wishin' a bite of vittles, I reckon we might manage to scare up a wee bit for some Jonathans. May'aps even a wee taste of grog, should you be wantin' it." A tall, swarthy man with his long hair neatly braided down his back and a blue cloth coat missing its lapels over none-too-clean white canvas trousers spoke to the visitors. "You'll just 'ave to fall in there at the foot of the mainmast on the weatherdeck when you 'ear the pipe. Reckon you'll 'ave to fend for yourselves at the mess, though." He looked at the Americans for a moment, thinking. "Which one of you is the captain of that wee vessel. I'd warrant one of you oughta be?"

Isaac stepped forward and haltingly, in a quiet voice, identified himself as such.

"You'll be eatin' in the Gunroom with the officers, since you're our guest. Reckon that Cap'n Porter ain't likely to be arskin' you to jine 'im an' the admiral in the Cabin. Har har."

He looked at the two disfigured sailors. "You two look like you might 'ave seen some action somewhere along the way. I'd warrant you met up with the Royal Navy afore?"

"Aye, and spent some time enjoyin' the hospitality of your lodgings at Melville Island on top of it." Jack smiled at the stranger. "Who might you be?"

"Taggert, Bosun. Since you're Jonathans, I'd warrant you lads was traded back quick as ever you please from Melville. Seems like only the Frogs manage to stay put there."

"Aye, was something like that, it were. We . . ." Jack's next thought was cut off by the pipe followed by the fife playing the call to dinner. None of the Americans recognized the tune, but Isaac immediately recalled the *Nancy Dawson* and again his former life rushed back to him. Fortunately Bosun Taggert moved away to supervise the grog line and Isaac grabbed Jack's elbow.

"Don't go tellin' any more 'bout your time in the prison, Jack. They might not take kindly to the way you — and Jake — was 'traded' back. Let's see about some grog." Isaac smiled for the first time since coming aboard and took a step toward the ladder leading down to the weatherdeck.

"'scuse me, *Cap'n* Biggs, but didn't that cove Taggert say you was 'sposed to take your vittles in the *gunroom* with the officers?" Clements comment was accompanied by a grin as he now fully returned to his easy-going self and tried to lighten the spirit of his fellows.

"Wouldn't know how to act in the gunroom, Jack. Rather be eatin' with you coves anyway, though only the good Lord knows why. Right now, I'm thinkin' we're better off stayin' close aboard each other, so if'n you ain't objectin', I'll just be an able seaman for a while." Isaac smiled back, more at ease since it was becoming apparent that they were not to suffer any ill effects of their 'visit' to the Royal Navy. His familiarity with the routine of the Royal Navy — and the fact that he was the only member of his crew with that familiarity — provided him with some comfort. "'sides," he added with a wink at Jake Tate, "it's some sharp-set I am right now, and I don't take much to the idea of waitin' an hour and more for the Gunroom mess to take they's vittles."

"Biggs! That you, by Gawd?" The voice came from forward, by the mainmast. Isaac started as though shot. He turned and peered through the gloom of the weatherdeck searching for its source, his smile vanishing. It took him a moment or two to realize he had stopped breathing.

Then the voice called out again. "Biggs! Over here. It's me, Wallace."

"Looks like you got you a friend here, Isaac. And you look a little peaked, of a sudden. You feelin' all right? Maybe you shoulda made for the gunroom after all!" Clements tone was cheery, but the implications — for all of them — were less so. Isaac continued to stare at the knot of seamen from where Wallace had called.

"There you are, Wallace. Couldn't smoke your voice right off; been close enough to two years since I seen your ugly face last. What are you doing here, in the flagship, no less?" Isaac hoped that his own cheery tone would help prevent disaster.

"Got put off'n the ol' *Orpheus* — and away from that damn flogger, Winston — in Bermuda last spring. We was 'eadin' for 'ome, and *Tonnant* was 'eadin' 'ere, needin' some hands. Winston sent me an' a dozen others over — seein's 'ow it were the admiral what was askin'. Reckon 'e felt it might do 'im some good — 'elpin' out the admiral. What 'appened to you? Last I recall, you and Cochrane and some others was sailing them prizes down to Antigua. With Burns, if'n I recollect rightly. Never did 'ear what happened to you. Some one of the officers once mentioned that the prizes wasn't in to English 'arbour, but ol' Burns never showed up again — nor any of the others. I'll tell you, lad, you're the last one I'd expected to see 'ere. Didn't you once say you was from somewhere north of 'ere — Massachusetts, if'n I recollect."

"Aye, Wallace. Massachusetts it is. An' the prizes got themselves took by some American privateers." Isaac brought his old friend and fellow topman up to date on his activities — leaving out a fair amount of detail, especially about his visit to Halifax a year back — and concluded with ". . . and I seen — well, I didn't actually *see* him — but I heard that Lieutenant Burns is now *Captain* Burns and has a vessel right here in the Bay. So I reckon he made it ashore down to Haiti and then found hisself a way back to the fleet."

Isaac made the introductions of his crew, and each responded to Wallace's greetings with a wan smile and a quiet voice.

"I surely hope you ain't plannin' to mention to some officer who I am, Wallace; that would make things right uncomfortable." Isaac smiled hopefully.

"Wouldn't think of it, Isaac lad. You got your own self off'n that hell-ship an' I admire that. No, I ain't gonna mention your time in the Royal Navy. Especially now you've got your own vessel. I collect that wee one trailin' astern is the one you mentioned just now?"

"Aye that it is, and soon's Colonel Skinner and Mister Key're done talkin' with your admiral, I aim to get it — and us — away from here quick as ever I might." Relief was evident in Isaac's voice and in the faces of his crew as the men got their grog and joined Wallace's mess for their dinner.

CHAPTER
TWENTY-EIGHT

By the time the last British ship had dropped its anchor, it was dusk. The weather had improved not a whit; in fact, the drizzle had evolved into a steady, soaking rain and the approaching night held the promise of little change. *Tonnant*, the American sloop still secured astern, and a dozen troop ships along with a few frigates had found their anchorages a mile off North Point. The Americans still aboard the flagship could see Royal Marines mustering in the troopships for what could only be a landing. *Tonnant*'s position in the center of the row closest to Baltimore city — but still a safe eight miles distant — allowed Isaac and his crew a good view of the ships to either side as well as those astern and, through the rain and gradually descending darkness, the frigates, brigs, bomb and rocket ships, and tenders as they anchored some five miles off Fort McHenry.

Jack and Jake had watched as the deeper-draft frigates (Jake stopped counting as the sixth passed) led by HMS *Surprise*, to which Admiral Cochrane had shifted his flag, spent a good part of the day tacking up the Patapsco River, running aground several times in the process, bringing smiles to the American faces. They also watched — in less good humor — as each in turn was pulled or kedged off the shoals and the bomb ships and rocket ships continued even farther, coming to anchor barely two-and-one-half miles from the massive fort.

"Them smaller vessels close in, Isaac; I seen 'em when they went by us. Looks to me like they's rigged to fire shells 'stead of shot. Them short-barrelled carronades they was sportin' could only be for shells. They could make some trouble for the lads in the fort if'n they can hit what they's aimin' at." Clements stood beside Isaac observing the activity of the fleet. He looked again and continued. "Reckon that cove what's in charge there — what was his name? Armistead or something, I recollect — would be right interested in knowing what them ships is plannin' on throwin' his way."

"Aye. I imagine he rightly would, Jack. You figgered a way we can get ourselves off'n this ship and sail in there to tell 'em? These rascals here ain't likely to just hand us down into the sloop with a tip of they's hats and give us a push toward the city so's we can warn 'em." Isaac paused and looked around the ship, his gaze finally settling on the American sloop where she tugged gently at her bow line some two hundred feet away. "Say Jack, what about your dog? Have you gotten an eye on him? I ain't heard him bark since we left him there. I don't reckon he's enjoyin' hisself settin' back there in the sloop." Isaac nodded astern of the two-decker.

Jack's face darkened as he looked aft. He could see little of the sloop save her rig and the top of the deckhouse. Carronade was not in sight, but Jack had no doubt the big dog was still aboard and waiting for him to return.

"How much longer you figger they's likely to keep us here, Isaac. I ain't real fond of standin' here bein' looked over by these Royal Navy coves like I was a piece of meat a-hangin' in a butcher's shop." Tate had noticed that many of the seamen aboard were treating the Americans as a curiosity — as were the officers and, most particularly, the midshipmen. They seemed to relish moving their guests around, ostensibly to get them out of the way, but it was obvious to all that the youngsters were merely exercising their limited authority to impress the Americans. And some took real delight in bullying them.

One midshipman who appeared to the American crew as the "runt of the litter," as Clive Billings had put it, seemed to spend most of his time waiting for the men to seek some shelter from the rain and then moving them to another place on deck — in the open. By now, the sloop's crew was thoroughly soaked, their hair plastered to their heads, and Sam Hay and Jake were actually shivering with cold in spite of the moderate temperature.

They had enjoyed some lively conversation with Wallace and his mates at their mess, and the American sailors realized that there was little difference between the men of the Royal Navy and themselves — none relished their existence — and most of the talk centered on life ashore or the pursuits each would follow when the war ended. Jack had again pointed out that the ship had still not been called to quarters to which his British messmates had only shrugged. One, a topman under Wallace's command on the fore-mast, had disdainfully pointed out, "We ain't got no need to go to quarters. Heard it meself, I did, from Mister Reed, that we ain't gonna fire or even put our marines ashore. Said we's just gonna set 'ere an' watch an' then when the frigates and bomb ships 'ave done they's work, we'll move in to put our lads ashore and meet up with the marines marching in from that spit of land yonder. Shouldn't be any trouble takin' this little place, 'specially after Washington!"

The comment had sparked a brief but lively round of comments from both sides of the fray; the Americans hoping this man's assessment of the situation was wrong, but fearing the worst, while the British seamen nodded knowingly at their mate.

Immediately after Cochrane had shifted his flag to the *Surprise* frigate, now anchored with the bomb ships and tenders close to the fort, Skinner and Francis Key had appeared on *Tonnant*'s deck and sought out Isaac.

"Looks as if we have been successful in convincing the admiral to release Doctor Beanes, Captain. But, unfortunately, the admiral has given orders that we are all to remain aboard this ship until the fight is over. He pointed out that it would do their effort no good at all should we go ashore and announce his plans — which I must add, we discussed in some detail at dinner — to our fellows defending the city. So it is here we shall stay for the moment." Colonel Skinner was pleased with their success in securing the doctor's release, but quite distressed at their apparent temporary captivity.

"You figger they might be willin' to let us get back aboard the sloop, Colonel? At least there, we'd be able to get outta the weather without Midshipman 'Runt' and his mates chasing us out of any lee we can find. And Jack, here, could see to his animal." Isaac's earnestness brought thoughtful frowns to the faces of the two negotiators, but Key responded quickly.

"I shall inquire of General Ross and the captain. Ross mentioned that he will be personally leading the troops who go ashore, but he is still aboard, I believe." The lawyer turned and stepped quickly aft toward the quarterdeck, his shoulders hunched up in limited defense against the still-falling rain.

The sloop's crew had moved to a position under the blue cutter on the weather deck, which offered some limited protection from the rain. Isaac noticed that Jake and Sam Hay kept an alert lookout for their nemesis, the bantam midshipman who seemed to delight in denying them any shelter. He also noticed that, now in from the rain, they had stopped their shivering. The colonel made idle conversation with Isaac, detailing the British plans he knew of and lamenting the fact that they were unable, for now at least, to do anything to help the American cause.

"If I could somehow get the word to Commodore Rodgers that General Ross is landing something on the order of four thousand marines and sailors to attack Baltimore by way of North Point, I am sure it would be helpful to him. I know he has seen the bomb ships, rocket vessels, and frigates already close in and I would assume their mission is quite obvious to even the most casual observer. But I don't know that he is expecting an attack from the land." Skinner's frustration was palpable, and, in the dim smoky glow of a nearby lantern, Isaac could make out the lines furrowed into his forehead.

"Colonel, I don't reckon you need worry your own self about that. Some of the lads and me met the commodore a few days past and he allowed as how he had right plentiful troops all set to the east of the city and ready to march out this way. Fact is, I'd wager he's started 'em out here already. Mayhaps these coves might be in for a surprise once they get 'emselves ashore. They's thinkin' Baltimore's gonna lay down and just let 'em march right in — just like down to Washington; from what I seen ashore, that surely ain't likely. I'll warrant these folks'll fight — and fight good. Rodgers is a pretty smart cove, 'cordin' to what most say and he seemed ready for whatever the British come up with."

"Captain, I do hope you are right on that score. As Mister Key mentioned to your . . . commodore? Captain Talbot? . . . if Baltimore falls, we are most assuredly sunk and, I fear, our cause lost." The agent for prisoner exchange shook his head. "I just wish there was some way we could get in there and be of some help."

Before Isaac could respond, Frank Key was back, his face wreathed in smiles. And he was accompanied by Midshipman "Runt" who drew himself up to his full five-foot height as he approached. A tall, elderly man, dressed in none-too-fresh civilian clothes, brought up the rear.

"In the absence of Admiral Cochrane, General Ross and Admiral Cockburn have authorized you . . . gentlemen," the young man stumbled on the word as though getting it out was an effort, "to return to your vessel." The Americans, to a man, brightened and Midshipman "Runt" went on before any could exclaim. "However, the boat shall remain secured to *Tonnant*, astern, as she is now, and you will be accompanied by a cadre of His Majesty's Marines. Just to ensure you remain with us until we have finished our work here." He showed a mirthless grin, delighting in the rise and fall of the men's hopes. It was more a grimace than a smile, showing a broken row of uneven teeth, the gaps between several a testimonial to the surgeon's skill, which did little to enhance his already gnome-like appearance.

The young officer-in-training went on, "The bosun will see that the boat is hauled alongside without delay. And I might add . . . gentlemen . . . it has been a pleasure having you aboard His Majesty's Ship *Tonnant*. I am hopeful we will meet again — after Baltimore has fallen." The little midshipman strutted away, filled with his own sense of importance.

"At least the company'll be better. Be right interesting to see how the — what did he call 'em, Isaac? a 'cad-ray'? — the Marines, I mean — take to spending time with ol' Carronade. Oughtta keep 'em entertained right nice." Jack was already heading for the ladder to the spar deck.

True to his word, the bosun had a dozen and more sailors, idlers, Isaac reckoned, hauling on the heavy hawser attached to the bow of the sloop. The dog aboard it, awakened by the movement, reprised his earlier concerto of barks and growls.

"You ain't leavin' us, Isaac? Cain't believe you coves would rather be on that little boat than nice an' dry — " Wallace smiled at his own joke, seeing the sodden jackets and trousers on the Americans, and continued with hardly a pause. ". . . and with all this lot for company — here on the finest of 'is Majesty's Navy!" Wallace had happened by and seen the sloop being dragged alongside. He watched with the crew as the sloop was secured to the British two-decker.

"Well, Wallace, it ain't we're actually leavin', exactly. And we will have some of your marines for company, since the general," Isaac nodded in a generally aft direction, "don't seem to think we'd want to stay close aboard without someone to make sure we do." Isaac put out his hand and the British topman took it. "A great surprise to see you again, Wallace. If you cross tacks with any of them other coves I knowed on *Orpheus*, let 'em know I'm still alive."

"Aye, and glad I am indeed to 'ave seen you as well. Mind you don't get yourself 'urt in the fightin' what's comin'. An' after . . ."

" 'ere, you, sailor. I am sure you must 'ave duties to see to — and likely more important than talking to these . . . gentlemen. Move along now." Midshipman "Runt" was back. Wallace glared at him, muttered something under his breath, and winked in the darkness at Isaac and his mates.

As the men waited for their escort of marines, they noticed that the bustle of activity on the troop transports seemed to have increased and that there were dozens of large pulling boats milling around the fleet.

"Reckon them boats is just waitin' on a signal to go alongside and start takin' the troops ashore. Looks like they're some serious 'bout this landing." Jack looked aloft. "Leastways, it looks to be clearing some. See? You can just make out the moon behind them clouds. Folks ashore gonna be able to see 'em comin', I'd warrant."

"Isaac, you think we might be able to cut that cable and sail away. Don't reckon a two-decker gonna come after us. And we can likely outsail any of they's pullin' boats, 'specially if this breeze keeps up." Jake Tate spoke in low tones to his captain, but Isaac was unable to respond beyond a shake of his head as a half dozen Royal Marines, apparently their guard, marched to the ship's waist and arrayed themselves alongside the hammock netting.

Without ceremony or so much as a 'good evening' from Midshipman "Runt", the American sailors, lawyer Frank Key, Colonel John Skinner, Doctor William Beanes — for that is who the older man turned out to be — and the six Royal Marines clambered down the battens on the side of the flagship and into the sloop and were welcomed by its keeper with a wagging tail and joyful barks — at least until the British soldiers appeared. Then the tail stopped and the barks turned to a most menacing growl, causing one of the newcomers to unship his musket and hold it at the ready. Isaac saw a disaster in the making and moved to head it off.

"You leave him alone and I'd warrant he won't bother you, save for some growls or snarls. He don't much take to the British. Now you coves just make yourselves right at home, but I think you'd likely better stay for'ard there out of the way." Isaac pointed at the bow of the little ship which looked even smaller after their visit aboard the eighty-gun flagship. The sloop's hawser was paid out and again she returned to her position astern of *Tonnant*.

"Captain Biggs," Mister Key touched Isaac's elbow seeking his attention. "We didn't have the opportunity to introduce you and your men to the object of our mission. This gentleman is Doctor William Beanes of Upper Marlboro who has, until now, been held captive by Admiral Cochrane. Doctor, Captain Isaac Biggs."

"I am indeed happy to make your acquaintance, Captain. And thank you for bringing Colonel Skinner and my good friend Frank out to rescue this tired old doctor. I should be hard pressed to know how I would have survived much longer as a prisoner."

Hands were shaken and introductions made by Isaac to Jack and Jake. The other Americans were forward, seeing to some none-too-happy Royal Marines.

CHAPTER TWENTY-NINE

J ared Talbot was overseeing a handful of his flotillamen as they labored shifting shot and powder at Fort Covington, where Addison and most of his men were indeed 'laid low' by illness. The fort, sited on a point across from Ridgely's Cove, could fire over both water and the land behind Fort McHenry. It commanded a clear view of the harbor and, beyond it some eight or nine miles, North Point. During the brief period of daylight when the rain had stopped, he and his sailors could see the masts of the British fleet as it came to anchor off the point, and more clearly — even through the rain — the bombardment fleet as the frigates and bomb ships took up their positions only a few miles away.

"I reckon you'll be lookin' out for Isaac and 'em what took them two coves out there eh, Jared?" Bill Andrews came up behind Talbot and spoke softly to the tall back with the braid reaching down its length. The two men had sailed together since before the war, when they ran sharp-built schooners up and down the Bay.

"Aye, you can bet on that, Bill." Talbot spoke without looking around. His huge paws rested on the embrasure which provided the gunport for a long eighteen-pounder. "Shoulda been back by now, I'da thought. 'Specially since them ships out there off North Point gotta be most of the fleet and, I'd warrant, one of 'em'll be Cochrane's flagship." The lights of the British fleet winked dimly in the dark, competing with the few stars that managed to appear from time to time through the thin overcast.

"Maybe the British took 'em as prisoners — wouldn't let 'em leave. Or mayhaps that 'truce flag' that agent cove had didn't answer and they got took under fire." Bill Andrews was never one to look for a silver lining.

The acting commodore turned and studied his friend and mate. After a prolonged silence he managed to produce a grunt in acknowledgment of the remark, but preferred not to dwell on it. After another moment he spoke. "Reckon they'll turn up after whatever the Royal Navy got in mind for us is done with. Less'n o'course they grabbed that doctor they was after and made a run over to the Eastern Shore. No tellin' what mighta happened." He turned and cast one more glance toward the harbor, taking in the smaller ships anchored at about four or five miles distant, as well as the larger ones — the transports and most likely the flagship — anchored almost hull-down off North Point. Then, followed by Andrews, Talbot made his way past the row of guns, speaking to each of the crews as he passed.

Most were flotillamen and included a significant number of the men who had arrived with Isaac and Jack some ten days earlier. They were unused to manning batteries on land, preferring instead the flexibility and maneuverability of their gunboats. It didn't seem quite right to most that they should be stationary targets for the British gunners they would be facing — even with the thick stone and mortar walls that surrounded the fort.

"Say, Jared. We gonna be stuck here — or we gettin' back to the boats so's we kin fight proper?"

"Aye, what about it Jared? We're sailors! This job o' work here is fer them army and militia coves."

"When you figger they's likely to start shootin', Jared. You think they can reach us from out yonder. Looks like pretty long range to me!"

"I reckon we'll know when they start shootin', Ike. You just set there and wait — an' stay awake. If'n them ships yonder decide they's gonna come in closer, we gotta be ready to turn 'em around." Jared raised his voice so all could hear. "You men. Hear me now. I'd warrant McHenry's gonna be takin' most of the firin', but this battery and the one there," he pointed in the dark toward the battery known as Babcock, "gonna be right important if'n the fort cain't hold 'em — or if'n the British try to get round the back in boats. You got to keep a sharp lookout and stay alert. No tellin' when this scrap is gonna get started, but I don't reckon we'll have to wait long. And I'd wager they're gonna give us everything they got."

His short speech was received with somber nods and a few anxious looks toward the dark harbor. A few of the men looked around and at each other, as if looking for a way out. But nobody left.

Talbot and Andrews continued moving around the battery, answering questions and trying to maintain their men's spirits. Both felt, as many did, that a shore-side battery was not where they wanted to be — especially with an entire fleet of gunboats anchored barely a musket shot distant, but this is where Rodgers wanted them, and by God, this is where they'd stay — and fight.

The American sailors enjoyed a sleepless night as they kept a "sharp lookout" and milled about the modest fort talking and smoking. The rain began again during the small hours of the morning, soaking most of the men since the limited cover available provided scant shelter. Not long after dawn had eased the black night into a gray day and the men had been fed their breakfast of burgoo and chocolate, someone heard the first sounds of conflict. Faint, to be sure, but carried on the wet easterly breeze, came the unmistakable sounds of musket and artillery fire.

"Sounds like they's fightin' over to the east, Jared. You reckon the British'll put troops ashore there like they done in Benedict?" One of the sailors who had come to Baltimore with Biggs and Clements spoke. "I seen 'em at Bladensburg an' if'n they put them same Marines ashore here, I reckon they can go anywhere they's wantin' to go. The militia sure ain't gonna stand up to 'em! Them so'jers're the same ones what was fightin' against that Frog cove — what's his name — Boney some-such or other."

"Well, sailor, I wouldn't be too sure about that; Commodore Rodgers put a whole passel of regular troops as well as militia out yonder towards the east and south. Reckon that's what we're hearin'. 'Cordin' to what the commodore told me just a few days back, we got plenty of men and artillery out there and they's set to stop the Royal Marines comin' in from North Point. Gotta be right hard for all of 'em out there, movin' through the mud and this damn rain. But what's goin' on over to North Point ain't my concern. Them ships yonder is all we got to worry about — at least for now."

Indeed, "them ships yonder" had come no closer nor had any fired a shot. And this troubled Jared. Why hadn't they come in some and begun the bombardment which they were clearly planning? He called Bill Andrews over to where he stood in the drizzle watching the fifteen or sixteen ships that he could see well out of range of both his guns and those at Fort McHenry.

"This waitin's takin' it's toll on the men, Jared." Andrews said when he showed up. He, too, looked out at the ships positioned to menace, but as yet, not do harm to the forts or the city. "You figger they're just a . . . what was the word . . . *distraction*, yeah, that's the one. Tryin' to make us think they's gonna fire on us and while we're watching them, they come in from the shoreside astern and catch us lookin' the other way."

"Could be, Bill. Mayhaps that's what's actin' over to North Point. We might never see a Redcoat; them English Marines could just march theirselves right down the point and into the city without no problem. 'Ceptin' for the army and militia what's out there. I'd be willin' to wager that them soldiers what's comin' down the point gonna run into something they ain't expectin' — 'specially after Washington. 'Cordin' to what I've seen round here, these folks is some riled up and they's gonna fight. You mark my words, Bill Andrews, this scrap ain't over by a long shot, and them ships out there ain't just there to look pretty — or scare us into surrendering." Talbot was clearly as anxious as his men, and it came through in his voice. But he believed to the very core of his being that what happened in the capital would not happen in Baltimore.

All day sporadic firing could be heard, carried on the still easterly but now drier breeze, as fighting continued on the eastern approaches to the city. But still the British ships remained passively anchored just a few miles off of Fort McHenry, maddeningly just out of range of the fort's guns.

As the flotillamen of Fort Covington were sitting down to their supper — if the scant rations available could be called such — a rider galloped in on a lathered horse.

"Message for Commodore Talbot from Commodore Rodgers here. One of you Talbot?"

Jared identified himself and took the proffered letter from the civilian, who immediately remounted and spurred the tired horse back toward the city.

"What's it say, Jared? We done? We can get back to our boats and go after them bastards out there?" Hopeful thoughts which they all, including their commander, shared.

"Don't look like it, lads. What this says is that the militia and army coves under General Stricker seen action most of the day and held. They are fallin' back toward the city, but it ain't a rout and looks like the British had a high butcher's bill. Says here they lost they's head general — some cove named Ross."

Silence greeted his words while the men digested their import. Almost as one, the sailors broke out in a lusty round of *huzzahs* at the first good news they'd heard. Maybe this wouldn't reprise Washington after all. Talbot ordered a small cask of beer opened to allow his men to toast the success. Smiles and an uneasy good humor flooded over the little fort and brave epithets taunting the British vessels were uttered. And eventually, all but the watch found restless sleep under the threatening sky.

No one was still asleep at about five in the morning when one of the lookouts found Commodore Talbot standing under an over-hang of the roof on the brick magazine, one of the few dry places still available after the rain had again begun its noisome torment just past midnight.

"Looks like something's actin' out there, Jared. Hard to see through this damn rain, but it sure looks like some few of them ships is movin' closer."

Talbot followed the sailor to the wall and peered through the wet darkness. After a moment, he turned, nodding. "Aye, that it does. Them smaller ones is closer by half. And still comin'. Rig them signal lights to let the fort know. They probably seen 'em their own selves, but it cain't hurt. And find Andrews."

"Reckon it's gonna be startin' right quick, now, eh, Jared? Looks like some of them rocket vessels have moved up closer." Andrews appeared and stood beside his commodore, staring out the gunport at the slowly approaching ships.

"And maybe a bomb ship inta the bargain. Lookee there — that one to the east. Looks bigger 'an them other two. Must be a bomb ship. Get the men ready; load the guns — use cold shot — and get the linstocks lit. They'll likely try McHenry first, but we might as well be ready."

Talbot moved restlessly around the small enclosure, making sure the men were at ease but paying attention, and that the can-non were loaded as he had instructed. In the pre-dawn darkness, he could make out few faces, save those near the now glowing slow-matches. Those faces, he saw, were drawn and tight, show-ing the concern at being stationary targets, clearly a difficult lot for men used to the mobility of ships.

The sky continued to lighten and once again the rain had eased its relentless soaking. Under a desultory drizzle, the British ships were plainly visible as they came to their anchors barely two miles off Whetstone Point. The flotillamen at Fort Covington, as well as their army and militia counterparts at McHenry and Babcock Battery, crouched behind their cannon, keeping the long barrels trained on the encroaching fleet of rocket launching ships and their bomb firing sisters. An occasional glance at McHenry showed Armistead's huge American flag waving weakly in the light breeze.

One of the frigates, HMS *Cockchafer*, had detached itself from the afterguard and, as the men watched, she moved through the re-anchored fleet and came to her own anchor. They could plainly see the cable was rigged with spring lines which would allow her crew to turn the ship, bringing her broadside to bear regardless of the wind direction.

After watching and waiting, the broadside was almost a relief; with synchronous perfection, the entire fleet — those which had moved in close to the shore — delivered their thunderous greeting. Buildings trembled from the blast and, though bombastic to the extreme, little damage, save to the walls of Fort McHenry, was wrought on the city. People rushed to rooftops — the same ones from which they had witnessed the distant glow of Washington's flames — to see the battle.

Major Armistead immediately returned the British fire, and several of the guns of McHenry found their targets; the rigging of the *Cockchafer* was damaged during the encounter and a cheer went up from Jared's men in Covington as they watched the frigate win her anchor, springs and all, and lead the fleet to a position just out of range of the Fort's guns. Regardless of the range, both sides continued their non-stop bombardment for nearly three hours.

"They's just wasting shot and powder, Jared. Them shots ain't touching them Royal Navy bastards. Landing short, every damn one. You reckon Armistead knows they's short?" Andrews, a veteran of several sea battles, questioned Talbot as they watched, frustrated by their battery's inability to bear on the British.

"I'd bet he's just lettin' them boys let off a little of they's frustration, Bill. He can see the shot-fall good's you and I can. Them mortar rounds the British is firin' is likely shakin' them boys up pretty good. The rockets ain't doin' much, but I sure ain't lookin' forward to havin' them big mortars landin' in here."

Both men could see the large iron balls, hollowed out and filled with explosives controlled by a fuse, flying and bursting all around the walls of Fort McHenry. Their concussion was awesome, felt by Talbot's men in Covington and as surely by those at Babcock; *it must be a living hell*, both men thought as they watched.

As if the major in command of the Fort had heard the conversation, American firing suddenly stopped. There was little point in wasting their limited shot and powder as none of the ships whose guns and mortars and rockets rained horror on the Fort were within range of American guns. The British guns continued without pause, maintaining their fusillade with relentless fury. The shells and iron balls fell at the rate of one every minute.

Sometime after what would have been dinner time had not the Fort been under siege, Jared and Bill Andrews watched as a British mortar round hit one of the twenty-four-pounders in the southwest corner of the Fort.

"Gawd awmighty! Did you see that? That musta been a direct hit. Them poor coves couldn'ta survived that." Andrews was standing on the barrel of a long eighteen-pounder watching the shelling over the parapet of the smaller fort. Jared watched impassively, his head clearing well the top of the wall as he stood next to the gun. The British shot had continued unabated and, for the most part, unrequited.

"Aye. Reckon you're right, Bill. They're gonna have to remount that gun if'n she's not busted up too bad." Suddenly he pounded his fist down on the top of the wall and turned inward. "You men! Stand by to fire. I know the range is long, but give it your best. Every barrel what'll bear . . . FIRE!"

With a deafening roar, the eight eighteen-pounders that had even the slightest chance of hitting a target belched forth a tongue of flame and smoke. The easy breeze barely had sufficient strength to clear the choking, lavender-tinted smoke hanging in front of the guns, so none of the flotillamen could see if their shots had told. Since they were actually farther from the bombardment fleet than even the guns of McHenry, it was unlikely, but as Jared told himself, and Bill Andrews, "It's good for the lads to join in this scrap. But I sure do wish them bastards would come in a little closer — just enough to let us hit 'em!"

"Looks to me like the Royal Navy got almost the same problem,

Jared; most of them balls the Brits're firing in here ain't got range enough to do a helluva lot of damage. See how they's just bouncing off'n the outer walls? Them shots is about spent. The mortars is all that's makin' they's lives miserable over there. And looks to me as if more'n a few of 'em's landing short or blowin' up in the air afore they even get here."

Within the hour, Andrews commented, "Looks like you're gonna get your wish, Jared. Them ships is underweigh. Looks to me like they's movin' in. Whoever's in charge out there must think he's got Armistead's lads on the run."

"Stand by, men. They's comin' into range. Sight your pieces careful and blow your matches." Talbot was standing on some upturned crates between two cannon and watched with complete concentration as the British ships moved carefully into the killing range of both forts. He trained a longglass on the activity at McHenry, pleased to see that the big flag still flew from the mast in the fort's enclosure and that the recently dismounted twenty-four-pounder was again ready for service. His command to fire was nearly drowned out by the deafening roar of the fort's huge guns.

The crews of both forts and the Babcock battery, frustrated by nearly six hours of forced inactivity, unleashed a barrage of iron shot as the British ships came within range.

Yelling over the deafening din, his long braid flying left and right as he turned from the battle to his guns, Talbot exhorted his men with reports of how their shots told.

"Keep firin', lads! You're hittin' 'em! Lookee there; that frigate's took one right a'twixt her wind an' water . . . there — that bomb ship's took a round! Watch there! They's another frigate comin' close. Fire, lads, fire!"

McHenry's guns continued their firing unabated as well and, as those who could watched, boats were lowered from a newly arrived second frigate to take in tow the rocket launcher, *Erebus*. *Cockchafer*, her tophamper still damaged, withdrew, followed quickly by the remaining vessels and, in less that an hour, the incident was over. The American guns again fell silent. But not the American soldiers and sailors; cheers broke out from all around the harbor front as the men saw the British pull back. Adding to the general feeling of well being, a military band in Fort McHenry broke out in "Yankee Doodle."

But the British bombardment continued, mortars and rockets

wooshing through the sky and exploding ineffectively as nearly-spent iron shot splashed into the harbor or thumped dully against the outer ramparts of the star-shaped fort. A supper of dry biscuit and some hastily thrown together lobscouse made up for the lack of dinner and the men in both forts settled down to wait for whatever came next, as the rain, absent almost all day, returned with a fury to make their night truly miserable.

"Jared . . .Jared! Wake up. We got something right out yonder!" It was nearly halfway through the middle watch as Bill Andrews shook his commodore out of an exhausted sleep. The urgency in his voice, combined with the rough shaking, brought a reluctant Talbot struggling up through the depths of unconsciousness.

"Wha . . . wha's happening? We bein' boarded? Wha . . . who . . . oh! It's you Bill. What's actin'?" Talbot was fully awake and stood as tall as the limited overhead in the magazine would allow. He scratched at his beard.

"Looks like some boats headin' in. 'Pears they's makin' for Ridgely's Cove. Or tryin' to get in behind McHenry. Best you come have a looksee for your own self. And the Brits've quit firin', too." Andrews, already hurrying back out to the fort's wall, threw the words back over his shoulder. In his haste to follow, Jared neglected to duck and his head made a dull *thud* as he walked squarely into the lintel of the low doorway.

Andrews heard the distinctive sound and, turning back, offered, "Mind your head, Jared!" He was still smiling when he reached the ramparts.

Talbot, on the other hand, appeared at the wall rubbing his head and cursing. Bill ignored the exclamations and pointed, all amusement gone.

"See there? Less'n I'm goin' blind, they's more'n a dozen row barges and maybe one of them rocket ships headin this way. There! Looks like a gig or something small leadin' 'em. Must be takin' soundings. You can hear the oars splashin."

"Aye, I see 'em. Turn out all hands."

As he watched, Talbot, and soon the others in Fort Covington, could see winking lights below them dimly glinting through the rain. "Hmmm. Lit slow matches, be my guess. Gives us something to aim at — and thankee kindly, Mister Royal Navy sailor!" Talbot smiled ruefully to himself as the fort came quickly and quietly to life and the guns were once again manned.

"Use them lights down there for your targets. Give 'em your best, lads! Make every shot tell! FIRE AS YOU BEAR! "

With hardly a moment's hesitation and, since all of the fort's guns could bear, the entire battery opened fire on the twinkling lights below them. In the ensuing silence and, as quickly as his hearing returned, Jared realized that the splash of oars had stopped. The lights he had seen stopped twinkling and grew brighter. "Reckon they're slow matches, all right." He turned to his sailors. "Keep your heads down, lads, they're gon . . ."

His words were drowned out by the British fire as gun barges and a schooner opened fire on both Covington and Babcock. In a brief lull in the firing, Jared yelled to his men, "Fire at the flashes, lads! At this range you cain't miss!"

And indeed, their shots told; in the silence between shots, shrieking and yelling from below the fort confirmed their accuracy. A few balls — likely from the schooner — thudded harmlessly into the walls around Covington and Babcock, now a full participant in the carnage. Several shots and more than a few rockets flew overhead, landing in the new works behind Covington where an additional battery was being built.

"By George, they'll blow us out of the water! Backwater; retreat!" The British voice drifted up from below them and the American sailors, still frustrated over their earlier inability to fire effectively, were inspired to greater rates of fire and accuracy.

A single rocket split the wet darkness as it flew straight up from the British squadron. "That's a signal, I'd warrant. Reckon they's headin' back to the deeper water," Bill Andrews laughed to Jared andpointed. Through the glow of the continued barrage, the men could see the British barges, rocket ships, and the single schooner as they worked their way back to the fleet, passing Fort McHenry to larboard.

The light gave the gunners manning the lower water battery at the fort a welcome target. As the bombardment fleet fired its mortars and rockets to cover the failed mission's retreat, the eerie wet glow created as the missiles sailed through the rain lit the barges adequately for the gunners at the fort to pick out targets. It only lasted for a moment as the row barges, gig, and schooner were soon beyond their range and out of harm's way.

Talbot and Andrews stood at Covington's wall, soaked through and through but smiling at their first real trial successfully met.

"You lads done right good, by the Almighty!" Talbot's voice boomed out. "We turned them bastards around. Tryin' to land 'long the shore here, I'd reckon, and get into the city behind the fort. Them Brits're findin' out that we ain't gonna lay down and die for 'em like them ones down to Washington done! Well done, lads!"

A round of "Huzzahs" broke out and was echoed by the sailors and soldiers at Battery Babcock only five hundred yards down the shore. The rain, coming hard and steadily now, was ignored as the men of Joshua Barney's gunboat flotilla celebrated and cavorted around the fort.

The British ships, rocket launchers and mortars continued their bombardment of Fort McHenry sporadically through the remainder of the night; each time they fell silent, the Americans prayed it was over and they would have to endure the exploding missiles and rockets no longer. But the shells would always start again and the soldiers and flotillamen manning the forts would hunch down and, like a beleaguered ship in a storm at sea, ride out yet another onslaught.

CHAPTER THIRTY

"How long do you figger this is gonna go on, Colonel? Any of them coves you was taking your dinner with mention that?" Jack Clements shifted his rump on the sea chest that served as his chair in the sloop's tiny cabin.

He, Skinner, and Frank Key had all crowded into the captain's cabin when they returned to the sloop along with Isaac and Jake. Carronade lounged at the foot of the ladder just outside the door and snored contentedly; the distant firing bothered him not at all. Wet tarpaulin coats, Key's cloak, and Colonel Skinner's sodden blue jacket hung, dripping in a corner. A single candle shared the table with a small cask of beer and a half empty bottle of wine; a pair of smoky lanterns hung from the overhead beams and cast a yellow glow which moved about the small room as the sloop rocked gently in the light chop running in from the Bay.

"The admiral mentioned something about continuing until the Royal Marines had successfully taken the city from the land. He fully expected that our militia and army would collapse under the onslaught, allowing the British quick access to Baltimore from the east. I would imagine he is somewhat surprised that it is not a *fait acompli* already." Skinner smiled at the sailors and reached into his waistcoat pocket for his watch. "Already past midnight, it is, and still they continue the bombardment; must be that Major Armistead and his lads are withstanding what can only be cruel punishment better than Admiral Cochrane expected."

No sooner had he spoken than the firing stopped. At first, none of the men realized what was missing, so accustomed to the firing had they become. In the encompassing silence, the creaking of the little ship as she worked at her tether, spars, rigging, and hull, making the noises sailors grow to love and expect, suddenly rang loud.

"Oh my God! It's over. The firing's stopped; it can only mean disaster!" Key leaped to his feet and, grabbing his wet cloak from the peg in the bulkhead, tripped over Carronade in his haste to get to the ladder. The dog, rudely awakened, sat up and in so doing, fouled Key's legs even more. The two of them went down in a heap.

Clements, closest to the door, stood and offered the lawyer a helping hand while he spoke quietly to the dog, still startled and looking for something to bite.

"I must get upstairs to see what's happening. Here . . . get that animal off me . . . damned cur stood up just as I was . . . *ooof* . . there's a good dog . . . thank you for the hand, sir. I will . . . keep the animal here, if you please." And Key was back on an even keel and headed up the ladder. Carronade, calmed by his master, lay down again and was soon snoring quietly.

Isaac and Jake shrugged into their still-wet coats and followed the lawyer topside. They found him gripping the low bulwark and leaning toward the shore, oblivious to the pelting rain. After listening to the bombardment for so long, it was indeed eerie to have it silent. There was little activity on *Tonnant* and, from what they could see, the other nearby ships had few men on deck.

"Oh my God. What has happened? Why have they stopped firing? Can the city — and Fort McHenry have fallen? Impregnable, we thought. Here, Captain Biggs: can you see anything out there through this cursed downpour? I can barely make out the ships inshore of us, let alone the fort. I can not believe that they would have stopped their damnable shelling for any reason other than their success."

"No sir, I cain't see much more than you. Maybe they's just restin' a bit. Firing the way they have been takes some toll on the men. Cain't keep it up like that forever. The men must be needin' a rest — some sleep."

"Let us hope you are right. Perhaps they will begin again when the men are rested."

Biggs and Tate exchanged looks; why ever would an American

want the shelling to continue? Surely he has to know that the men on the shore — on the receiving end of the bombardment — must have had enough by now! Jake mentioned it.

"Uh . . . Mister Key? Why're you so anxious for 'em to start firin' again. Reckon them lads in the Fort likely feel some different about it. They're prob'ly right pleased that it's quit."

"Think, boy! If the firing has ceased, it can only mean the fort — and the city — has surrendered. Why else would they stop the bombardment? Unless, of course, your captain is correct and the men are resting. As long as the firing continues, it means that the fort — and Baltimore — stand." Key shook his head in the dark; it was incomprehensible that anyone could be so stupid.

For some time the three men stood silently watching for the trail of a rocket or the explosion of a mortar shell. One of the Royal Marines, quite soaked from being relegated to the sloop's foredeck, approached the Americans. The claying from his white pants had run onto his boots, streaking them gray and his sodden red jacket appeared almost black.

"I'd quite imagine my lads and I will shortly be returning to *Tonnant*, now that the battle appears concluded. A pity you colonials can't defend yourselves. Of course, most of 'is Majesty's troops who have taken your city are veterans of our recent victory over Napoleon. Fought under the Iron Duke, you know — the Duke of Wellington? In point of fact, it was 'e what recommended General Ross to 'is command 'ere. Quite a fine leader, 'e is. Certainly would appear 'e 'as 'ad little difficulty in bringin' you Jonathans to 'eel!"

Even though the Americans were unable to see the sneer the Royal Marine sported, they surely could hear it in his voice, supercilious and overbearing. The tone and his words did little to ease their concerns. It was as the British regular finished speaking that Carronade chose to come on deck to see what might be happening. Out of the corner of his eye, the Royal Marine caught movement, low and dark, emerging from the scuttle; at the same time, the dog saw the red coat and white pants over black boots in front of him and immediately began to growl.

Carronade stopped in his tracks just out of the hatch and stood, teeth bared, growling a low, menacing tone that caused the Englishman to take a step backwards. Even in the dark, the Americans could see the line of raised fur down the length of the animal's back.

"You probably'd be best stayin' still, you don't want to get bit, I'd say. He don't much take to you Redcoats." Isaac suggested quietly. He saw Jack's head emerge from the scuttle behind the dog.

The Royal Marine had unslung his musket and was raising it to his shoulder when Jack yelled.

"Don't shoot, for God's sake! Ain't no need for that!" He quickly scrambled out of the hatch and dove for the dog, attempting to get a hand on its neck, but it was too late.

As the gun went off, sharp and unnaturally loud it seemed, Carronade launched himself at the soldier. Months of restraint coupled with a hated memory of abuse at the hands of like-appearing men fueled his spring and his jaws clamped onto the Englishman's forearm. Of course, the shot went wild, burying itself in the bulwark, and bringing the watch to the stern taffrail of *Tonnant*. Amid snarls and screams, the pair fell to the deck; the musket clattered as it fell from the marine's hands and slipped under the bulwark to land with a soft splash in the water alongside.

Jack grabbed Carronade's shoulders and, shouting "Let go, boy! Leave him be!" to the dog, pulled him off his terrified victim. But not before the animal's powerful jaws had ripped through the red jacket and well into the man's flesh.

"'ere — whot's 'appenin' down there? Whot's all the caterwaulin' about? Who fired the shot? Lieutenant Parker: over 'ere, sir. I think there's trouble on the Jonathan's wee boat." The quarterdeck watch on *Tonnant* was peering over the rail at the sloop. He could not see what had happened, but surely heard the shot and the subsequent screams and yells.

"Nothing to worry about, young man. Just a minor altercation between one of your Marines and our dog." Key responded quickly. "The shot was fired when the gun slipped from his hands. Go about your business, now." Jack noticed that suddenly "that damn beast" had been replaced by *our* dog. He smiled in the dark as he pushed and pulled the animal back to the scuttle, lifting Carronade's front paws over the lip and starting him down the ladder.

The wounded British Regular had regained his feet and, in the dim light of a nearby lantern was examining his arm, clearly alarmed at the blood flowing freely from the wound.

"My God! That animal has bit me through and through. Look at me arm; I'm bleedin' to death, by God!" He held his arm close to the light and then waved it in front of his mates who had hustled aft, drawn by the shot and the noise. One of them took the arm to steady it and looked carefully at the bite.

"'Ere, now, Dicky, you ain't 'bleedin' to death' 't'all. Barely scratched you , 'e did. You're lucky 'e didn't take your bloody arm right off! Big dog like that. You shoulda shot 'im soon's 'e showed up." The marine, a sergeant and apparently in charge of the detail, looked at Isaac, Key and Jake. He shook his head, causing rain drops to fly from his hat.

"As for you Jonathans, you'll keep that animal out of our way or I will damn sure shoot the beast my own self! Keepin' a bloody dog aboard a boat, indeed. 'Ave you by chance something that might answer as a bandage for this? Or should I 'ave the watch aboard *Tonnant* 'aul us back alongside to take us all on board and 'ave the surgeon 'ave a look while you and your men are put in irons for attacking a soldier of the Crown?"

"I reckon we might have some cloth below that'd serve right fine for your friend, Sergeant. And I'll see the dog stays below. You and your men get back up to the fo'c'sle. Best you stay there, like you done afore." Isaac started for the hatch and saw the marines turn to go forward as his head disappeared below the deck.

Jack was grinning broadly and patting the big dog on the head. "How 'bout that, Isaac? Ol' Carronade got his own self into this scrap even if we're stuck out here." He bent over the dog. "Good boy, Carronade. You showed him 'bout pointin' guns at us 'Jonathans,' by God!" The dog responded with an enthusiastic thump of his tail.

"Jack, you're gonna get us sent back on board that two-decker and locked up, like as not, you don't keep him under control. Don't be so damn happy about it!" Isaac tried to maintain some level of the stern commander in his voice, but his pleasure at putting one of their "guard" out of action — even temporarily — came through and Clements called him on it.

"Isaac, lad, you're just as happy as me 'bout what Carronade done, and don't try to hide it. I know you've come to like him just fine — near as much as me — and I reckon you'd be some put out if'n it'd gone the other way; if'n that Redcoat hadda shot him. You know that. 'Sides, Carronade was just gettin' him some pay-back for that splinter he took down to the Patuxent! And we ain't gonna wind up back in *Tonnant*; them Navy lads ain't got no want for the likes of us. They got much more important fish to fry, 'specially if'n they took the city."

"Aye, I'd warrant you're right about that, Jack." Isaac smiled at his friend and reached down to scratch Carronade's head. "But all the same, try to keep him in your lee. Ain't no . . ."

"Captain Biggs! A boat is coming alongside the *Tonnant*. You had better come up here and have a look. No telling what is happening." Key shouted down the ladder and Isaac turned to go back into the wet night, his collar turned up and his shoulders hunched against the steady downpour in a futile attempt at keeping the rain from running down his neck.

"Seems to be quite a flurry of activity there. More 'an a few officers turned out up there where the boat landed, it appears." Key's attention was riveted on the men climbing up the two-decker's massive side. Colonel Skinner, on deck since the altercation, stood beside the lawyer and was equally intent. Isaac noticed that yes, indeed, there did seem to be quite a number of officers turned out awaiting someone's arrival. A few words drifted back, carried on the breeze from the ship ahead as the messenger from the boat reached the deck.

" . . . Ross . . .blood . . . Jonath . . . olding . . . not moving for . . . Cockburn and Colonel Brook say . . . off . . ."

The words were meaningless to the Americans. They could only hope it was good news and that the lull in the shelling of Fort McHenry did not tie into a victory being reported to the flagship. Skinner turned back to Isaac and Frank Key.

"I think the British are having some trouble over there. From what I could hear — which was precious little — they didn't sound like they were reporting victory. It just could be that Stricker's troops held and turned the enemy back. Admiral Cockburn wouldn't allow the Royal Marines to retreat, I'm sure."

"No, I reckon not. He's a fighter. He's the one followed Commodore Barney's flotilla all the way up the Patuxent to Pig Point just so's he could burn our boats." Isaac chimed in with his own personal experience with the British admiral. And then the firing started from shoreward.

"By God! That's a good sign. Firing again. Captain, have you a nightglass, by any chance?" Key was again at the rail, straining to see through the dark and rain as the deep *booms* and distant flashes resounded dully. The streaks left by Congreve rockets winked red in the wetness.

The Georgetown lawyer peered through the provided glass for a moment then exclaimed "That's our guns firing, by the Almighty! They must have got within range of the fort." He seemed to dance in place, then shouted out, "Give it to 'em lads, keep pouring it into 'em!" Only those on the sloop and a few still on deck on the British ship could hear his encouragement, but the firing did, in fact, keep up for some time and eventually was answered by the entire bombardment fleet. Congreve rockets and mortar shells could be seen quite clearly, even through the rain, as they flew from the warships into, around, and over the Fort.

"Well, I'd warrant that settles that! They wouldn't keep firing into a fort they had taken, by God! Armistead has not surrendered — and I would presume, neither has the city! Oh, how I hope this is a harbinger of what is to come." Key was more animated than even Colonel Skinner had ever seen. "You gentlemen may retire downstairs, if you wish; I shall remain here and watch — and pray." He hauled a watch from his pocket and considered it for a moment. "Should be dawn within a few hours now. They can not possibly maintain this bombardment for very much longer — but should they be able to, I pray that those brave lads in the fort can withstand the onslaught as long as they have to. Been at it nearly twenty hours." Completely oblivious now to his departing shipmates, he continued, mumbling under his breath, "Inhuman, absolutely inhuman. No one should have to bear that punishment! What an unholy ordeal!"

He lowered the glass from his eye and looked around the fleet anchored close at hand. More activity on the ships' deck; more people seemingly interested in what was happening in the harbor. Even the marines taking their ease — as much as they could given the cramped space and steady rain — on the fo'c'sle seemed to have taken a new interest in the bombardment. They talked among themselves, cursing Jonathans, the rain, and a host of officers who apparently were responsible for assigning them this miserable duty on the American sloop. Their voices drifted aft to the lawyer's hearing.

"Well, lads, we mighta been over on the shore, just as wet, but with the added joy of flying shot into the bargain!" One of the marines got it right and the others eventually returned to silent suffering.

Below, Isaac, his crew and John Skinner each found some

room to, if not stretch out, at least to recline enough to sleep; and sleep they did, lulled off to an exhausted slumber by the continuing dull booming of the ongoing punishment being delivered to Fort McHenry and the city of Baltimore.

CHAPTER
THIRTY-ONE

"I can not see through this blasted fog. First rain and now this fog! Damme! And I could see stars earlier! The guns are finally still, but did they hold through the night? Damn the fog!" Frank Key greeted his shipmates with his back as they emerged from the cabin and hurled epithets at the fog.

"What do you see, Frank?" John Skinner asked unnecessarily. The fog blew in wet sheets across the harbor. One could barely make out the British bombardment fleet at anchor — and of them only their topmasts were visible. There was no sign at all of the target of their attack through the preceding long day and night.

"Blast all! Not a thing! The tops of some of the masts of the ships yonder, but nothing beyond them." He glared through the longglass again, savagely jamming it into his eye with a force born of frustration and anger.

The colonel and Isaac flanked the lawyer while Jack and Jake stood with Doctor Beanes behind them staring into the whiteness. The doctor had missed the doings of the early morning, managing in his exhaustion to sleep through most of the night. Carronade remained below, out of the sight of the Royal Marines still camped on the sloop's bow. Isaac noticed that Key's free hand was clamped onto the bulwark with such a force that his knuckles had turned white. His cloak hung, sodden, from his shoulders, the bottom of it so waterlogged that it barely moved in the increasing wind.

"With this wind gettin' up, the fog ain't gonna be 'round for long, Mister Key. You'll be able to see the shore right quick, I'm thinkin', now they's a breeze." Jack Clements looked around, sniffed the air, and made his pronouncement. Which, as it quickly developed, was right on the mark.

"There! There it is! Oh my God! Is that the most beautiful sight you've ever beheld? Look. Armistead's flag is still there! We held through the night and that ungodly punishment! Oh, thank God!" Key was doing his little dance again, this time a dance of joy and excitement and, indeed, the others could see through the torn wisps of fog, as the wind moved it away, the huge American flag waving from its mast in the yard of Fort McHenry. It was truly a stirring sight and none could take their eyes off it as it flew, a little tattered and holed, but still high over the ramparts.

As the Americans watched the flag, they could not help but notice that the bombardment fleet was beginning to stir, winning their anchors and making their way back down the harbor toward the rest of the fleet. And suddenly, it seemed, the deck of *Tonnant* was bustling with activity.

A barge had appeared, rowed smartly and quickly to under the side of the flagship. Oars were tossed on command and the boat coasted in under the towering side. Isaac, his days as a Royal Navy tar coming back to him yet again, watched and recognized a very senior officer — likely an admiral, he thought — climb quickly from the sternsheets and up the battens to the deck where he was greeted with appropriate ceremony. The bosun's pipe and a marine drum signified the new arrival's importance. Within a few moments came a hail from the *Tonnant.*

"Ahoy . . . on the American sloop. We'll be bringin' you 'longside, 'ere." A voice from an unseen officer or midshipman shouted down from the taffrail high above them.

"Well, now what? I certainly hope they haven't changed their minds." Dr. Beanes voice was tight with concern.

He didn't need to elaborate; there was no doubt about what William Beanes was thinking. Isaac and Jake started forward as the sloop gathered way, pulled by unseen heavers on the spar deck of the British vessel. The lawyer, prisoner exchange agent, and their prize remained with Jack Clements in the waist of the sloop.

"Well, glad to see *you're* still alive! Maybe you was a little quick with your comment last night, soldier. And how's your arm?" Isaac smiled at the Royal Marine who had visited them during the night.

Isaac got a glare from the man for his trouble. "Looks as if you lads might be about ready to get yourselves back aboard the flagship. I hope your night was not too uncomfortable. We have such little space for passengers."

A voice called down from the deck above them. "The admiral'd like to 'ave a word with Colonel Skinner, if you please — and you can send up our marines. Then you'll be free to go on about your business, Captain, as soon as your passenger returns. Admiral Cochrane sends his apologies for any inconvenience he may have caused you and asked me to wish you a speedy return to port."

"Reckon that's who was in the boat then, Jake. I guess it's over. They must be gettin' ready to leave." He turned and called to the agent for prisoner exchange. "Colonel Skinner: seems as if the admiral wants a word with you, sir. You can get up there soon's we're secure 'ongside."

Isaac waited on the fo'c'sle for the American's return, which happened within the space of half an hour. The Royal Marines had already made their way up the *Tonnant*'s side, pleased to be back on the deck of a *real* ship. The sloop's crew was chafing at their lines to get away from their forced confinement and, as soon as Skinner's feet touched his deck, Isaac grinned at Jake and said, "Let's cast off this line, here Jake, and get ourselves back to Talbot an' 'em."

Jake nodded at Isaac and, even before the words were finished, was working one-handed at the post holding the sloop's tether to the warship.

"Stand-by to make sail. Jack, Sam! Get the mains'l unfurled. Clive: same on the jib. Stand-by the halyards!" Isaac turned to Jake. "Soon's the mains'l's up, cast off and give a holler. I'll get aft."

As Isaac made his way to the tiller on the sloop's tiny quarterdeck, he noticed the Georgetown lawyer busily scribbling on the back of a well-worn piece of paper. Judging from its damp appearance it had spent the wet night somewhere on Key's person. The man, Isaac noted, was totally engrossed in what he was about and quite oblivious to the fact that he was still soaked to the skin; that they were getting underweigh at long last did not signify in the slightest. He did not even look up as Biggs and Skinner passed him.

Within a few moments, the sloop, free from her twenty-four-hour captivity, was making light of the chop as she scooted on a close reach toward the harbor and the flotilla anchorage in Ridgely's Cove.

"What was all that about with the admiral, Colonel? If'n it's any of my business, that is?" Isaac guided the sloop toward Baltimore, the tiller resting against his leg and his glance alternating between the set of his sails and the agent who stood nearby watching the approaching British ships.

"Oh, not a great deal. Cochrane apologized for detaining us and wondered how the lads in McHenry could have withstood the barrage the fleet poured into them. Said it was quite a testimony to their will and courage." Skinner paused and looked back toward HMS *Tonnant,* still a hive of activity and, even from the short distance the sloop had gained, standing large in the fleet. "He also said something about sunken hulks between McHenry and Fells Point; had they not been there, he mentioned, the British would have been able to rush past the fort and cut off the city. Those hulks made it impossible for the naval support of the marines to have any real impact. Probably helped defeat the siege. That of course, and the militia units on North Point. I collect that was a complete disaster. Never in his wildest dreams did he expect to find a well-trained and competent militia . . . with apparently decent leaders. Mentioned also that General Ross was killed. Too bad that; I kind of liked the man."

"Them hulks bein' sunk where they was was the flotilla's doin's. Glad we was able to help. He say what they was gonna do next?"

"No. He did say that they considered this a diversionary raid. I can't imagine why, but that's what he said — and no point in continuing it with the resistance they met. Cut their losses, I figure. But he did indicate — obliquely, to be sure — that they would be getting their marines back into the ships quick as ever they might, so my guess would be they'll be heading somewhere else to wreak their misery and havoc."

The sloop continued in toward the city, its crew silent. Isaac noticed from his post at the tiller that Key continued writing whatever it was he was writing, head down and scribbling intently.

Closer in to Whetstone Point and its beleaguered fort, Jake called out from the bow where he had been watching the British bombardment fleet sail by them on its way to rejoin *Tonnant* and the others still anchored off North Point.

"Something in the water, Isaac, just comin' up on the wind'ard bow." He studied the object for a moment, then called out again. "Looks like a body, Isaac!"

Biggs let the sloop's head come up some and shivered her sails, slowing her dash up the harbor. He peered over the side as the body drifted by.

"Aye, Jake. A body it is, and from the uniform, British . . . an officer, I'd reckon. He's still got the swabs on his shoulders." Isaac pointed at the epaulettes waving languidly from the blue jacket as the body was lifted on the crest of a small wave. "Reckon some of them shots the lads at McHenry fired found they's mark!"

"There's another yonder, comin' up in our lee," Billings irritating voice chimed in. "Missin' a limb, it looks like." He pointed at the corpse as they approached the grisly sight. "Watch it, Isaac. They's somethin' sunk right by it . . . looks like a boat — or a piece of one, by God!"

"Them lads done right good, I'd warrant, Isaac. Looks like more 'an a few of they's shots told!" Jack Clements was peering over the side as the body and the remains of what might have been a row barge bobbed in the chop and passed by under the sloop's lee. "Damn! It sure is nice to see some British vessels busted up 'stead of ours!"

As they approached the shoreward ramparts of the fort with its waterbattery of forty-two-pounders poking ominously out from the earthern redoubts, all eyes studied the beleagured fort.

"Would you have a look there! What a pounding they must've took! Lookee there; you can see where some of them big shells landed. And look at the wall there — whole pieces missin' from it!"

"They's still some of them shells — mortars, I'd warrant — settin' there at the water's edge. Must not've exploded like they shoulda!"

"There! You can see where they musta fired into the side of her. See, the wall's all pocked and missin' pieces." Jake pointed out the results of the early morning attack from the row barges and, as Isaac eased the boat into the mouth of Ridgely's Cove, he exclaimed again at the condition of Fort Covington.

"Them poor bastards musta took a beatin', there in — what's that one called, Isaac?"

"Recollect Jared called that one Covington, Jake. Looks like they got hit some in there. Musta been wild shots. Don't seem like much of a target, less'n they got tired of shootin' at McHenry."

"Ahoy! On the sloop. Isaac — that you? Up here, lad. In Covington. Here!"

Isaac looked up again at the fort, and saw a figure — from the size it could only be Jared Talbot — waving and hollering from the wall.

"Jared! What're you doin' up there? Figgered you to be chasin' 'em outta the harbor with the flotilla!"

"Get yourself into the cove. I'll meet you there and tell you what's been actin'." The voice boomed down and even before its echo died out, the figure disappeared from view.

"Reckon ol' Jared got hisself assigned up there by Commodore Rodgers. Remember, Jack? Rodgers told us them army coves was took sick with something or other. He sure had a view of the fightin' from up there!" Isaac smiled, relieved to see his friend, and happy to be almost home.

As the sloop eased into the anchorage, still crowded with a dozen and more gunboats, Isaac brought her onto the wind, ordered the sails handed and brought her to anchor barely a pistol shot from the short wooden pier. They could hear hollering and singing coming from the shore and Clements, his eyes crinkling even more than usual, smiled knowingly at his skipper. The flotillamen were celebrating.

Even as the sloop came to her anchor, Frank Key remained intent on his work. The proximity of shore and the sounds of the celebration didn't signify. The scrap of paper was filled with words, strike-outs, and more words. He studied it for a moment, pausing in his labors and, wetting the stub of a pencil on his tongue, wrote furiously again.

"Say, Frank. Captain Biggs says a boat's coming out to take us ashore. You had best put your journal aside for a bit and get your effects together. I, for one, am quite anxious to put my feet on American soil again." William Beanes smiled at his friend but received a blank, glassy-eyed stare in return.

"Uhhh . . . oh, we're in already?" Key carefully folded the paper and started to put it and the pencil into his pocket. Realizing it was still quite wet, he thought better of it and, carrying both in his hand, stepped to the scuttle to "get his effects together." "It's not a journal, Bill; I've been writing verse. Seeing our flag this morning after that hellish night has moved me more than anything I've ever experienced and I wanted to set it down while the feelings were still with me. It's not quite complete yet, but I shall soon be satisfied with my effort. Perhaps you'd be good enough to read it when we get ashore and give me an opinion?"

"With pleasure, Frank. You know I've always admired your poetry. But let us find a quiet place in the city where we can talk. Now that I've rested, I want to tell you of the travails I have suffered these three weeks and more since Admiral Cochrane snatched me right from the dinner table in my home."

CHAPTER THIRTY-TWO

There was not a "quiet place" to be found in the city; indeed, the citizens of Baltimore were packed into every ale house, tavern, and coffee house celebrating their survival and the withdrawal of the British bombardment fleet. Even with the hour being barely dinner time, more than a few were glassy-eyed drunks, some passed out at tables, while others danced and cavorted like folks possessed. Singing, shouting, laughing people spilled out of doorways into the streets making it difficult at best to move past any establishment serving ale or rum.

Sam Hay and Clive had gone off with other members of the flotilla to celebrate, and Isaac, Jack, and Jake Tate had joined forces with Bill Andrews and Jared Talbot. They walked slowly through the choked streets of Baltimore while Jared told them of the long day and night in Fort Covington and the British attempt to flank them in boats. Andrews filled in whatever the big flotillaman left out.

"It was about the onliest chance we got to do any real firin', Isaac. Them bastards stayed just out of our range most of the time. Even the forty-two's at McHenry had trouble reachin' 'em some of the time. But when one of the lookouts heard them oars splashin', Jared, here, knew we was gonna be in for it! Opened up with the whole battery we done, by Gawd, and them coves at Babcock jumped right on it too! Reckon we busted 'em up right good from the sound of it. Heard a lot of hollerin' and wailin' from they's boats, so we knew the shots was tellin'. Then when they pulled back, they hadda get by the lads at McHenry and they had a turn at 'em as well. It was right nice, I'm tellin' you!" Andrews was animated, gesturing dramatically as he described the early morning fight, expanding on what Talbot had just mentioned.

Isaac looked at Jake. "Reckon them two dead Royal Navymen and that ruint boat we seen comin' in was on account of that, then." He saw the questioning look from Andrews. "Aye. Seen a couple of 'em — one for sure was an officer and, thinkin' on it, a fair senior one to boot — and a boat pretty well shot up, it were. Probably four or five miles off Whetstone Point. Musta got carried out there on the tide. You coves done right good, I'd say. Yessir, right good, indeed!"

"Bein' on the receivin' end of that bombardment musta been like bein' in Hell, I'd warrant. Can't imagine what it musta been like with them mortars and shells goin' off all around." Jake was awestruck as Jared concluded his description. "Iron shot is one thing and we all done that, but them bombs blowin' up overhead musta shook more'n a few of you coves, I'd wager." He bobbed his head, seeing Talbot and Andrews in a new light and with new respect.

"Here, lads, this talkin's thirsty business. Let's get us a glass o' something in there." Jared was already pushing his vast bulk through a doorway crowded with revelers. He used his size to open a path and the others followed closely in his wake.

After they had elbowed their way to the back of the tavern and secured a large tankard of ale for each, the four of them stood in a corner and shouted over the din.

"One of the coves what'd been in McHenry told me the British fired above fifteen hundred shells at 'em. Weren't but four of 'em got 'emselves killed in it, too. Hard to reckon that with how long it went on, by Gawd. Heard they was two dozen or so what got hurt — some cruel, to be sure — but still right lucky, I'd say. Most of the damage come from them damn mortar shells blowin' up aloft; some exploded after hitting the ground, as well." Jared's deep voice carried well over the din and he had taken it upon himself to do most of the talking. "And I heard from one of the army or militia coves who was with Winder . . ."

"Winder! That bag o' wind was here? I figgered after the mess he got into at Bladensburg that he'da been hidin' out somewhere or crawled off into some corner to lick at his wounds! With him in charge it's a wonder them militias didn't run off like they done at Bladensburg." Isaac couldn't believe that the stout general he had met at the River Rose ale house in Nottingham — which seemed like years ago, but was only July — was actually in charge of anything.

"Oh, he wasn't really in charge, Isaac. General Stricker was givin' orders, I reckon, and o' course, Commodore Rodgers and General Smith were tellin' him what to do. But gettin' on with what I was tellin': that cove tol' me that they killed the English general early on — right quick after the shootin' started — and the whole thing was damn near done then. The British didn't know what to do 'til some other general or colonel or something took charge. The Americans gradually fell back, skirmishing as they did, 'til the British was right up to the Philadelphia Road. Then they seen Rodgers guns and entrenchments up to Hampstead Hill and had 'em some second thoughts, by God!" Talbot laughed a great booming laugh at the way the Americans had drawn the hardened British regulars into a trap.

"Reckon they just sat there then, trying to figger out what they was gonna do. Tested the line some and get sent back, they's tails a'tween they's legs." He laughed again. "Puttin' together the way it happened, I'd wager a fair piece that that run they made in boats toward us at Covington had something to do with them gettin' stuck there under Rodgers' guns. They was takin' a poundin' there, I'd warrant, and maybe the navy was tryin' to draw some of our so'jers away from where they was. Didn't reckon on findin' the flotillamen lookin' down their barrels at 'em, har har!"

A disturbance near the entrance and the sudden easing of the noise ended Talbot's second-hand description of the battle of North Point.

"They's regroupin'. Get back to your posts. The British are formin' up again. Comin' from over to North Point, they are!" Someone shouted out the grim news and after a long hush born of disbelief, the floodgates of noise reopened. Everybody was shouting, some trying to debunk the news while others shouted encouragement.

"Cain't be! Sent 'em packin', we done, by the Almighty! We seen the ships sailin' for the Bay with our own eyes!"

"Hell's fire, lads! We whupped 'em once, we can do it again. Teach 'em good an' proper this time. Let's get back to the lines! Bring 'em on!"

Regardless of which side one took, the boisterous crowd soon found itself pushing out of the ale house. In no time at all, the establishment had disgorged most of its occupants — those who could walk or stagger — into the street. Confusion as to the veracity of the report had the people running to and fro, bumping into their fellows and, in some cases, knocking the smaller ones off their feet into the thick mud beyond the walkways.

Some of the men ran to horses, carts, or other means of conveyance which they mounted, then dashed off to their duty-stations from the night previous; others discussed the situation, finally deciding to go up to Hampstead Hill and see " . . .what the devil this was all about!" Still others, the flotillamen most notably, walked quickly to Ridgely's Cove and, rounding up a few sober sailors, set out to the harbor in a pair of gunboats.

"They sure don't look like they's headin' back this way, lads. Looks from here like them bomb ships and frigates are just waitin' out by the flagship. 'Ppears they's anchored, near as I can see." Jared had a longglass to his eye while Bill Andrews steered the boat. He steadied himself against the larboard shrouds and peered through the glass again, studying the scene some five and more miles away with intensity.

"Jared! You see them boats? The ones coming over toward the shore yonder? They's full of Marines. Looks like they's headin' *out*, not *in*. Might be they's bringin' 'em back from North Point." Clements' voice floated over the water from the gunboat that he, Jake, and Isaac, along with a few others to man guns should they be needed, had commandeered from a crew too drunk to manage.

Jared swung his glass and studied the scene for a moment. His booming voice carried easily to the other vessel. "Looks like you're right there, Jack. They must be haulin' 'em back to the ships. We'll get us some closer. Cain't hurt and we might be able to see more."

The two gunboats, American flags flying proudly at their peaks, sailed further from the harbor and closer to the enemy ships anchored in a light chop and growing breeze off North Point. A steady stream of boats plied the waters between the shore and the transports, some coming from the mouth of Old Roads Bay while others came from the point itself. And they were loaded to the gun'ls with red-coated Royal Marines. More could be seen with the glass as they clambered up the sides of the hulking transports, while still others waited, lining the shore to the east.

Boom! A dull thud of a cannon firing caused all hands to shift their gaze to a sixth-rate frigate, identified by the small cloud of lavender-tinged smoke just blowing away from her side. She was anchored on the outer edge of the formation and apparently the American flags flying from the two gunboats had aroused some attention in that quarter. The ball fell far short and, from the splash, Jared decided a small bow or stern chaser had been used.

"I don't reckon they're gonna get under weigh and come after us, Isaac, but let's not give 'em the idea! They's likely none too happy with the position they's in and might be thinkin' on takin' it out on us." Jared emphasized his words by nodding at Andrews who put the tiller down, bringing the boat's head around through the wind and settled her down on the other tack, heading back toward the city. Isaac followed suit, Carronade barking insistently at the British fleet now receding astern.

Within a few days, the people of Baltimore were again jubilant, celebrating with undiminished fervor, as they watched the British fleet sail from the mouth of the harbor; they had recovered their marines, buried their dead, and won their anchors. A rider had brought the news from Patapsco Neck early on the morning of September sixteenth. And this time, there was no stopping the delirium.

Revelers overflowed the taverns and lined the streets. They had done it! The militia and the townspeople had turned the mightiest army in the world — the one which had put down Napoleon Bonaparte — and withstood a twenty-four-hour bombardment by the Royal Navy. The disgrace of Washington's defeat was forgotten and there was singing in the streets.

Isaac, in the company of Jared Talbot, stood along the wall of a tavern shouting at each other over the tumult. Suddenly, Jared noticed that Isaac's eyes had fixed on something — or someone — beyond him. He turned and looked. In a corner of the establishment was a crumpled figure, the well-worn and dirty clothes marking him as a sailor.

"What're you lookin' at so hard, Isaac? Not that drunk yonder, is it? Just some washed up sailor, I'd warrant." Jared shouted into Isaac's ear.

"No, Jared. I mean, aye, that's what I'm lookin' at. But I'm right sure I know that cove; sailed with him back a few years. I'm gonna have a look." Isaac pushed his way through the few men to get to the corner and the table over which the sailor was slouched. A tarpaulin hat, torn and ragged, was pulled down low on his forehead. As Isaac stood over him, the seaman looked up with bleary, reddened eyes that squinted, even in his torpor, with a malicious cast. A ragged growth of beard, the filth on his plaid shirt, and the aroma emanating from his form gave perfect testimony to his unemployment and destitute state.

"Wha ya want? 'Less'n yer gonna get me a drink, go 'way. I . . . hey! You look some familiar. Who are you. You mebbe need a prime hand fer yer ship?" The man shook his head to clear away the stupor and tried to focus on Isaac. He reeled some in his chair and clapped onto the edge of the table to steady himself.

"I thought it looked like you, Mister Jakes. You remember me? Isaac Biggs — off'n the *Anne*." Isaac stepped back a bit and wrinkled his nose. He noticed that he had lapsed easily into the 'mister' form of address, a habit left from the days when Jakes was third on the bark and he was a topman.

"Biggs, is it? Aye, I 'member you." He rubbed a grimy hand across his face and beard. "Pain in my arse, you were. Thought you was in the Royal Navy, now. Har har! What happen, they t'row you out?" Recognition crossed the drunk's face and, as the memory of where he had known his visitor filtered into his rum-soaked brain, was quickly replaced with hate.

"Why aren't you sailin', Jakes? How long you been ashore, anyway?"

"Smalley, that damn scoundrel, put me ashore soon's *Anne* got into St. Bart's. Didn't take kindly, he said, to me sellin' ship's stores. He never proved a damn thing, but he put me on the beach just the same, the bastard! Wouldn't even bring me back to Boston, damn his eyes.

"Got myself back home but couldn't get more'n a seaman's berth by the time that rascal got done tellin' folks why he put me ashore. Ain't been out in a year — how long's this war been goin' on? Aye, three it is, and ain't been out since afore it started. All on account o' that bible spoutin' whoreson. An' you, I reckon. You musta had something to do with it, 's'well. Hard times for Ben Jakes it's been!" The drunk started to rise and reach for a knife, realized it wasn't there, then shook his head and slouched down again in the chair.

Realizing he had nothing more to say and that Jakes likely

was incapable of saying more, Isaac returned to Jared, still leaning on the wall where they'd been. He responded to Talbot's questioning look.

"Cove I used to sail with — back before the war. He was third on a merchant outta Marblehead. I was in the foretop back then . . . afore I wound up in the Royal Navy. Hasn't been to sea since the war started, he said. Can't get a berth. Reckon he's not likely to get one any time soon, neither!"

Jakes was forgotten as the two men continued celebrating with the crowds, telling stories at the top of their lungs, and enjoying the gayety and festive atmosphere of the city.

At the same time, Jack Clements and Jake pushed their way, laughing, down a waterfront avenue and bought a newspaper — *The Baltimore Patriot* — from a boy for a few cents. The headlines proclaimed the 'wondrous victory' and every page was filled with stories of the horrors and triumphs of the 'siege of Baltimore.' There were lists of dead, wounded, and missing. Stories from eyewitnesses to the bombardment. And near the back, by itself, was printed a poem.

"Lookee here, Jake. This is right good. Writ by some cove called Francis Scott Key. Hang on there; wasn't that the lawyer cove we carried out to *Tonnant?* He calls it 'Defence of Fort M'Henry'. Musta been what he was workin' on all the way back in."

"Aye, Jack. He said something about bein' 'moved' by seein' our flag that morning after the shootin' quit and I heard him say to the doctor he was writin' verse. Must be what he come up with." And he kept walking.

Jack Clements was not listening to his young, one-armed friend; he had stopped walking and was completely engrossed in the verse. He had begun to read it aloud, but his voice, becoming a little shaky, just trailed off into silence. Finally he looked up, surprised to see Jake studying him from close aboard, a quizzical expression in his eyes, and even more surprised to discover that his own rough cheeks were wet.

CHAPTER
THIRTY-THREE

"Damn nice of Jared to let us take his sloop. Sails nicer than that one we took out to the British fleet back in September, eh, Isaac?" Jack Clements eased the tiller down a trifle and the handy little sloop pointed her bow even higher into the brisk southwesterly, proving his point. Isaac was leaning on the weather rail watching the water rush by in a foamy torrent as they made their way down the Chesapeake. He was lost in thought, and Jack's voice was just a distant buzz that mixed easily with the sounds of the sloop.

"Isaac? You still with us, lad? You ain't hardly said a word since we cleared Bodkin Point." No response. "ISAAC! I'm talkin' to you, lad. Where're you at, anyway?" Carronade, disturbed from his siesta by Jack's raised voice, lifted his big head and looked around. Seeing everything was as it should be, he put his head back down on his forepaws and quickly went back to sleep.

"Sorry, Jack. Reckon I was tryin' to figger out what to do. Only thing I know for sure is that I want to be with Sarah. But what else, I got no idea. Course, she may not want to tie her line to a sailor and what I been workin' on in my head is what I'll do if'n that's her mind. I don't know anything else. Cain't see myself farmin' or drivin' a team somewhere. Or tendin' to some store, helpin' folks pick out notions." Isaac shook his head and pushed a hand through his curly hair.

Jack squinted his eyes at the water ahead and said nothing.

His friend had been like this since all the celebrations had died down back in Baltimore and the city had regained its composure. Most of the militia units had been sent home and the army units had departed as well. Repairs were proceeding apace on Fort McHenry and those areas of the waterfront which had suffered in the bombardment.

The gunboat flotilla was still functional and Joshua Barney, still ailing from the wound he suffered at Bladensburg, had returned to Baltimore to resume command. His first assignment had been to escort a prisoner exchange vessel, loaded with the surviving British casualties from Bladensburg, to Hampton, Virginia. Since only a few of the boats were required for that duty, he had given Isaac and Clements, along with a few of the others, leave and authorized the use of Jared's sloop. That was in early October, and Clements and Biggs, with a small crew, had departed soon after. In an eloquent and moving speech, Barney had promised all the flotillamen that he would continue to badger Congress for their back pay and other compensation.

After several more minutes of silence, Jack spoke again to his former captain and friend. "You know, Isaac, if'n Jake has really swallowed the anchor and gone ashore for good, ain't no reason why you cain't. Last words outta his mouth afore he shoved off for — where was it Miss Charity's family is at? — Frederick, I think — was something about him not lettin' her outta his sight. And I kinda thought she felt the same way 'bout him! Reckon he's gonna try his hand at farmin' her daddy's place there." Clements smiled, his eyes bright, at his unintended humor.

Isaac returned the grin and shook his head. "Try his *hand*? You ain't never gonna change, are you Jack. I think you say them things without even tryin'! But what would you do in my place? Pickin' up a shovel or chasin' a plow astern of some old plug don't seem to answer for either Jake or me. I don't know how he's gonna do it; I ain't sure I could."

"Why'nt you sail them waters when you get to 'em, Isaac? You ain't got to figger all that out now. Fact is, you don't know for sure if Miss Sarah'll even have you! Now that's something to worry on!" Jack's laugh roused the dog again and even Isaac smiled. "Aye," he went on in the same vein, "she's likely run off with some dashing militia man what owns a mercantile or some such. You think a pretty miss like her is just gonna sit around and pine after some sailor what's run off with a bunch of little gunboats? Ain't even sailin' in something pretty — like a frigate or some such!"

Isaac's face clouded briefly at the suggestion that his feelings were unrequited, then smiled again as he dismissed the thought as completely unthinkable! After all, *she* had kissed *him* first, and taken him home to meet her father, and walked all over the town of Benedict with him, as often as not, holding hands. Surely not the action of a lady who did not care for him! On the other hand, she had not responded to his letter, posted just after he arrived in Baltimore. Well, that was likely on account of the war and she probably didn't know where to address a letter to him. He realized Jack was talking to him again.

". . . turn Drum Point, right?"

"Sorry, Jack. Didn't catch all you said. Something about 'Drum Point'?"

"Isaac, stay with us here, lad. We'll have you in the arms of your lady quick as ever you please, but right now, we got to sail this here boat. What I said was, 'We'll likely have to wait on the tide to be fair after we turn Drum Point.' Thinkin' we could tuck in behind Point Patience there and wait if'n we got to. Reckon that'll bring back some memories, eh?"

"Aye, that would answer nicely, Jack. And I'm sorry about wanderin' off like I been doin'; it's just . . . I can't get her outta my mind — and now I'm gonna see her in a day or so! I'll try to stay aboard — least 'til we see Benedict; no tellin' what I might do then . . . maybe jump overboard and swim if'n the barky ain't sailing quick enough!"

"Any o' you coves want some vittles?" A disembodied head belonging to Sam Hay popped out of the scuttle. He and another had shipped with Isaac and Jack mainly for want of something do to.

Clements welcomed the interruption; maintaining his good humor all the while listening to Isaac's most likely groundless worries was trying. "Been thinkin' on that very thought, Sam. Gettin' some sharp-set, I am. What've you got down there? How 'bout it, Isaac? Reckon some food might take your mind off'n your troubles?"

The sloop turned Drum Point just as the darkness descended and, as Jack had prophesied, right into the tide which had begun to ebb. An easy reach, albeit slower than Isaac would have liked, took them around the end of Point Patience where they anchored for the night.

After a supper of dried peas and some left-over lobscouse from dinner, the men remained in the sloop's small cabin; the wind had died and, under a clear sky flecked with brilliant stars, the temperature dropped, making the warmth of the cabin most welcome.

"You hear 'bout what them lads up on Lake Champlain done? Quite a scrap they had, I heard. Just afore the fightin' at Baltimore, I think." Sam Hay looked around at his messmates. Seeing mostly blank looks, he continued. "Aye. Some cove come down to Baltimore just afore we shoved off — last night, I reckon it was — and was tellin' 'bout how MacDonough whupped the freshwater Royal Navy right fine. Better'n we done in Baltimore, sounded like. Off a town called Plattsburgh, it were. Fought damn near the whole thing from they's anchors, if'n you can believe that! Used spring lines to wind 'em around so the guns'd bear wherever he needed 'em to. That cove MacDonough done us proud, though. Had most of his ships cruel hurt, but even after he lost the whole larboard battery on *Saratoga*, — she's a corvette of twenty-six guns — he hauled on them springs and turned the other side to firin'! Hammered some Royal Navy vessel — their flagship, a frigate of thirty-seven guns, I'm told — damn near into matchwood. Musta been one merry hell of a fight! Yessir, I reckon them lads on the fresh're walkin' tall after that one!"

At the mention of 'the fresh', Isaac shot a look at Clements. "You reckon Coleman and that gunner . . . Tim Conoughy, right?" He received a nod from Jack and continued. "You think they mighta been involved in that one, Jack? They was headed up that way last Fall when we come down here." He shook his head. "That sure seems like a long time ago, don't it, Jack? Been some doin's since we left Salem. I ain't heard a word from them two since Salem. Wonder if'n they seen any action up there. I recollect how Tim was always complainin' he didn't have any 'real' guns to shoot. If he was up there — where'd you say, Sam? Plattsburgh? — I reckon he mighta got his fill. Sounds like something he'd be smilin' and dancin' about."

Jack and Isaac smiled as they reminisced about their former shipmates, Coleman, Conoughy, and others, and the night passed, cold and clear, as the sloop swung into a stiff westerly just before dawn.

A fair tide and the westerly carried them up the Patuxent River late the next morning, passing St. Leonard Creek with its memories and the other points that had occupied their attention during the hot summer while the flotilla dodged and tracked the British ships which were focused on rooting out the gunboats and destroying them. Each memory brought a comment and, from time to time, even a bark from Carronade, who had resumed his old post in the bow of the sloop. His ears blew back and the fur on his back riffled as he lifted his nose to the breeze.

By supper time, the dock of Benedict hove into view and Isaac could barely contain himself. Gone was the cool, reserved, and seasoned fighting sailor who had seen frightening and bloody action on vessels large and small against the enemies of two nations; in it's place was a nervous young man, consumed with questions for which he had no answers. He paced the length of the deck, unable to stand still or even eat as the rest of the crew wolfed down a quick meal.

His eyes darted around the river, taking in the banks on both sides and the water and shoals ahead of them and behind, but always returning to fix upon the pier at Benedict. He remembered the first kiss he and Sarah had shared there just inshore of the dock and smiled.

By the time the sloop was made fast to the dock, Isaac was beside himself. There had been no one on the dock to greet them in, but then no one had known they were coming; there was no sign of life, save a few windows showing the yellow glow of a whale oil lamp. A horse was secured to a rail not far from the dock and it stamped its feet, shifting its weight and stirring up little clouds of dust that shimmered in the last rays of the sun.

"Jack, I got to get over there. No tellin' when I'll be back, but I can't wait a moment longer." And he vaulted the bulwark and tried to walk calmly down the pier. A look back at the sloop showed Jack and Carronade, his forepaws on the bulwark, watching him stride away.

Sam Hay joined the pair and stood silently for a moment, watching Isaac move purposefully toward the town. Then he turned to Clements, the beginnings of a grin working at the corners of his mouth. "I'd warrant the evening gun has fired, eh Jack? Leastaways, for Isaac." Jack smiled and nodded, his eyes never leaving the sight of his departing shipmate.

Hurrying along, but trying not to appear as if he were hurrying, Isaac heard Jack shout something — he couldn't make it out — but he didn't stop. He would brook no delays now! His focus was as complete as it would be were he going out on a swaying yard to hand a flogging tops'l. To a bystander, Biggs looked liked any other sailorman ashore; his rolling gait and confident smile were testimony to the calm untroubled life of a seaman.

Inside, however, he was anything but calm, his thoughts churning and reeling with horrible visions, then wonderful ones. He noticed he had begun to sweat even though the air was pleasantly cool with a nice breeze. Across the little green — none the worse for the recent visit from the British — down the street lined with mostly plain, simple homes, and then there it was: Colonel Thomas' house. More memories flooded back, thoughts of his several meals there and his conversations with the colonel. Of secret smiles shared across the table with Sarah and the occasional touch from her foot under it. He started down the street, his heart pounding. Barely a pistol-shot away, his head filled with misgivings, he hesitated, then moved — almost cautiously — forward. Somehow, her house seemed much closer to the dock than he remembered it! He needed to think a moment. He stopped as he got to her walkway, a hand on the fence.

My God, what if she don't want to see me? What if she ain't there any more? What if her father . . . No, Isaac. It ain't gonna be that way. She's gonna be . . .

"Isaac! Oh my God, Isaac! I thought that was you from the way you walked! I just knew you'd come back to me! Oh, Isaac! I'll not let you out of my sight again." And, her eyes streaming with joyful tears, Sarah Thomas flew out the door, down the walk lined with fall flowers, and into his arms.

AUTHOR'S NOTE

The British blockade, brought to a fine degree of efficiency by the availability of additional naval assets in 1814, essentially closed the eastern seaboard of the United States, not only to commerce, but also to the United States Navy. Frigates, brigs, and tenders were distributed up and down the coastline, from Massachusetts to Charleston, grounding "on their own beef bones." That the British returned their forces to the Chesapeake Bay was indeed intended as a diversion, as Admiral Sir Alexander Cochrane had mentioned to Colonel John Skinner aboard *Tonnant*. The object of the diversion was to force the Americans to move resources from the inland lake areas where the British were being overwhelmed. This tactic failed, but not before it had caused some considerable grief to the United States.

Having mapped and charted the Chesapeake quite thoroughly in 1813, the English ships moved with some impunity around the Bay, raiding waterfront towns and local shipping at will. The only thorn in their side was Joshua Barney. His flotilla of gunboats created a problem for the British that had to be removed.

Commodore Barney, a hero of the American Revolution, was somewhat unique in the Navy; he reported directly to the Secretary of the Navy, William Jones. Moreover, he was given a quite free hand in his operations.

While the sloops that Isaac Biggs and Jack Clements commanded early in the story are the inventions of the author's imagination, Barney did have a schooner, *Asp*, and a cutter, (actually a "block sloop") *Scorpion*, under his command. In fact, there is every reason to believe that Barney's flag was carried on *Scorpion* more than on any other vessel.

The action that took place in St. Leonard Creek on June 10, 1814, was referred to as the "First Battle of St. Leonard Creek" and the subsequent action in which Barney actually escaped to sail further up the Patuxent was named, logically, the Second Battle of St. Leonard Creek. Immediately after the battle, the army and militia had removed to safety the artillery pieces and the wounded that had been abandoned in the initial retreat, not some days later, as told by Biggs.

It might be noted at this point that there is, in fact, some confusion surrounding the name of this locale; is it St. Leonard or St. Leonards? The creek is still known today as St. Leonard (no 's') while another town across the Patuxent River is called Leonardtown. Underwater archaeological exploration, conducted jointly by the Calvert Marine Museum in Solomons and Nautical Archaeological Associates over a period of over twenty years, has uncovered artifacts and parts of Barney's gunboats in St. Leonard Creek. Further exploration discovered that a pylon of the Route 4 bridge at the junction of Route 301 in Maryland was positioned *through* the remains of one of the scuttled gunboats near Pig Point.

Dr. Plumm is a creation of the author's imagination, but his attitude is consistent with the mindset held by many of the area residents. They wanted no part of the war and resented Barney for bringing it up the river to them.

That the British burned our national capital was the inspiration of Admiral Cockburn and not part of his original orders; he realized that with the fleet already up the Patuxent, Washington was a relatively short march away and he convinced General Ross that it would be an easy victory, and fine retribution for the American destruction of the Canadian city of York (now Toronto) in 1813. British ships were already raiding on the Potomac and confusion would be rampant. The troops the two men commanded did, in fact, include many of the battle-hardened veterans of Wellington's army who had only recently brought Napoleon Bonaparte to heel, as suggested by one of the flotillamen later in the story.

As indicated by General Winder, there was great apprehension about where an invasion would occur; Barney and Secretary Jones had few supporters for their theory that Washington would be the target. But when the attack came, orders were issued to burn everything that might be of use to the enemy. Most particularly, the Navy Yard and rope walk.

Interestingly, among the vessels ordered burned in the Washington Navy Yard was one that simply would not take the flames: the 1799 frigate *New York*. The ship, built by subscription by the city of the same name for the Quasi War with France, had been abandoned there in ordinary (decommissioned, in modern parlance) by Jefferson's administration as unnecessary and was so waterlogged that she would not burn.

The story of the Battle of Caulk's Fields is told of by one of the flotillamen. It did indeed happen and was the only land battle fought on the Eastern Shore of Maryland during the entire conflict. Sir Peter Parker, a favorite of the Royal Navy, was killed in that action. He was brought to Mitchell House (today a lovely bed & breakfast) in Tolchester where he died (some accounts report that he was already dead when brought to the house). Subsequently, his remains were carried by Lt. Henry Crease, his ultimate successor, in the frigate *Menelaus*, to an anchorage in mid-Bay (near Poole's Island, not to the south as suggested by one of Talbot's flotillamen) to avoid harassment from the gunboats. He was there preserved in a barrel of rum (much the same as Admiral Sir Horatio Nelson was after Trafalgar) and taken to Bermuda, where he was temporarily buried. Sir Peter was ultimately brought to a final resting place in London. The battle was essentially as the gunboat skipper Morris told it. The nineteenth-century town of Belle Air is now called Fairlee.

At Fort McHenry, the outer guns — the "water battery" — were actually forty-two-pounders salvaged from the French ship *L'Eole*, on loan from the French government. Some of the same guns were also sited at Forts Covington and Babcock. They were manned by sailors from Joshua Barney's gunboat flotilla and from the United States frigate *Guerierre*. (Built by the United States and launched in June 1814, but not yet ready for sea, the vessel was named for USS *Constitution*'s first — and perhaps most notable — adversary of the war.) Additionally, the neighboring forts of Covington and Babcock were also manned by flotillamen.

HMS *Surprise*, the frigate to which Adm. Cochrane shifted his flag prior to the bombardment, was a real vessel in the Royal Navy and was commanded by the admiral's son. Together with the mortar and rocket ships, the frigates of the bombardment fleet fired nearly eighteen hundred round shot and mortars at Fort McHenry. The mortars were mainly ineffective in causing any physical dam-

age, as most were fused incorrectly and did indeed burst in the air. However, many of the men were killed or wounded within the walls of the fort as a result of airbursts from these shells.

One shell actually landed, but mercifully did not explode, in McHenry's magazine.

John S. Skinner served at Annapolis during the War as agent for British packets, flags of truce and dispatches, and as agent for prisoners. His frequent contact with the British fleet provided the Untied States with an important source of intelligence.

When he and Francis Scott Key needed transportation to the British fleet to negotiate the release of Dr. William Beanes, they hired a sloop from a Mr. Ferguson which became a "private truce vessel." Barney's flotillamen were not involved with Skinner and Key. The two men, with Mr. Ferguson, sailed from Baltimore on September fifth, locating the British fleet on September seventh at the mouth of the Potomac River, not off Eastern Bay as indicated in the story. Based on documents from those involved, historians now agree that Colonel Skinner did the lion's share of the negotiating for Dr. Beanes' release.

Key's poem, *The Defence of M'henry*, (sic) was completed in his boarding house when he returned to Baltimore. He then showed it to his brother-in-law, Joseph Nicholson, who had been in command of the Baltimore Fencibles stationed at McHenry during the bombardment and, at his insistence, the poem was published on a broadsheet shortly thereafter. Within a few days, it was published in the newspapers with a notation that it was to be sung to the tune of a most popular old English drinking song, *To Anacreon in Heaven*. And in October, an actor, calling it "The Star Spangled Banner," sang it on the stage in its first public performance. One hundred sixteen years later, it became our National Anthem. Writing poetic tributes to the young nation and its heroes was not a new undertaking for Key; some nine years earlier he had written a poem celebrating the heroism of our sailors, particularly Steven Decatur, in the action against the Barbary pirates of Tripoli (now Libya). Coincidentally, that song was also set to the tune of *To Anacreon in Heaven*.

After the British left the Patapsco River, there was minor raiding and skirmishing as they headed south on the Bay. Beginning October 11, 1814, coast watchers noticed an increasing number of ships anchoring in Lynnhaven Bay (Virginia). The fleet left, headed for New Orleans, on October fifteenth. A small cadre of ships remained active in the Bay through year's end, keeping the Eastern Shore Militia in a state of readiness.

Even though the purview of this volume and its predecessors did not include the action of the fresh-water navy, it was none-the-less most important to the ultimate outcome of the war and must be mentioned here.

Most particularly, the Battle of Plattsburgh, fought on Lake Champlain, was a major triumph for the Americans. More or less as described by Sam Hay in the story, MacDonough's victory caused General Prevost to recall General Sir Frederick Robinson who was about to attack Plattsburgh by land; a retreat was ordered due to the fear that the British supply lines would be cut by the American fleet, which now controlled the Lake. Had the British been successful in their attempt, it is likely that they would easily have been able to control the entire Hudson River Valley, and the outcome of the war might have been substantially different.

Combined with the failure of their attack on Baltimore, MacDonough's victory brought the British back to the peace talks with a more focused outlook and ultimately, on Christmas Eve 1814, the peace, called the Treaty of Ghent, was signed. And yes, the Battle of New Orleans, one of the most famous of the war — and well- known of the American victories — was fought after the signing of the treaty. In fact, ships at sea — of both sides — were unaware of the treaty and continued the hostilities unabated until June of 1815.

For the reader interested in learning more of this oft-neglected period of our history, I have appended at the end of this volume a short list of non-fiction works (not to be construed as a bibliography) that might shed further light on the War of 1812. Some are quite specific, while others deal with the entire effort in a more general context. Additionally, for the many who are not aware that our National Anthem, *The Star Spangled Banner*, has *four* verses, I have presented it in its entirety. It is quite stirring.

William H. White
Rumson, NJ
2001

The Defence of M'Henry [sic]
(The Star Spangled Banner)

tune: *To Anacreon in Heaven*
by: Francis Scott Key, September 14, 1814

O! say can you see by the dawn's early light,
What so proudly we hailed at the twilight's last gleaming,
Whose broad stripes and bright stars through the perilous fight,
O'er the ramparts we watch'd, were so gallantly streaming?
And the Rockets' red glare, the Bombs bursting in air,
Gave proof through the night, that our Flag was still there.
O! say does that star-spangled banner yet wave,
O'er the land of the free and the home of the brave?

On the shore dimly seen through the mists of the deep,
Where the foe's haughty host in dread silence reposes,
What is that which the breeze, o'er the towering steep,
As it fitfully blows, half conceals, half discloses?
Now it catches the gleam of the morning's first beam,
In full glory reflected new shines in the stream.
"Tis the star-spangled banner, O! long may it wave
O'er the land of the free and the home of the brave.

And where is that band who so vauntingly swore
That the havoc of war and the battle's confusion,
A home and a country, shall leave us no more?
Their blood has washed out their foul footsteps' pollution.
No refuge could save the hireling and slave
From the terror of flight or the gloom of the grave,
And the star-spangled banner in triumph doth wave
O'er the land of the free and the home of the brave.

O! thus be it ever when freemen shall stand,
Between their lov'd home, and the war's desolation,
Blest with vict'ry and peace, may the Heav'n rescued land,
Praise the Power that hath made and preserv'd us a nation.
Then conquer we must, when our cause it is just,
And this be our motto — "In God is our Trust;"
And the star-spangled banner in triumph shall wave,
O'er the land of the Free and the Home of the Brave.

Suggested Additional Reading

The Battle for Baltimore, 1814. Joseph A. Whitehorne. Nautical & Aviation Publishing Co., Baltimore, MD.

The Burning of Washington: The British Invasion of 1814. Anthony S. Pitch. Naval Institute Press, Annapolis, MD.

Guns off Cape Ann. Kenneth Poolman. Rand McNally & Co., New York .

Millions for Defense, The Subscription Warships of 1798. Frederick C. Leiner. Naval Institute Press, Annapolis MD.

Fort McHenry. Scott Sheads. Nautical & Aviation Publishing Co. Baltimore MD.

War of 1812, A Short History. Donald R. Hickey. University of Chicago Press, Chicago.

Hangman's Beach. Thomas H. Raddall. Nimbus Publishing, Halifax

The Prize Game: Lawful Looting on the High Seas. Donald Petrie. Naval Institute Press, Annapolis, MD.

America and the Sea. Labaree, Fowler, Hattendorf, Safford, Sloan & German. Mystic Seaport, Mystic, CT.

History of the Navy, Volume I. Edgar S. Maclay. D. Appleton & Co. New York, NY (out of print).

About the Author

Photo by Tina/Visual Xpressions

William H. White, a life-long sailor and amateur historian, has been a commercial banker, professional photographer and served as an officer in the U.S. Navy during the 1960s. He has been involved in both sail racing and cruising, primarily on the East Coast in one-designs and offshore boats, for over fifty years. He resides in New Jersey with his wife of thirty-four years. They have three grown sons, all fine sailormen. *The War of 1812 Trilogy* was born out of his love for history and the sea. More information on the author and his books can be found on his website: ww.1812trilogy.com.

About the Artist

Paul Garnett began drawing before he could write his name. He was a shipwright on the vessel *Bounty*, built for MGM's 1962 remake of "Mutiny on the Bounty," and his paintings have been published twice by the foundation which now owns the ship. His art has also been showcased on A&E's television program "Sea Tales"; the History Channel's "Histories Mysteries: What Really Happened on the 'Mutiny on the Bounty'"; and by *Nautical World* magazine.

A PRESS OF CANVAS

Volume One
in the War of 1812 Trilogy
William H. White
Illustrated by Paul Garnett

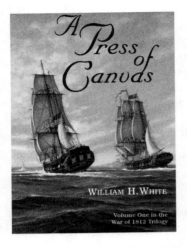

Softcover, 5½"x8½", 256 pages, illustrations.

A Press of Canvas, W. H. White's action-packed novel, introduces a new character in American sea fiction: Isaac Biggs of Marblehead, Massachusetts. Sailing from Boston as captain of the foretop in the bark *Anne*, his ship is outward bound with a cargo for the Swedish colony of St. Barts in the West Indies in the fall of 1810. When the *Anne* is stopped by a British Royal Navy frigate, Isaac and several of his shipmates are forcibly pressed into service on the *Orpheus*, actively engaged in England's long-running war with France.

The young Isaac, naive and inexperienced, faces the harsh life of a Royal Navy seaman and a harrowing war at sea. His new life is hard, with strange rules, floggings, and new dangers. Then the United States declares war on England and Isaac finds himself in an untenable position, facing the possibility of fighting his own countrymen. A chance meeting with American privateers operating in the West Indies offers him a solution to his dilemma and a reunion with an old friend.

Written from the aspect of the fo'c'sle rather than an officer's view and through the eyes of an American, *A Press of Canvas* provides new perspectives and an exciting story of this often neglected period in American history. Tiller Publishing is proud to offer this carefully-crafted tale as its very first fiction title.

"Sailors everywhere will rejoice in the salt spray, slanting decks and high adventure of this lively yarn of the young American republic battling for its rights at sea."
Peter Stanford, President
National Maritime Historical Society

"A great read . . . a very engaging story with believable, honest characters . . . taught me a lot about this period of history . . . just fabulous!"
John Wooldridge, Managing Editor
Motorboating and Sailing

A FINE TOPS'L BREEZE

Volume Two
in the War of 1812 Trilogy
William H. White
Illustrated by Paul Garnett

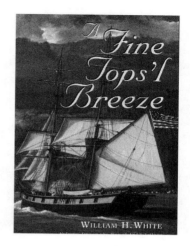

Softcover, 5½"x8½", 288 pages, illustrations.

A Fine Tops'l Breeze, W. H. White's action-packed novel, continues the adventures of the newest character in American sea fiction: Isaac Biggs of Marblehead, Massachusetts. In the second volume of the trilogy, Isaac ships as Third Mate on the Salem privateer *General Washington* in February 1813. At the same time, his friends from the British frigate *Orpheus* and the Baltimore schooner *Glory* find berths on the American warship USS *Constellation* and, eventually, they wind up on the USS *Chesapeake* in Boston just in time for her disastrous meeting with HMS *Shannon*. Throughout the spring of 1813, Isaac and the *General Washington* roam the waters between Massachusetts and Nova Scotia, taking prizes and harassing the British. When the American survivors of the *Chesapeake/Shannon* battle are confined in Melville Island Prison in Halifax, the *General Washington* and Isaac play an important role in securing their freedom.

Written from the aspect of the fo'c'sle rather than an officer's view and through the eyes of an American, *A Press of Canvas* and *A Fine Tops'l Breeze* provide new perspectives and exciting stories of this oft-neglected period in American history. The final book of the trilogy, *The Evening Gun*, will be available late this year. Tiller Publishing is proud to offer these carefully-crafted tales as its very first fiction series.

By the publication of A Fine Tops'l Breeze, *the second of his War of 1812 Trilogy, William H. White has taken his place in the charmed circle of writers of really good fiction about the days of fighting sail: Melville, Forester, O'Brian, Nelson, and Kent. Like them, his attention to the detail of ships and their hulls, spars, rigging and sails is meticulous.And, like them, his characters are not only credible, but memorable. He is a thoroughly welcome writer to this genre, which has brought so much pleasure to so many.*
Donald A. Petrie, author of *The Prize Game: Lawful Looting on the High Seas in the Days of Fighting Sail* (1999)

Through Bill White's evocative prose, one smells the salt breeze and feels the pulse of life at sea during the War of 1812.
John B. Hattendorf,
Ernest J. King Professor of Maritime History, U.S. Naval War College